Acknowledgements…

The foundation of this book is based on The Rock, who is first and foremost, the Lord Jesus Christ. My justification before the holy throne of the one true God stands on Him alone. However, since my conversion nearly a decade ago, my walk has flourished because of the sound teaching and loving discipleship of so many others. (My walk seems to flounder when I totally rely on my own resources for some reason, hmm…)

I am forever indebted to my brothers and sisters at Wellington Presbyterian Church, who graciously took a spirited, but too often stubborn, infant in the faith and tenderly fed him the nourishing truths of scripture. I hope I have in some small way humbly rewarded your patience and perseverance. I am especially thankful to Chuck and Sue Schaefer, who enlightened me by introducing this young convert to the works of many of my heroes in the faith.

The teachings of Dr. R.C. Sproul have been fundamental in guiding my reformed perspective of the deep love of Jesus for his saints. Dr. Sproul is truly one of the great minds in Christian theology and philosophy today. I have liberally used the knowledge I have received from his teachings in this book, especially in the first chapter. (The T.U.L.I.P. is my favorite flower as well).

Another heavy influence in the writing of this novel is the evangelistic methods of the late Dr. D. James Kennedy. I was exposed to his course known as Evangelism Explosion early on in my own walk with Christ and its impact has been invaluable in my efforts to share the gospel with the lost. Those who have also been trained in "E.E." will find the conversation between Franklin Edwards and Joe Beacon in chapter three very familiar.

In addition to the great saints mentioned above, I am eternally grateful to every Christian in my life who has helped push my walk forward. There are so many pastors, teachers, elders, deacons and others who have contributed to the writing of this book in a spiritual sense, I fear it would take another chapter (or book) to acknowledge all of them. Many of you already know who you are and what your love has meant to me, so I thank you for your faithfulness. And may we all praise our precious Savior for his faithfulness to us as well.

In his grace forever,
John Strassel

Dedication...

This book is dedicated to the three most memorable women in my life: my adoring wife Michelle; my faithful mother-in-law Jackie; and my dearest mother Millie. I love you all in a manner my mere words could never fully express.

Disclaimer...

All the characters in this novel are fictitious and any resemblance to actual persons living or dead is purely coincidental. All scripture references are from the Holy Bible, either the New International Version (NIV) or the New King James (NKJ) version.

"...being confident of this, that he who began a good work in you will carry it on to completion until the day of Christ Jesus."
(Philippians 1:6)

Chapter I

As the buzzer sounded over the intercom signaling the beginning of the day's classes at Good Shepherd Christian School, Franklin Edwards' mind began to drift back to his awkward adolescence.

Could it really have been be almost twenty years since he was a wafer-thin, acne-faced teenager, plopping his text books down and slumping into one of the old wooden desks in the very same classroom?

It's true that much had changed in Franklin's life over the past two decades, as well as at the Fort Lauderdale parochial school. The uncomfortable desks he used to call the "school stocks" because they left a student's body feeling like a confined contortionist, had long been replaced by shiny, metal and plastic tabletops with chair-back seats, which were downright cozy by comparison. The dull institutional green paint once covering the walls had since been sprayed over with a less-dreary cream and burgundy combo. Those and many other costly upgrades made Good Shepherd seem more blessed than quite a few of the less-fortunate schools in the area. Its reputation had become both respected and envied in the community.

But while the newly bulked-up and baby-faced Franklin looked back fondly on his schooling, as well as the solid preparation it had given him in his adult life, he knew the makeover on the sprawling grounds felt just a little too cosmetic.

Ever since Franklin began teaching advanced bible and history classes at his alma mater nearly five years before, he'd noticed a significant difference in the aura of the place. It bugged him that he couldn't pinpoint what was spiritually ailing the campus. For sure, most of the faculty members were conscientious, caring Christian folk with a deep concern for their students' academic and moral well-being. In fact over the years, many of the teachers had developed life-long mentoring relationships with their pupils. Franklin was keenly aware that his best friend, Dr. Samuel Simmons, had spent a generation nurturing him since his own impetuous youth. No, Franklin reasoned, the faculty wasn't the cause for his concern.

Yet, quite often, while teaching during recent months, Franklin sensed a satanic presence lurking nearby. Sometimes when the eerie feeling came over him, he would silently recite to himself First Peter chapter five, verse eighteen: "Be self-controlled and alert. Your enemy the devil prowls around like a roaring lion looking for someone to devour." In fact, the well-known Bible verse had come to mind at that very moment.

Franklin's students began to make their way into the classroom as the final buzzer blared; it's shrill almost commanding the kids to take their seats immediately.

They were a varied group of seniors with a wide range of spiritual and secular influences. Some came from well-to-do families while others were just grateful the church congregation was affluent enough to offer the scholarships that enable poorer kids to attend an expensive, private school.

Taking his usual seat front and center in the classroom was princely Troy Battles, whose swagger everywhere he went reflected his regal upbringing. Though not really royalty, the Battles clan was an unseemly wealthy bunch, who had no problem flaunting their grand fortune. Troy, the sole heir, impressed almost all who came in contact with him. His teen idol looks, from the jet black coiffure and midnight eyes to a brawny physique, caused the girls to swoon so much they practically performed cartwheels down the school's hallways in hope of having him notice them. But only one lovely lass had ever been able to capture his full attention.

Troy basically chased Gretchen Bjorn since they played together as young kids in the Battles mansion. From the time Gretchen's father Erik went to work as an accountant for Troy's dad's import business, the Battles and the Bjorns remained inseparable. Still, it wasn't until they reached their teenage years that blond-haired, blue-eyed Gretchen allowed her dashing playmate to pursue her romantically. Troy finally caught the Swedish beauty and then never let her out of his sight. So there was Gretchen slipping gracefully into the desk beside him.

As Franklin outlined the morning's lesson on the whiteboard, the rest of the small class chattered among themselves. That particular Monday was the first day back after the long Easter break and Franklin knew he would have some difficulty refocusing his students' attention back on their studies. To make matters worse, graduation was only a mere two months away. Although their bodies were still stuck in high school, their minds were already daydreaming of college in the fall. Franklin could relate to their pleasant reverie and often found himself flashing back to his university days, especially crisp autumn afternoons at The Swamp in Gainesville.

"Who do you think God roots for on the gridiron?" Franklin

quipped to his class. "You know, what his favorite football team is?"

"The Cardinals, either Stanford or Louisville," claimed one boy.

"Probably Texas Christian or Southern Methodist," shouted another.

"No you fools," Troy replied. "It has to be the Fighting Irish. Who else? Notre Dame has Touchdown Jesus, after all."

"I didn't say it had to be college," answered Franklin coyly. "Everybody knows the Lord loves the Saints."

The bemused teacher listened to a few hisses and sighs resonate throughout the room before posing another question to his attentive students.

"What is you favorite flower and why?" Franklin asked. "Take a few seconds to think about your answer before you raise your hands."

First to reply was Stephanie, a dainty little redhead who reminded Franklin of his wife Sara in one of her own teenage photos. "Roses are my favorite. Their form is perfect and their scent is delightful."

Franklin nodded agreeably.

"I like the smell of the citrus blossom," noted Keira, a studious, bespeckeled young lady. "They are tiny, but pretty in a quaint sort of way. Besides, it's our state flower, you know."

Interesting answer, Franklin thought to himself. "What about you Gretchen? What's your favorite flower?"

Pausing for a moment after being caught off guard by her teacher asking her directly, she offered the lily as her response. "I love them because they remind me of Easter. Being horn-shaped, they almost seem to be announcing the resurrection of our Lord and Savior,

Jesus Christ. I think their white color reflects his pure beauty."

"What a sweet notion Gretchen," the highly-pleased teacher remarked.

Rolling his eyes, Troy restlessly blurted out "Who cares about flowers? What's the point of all this anyway Mr. Edwards?"

"I'm glad you asked Troy because my favorite flower is the tulip and I'll tell you why that is."

Franklin walked over to the whiteboard and pointed not to a picture of the aforementioned flower, but to the word T.U.L.I.P. spelled out in big bold letters. He explained to his students that the term is an acrostic signifying the five points of the reformed faith, which was to be the subject of the day's lesson.

"I believe this little flower goes a long way in helping us Christians to explain why we believe what we believe. But can any of you first tell me what our salvation means to us?" Franklin asked his class.

Troy was the first to raise his hand. "It means we are saved from the scorching flames of hell."

"That's true Troy, but what else?"

"Salvation to me," said Gretchen, "means spending eternity in the loving arms of Jesus. His affection for us is why he was willing to suffer so greatly on the cross. What a dear love He has!"

"Also correct," Franklin responded approvingly. "But why would God's only begotten Son need to go through such pain and suffering so that we could live eternally with him?"

A pause stifled the discussion momentarily.

"Because we're sinners?" timidly replied Daniel, whose soft-spoken answer was barely audible to the rest of the class.

"Speak for your self, Danny boy," Troy told the gawky kid, who cast his eyes downward. "I'm just razzing ya. Of course, we're all sinners and need forgiveness."

"You are absolutely right Troy," the teacher interjected. "Yet, why didn't the Father just forgive our sins outright and not send his Son to the cross?"

A few seconds lingered before Troy raised his hand and answered. "Because God is perfectly holy and somebody had to pay the penalty for peoples' sin in order for us to enter heaven."

The teacher wanted more from the smug Battles boy.

"Well, because Jesus died for our sins," Franklin stated, "does that mean everybody receives forgiveness and therefore goes to heaven? Why then does God send some to hell Troy?"

Once again irritated by Franklin's challenging manner, Troy bit back.

"Because they don't accept his forgiveness when it's offered freely to them. Some people hate Jesus and reject him. Others think they can earn their way into heaven by doing good works. But it's only faith in God's son that saves you."

The teacher again pushed his brash student.

"Great answer Troy, but you haven't fully grasped the direction in which I'm heading. From where does that faith come? From us or from God?"

Troy verbally fought back, his smirk casting shades of disrespect.

"It's up to every man to respond to God's call," Troy claimed. "God offers every one the opportunity to avoid hell, but we must accept that offer individually. It's each person's responsibility to accept God's grace and not every one does. So, if you end up in hell instead of heaven, it's your own fault. You had your chance."

Troy smiled smugly, believing he had pretty much summed up the day's lesson.

"The great reformers like John Calvin would think differently Troy," Franklin replied, strongly challenging his student's claim.

Frowning because he realized the disputed path his teacher's lesson had taken, the well-read Troy muttered to himself "Calvinism, that's like a different religion."

Not wanting to begin a lengthy debate with the bright Battles boy over his dimwitted view of one of the Lord's greatest saints, Franklin pretended he didn't hear the snide remark and began to dish out the meat of his lecture.

"It's certainly true that every person must decide whether they will accept God's gift of salvation or not. But therein lays the real problem. No one has the heart to accept such a gift, which leads us to the first letter in our acrostic."

Mr. Edwards strolled over to the board and tapped on the word of the day with his pointer.

"The T in T.U.L.I.P. stands for the theological concept known as Total Depravity," he said. "It means that all men and women are born spiritually dead and not able to believe the gospel without the Holy Spirit breathing new life into each one of them. This fact is scripturally backed up early in the second chapter of Paul's epistle to the Ephesians."

Franklin felt like one of his old college professors as he spoke with authority. He loved teaching his students on topics that would challenge both their mind and their faith.

"You see," Franklin continued, "ever since our parents Adam and Eve first sinned in the Garden of Eden, all of their children, which encompasses every person who has ever lived, are also guilty of that sin. This means that we are born with a sinful nature or what is called original sin. It's why we all sin. King David knew this when he cried out to God in Psalm fifty-one verse five."

Franklin found the pre-marked passage in the Bible on his lectern.

" 'Behold,' "he stated from the text, his right index finger raised in the air, " 'I was brought forth in iniquity, and in sin my mother conceived me.' " Franklin paused for emphasis and looked out at his class. "So when we enter this world, sin doesn't just make us ill, it kills us spiritually. Any questions so far?"

Keira quickly raised her hand.

"Mr. Edwards," she said, "I know the Bible states 'all have sinned and fall short of the glory of God.' And I also realize that some people are far greater sinners than others. But isn't it true that most people are basically good at heart? I know that there are a lot of good people in the world."

The teacher shook his head forcefully against such flawed thinking.

"The humanists would like you to think that Keira," he replied. "But Biblical Christianity teaches that sin penetrates the very core of all of our lives. There is no part of us left untouched by sin. That's why we call this condition total depravity...Now, while we are not utterly depraved because we are not as sinful as we could be, the Bible also says 'no one is righteous, not even one.' And because of the state in which sin renders our heart, the Bible calls us 'dead in our trespasses and sins.' It is only when God's Holy Spirit revives our hearts will our souls be brought back from death unto life...And that is strictly God's choice. Which brings us to the U in T.U.L.I.P."

At that point, most of the students were still keeping up with the gist of their teacher's lesson and some were even beginning to realize the depth of the spiritual points being made. Hearing no further questions, Franklin moved on.

"Simply put, Unconditional Election means that God's choice to save certain totally depraved sinner's rests solely in his sovereign will. God does not look down the corridors of time and pick those who pick him, as many people believe. In fact, one of Calvin's rivals, Arminius, taught such doctrine, but we will try to discuss their battle later if we have time."

Shaking his head, Troy thought to himself *why not debate this dispute now?* But with the teacher moving briskly through the lesson, Troy didn't get the chance to raise his hand and challenge Mr. Edwards' position.

The teacher walked back to the lectern and flipped to another passage in scripture.

"I want you all to turn in your Bibles to Ephesians chapter one and read what Paul writes about God's perfect will," requested Franklin, who gave his students a few moments to look up the text.

"In verses four through six, Paul writes: 'For he (God) chose us in him before the creation of the world to be blameless and holy in his sight. In love he predestined us to be adopted as his sons through Jesus Christ, in accordance with his pleasure and will -- to the praise of his glorious grace, which he has freely given us in the One he loves.' " Franklin looked up and smiled at his students. "The One whom Paul is writing about here is Jesus, the only person who ever followed the Father's will perfectly. The Father has loved the Son through all eternity. Jesus is the only One who deserves the Father's love. Because of our disobedience, we are objects of the Father's wrath, and deservedly so. But when he looks at us through Jesus, we become objects of his love if we have faith in the One he loves. Do you understand?"

Jake, a hard-working Catholic student, who was one of Franklin's most inquisitive pupils, posed to his teacher: "What does predestined mean? I've heard the term before, but I really don't know what it means."

Franklin scratched his chin while pondering just how to answer Jake's question on one of the most controversial doctrines of the Christian faith. In the meantime, wily Troy smirked as he hoped to catch his teacher stumbling on the forthcoming definition.

"Essentially Jake," Franklin sighed, "what predestination means as far as salvation goes, is that whether we end up in heaven or hell is decided by God not only before we get there, but before we are even born. For is own glory, God mercifully chooses some individuals to live eternally blessed with him in heaven while he passes others over, allowing them to pay the consequences of their sins in anguish forever in hell. Many churches believe in predestination, but differ on how God chooses his elect."

The teacher folded his arms and scanned the room. He noticed a few yawns failing to be stifled.

"We spoke briefly before about the Arminian view," he said before clearing his throat. "Where God has foreknowledge of those who will choose him and thus picks those who pick him. But that means the decision is primarily up to each individual...I just don't see how a sovereign, all-powerful God could possibly leave such a consequential decision in the hands of fallen people, whose depraved hearts make them incapable of choosing him. This was also the view held by the reformers like Calvin. We only choose God because he chose us first. Read Malachi one verses two and three." Franklin turned to the passage. "It says: 'I have loved Jacob, but Esau I have hated.' Or Exodus thirty three, nineteen: He quickly flipped through his Bible. "'I will have mercy on whom I will have mercy. I will have compassion on whom I will have compassion.'

Being a just God, it's amazingly loving that he has mercy or compassion on anybody...Which takes us nicely to the L in T.U.L.I.P."

Franklin tapped his pen on the L three times.

Troy, realizing he would have to wait to cross-up his highly-prepared instructor with an alternative theology, squirmed anxiously in his seat.

"Anyone have an idea what this L might symbolize?" Franklin asked. "Oh, Gretchen. Alright, what does the L mean to you?"

Batting her doe eyes in a winsome fashion, Gretchen replied demurely, "it should stand for love, Mr. Edwards. Like John three, sixteen says 'For God so loved the world that he gave his one and only Son, that whoever believes in him shall not perish but have eternal life.' "

Franklin smiled at Gretchen's charming answer, but then gently corrected her.

"Yes, while it's definitely true that God loves his creation; his Word says that he only saves some of it. God's salvation is limited to those he unconditionally elects. Hence, the L stands for Limited Atonement."

As he wrote out the definition on the whiteboard, Franklin continued his explanation.

"Now, to atone for something means to make amends or pay for a mistake that has been made. For example, if you are caught speeding by the police and they write you a ticket, you make amends for your mistake by paying the fine. If you don't pay the fine, the authorities can send you to jail. But with God, humans are incapable of making the payment due to forgive their debt. We have so many sins credited against us that we could never reconcile such a high debt. And because we can't repay a Holy God for our transgressions, He must send us to Hell to punish us."

Franklin pursed his lips and raised his palms up in resignation.

"But as Gretchen noted," he continued, "God, thankfully, does love us so much that the Father sent his sinless Son to the cross as the substitute who satisfied the debt we owe. And the Son paid the debt we owe willingly. He was not coerced or forced to do so. It's important to remember the Father and Son worked in harmony to effect our reconciliation."

Pausing to give his students a chance to catch up writing down their notes, Franklin noticed Troy gazing aimlessly out the window.

"Something troubling you Troy?"

"No sir. I'm just contemplating what you are saying."

"Very well," said Franklin, focusing his eyes back on the rest of the class. "Okay, all Christians believe in the doctrine of atonement. Where we differ is on how that atonement is offered. Some Christians are known as Universalists because they believe Christ died for the sins of the whole world without exception. They cite verses such as First John two, two to back them up scripturally. Will someone read that verse for me?"

Troy promptly raised his hand and quickly flipped through the delicately thin pages of his well-worn bible to the requested passage.

"First John two, two," proclaimed the now re-energized would-be theologian. " 'He,' meaning Jesus, 'is the atoning sacrifice for our sins, and not only for ours but also for the sins of the whole world.' "

Troy couldn't resist trying to show off his smarts to both his teacher and the class. Pride always got the better of him. He raised his head from the Bible and looked his teacher squarely in the eyes.

"What this verse seems to be saying, Mr. Edwards is that Christ's death was intended for everybody. But if that were true, then Christ's death on the cross would satisfy God's wrath toward everybody, and everybody would be saved. But if you believe that, then you can't believe in hell. The bible says hell exists, right? So therefore, I think when John wrote the "whole world', he meant the whole world that believes the gospel...It's still a matter of accepting Jesus' sacrifice as to whether you are saved or not. It's your choice."

Thoroughly pleased with his explanation of the bible verse, Troy folded his arms and nodded his head in a highly self-satisfying manner.

"Not bad Troy," Franklin said with a wry smirk. "But also remember that if Christ died for everybody's sins, not only would everybody go to heaven, but God would be also unjust. Like you said Troy, there is a hell and God does send people there. So actually this bible passage proves more than the Universalists want it to prove. They are too broad with their definition of atonement. I liked your answer Troy, but it too was not quite specific enough."

Troy gasped a heavy sigh and rolled his eyes while tilting his head back in frustration. Reflecting on the numerous times this year Mr. Edwards had called him out for not giving a thorough response to a pointed question, Battles felt like telling his teacher to go to the foreboding place they were just talking about. Instead, Troy bit his tongue and waited patiently in cold silence for another opportunity to launch some more verbal weaponry in the blooming rivalry.

Turning back toward the whiteboard, Franklin was hardly aware of Troy's simmer and moved on with the lesson. Underling the word Limited, the teacher stated: "This is the other key word in our definition.

"Now some prefer the word definite instead of limited when speaking of atonement. And while it is probably a little more accurate to say definite instead of limited, it makes our acrostic T.U.D.I.P. instead of T.U.L.I.P. So for our purpose today we will stick with limited."

A slight snicker spread across the room as the teacher continued.

"Since we've previously discussed that some people will justly end up in hell when they die, then atonement must be limited to the elect when it is offered. You have to remember the time period when John wrote this passage and to whom he was writing it, namely first-century Jews who converted to Christianity. You see, in Old Testament times, the Jews believed that their sins were atoned for through the sacrifice of animals such as lambs. But such sacrifices really didn't save them; it was their faith in God's promise of the Messiah that saved them."

Franklin sat down on his wobbly metal stool and put his elbows on the lectern.

"When Christ, which is Greek for Chosen One, came to earth, he was that long-promised Messiah. Jesus is the perfect lamb who was sacrificed for his people. In fact according to Matthew one, twenty-two, the Virgin Mary was told to name her unborn son 'Jesus, because he will save his people from their sins.' This salvation that Jesus bought for his people with his own blood is not in vain, but it is definite because it fully paid the price for their sins."

The teacher glanced around the room. Gretchen flashed a delightful smile at him.

"Now at the end of Matthew," he continued, "the risen Christ told his disciples to go to the ends of the earth and spread the gospel. Yet while Christ's shed blood is sufficient to save everybody, it is only effective to those who believe the gospel. Those known as the elect, who as we said before, were chosen by God before creation. So John's teaching that Christ died for the sins of the whole world means that the elect are not limited to Israel but found throughout the world. And all for who Christ died are redeemed by his sacrificial act.

"Any questions or comments before I proceed?"

Stephanie, who had been surprisingly quiet throughout the whole lecture in spite of her normally doubtful disposition, asked: "If all you say is true, Mr. Edwards, then how can we know for sure if Christ died for us? Is there truly a way we can tell if we are elected or not?"

Franklin endearingly reassured his uncertain pupil.

"Don't worry Stephanie; God gives both salvation and assurance through the power of his Holy Spirit. This is where the I in T.U.L.I.P. comes from."

Mr. Edwards returned the whiteboard and drew with a black marker a picture of a heart with a jagged crack split down the center of it. To the right of the black heart, he then drew with a bright red marker a perfectly formed heart shape, symmetrical on both sides. Though his artistic skill left much to be desired, Franklin surmised the illustration would serve his purpose.

"Remember earlier in our lesson we said that every man, and every woman for that matter, is born spiritually dead?" Franklin asked the class. "Well, the black heart on the left side of this illustration represents our condition at birth. Though our bodies are alive and physically grow, our dead, black hearts leave us without any spiritual desire for the ways of God and we never mature unto what is called a saving faith. So in order to claim the redemption Christ gained for us and enable us to enter heaven, we need a new heart."

Franklin pointed to the red heart on the board and glanced

quickly around the subdued classroom to make sure none of the kids were dozing off. So far, so good, but Franklin knew the topic might be better served if the students could continue to actively participate.

"Everybody turn in their Bibles to Ezekiel thirty-six, verses twenty-six and twenty-seven."

A few moments passed before Franklin asked Stephanie to recite the passage aloud. She cleared her scratchy throat before reciting the two verses.

"It says 'I will give you a new heart and put a new spirit in you; I will remove from you your heart of stone and give you a heart of flesh. And I will put my spirit in you and move you to follow my decrees and be careful to keep my laws.' " Stephanie lifted her suddenly tearing eyes from the page and turned them curiously toward her teacher. "How do we know when we have a new heart Mr. Edwards? I certainly hope I have new one!"

Franklin smiled sweetly at the disconcerted girl and then asked the class to offer some comforting words. "Can anybody dispel Stephanie's worries about the state of her heart?"

Displaying her always-present ability to calm a person's anxiety, Gretchen walked across the room and gently placed her hand on Stephanie's shoulder.

"Stephanie dear, I bet Jesus' own disciples felt the same way as you," Gretchen said as she reassuringly rubbed her friend's shoulder a couple of times. "It's okay to wonder about where you stand with God. But don't overly trouble yourself with worry. I think the fact that you care so deeply about your salvation shows how much you love him in your heart. And Jesus says he will always love you and never leave you."

As Gretchen wiped away a slowly dropping tear that was

running down the girl's cheek, Stephanie nodded affirmingly and replied softly in between sniffles: "Thank you sweetie. You always know the right thing to say."

Gretchen winked and returned to her seat.

"Oh brother," said Troy, shaking his head at the sisterly moment. "Why don't you give her a kiss on the forehead next time?"

Gretchen punched Troy gently in the shoulder and stuck her tongue out her smart-mouthed boyfriend.

"Thank you Gretchen," Franklin said. "Troy, you could learn a thing or two about grace from her."

Troy shrugged and returned his eyes to his notes.

"Speaking of grace," Mr. Edwards continued. "That's exactly what God is showing us in the Ezekiel passage. Because of the Father's love for those the Son has redeemed on the cross, the Holy Spirit calls us to Christ by giving us the right heart to accept this free gift of salvation. Without our hearts being renewed by the Holy Spirit, there is no way we can accept this gift of grace. And this grace given to us is a gift we can't refuse. That is why it is called Irresistible Grace."

Not bothering to raise his hand, Troy quickly blurted out, "but some people do resist this grace Mr. Edwards. It happens all the time."

Nodding, Franklin responded, "You're right Troy. People do hear God's outer call of the gospel and reject it. That's because the Holy Spirit has not changed their hearts, they are still as black and broken as the day they were born." Edwards firmly tapped his pointer on the split black heart on the whiteboard and stared directly at Battles.

"But the Holy Spirit's inward call is always effective. It never fails to produce His desired results. You've heard the term "born again' haven't you Troy?"

"Of course I have Mr. Edwards."

"Well then, are people really born again Troy?"

"In a sense. Because they have accepted grace, they are a new person. Jesus told Nicodemus that he could not enter heaven unless he was born again."

"But who does the so-called rebirthing?" Franklin asked as his brow rippled with frustration toward Troy's somewhat sarcastic response.

"God does change our hearts, but only if we let him. We must prove that we have faith in what Jesus did on the cross. We have free will Mr. Edwards. Even your friend Mr. Calvin wouldn't deny that we have the will to choose whatever we desire."

"Yes Troy," Franklin retorted. "But even Calvin's rival Arminius would admit that our will is not free to choose what it does not desire. So therefore, with regard to salvation, the question of the freedom to choose God or not is really a matter of our desire. And because sin has killed our hearts spiritually, we have no desire for God. He must give us that desire. Maybe regeneration is a better term that rebirth. When the Holy Spirit regenerates us spiritually, he changes the disposition of our hearts and plants a desire for himself within us."

Troy paused for a moment to process what he'd been told before again responding. "Okay, so where does faith fit into this scenario?"

"Rebirth or regeneration precedes faith," the teacher replied sternly. "We do not choose to be regenerated. God chooses to regenerate us before we will ever have the desire to embrace him. After we have been regenerated, we do choose to believe in Christ and follow him. But it is God himself who gives us that faith."

Troy was rendered speechless by what he had just heard, so Franklin pressed on.

"Now, when God gives us this faith, he will never take it from us. This brings us to the final letter in our acrostic: the P."

Realizing less than five minutes remained before the end of class, Franklin requested that his students not ask any more questions until he finished a brief definition of the doctrine known as Perseverance of the Saints.

"Now, the P in our acrostic," said Franklin, pointing to the letter on the board, "really can stand for two words."

Franklin wrote both perseverance and preservation in red letters on the board.

"Webster's dictionary defines to persevere as 'to persist, as in an undertaking, in spite of difficulties.' In reference to our faith, this would seem to imply that we will keep our faith until we die so long as we persist in our efforts to please God, even when we encounter troubles in our life. That if we fail to please God by our sin, we must somehow make up for our sin by performing good works to get back in God's good graces...To me that sounds like we will lose our salvation if we fail to persist in acting like a good Christian should. But that kind of thinking is not only bad doctrine, it is completely untrue, both biblically and practically."

Franklin paused after the previous statement to make direct eye contact with some of the Catholic students in the class. Remembering their teacher's request for silence, the kids just sat and listened attentively.

"Sure, we could fall from grace if our salvation was up to us," Franklin continued. "Look at Adam and Eve. God told them not to eat from the forbidden tree or they would surely die. But after being tempted by the serpent, Eve ate from the tree and gave some fruit to Adam as well. They should have died instantly at that point, but they didn't. They realized their sin and tried to hide from God, knowing they could do nothing to make up for what they'd done. When God found them, did he immediately put them to death as he had every right to do? No! Did he start over with a new couple? No! What he did was show them grace."

Franklin quickly flipped threw the pages of his blue paperback copy of Webster's Dictionary to find the word preserve.

"To preserve means," said Franklin, briefly glancing above the tattered book's pages at his students, " 'to keep safe, to guard, to protect.' That's what God did for Adam and Eve. Despite their disobedience of his command, God chose not to destroy those he created in his own image, but instead, preserve them...Oh, there were consequences for their actions. They were forced to leave the paradise of the garden for one thing. But Adam and Even didn't totally fall from their Creator's hand. He held them up and through that couple, the rest of mankind was born, albeit in sin."

Noting the clock slowly counting down the time, Franklin summed up his lesson rapidly in the few remaining seconds.

"This is one reason that the P is my favorite letter in our acrostic. Despite being a wretched sinner, God still preserves me," Franklin said.

Troy smirked, wondering what was so sinful about his teacher. Franklin noticed Troy's expression, but pushed forward with his lesson.

"By the power of the Holy Spirit, I will not fall so badly that I can never get back up again. I persevere because God preserves me. He guarantees my salvation. All whom the Father elects, he brings to glory in heaven. No matter what I do, I can't ultimately lose my faith and therefore my place in heaven. It's impossible..."

The buzzer's blare over the intercom interrupted Franklin in mid-sentence.

"There are a few more points I'd like to make on this subject, so contemplate what I've told you today and we'll continue in our next session."

As he and Gretchen gathered their books to leave, Troy glared back at Franklin and sighed, wishing he had the chance to get in a few more blows to his teacher's doctrinal views. Battles vowed to himself that he would be fully armed next time to refute Edwards' points. Gretchen, sensing her boyfriend's frustration, lovingly took his hand in hers. As Good Shepherd's premier couple exited the classroom, Gretchen looked back at the teacher with a becoming smile and a slight wave.

Franklin nodded in return while putting away his own lecturing material. He felt that he probably left his lesson lacking due to time constraints. Franklin wished he had the chance to explain why some people profess faith in Jesus and then turn their back on him. Those who appear to fall away never really had faith in Christ in the first place, an instance Franklin had seen often in his thirty-plus years of walking with the Lord. He realized that statistically some of his own students who had vocalized their belief in God's only son as their Lord and Savior may never display the true saving faith that proceeds from a regenerate heart. It was a fact that troubled Franklin deeply. But all a teacher can do is present the facts to the best of his ability and hope the Holy Spirit applies that knowledge. Franklin rested in the fact that his students who are true believers can never be snatched from God's hand.

Franklin was pondering his own assurance of salvation as he turned out the light and left the classroom. Heading to the teachers lounge down the brightly-lit corridor, Franklin remembered his assurance came from his understanding of the Word of God coupled with the testimony the Holy Spirit placed in his own heart. Knowing that Jesus nailed every one his deepest and darkest sins to the cross brought Franklin great comfort. His quieted heart prompted the teacher's mind to recall Gretchen's sweet words about the Savior about an hour earlier: *What a dear love He has.*

"He most certainly does," Franklin said to himself. "He most certainly does."

Chapter II

"Do I really want to open my eyes?" Franklin asked himself, fully aware that the sun's laser-like rays were pinpointing his covered pupils through the tiny slats on the blinds draping his bedroom window. He thought it almost tortuous to be so rudely awakened on a beautiful Sunday morning. Wasn't sleep such a precious gift bestowed by God on his creation that to interrupt its purpose of rest and renewal would be downright sinful? After all, didn't the Lord himself create a Sabbath after six days of arduous labor?

But the more Franklin questioned the worthiness of breaking his slumber, the fewer valid excuses he could muster. Oh well, at least when he did pry open his weary eyes, Franklin awoke to the lovely sight of Sara lying peacefully next to him. Her auburn tresses seemingly kissed her fair white cheeks and pursed ruby lips. Even while she slept, Sara appeared almost radiant to her still youthful-looking husband.

Franklin knew how truly blessed he was when the Lord yoked him with Sara during their freshman year in college. Only God could link such a shy, gawky fraternity pledge to a charming, confident future sorority president. Besides her obvious beauty, Sara had always been one of the most outgoing and friendly persons anybody would ever wish to meet. And there she was, softly sleeping next to him in their cozy, queen-size bed. The couple had often thought about trading in their mattress for a larger model, but they didn't want to sacrifice being able to lovingly brush up against each other during the night. Franklin thanked God daily for his bride, as well as the two precious children their union produced.

Because ten-year-old Brianna and her two-years younger sibling Ashley were apparently still asleep early that Lord's day, Franklin felt it would be romantic to wake Sara with subtle kisses on her neck. He began to lightly touch her with his lips, bringing a faint smile to her face. Franklin tenderly caressed his wife's shoulder, causing her to roll over onto him and plant a kiss firmly on his mouth. Sara just then glimpsed a twinge of movement from the corner of her eye.

"Good morning sweetie," Sara said to the tiny blonde tyke standing in the doorway. "How's mommy's little girl today? Come here."

Ashley quickly dashed over and jumped onto her parents' bed, giggling as she leapt. Franklin had never minded either of his daughters climbing into bed with him and Sara some mornings, but he was wishing Ashley would have waited just a little longer that day. He was certain Brianna wouldn't be far behind.

Sure enough, just a few seconds later the older sister also slipped between the sheets, making for a boisterous beginning to a usually calm Sunday morning.

After a couple of minutes of playfulness, Sara put on her robe and got up.

"Okay gang, time for mommy to make breakfast," Sara said, as she flashed a bright smile and offered a consoling shrug to her understanding husband.

"No sliding down the balcony Brianna, you're gonna hurt yourself," Franklin heard Sara yell to the eldest girl, who stopped abruptly midway down the banister.

Franklin realized he might as well head to the shower as Sara prepared breakfast. Maybe a cold dousing would be appropriate this morning he mused, knowing the lovemaking was to be put on hold for the time being.

Sundays had always been the favorite day of the week for the many generations of the Edwards clan. Franklin recalled that fact as he readied himself for church.

<hr />

South Florida was a much different place when Jordan Edwards relocated his young bride Gracie to the balmy peninsula in the late 1960's. While the rest of the nation was enduring a period of great social upheaval, it was a part of the country that seemed a fairly calm place to begin a family. Florida was nowhere near as populated then as it was to become and Franklin's father took comfort in the laidback lifestyle. A college professor in Boston for nearly a decade, Jordan was happy to leave the big-city pace once he married his small-town sweetheart.

Gracie was almost ten years younger than her new husband, whom she met at a Lutheran church picnic her best friend Lillith had invited her to during one of the northeast's most blistering summers. Jordan's distinguished presence caught Gracie's notice the minute she laid eyes on him. Even in his dingy jean-shorts and white T-shirt, Jordan cut a striking figure as he stepped up to the plate while play- ing in the picnic's softball game. Promptly swatting a bases-clearing home run, Jordan politely tipped his hat to the ladies in the stands as he triumphantly rounded the bags that hot Sunday afternoon.

"He's a bit of a showboat," Gracie remarked to Lillith, "nice looking though."

"Want to meet him?" Lilith quickly responded with nodding approval. "He is one of my brother's best buddies. Come with me. I'll introduce you."

Grabbing Gracie's arm, Lillith promptly led her friend in the direction of Jordan. Gracie was a bit timid at the thought of such an impromptu introduction, but Lillith always acted rashly while trying to play cupid for her somewhat shy friend. Jordan was pouring a cup of ice water over his head under the cool of a tall shady elm tree when Lillith startled him with a shoulder tap. Some of the water splashed onto Gracie's curly brown hair, but she pretended not to notice.

"Jordan, this is my best friend in the whole world, Gracie," Lilith said in her delightful Tennessee drawl. "She admired the way you handled yourself out there and likes the cut of your cloth."

"Lilith!" Gracie exclaimed, amazed at how her friend's brashness contradicted her own strict Baptist view of potential courtship.

Grinning, Jordan reached out and firmly shook Gracie's tiny hand. "Nice to meet you, my dear. Any friend of Lillith's must like to laugh a lot and have fun. I know fun is your middle name, huh Lilith?"

Winking at Jordan as she walked away, Lillith answered "You be a gentleman now Jordan. I'll be right over at that table Gracie if you need me."

Gracie was curious about her friend's sly comments, but wouldn't find out until much later that Jordan was quite the ladies man in his youth, a fact well-known by Lillith. But after coming to Christ in college, Jordan had walked far from his previously wanton ways. He had since developed a liking for nice Christian ladies, however, most who had come across his path were neither nice, Christian, nor ladies. Yet, standing there right in front of him appeared to be a woman who possessed the distinct qualities for which he had been longing.

"You from around here?" Jordan asked Lillith's pretty, young friend.

"No, I'm from the Midwest, Kansas actually," answered Gracie.

"So what brought you to this part of God's glorious creation?" queried Jordan, making sure to invoke the Lord's presence in the conversation.

"I came here on a volleyball scholarship to Boston College. Just finished my senior year and hope to attend graduate school in the fall."

"What's your major?"

"Accounting and finance," replied Gracie, continuing the awkward small talk. "What do you do for a living?"

"I'm currently teaching the history of religion at Boston University. But I'm looking for a change. I think college students today are becoming way too liberal for my liking...Anyway, Gracie, can I buy you a hot dog?" Jordan asked as he nervously nibbled the end of a drinking straw.

"I thought they were free?" she answered quizzically.

"Of course they are," said Jordan, slightly amused by the curious sparkle in the woman's big brown eyes. "It is just my way of asking you if I can continue our conversation."

"Oh," Gracie said as she smiled back at her handsome new suitor. "I'd love it if you would buy me a hot dog."

Jordan cocked his arm by his side, allowing Gracie to lock her arm into his as the couple strolled over toward the refreshment table under one of the park's old wooden pavilions.

⪧✦⪦

What a humble start to a life of walking hand-in-hand with the Lord, Franklin thought to himself as he remembered his mother's version of meeting his father all those years ago. Just as he was adjusting the knot in his tie in front of the mirror, Sara walked into the bedroom to inform Franklin that his breakfast was ready and waiting.

"Ah, another Sunday tradition I love," Franklin said to his wife.

Sara walked over and gave Franklin a mushy peck on the cheek.

"Maybe we can start a new Sunday tradition this evening," said Sara, as she gently smacked Franklin on the seat of his pants. "But hurry down now before your breakfast gets cold."

Franklin dutifully followed his wife down the stairs, sliding on the banister just like Brianna had done before.

"Well, I see where she gets it from," noted Sara, shaking her head at her husband's childish antics. "You know. You are not setting a very good example honey."

Feigning a boy pouting at his mother's scolding, Franklin took his place at the breakfast table and asked for the Lord's blessing on the food, as well as the Sabbath day.

Devouring a hearty helping of Sara's fluffy scrambled eggs, crisp bacon and lightly toasted English muffins left Franklin feeling satisfied in the belly, and also helped to whet his appetite for the spiritual meal he would partake later that morning.

Communion Sundays at Good Shepherd Presbyterian never failed to summon a deep reverence for Jesus all the way to the very core of Franklin's soul. To think that day he would again feast at the Lord's Table and commune with the divine nature of Christ, brought tears of remorse in Franklin's eyes. Knowing that his innocent Savior willingly suffered an indignant death on a tree rightly belonging to sinners like himself, always brought Franklin to repentance when he ingested the bread and wine. It wasn't that Franklin had not been known as what the secular world would call a "good person." He knew he wasn't all bad. But compared to Jesus, Franklin severely lacked any justifying righteousness. He lamented his woeful deficiency, but the promise of salvation that came with each communion always brought Franklin to his knees in worship.

"Praise God that He spiritually nourishes us with his body and blood," Franklin exclaimed to Sara as they loaded the two girls into their van and hurriedly headed off to church. "I can't wait until Jesus returns and we can feast on his glory forever in heaven."

"You and me both honey, Hallelujah," Sara replied with an almost mocking smile. "I've always loved the way you express your love of the Lord. It's like you're always in communion with God. That's comforting for me and the girls."

Franklin mouthed "I love you" to his wife as he started the engine. A gracious respect for her husband's soft heart was one of Sara's most endearing Christ-like character traits. Franklin had lovingly enjoyed discovering his bride's other admirable qualities over the years they'd been together.

As Sara began to sing with the kids the new praise song they learned the previous week in Sunday school, Franklin recollected the days sitting in the pews at Good Shepherd as a young boy with his family.

Back then the preacher, Pastor Thomas, was a somewhat frightening figure to the pre-adolescent Franklin. The elderly gent with a coarse voice, soul-piercing blue eyes and snowy long hair parted unevenly to one side, often scared Franklin with his gaze from atop the pulpit. It seemed like the high-priestly old man, draped in a flowing black robe accented by a white collar, was speaking directly from God when he belted out verse after verse from his oversized Bible. And Franklin was certain the most pointed passages about sin were sharply directed at misbehaving little boys like himself. The past week's youthful transgressions would race around in his head as Franklin listened to the pastor recite the sermon.

What a woeful place church is, Franklin thought back then as he squirmed uncomfortably in his seat. Gracie would lightly smack the young boy on the leg to keep him still.

"Is the service almost over mama?" Franklin would ask, but Gracie would just bring her index finger to her mouth and quiet him quickly.

As the Edwards family left the church each Sunday, rickety old Pastor Thomas would shake each of their hands and tell them to "have a blessed week." The preacher never seemed as foreboding to Franklin at the back of the church as he did from the pulpit. The old man was in fact sometimes downright friendly to the lad as he once again crossed the threshold to the freedom of the outside world.

Sundays were also fun days for the Edwards clan, and Franklin especially loved when they would have a picnic after church.

<hr/>

"That's not a bad idea," Franklin said to himself as he pulled the van into the church parking lot.

"What's that dear?" asked Sara.

"Why don't we go to the beach after church today and have a barbecue," Franklin answered. "Does that sound like fun to you girls?"

"Yeah daddy!" the youngsters gleefully responded, almost in unison.

"That sounds like fun, but you girls have to behave in church," Sara sternly told the sisters. "No messing around today. Okay?"

"We'll be good mommy," Brianna said assumingly as she held her little sister's hand while they took the short jump down from the van and ran toward the church together.

Once inside, the service again proved to be a blissful experience for Franklin. From the first notes of opening hymn, through Pastor Reynard's remarkable sermon on Christ's Ascension into heaven and culminating with the sacrament of Holy Communion, Franklin knew he surely felt the Lord's presence in the modestly-filled sanctuary that wonderful day.

"Great job Chris," said Franklin, backing up the compliment to his pastor with a brotherly hug. "I sometimes forget that our Savior is alive and well. His tomb's still empty. Thanks for the reminder."

"You're quite welcome," responded Pastor Reynard, whose youthful appearance and engaging smile always made Franklin and his family feel at ease in church, a stark contrast to his worship experience as a kid in the same old, but well-kept, wood-framed sanctuary. "You all have a blessed Lord's Day now."

Franklin and Sara tried to mingle with a few friends under the vast foyer outside the church, but were quickly halted by their daughters' persistent pleas to hurry off to the beach. Although they were somewhat nagging at that moment, the youngsters had earned their parents' favor by their stellar behavior during the service. They'd also received high praise earlier that morning from their

Sunday school teachers, so both Franklin and his wife were more than willing to reward the girls with an afternoon of fun in the late April sunshine.

The Edward's happy homestead was located a good ten miles from Good Shepherd in the suburb of Plantation, so Franklin scooted the family van briskly down Interstate 595. The pace was a little too quick for Sara's liking.

"Honey, I know you love racing your sports car, but this is not Friday night at the speedway," Sara scolded. "We'll get there soon enough."

Franklin rolled his eyes, but immediately let up on the gas pedal. A few minutes later, they pulled up into the driveway and another mad dash began.

Sara hurriedly dressed the girls in their swimsuits while Franklin loaded up the large blue cooler with barbecue fixings and ice. Sara and Franklin made quite the team whenever a family outing needed to be hastily thrown together. On this occasion, the Edwards party was off and rolling again in a scant fifteen minutes.

"Near record time," Franklin mumbled to himself as he again started the van.

"Where's you're swimsuit?" Sara asked her husband.

"I thought I'd just go skinny dipping," Franklin answered with a comical smirk that garnered a few giggles from the girls. But seeing Sara was not amused, he quickly changed his response.

"It's under my shorts honey. I'm just funnin' with ya. Let's roll."

"Not too fast dear. Let's get there in one piece."

Franklin teasingly made engine-revving and tire-squealing sounds at Sara while pulling the van onto the street. Sara just shook here head while the little girls delighted in their daddy's antics.

Franklin then remembered how his own father's playfulness used to vex his mother to no end.

Jordan was quite the prankster in his day and Gracie often bore the brunt of his amusing actions. Franklin recalled one occasion when his mother was, for months, the helpless mark of his father's tomfoolery.

⚜

Gracie received some expensive imported coffee from Columbia by her favorite aunt one Christmas. Jordon overheard his wife raving on the phone to Aunt Beatrice a few weeks later about the coffee's delectable taste and delightful aroma. When Gracie told Beatrice she wished the five-pound can would never run out, Jordan's mischievous nature drove him to conjure up a clever ruse.

He set the scheme in motion by phoning the elderly aunt and asking her if she could ship him a few more cans of the coffee when she returned to Bogotá after her year-long missionary furlough ended that February. Jordan told Beatrice he thought another shipment of the java would make a nice birthday present for Gracie that spring. Beatrice agreed and said she would send the coffee as soon as she arrived in Columbia.

Beatrice shipped the bulky package to Jordan's office at Good Shepherd, where he was then employed as Dean of Academic Affairs. Jordan took one of the cans home and left the other three safely tucked away in his office closet. Gracie wasn't there when Jordan arrived home that cool March evening, so Franklin's deceptive daddy hurried into the kitchen. He opened up the tin coffee canister and made precise note of the amount of the contents inside. *Just about half full,* Jordan thought to himself. He then carefully scooped up a cupful of the coffee Beatrice had sent him and poured it into the canister.

Jordan knew that every morning Gracie would brew exactly one-quarter pot of the coffee, making just enough to fill her thermos for the day. So every four days before Gracie awoke, Jordan would slip into the garage where he hid the can he brought home from work and replace the coffee Gracie had used during the previous days. After a couple of months, Gracie was astonished how much coffee still remained in the canister.

"Boy Jordan, I'll tell you what," Gracie remarked to her husband at the breakfast table one Saturday morning. "This coffee Aunt Beatrice gave me certainly goes a long way. It's been five months and I've only used about half of it. I can't wait to tell her it's like a never-ending supply she gave me. Amazing!"

After nearly blowing orange juice out his nostrils trying not to laugh, Jordan said "Maybe it's a miracle, like the one the Lord performed for the widow of Zaraphath."

"Huh?" Gracie responded quizzically.

"Yeah, you know," Jordan answered, "the lady in the Bible who graciously offered Elijah the last meal she was gonna make for her son and herself, despite having only a small jar of flour and a little jug of oil. Because of the honor she showed one of God's men, the flour and oil never ran out. You show such great love to me and our son, maybe the Lord's doing the same for you. Who knows?"

Gracie laughed slightly and continued to brew her coffee while Jordan winked at his curious nine-year-old son. Franklin remembered the prank continuing for a few more months until Aunt Beatrice wrote to Gracie and told her she thought Jordan was so sweet for buying his wife such a pricey birthday present. Those four cans of Columbian coffee cost well over $100 to ship overseas, which was very expensive for 1977.

Jordan knew the jig was up when Gracie presented him with the letter that night as they readied for bed. Gracie wasn't really angry at her husband, just disappointed that she had once again fallen victim to another one of his pranks.

⚜

Franklin chuckled aloud as the family van pulled into Hugh Taylor Birch State Park on Fort Lauderdale's world-famous beach. Sara queried her husband about what was so amusing, but Franklin said he would share with her later.

"Oh, honey, look there's a spot open right over there," Sara said as she pointed to a near-perfect location with an open picnic table and grill under a patch of tall, shady Australian Pine trees. "Let's grab it quick."

Franklin made a sharp right turn into the parking spot in front of their chosen area, cutting off another vehicle with the maneuver. After nodding apologetically, Franklin rolled down his window and offered the parking space to the perturbed driver in the other car, a souped-up lime green Mustang convertible. But the annoyed young Hispanic man gave Franklin and his family the one-finger salute and drove off.

"We'll that wasn't very nice," Franklin muttered, rolling his eyes.

"Don't worry about it dear," Sara said. "You tried to make amends. He didn't want to accept your offer. Maybe he's just having a bad day."

"We'll, he's not gonna ruin mine!" Franklin exclaimed. "Let's party!"

"Yeah!" the girls screamed in delightful response and quickly unbuckled their seatbelts in anticipation of the fun that was about to begin.

Sara helped Franklin unload their supplies from the van and carry them over to the chosen picnic table. Brianna and Ashley were already pleading with Sara to take them to the beach.

"We'll go as soon as I help daddy set up the area for our barbecue," mother somewhat sternly told the eager duo. "It will just take a couple of minutes. Be patient."

"Aw, their just excited honey," Franklin said with a smile and a slight shoulder shrug. "They only wanna have fun."

"We'll they need to learn some patience also!" Sara snapped back.

"Hey. What's wrong with you?"

"Nothing," Sara softly murmured after realizing her tone toward both her husband and the youngsters was surprisingly sharp. "I'm sorry dear. You know I sometimes get like that when I get rushed."

Franklin put his arm around his wife's shoulders and gave her a quick peck on the cheek. Sara hugged him back and kissed Franklin softly on the lips. The girls giggled at their parent's public display of affection, despite being accustomed to seeing mommy and daddy's frequent openness about showing their heartfelt love for each other.

"Why don't you take the girls to the ocean," Franklin suggested to Sara as they released their embrace. "I can handle things here."

Tilting his well-worn Miami Dolphins ball cap to one side and donning his cliche'-ish "Kiss the Cook" apron, Franklin picked up a pair of tongs and a spatula in each hand and flexed his biceps.

"I'm Captain Cookout you know!" he exclaimed with a deep voice, nearly stumbling when he slipped on some grease while striking the foolish pose.

Now Sara was also chuckling, as was an elderly couple who

were watching the family's antics from the next picnic table over.

"Okay girls, you win," she said, directing a quick wink at her husband as she flung a beach bag full of gear over her shoulder and held each daughter's hand while they hurried away.

"Come back in an hour or so and I'll have a yummy dinner ready for you," Franklin shouted to Sara and the girls as they walked toward the dimly lit tunnel leading under State Road A1A, which separated the park from the beach. Sara waived back after glancing down at her watch.

Franklin returned to his assignment, brushing out the ashes left in the nasty public grill by the previous user. He hated using the park grills, but he didn't feel like lugging his much-preferred propane-powered cooker from home in the van that time out. So instead, Franklin ripped open a medium-sized bag of charcoal and meticulously placed the briquettes to form a perfect pyramid. He then thoroughly doused the coals with lighter fluid and flicked a lighted stick match on them. The flames exploded upward, quickly engulfing the dark, black briquettes.

"That's what God will do to Satan and his minions one day," Franklin mused to himself.

After scraping the slimy baked-on crud off the rusted grill rack, Franklin covered it with tin foil and set it to the side of the grill. It would take about 15 minutes for the coals to be hot enough to begin cooking the chicken breasts and wings, so Franklin went to the cooler and pulled out an ice cold soda. He would have preferred a beer, but couldn't remember if alcohol was allowed in the park, so he left his stash of brew at home. He thought maybe he would indulge in a couple adult beverages later that evening with Sara before resuming the smooching that was abruptly interrupted earlier that morning.

While sipping on his soda, Franklin gazed around the park on the beautiful spring afternoon. The sky offered a magnificent shade of light blue, accented by a few puffy, white clouds. The temperature was hovering in the steamy upper 80's, but the steady sea breeze stirred the air just enough to offset the heat a little bit. Franklin also noticed it was certainly warm enough for many of the young ladies to walk about in just their swimsuit tops and a pair of shorts. In fact, an ample, blonde in her early twenties spotted him unwittingly staring at her and flashed a coquettish grin at him. Franklin smiled back and then swiftly looked away, realizing his unintended offense. He tried not to look in her direction again as he walked over to the cooler, but he couldn't help but sneak one more fleeting glance. The lady had since turned around with her back toward Franklin, so he didn't get another chance to peer at the part of her swim top that had first caught his eye. Good thing Sara wasn't around or he was quite sure she would have smacked him good for his lustful looks.

Franklin refocused on the task at hand, preparing the customary barbecue supper for his lovely wife and kids. He was determined to make the chicken taste delicious despite the fact it was cooked over charcoal instead of gas, which Franklin swore always gave food a much cleaner flavor. He was being deliberate in his cycle of turning and saucing the chicken and stirring the baked beans, so as not to look over at the blonde again. Meanwhile, Sara and the girls quietly slipped up behind him and yelled "Boo!"

Startled, Franklin jumped back while the girls laughed with delight.

"Did we scare you daddy?" Brianna said with a broad grin and dripping red hair that looked just like her mother's when wet. "Mommy told us to scare you."

"And you certainly did," Franklin said as he picked up his

daughter and lifted her high above his head. Brianna screamed a lit bit while her daddy spun her around like dive-bombing airplane. She just loved it when he played like that with her. Franklin gently landed his daughter back on her feet.

"My turn daddy, my turn," Ashley yelled.

Franklin scooped up the tiny tot, who shrieked with glee as he performed the same sweeping maneuvers, albeit a little more slowly. After another soft landing, Franklin asked Sara: "Your turn?"

"Don't you dare," Sara replied, sternly waving her index finger at her husband as he playfully approached her. "I'm not as skinny as I was in college."

"You still look light enough to me," Franklin said as he reached out to Sara, who was still only about ten pounds heavier than she was in college. "Girls, should I give mommy an airplane spin? What do ya think?"

"Go for it daddy," Brianna yelled as Franklin wrapped his arms around Sara's waist.

"Franklin stop!" Sara exclaimed, boldly shoving her husband's arms down.

Not wanting to push the issue, Franklin dropped his arms to his side before folding them across his chest. "Mommy's no fun girls, is she?" he said with a pout.

The children laughed at their father as Sara smirked and rolled her eyes.

"I just think you might want to save you're back for later to-night," Sara said with a wink.

Franklin quickly turned and walked toward the grill

"Okay girls, I think supper's ready," he said flashing a grin back at Sara while picking up a slightly blackened chicken breast with the tongs. "Yep, looks done to me. Let's eat."

The girls helped Sara set the table while Franklin took the meat off the grill. One of the wings slipped out of the tongs and landed in the dirt.

"We'll I guess the ants need to eat too," Franklin remarked, shrugging his shoulders. "No five-second rule when food lands in dirt."

Sara grimaced at Franklin's comment as she continued to spoon out a helping of potato salad on each plate.

"Alright gang, have a seat," Sara commanded the family. "Brianna, honey, would you say the blessing today?"

The girl eagerly clasped her hands together and bowed her head.

"Dear Jesus," Brianna prayed in a determined, yet humble voice. "Thank you for this food we are about to eat. Thank you for mommy and daddy and Ashley. Thank you for the beach. And may we continue to have fun today. In Jesus name. Amen."

"Thank you Bri," Franklin said as he nodded approvingly at his little girl before taking a big bite of his crisp chicken breast.

"Are we going to go back in the water after we eat mommy?" Ashley asked.

"We will have to wait about a half-hour before we go in," Sara responded. "We don't want to get a cramp. But we can make sand castles until then."

"Are you going swimming too daddy?" Brianna asked. "The water is a little cold, but you get used to it."

"Sounds like fun. Are there any waves today?"

"Just little ones daddy. You can't surf them."

"That's okay. I didn't bring my surfboard anyway. Maybe we can just body surf the waves Bri?"

"I wish we had a raft."

"I know. I forgot it at home."

"That's okay daddy. It'll be fun anyway," the child said with a shrug and finished the rest of the food on her plate.

"Wow Brianna, you must have been hungry," Sara noted. "Good job."

"Swimming always makes me hungry mommy. Can we go to the beach now?"

"As soon as you're sister is finished and we clean up."

"I'm done too mommy," Ashley quickly said, knowing the beach was more appealing than her supper.

"A few more bites dear," Sara said. "I don't want you to be hungry later."

Ashley rapidly gobbled up a couple more pieces of chicken and a spoonful of beans before popping out a small burp.

"Good one," Franklin said to the smiling child. "Better from the top than the bottom your grandpa used to say."

Sara shook her head and smirked as Franklin and the girls laughed about Ashley's slight belch.

"Alright now," Sara said as she daintily tapped her lips with a napkin. "Girls, help me clean off the table while your father puts the rest of the stuff away."

As the family went about their respective duties, Franklin heard a familiar revving sound coming from a car in the parking lot. When he peered across the park, he noticed a sleek white corvette backing sharply into a parking spot with its tires squealing. The guy and girl who hopped out of the vehicle a few seconds later were none other than Good Shepherd's most dashing couple: Troy and Gretchen.

They appeared to be arguing, but Franklin couldn't really tell for certain. A couple of minutes went by before the green Mustang Franklin had encountered earlier pulled up next to the corvette.

The driver, who flipped off the Edwards clan a couple hours before, got out and walked over to Troy. The young men talked for a short while before shaking hands. Gretchen threw up her arms in apparent frustration with their discussion and walked quickly toward the beach tunnel.

"Don't worry about her, she'll be okay with it," Franklin thought he heard Troy say to the other guy in a voice loud enough to be audible to Gretchen, who starred back with a piercing scowl.

Franklin felt a hand on his shoulder.

"What are you looking at dear?" Sara asked her husband.

"A couple of my students, Troy and Gretchen, just got here," Franklin answered. "They look like they had a lover's quarrel over something."

"That Battles boy is trouble," Sara responded with a heavy sigh. "I don't know why Gretchen stays with him. She's such a sweet young thing."

Then Sara noticed the green Mustang.

"Hey, isn't that the mean man from before? What's Troy doing talking to that guy?"

"I don't know," Franklin said. "Let's just mind our own business and take the girls to the beach."

Sara agreed and the family gathered up their beach bags and headed to the ocean.

❧❖❧

Despite it being late afternoon, the beach was still a bit crowded. But the Edwards clan was able to find some open space just back from the shoreline about fifty yards to the north of the tunnel. Mom and dad spread out the blanket and secured the spot while the youngsters took their shovels and pails down by the water.

"This looks like a good place to build our sand castle Ashley," Brianna stated. "The sand is just wet enough to hold it together. Let's start digging."

Ashley nodded in agreement with her big sister, who took on the foreman's role in their miny construction project. Brianna could be a little bossy at times, but was mostly gentle when giving instruction to her soft-spoken sister. Ashley followed Brianna's lead no matter what they were doing, always looking up to her older sibling. The duo was inseparable playmates, who rarely argued with each other. Their Christlike love for one another, even at such a tender age, didn't escape their parents' notice.

"They play so well together," Franklin said to Sara as he removed his NASCAR T-shirt and plopped himself down on the green and red plaid horse blanket. "I'm truly blessed to have two beautiful, well-behaved little princesses."

"Your little queen isn't too shabby either is she honey?" Sara quipped, striking a flirtatious pose with her hands on her hips.

"You still look as gorgeous today as the day I met you," Franklin commented as Sara removed her white shorts and T-shirt, unveiling her conservative, yet appealing one-piece royal blue swimsuit. Despite birthing two children, she had managed to maintain her girlish figure through a healthy low-carb diet and a steady workout routine. Franklin so appreciated his wife's fitness regimen that he began low-impact weight training a few months earlier. The results were beginning to show on him also.

"You're looking pretty hot yourself, as I noticed this morning," Sara said as she slowly rubbed Franklin's slightly-tanned biceps. "I can't wait until tonight."

Sara kissed Franklin quickly on the lips before glancing back toward her daughters. The sand castle was taking shape, but the tide was also starting to creep in. Ashley found an old drinking straw and placed it atop one of the towers like a flagpole. Meanwhile, Brianna started setting seashells around the base of the castle, forming a decorative fence. Sara got up and walked over to help her girls complete their masterpiece.

Franklin gazed out to sea while Sara busied herself with Brianna and Ashley. He observed a large cruise ship chugging along the relatively calm ocean. The ship cast off good-sized waves as it navigated its turn into Port Everglades to dock. Franklin had loved to surf since he was a young boy and often wondered if it were possible to ride the overhead waves generated by the big boats. Despite the occasional winter north swell, South Florida offered mostly ripples to die-hard locals like himself.

As Franklin continued to ponder the preposterous prospects of cruise ship surfing, the buxom blonde from the park, who had previously caught his attention, walked through his line of sight. Franklin couldn't help but notice she was now donning a slinky, black, French-cut string bikini that didn't leave much to the imagination. Displaying very little modesty, he thought she had to be employed as either a fashion model or exotic dancer. Blondie smiled at Franklin as she strolled south down the shoreline. He acknowledged her subtle greeting before quickly reminding himself of the many ways Satan places temptation in a man's path. So Franklin locked his sights back on Sara and the girls

At that moment, a small wave came and washed over the sand castle. The girls folded their arms and sighed in frustration. Sara patted them on their heads, pointed at Franklin and whispered something in their ears. Brianna and Ashley suddenly sprinted over to their father and dove on top of him.

"Woe!" Franklin exclaimed. "I guess this is daddy's day to get attacked by some little beach monkeys."

"That's right daddy!" Brianna shouted back as she started patting her hands on her father's chest and head. "Ooh, ooh, ooh. Ah, ah, ah."

Ashley followed her sister, mimicking the scene they often played out when Franklin came home from work and called for "his little monkeys" as he walked through the front door.

The revelry continued for a minute or so until Sara walked up.

"Enough monkeys, quit beating up daddy," Sara said. "Why don't we all go for a swim?"

The girls abruptly ceased their harassment, jumped off Franklin and ran toward the ocean.

"Hold on, wait for us!" Sara cried out.

The girls stopped at the water's edge.

Sara grabbed Franklin's hand and helped pull him up off the blanket.

"They mugged you pretty good, huh?" she said.

"Wouldn't have it any other way," Franklin answered. "Ready for a dip?"

Sara nodded. Mom and dad caught up to the girls and led them by the hand into the surprisingly chilly water. Franklin winced as he entered the ocean, reminding himself that the sea was usually cool that time of year, even in South Florida.

As the family splashed around in the smallish surf, Franklin looked down the beach and again saw Troy and Gretchen. The couple was sitting on the shoreline, allowing the water to wash over their bare feet. Not wearing beach attire, they obviously hadn't come to the ocean to swim. Franklin wondered what they were discussing as Troy appeared to be almost pleading with Gretchen to listen to him.

He thought it might be Troy's aversion for drag racing his Corvette. Gretchen had never been a fan of her boyfriend's need for speed, especially when it came to illegal street racing on the lightly-traveled dirt roads in western Broward County. Maybe the guy in the green Mustang had challenged Troy to a drag race? Franklin knew Troy was cocky enough to take on all comers, having raced his own barely-legal Camaro against Battles in a sanctioned dual the Friday night before Easter break. Troy definitely wasn't too pleased when Franklin smoked him on the quarter-mile strip that night at the track near where the old Hollywood Sportatorium used to be located. Troy was such a sore loser that he wouldn't even shake Franklin's hand after the race. Not one in the Battles family had ever been accustomed to not getting their way.

The apparent spat taking place between the couple went on for a few more minutes before Gretchen beamed a broad smile and threw her arms around Troy. The embrace turned into a long kiss before the two of them clasped hands and made their way up the beach and back into the tunnel.

"I still don't get what she sees in him," Sara muttered to Franklin, who didn't know his wife had been observing the action.

"What can you say," said Franklin, shaking his head. "They're young and in love."

"I guess," Sara responded. "I'm just glad I don't have to date anymore like Gretchen does. And I know my man only has eyes for me. Right honey?"

"You can believe that's true," answered Franklin, who kissed his wife on the cheek while considering whether Sara had seen him eyeing the sexy blonde beauty a short time earlier. He certainly hoped not, because such a misstep might cost him dearly later on that evening.

The sun was starting to set when the family loaded up the van and headed back to their Plantation homestead. Drained from their long day in the sun, the girls fell sound asleep on the ride home with Ashley laying her head on Brianna's shoulders.

"Isn't that just adorable," Sara said as she looked in the back seat at the two girls. "They got most of the sand off in the beach shower. I should probably put them right to bed when we get home and let them take a bath in the morning."

"Great idea honey," Franklin said as he rubbed his hand on Sara's thigh. "Then we can get busy."

"I thought that would get you excited dear," Sara said with a sly smile and a twinkle in her eye.

Once home, Sara hustled the kids off to bed while Franklin cleaned out the van. Being exhausted, the girls didn't put up too much of a fuss and quickly fell asleep.

Sara then rushed off to join her husband in the shower.

As she slipped out of her shorts and swimsuit, Sara noticed a small carafe of their favorite white zinfandel sticking out of an ice bucket on the dresser. Next to the bucket, in between two crystal wine glasses, stood a miny vase with a slightly-wilting single red rose inside. A tiny white card was propped up against the vase. Sara picked up the card and read the short, but endearing message to herself: "Though the most fetching of flowers must fade with time, the blossom that is my love for you shall bloom eternal."

Tears of bliss welled in Sara's eyes as she practically waltzed over to the bathroom. The rush of steam that drifted by when she opened the door seemed a fitting prelude to simmering sensual symphony about to commence. Franklin slid open the see-through shower door and smiled lovingly at his bare beauty. Sara threw her arms around her man and submitted to his passionate kisses with unabashed fervor.

The love they made that joyous spring evening conjured up memories for both of their wedding night celebration from just over a decade ago. Their fiery desire for each other still blazed like a searing wildfire in the dry Florida brush. What, if anything, could quench so hot a flame?

Chapter III

Hallelujah My God, Hallelujah, for saving one like me. Praise for your grace, and tender mercies, that set sinners free. Hallelujah My God, Hallelujah...

Sara firmly, yet gently tapped her fingertips on the snooze button of the clock radio to abruptly cease the praise song emitting its triumphant lyrics through the dimly lit bedroom. She loved the reminder of hope the tune's message boldly presented, but would have preferred a slightly softer melody in which to awaken.

Monday mornings always presented a challenge to Sara, who could never seem to get quite enough sleep. But arising that particular day was even tougher due to the previous evening's thoroughly exhilarating liveliness. As she eased herself out of bed, Sara remembered the red-hot love she and Franklin made the night before. Although her husband had always been the consummate lover, Franklin seemed to lift Sara to new heights of bliss last night. What had gotten into him, she wondered, as she quietly opened the bathroom door? The small nightlight cast just enough illumination into the bedroom to cause Franklin to wince slightly as he opened one eye.

Sara smiled at him and mouthed "sorry" for waking her man

from his slumber. Franklin smiled back, appreciating his wife's still-nude silhouette through the faint, but adequate lighting. He rolled over as Sara closed the door and turned on the shower. What a great sight to start a new week Franklin thought to himself, wishing he and Sara had time for an encore performance.

He flashed back to their wedding night, when two nervous, adoring young virgins united as one flesh. Franklin noted how much their prowess in the bedroom had increased over the years. So much so, that they finally thought of themselves as experts. Franklin found himself getting overly excited by his reflections as Sara exited the bathroom wrapped only in a towel. Could they squeeze in a quick session, Franklin wondered, while he gazed at his mate as she dried off?

But Sara quickly dressed before walking over to Franklin and giving him a tender peck on the forehead. He decided to get up and take cold shower for the second straight day as he heard Sara wake up the still sleeping children.

While getting himself ready to begin a new work week, Franklin remembered the van running a little bit hot on the way home from the beach the day before. He decided it would be better to switch vehicles with Sara that morning, even though he knew his wife hated to drive his racy car. Sara was racing around trying to get the kids ready for school when Franklin went downstairs and gave her the news.

"I know you don't want to hear this, but I need to take the van into the shop today," he told Sara.

"Why?" she said with a deep sigh as she fixed the collar on Ashley's white uniform blouse.

"I think something's wrong with the cooling system. The temperature gauge was well above the half-way point when we got home last night."

"Did you check the water?" Sara asked. "Maybe it's just low."

"Have you noticed the van running hot lately?" Franklin responded rather sternly.

"No. But I really didn't look."

"You need to keep an eye on the gauges honey," Franklin said more gently this time, realizing Sara didn't appreciate his previous tone of voice. "That's okay. Just take the kids to school in my car. I'll get Joe to take a look at the van before I go to work. There's an early assembly today, so I have a little extra time."

Sara reluctantly agreed and continued to ready Brianna and Ashley for school. A few minutes later she loaded the girls in Franklin's royal blue Camaro, which was decked out with shiny silver chrome and louvers. "Boys and their toys," Sara said as she turned and kissed Franklin goodbye. He just shrugged his shoulders and smiled back as he held the door open for his wife.

The sun tried to peek over the horizon that mostly cloudy morning. The darkening skies and rumble of thunder rolling in from the ocean warned of a difficult drive ahead.

"Great. Where did this come from?" Sara mumbled, recalling the beauty of the previous day. "You girls all buckled in?"

"Yes mommy," the daughters answered in unison.

Sara adjusted her seat, put the key in the ignition and started the car. She accidentally pressed the gas pedal too firmly, causing the engine to rev loudly.

"Hey, you want to borrow my helmet?" Franklin shouted with a slight smirk.

Sara shook her head and responded with a curt grin. "I hate this car," she said, but Franklin couldn't hear her through the rolled up window. Sara put the Camaro in gear and slowly let up on the clutch. The car popped out of gear and quickly stalled.

"Easy!" Franklin shouted to his wife.

"I know!" she angrily mouthed back.

Sara placed the stick shift in neutral and turned the key again. Once more, she put the vehicle in gear. This time, though, she managed to synchronize the gas and clutch properly. Sara did squeal the tires a bit as she exited their circular driveway and made a right turn onto the street.

As she progressed down the road, Sara began to feel more comfortable with the full stable of horsepower under the hood. Although auto racing was too macho for her taste, she realized her husband delighted in the sport. His love for fast cars predated their college days. Franklin's dad got his son hooked on the sport as a kid. Sara didn't like the competition for her affection back then, but Franklin scaled back his zeal for racing greatly once they were married. After the children were born, Sara demanded her husband further limit his time on the track. Realizing his passion for cars was fast becoming an idol, Franklin agreed to race only one Friday a month at a track up in Palm Beach County. He did, however, tinker with the Camaro enough to keep it performing like a finely-tuned instrument.

Sara was impressed with how great the car always ran when she was forced to drive it. The vehicle didn't have a radio, so Sarah suggested she and the girls sing a song on the way to school.

"What do you want to sing?" she asked.

"I don't know. Let me think for a minute mommy," Brianna answered, placing an index finger to her mouth.

Like usual, Ashley mimicked her sister's action. A few seconds passed.

"Oh, I know," Brianna declared. "Let's sing Hallelujah My God."

"Good choice dear," Sara said with a giggle, remembering the tune that woke her up earlier. "Go ahead and start."

The daughters began to sing as Sara turned the Camaro onto Interstate 595.

⚜

Back at home, Franklin popped the hood on the van and took off the radiator cap. The fluid level was fine, so he put the cap back and turned on the ignition. Everything sounded like it was working okay. Franklin decided to drive over to his mechanic's garage about a mile away.

Joe Beacon was a longtime friend of the Edwards family. Franklin's father met Joe back in the 1970's while racing stock cars at the old Hollywood Sportatorium complex west of town. The place was a dump, but from an amateur standpoint, the racing was first-rate. Jordan and Joe would have some fierce duals on the tiny dirt oval in those days, but the contests were always fair and their respect for each other mutual.

Franklin tried to imitate their friendly competition when he raced. Joe liked Franklin's high regard for the sport and was quick to offer helpful tips to his friend's son.

Franklin tooted the horn a couple times as he pulled up to the old brick building where Joe repaired cars. The place didn't look like much. The parking lot needed to be repaved. The sign hanging above the faded brown garage doors was tilting slightly to one side. It was hard to read the establishment's name because the sun had bleached the black lettering so badly. In fact, the city's Code Enforcement Department was always trying to get Joe to fix up the joint.

But the locals all knew that Beacon's Auto Repair was the place to go to get excellent work done at a reasonable price. Porsche or

Pontiac, no job was too complicated or too simple for Joe. He would even fix flat bicycle tires for some of his patrons' kids.

Franklin honked the horn again as a moderate drizzle began to fall. One of the rickety old garage doors began to open. When the door had finally locked itself into place, a stout, gray-haired man in well-worn overalls motioned Franklin to drive the van in. The garage door creaked back down after Franklin entered.

"Hey sport, how ya doin'?" said Joe in his usual southern twang, as Franklin exited the van.

"Not too bad. What's been going on with you Joe?"

"Aw not much. Just keepin' my fingers dirty tryin' to make ends meet ya know," the old man answered as he gave Franklin a strong hug and a firm handshake. "It's great to see ya. How's that pretty little wife of yurs and them yung-uns?"

"They're doing well. Doing well."

"Great to hear it. I see yur makin' her drive that racin' car of yurs. I reckon she's none too happy bout that."

"Well the van was running hot yesterday. I didn't want her to get stuck on the side of the road with the kids. It seemed to be fine on the way over here though."

Joe walked around to the front of the van and placed his hand on the hood. Not hot to the touch he noted.

"Pop it open and let's take a look-see," he said to Franklin, who reached in and pulled the hood release.

The old man yanked on a couple of the hoses before opening the reservoir cap.

"I gave it a quick look over before I drove here this morning. Didn't see anything obvious," Franklin told Joe, who dropped down to look under the vehicle.

"Nuttin' leakin' down here."

Joe popped back up rather spryly for a gent well into his sixties.

"Can ya leave it?" he asked. "That way I can hook her to my computer and figure if it's an internal problem."

"I guess. Can you give me a ride into work?"

"I reckon I can do that fer ya. Just give me a few to make a couple calls first, awright?"

"That would be great Joe. I sure appreciate it."

"Not a bother. That's what buds are fer."

The old man turned and shuffled over to his tiny office in the back of the garage. Franklin leaned up against the van as he watched Joe leave. He had looked up to the old guy for years, kind of like an eccentric uncle whose quirky ways often brought about a smile. Joe was lonely after his wife died of cancer nearly twenty years before. He found solace in his work and became one of the finest mechanics on the local racing circuit. Franklin's dad appeared to be Joe's only true friend, as the widower kept mostly to himself and his cars. Jordan used to try to get him to socialize some, inviting him to church gatherings. But Joe would always seem to back away at the last minute. Franklin thought the old man was mad at God for taking his wife so young. But nevertheless, Jordan continued to sow the seeds of the Lord's grace in Joe right up until his own passing five years earlier.

Franklin tried to further the witness and was surprised to find Joe responsive to the gospel at times. In fact, about a week before Joe had gone with Franklin to place some fresh flowers at Jordan's grave. Franklin reflected back on that opportunity while he waited for Joe to make his phone calls.

Their light conversation turned to religion that dreary Saturday morning at the cemetery when Franklin remarked that he likened the rain to God's means of rinsing away some of the world's filth. Joe didn't respond until he and Franklin walked up to Jordan's tombstone and placed some tulips in the metal cylinder next to the grave.

"Yur daddy used to tell me that he longed for the day when he would see God face to face," Joe said as his eyes began to water. "I thought him crazy as a coot and I told him such. But ya know son, he was always so sure he was headed fer heaven. Ol' Jordan, he just knew so. He was the best fella I'd ever like to meet. I miss him a whole lot, like I reckon ya do."

Franklin placed his arm around Joe's broad shoulders and nodded in agreement.

"Joe, can I ask you a question?"

"Sure son."

"You know we're all going to die one day right?" Franklin said.

"Yep. Can't do nuttin' else," Joe replied.

"Well, in that case, let me ask you this," Franklin continued, "if you were to die tonight, do you think you would go to heaven or would you say that is something you're still working on?"

The old man paused for a moment before responding "I don't rightly know. But yur daddy sure did seem to know where he was headin' didn't he now Franky?"

"That's right Joe. My father knew for sure where he was going when he died. And you can know also Joe, if you want to."

"Well, I don't reckon I know where I'm fixin' to go, but I bet yur gonna tell me, huh?"

"Like I said, if you want me to I can explain how you can know for sure whether you'll be with God or without him when you die."

Joe smiled at Franklin, who displayed the same sort of passion for declaring the gospel as Jordan had done when he was alive. "Awright," Joe said nodding. "Yur daddy was pretty good at such talk. I'd kinda like to listen to yur take. Go on now."

Franklin and Joe sat down on a bench near the grave. The rain had slowed to a slight sprinkle.

"Joe before I tell you how you can know for sure whether or not you are going to heaven, can I ask you another question?"

The old man nodded yes.

"Okay, if you were to die tonight and God were to ask you 'Why should I allow you into my heaven?' what do you think you would say?"

Joe folded one arm across his chest and placed his chin on the palm of his right hand. He thought for a few seconds before replying.

"Well, I've always tried to be a good fella and not hurt too many folk."

Franklin agreed with Joe's statement.

"I think you're a great fella Joe, one of the best I know. You always go out of your way to accommodate people when their cars break down. I'm sure God appreciates an honest mechanic."

"We'll, my mama told me to be nice to folk, especially when theyz in trouble," Joe responded. "People these days don't seem to wanna help each other much. It's sad."

Franklin smiled at his friend.

"You know Joe, you're absolutely right. It is sad that people don't want to go out of their way to help one another. In fact, I'd go so far as to say many people in this world seem to want to hurt their fellow man more than help him."

Joe shook his head in agreement.

"I know Franky. Yur daddy and me used to talk about that a lot.

I'd tell him I thought the world was goin' to hell in a handbag. Jest look at the news on the TV. Damn shame."

Franklin chuckled and threw his head back. He loved the old hick's Tennessee candor.

"You crack me up Joe."

"We'll I jest get tired of bad news all the time. It's all killins, robbries, rapes. It ain't right the way folk act today. It seemed a whole better when I was a young un, that's fer sure."

Franklin again nodded his head in agreement, pausing a few seconds to gather his thoughts before speaking again.

"There is a lot of bad news in the world today Joe. And at one time, I felt the same way as you do right now. Having been raised in the church, I was wondering where God was in this whole mess. But then my father told me something one day when I was a teenager that changed my whole outlook on life. In fact, it was the greatest news I'd ever heard. Can I share it with you?"

"Absolutely Franky. Go on now."

Franklin swallowed hard and wiped away a tear that was brought up by thinking fondly of his father.

"The reason my dad was so sure he was going to heaven was that he knew eternal life, or what we call heaven, is a gift that is freely given to us by God himself. There is nothing we can do to earn this gift that we certainly don't deserve."

Joe looked at Franklin quizzically. "Then how do we get it?"

Franklin pulled out a small version of the Bible from his coat pocket and held it up.

"My dad and I both believe that God tells us how to go to heaven in His Holy Word."

Joe smiled and nodded affirmingly. "Ah, the Good Book. I was wonderin' when you'd brang that thing out."

"Is it okay Joe? I always find comfort in the Bible."

"Sure. Go right ahead."

Franklin thumbed through the thin pages before settling on Romans chapter three, verse twenty-three.

"We can see more clearly that heaven is a free gift that can't be earned or deserved when we see what the Bible says about man," Franklin said, staring straight into Joe's somewhat bloodshot brown eyes. "Every man, and woman, is a sinner. The Bible states clearly 'all have sinned and fall short of the glory of God.' This fact by itself is a huge problem for all of us when we die and stand before God. But the problem is really even worse than we realize when we continue to look at ourselves through God's eyes as told in His Word."

"I thought ya said this was good news Franky."

Franklin smiled reassuringly at his friend. "It is Joe. Bear with me for a while."

The old man nodded and smiled back as Franklin continued.

"Joe, when we were talking about the news on TV, you mentioned some obvious sins that people commit like murder and robbery. But do you realize there are other sins that we all do that are not so obvious?"

"Oh yeah, I know," Joe answered. "Yur daddy used to say we're so rotten its amazin' God wants anythin' to do with us at all. I always thought such talkin' was a bit strong though."

Franklin tilted his head slightly to one side and gently bit his lower lip before he responded in disagreement.

"Mmm, not really Joe, especially when you look at sin from God's point of view. You see, the Bible says that sin is anything that doesn't please God or breaks his law. And He means anything!"

"Well, tell me what the Good Lord means by anythin' Franky,"

Joe replied in a somewhat curious tone. "I'm not quite followin' where yur headin' boy."

Franklin paused to gather his thoughts, realizing he was sounding a bit preachy to his friend.

"Oh, I'm sorry Joe. I just get a little excited when I talk to people about our amazing Lord and how he deals with us."

"Aw shucks, that's awright Franky. Go on now."

Franklin had to stifle himself from breaking out in laughter at the old guy's backwoods mannerisms. Joe had always been such an endearing character for Franklin and his dad. He really did love the old coot.

"Joe, what God means by anything is this: a sin is not only doing anything we do that we shouldn't do, like stealing or lying; but also not doing anything we should do, like praying or reading his Bible."

"We'll I'm in big trouble then boy cause I hardly never pray or read the Good Book."

Joe looked away from Franklin and peered at the damp ground while shaking his head somewhat shamefully. Franklin placed his hand on Joe's shoulder to try and restore his confidence.

"I'll tell you Joe, I'm the same as you."

The old man looked up quizzically.

Franklin nodded with a frown on his face.

"That's right. In fact, I may be worse Joe. I'm a teacher at a Christian school and there are many days I forget to pray and read my Bible, among a whole lot of other sins I commit. You would think I would know better."

Joe looked at Franklin with a crooked smirk.

"Now come on Franky. I know yur daddy was proud of ya and I sure the Man upstairs is too. Yur a good Christian husband and daddy for God's sake. I reckon you've earned yur place in heaven."

Franklin pounced on the opportunity to explain to his buddy that nobody can be good enough to save himself from God's righteous wrath.

"That's the whole point Joe. The Bible says exactly the opposite of what many people think. Being a good person doesn't get you into heaven."

"It doesn't?"

"Nope. In fact, Jesus himself often scolded a certain group of people who thought they could earn their way into God's good graces. They were called Pharisees."

"Never heard of 'em," Joe said.

"They were a class of Jewish leaders in Jesus day that prided themselves on their performance of keeping God's commandments," Franklin carefully explained to his friend, not wanting too overwhelm him with too many details. "The common people looked up to the Pharisees, thinking they were the most holy men of their time. But the Pharisees were fools in thinking that God would honor their so-called standard for doing good works. Jesus set the record straight during his famous Sermon on the Mount for just how good a person would have to be to earn his way into heaven. Do you know what he said Joe?"

"I have no idear."

Franklin quickly flipped to the fifth chapter of the book of Matthew.

"Jesus was preaching to the people about loving their enemies and treating everyone with respect and honor. Not just those so-called good people like the Pharisees. In fact, earlier in the sermon he had told them that they would have to be even more righteous than the Pharisees to enter the kingdom of heaven. Jesus finally let them know that there was only one sure way to enter. He said 'be perfect, therefore, as your heavenly Father is perfect.'"

"Perfect?" Joe responded curtly, crinkling his scaly brow. "Fer cryin' out loud Franky, no one is perfect!"

"I know Joe. So do you understand why getting into heaven is about more than just being a good person?"

"Yep. I kinda do," Joe answered, looking a bit confused.

Franklin again reassured the old man.

"Don't worry Joe, we can see this all a bit better when we look at what the Bible says about God."

Franklin turned to Saint John's first epistle in the tiny Bible. He could tell that Joe was getting a little restless. The old man was nervously shuffling his feet on the slick concrete under the steel bench. The almost drum-like beat he kept while tapping his arthritic fingers on his knees seemed to signal Franklin to pace their discussion more quickly

"Joe, here the Bible says that 'God is love,' " said Franklin, pointing to the passage in the epistle's fourth chapter. "He is merciful and He doesn't want to punish us."

The old man quickly interrupted, his thick, gray eyebrows raised and crooked index finger pointed at Franklin.

"Aw, but wait a second now Franky. I'm fer certain God's fixin' to send bad folk to Hell now. Ain't He?"

Franklin didn't like getting cut off in his lecture, but he was pleased by Joe's comment.

"You're absolutely right Joe," Franklin responded, holding up the pocket-sized book. "This same Bible that tells us God is merciful and loving also tells us He is just. Therefore, He must punish sin. In fact, it says that 'wages of sin is death' and He 'will by no means leave the guilty unpunished.' "

Franklin paused a moment to gather his thoughts and make sure Joe was still following along. "So I guess we have a bit of a dilemma here don't we Joe?"

"Yep. Kinda like catchin' the coyote in the hen house. Don't really want to shoot 'em, but ya have to, uh Franky?"

Franklin giggled and tossed his head back.

"Yeah, but it's a whole lot worse than that. Let's review quickly how we got here Joe."

Franklin folded his arms across his chest and let out a deep sigh before continuing.

"Now, I told you that heaven is a free gift that we can't earn and we don't deserve. That's because man is a sinner and he can't save himself. But God loves us and doesn't want to punish us right?"

Joe nodded in agreement.

"Still, God is also holy and just, so He can't tolerate our sin. He must punish us for our sin. But Joe, while this is a dilemma for us, it's not a problem for God."

"How so Franky?"

Franklin smiled compassionately at the now fairly-intense old guy, who gazed back at him with his rippled brow and stern, boxed chin.

"You see Joe, God solved this problem for us in the person of Jesus Christ. You've heard of Him, right?"

"Of course Franky," Joe responded, with a slight roll of his eyes and a mock grin. "Every yung un in Sunday school has heard of Jesus."

Franklin nodded.

"Well Joe, who would you say that He is then?"

Joe paused, placing his index finger on his upper lip before answering.

"They say He is the Son of God."

"Who are they Joe?" Franklin asked with his palms raised up

and a smirk on his face.

Joe pursed his lips.

"You testin' me there boy?"

"Oh no Joe," Franklin answered back quickly, hoping he hadn't offended his friend's intelligence. "It's just that there are many different ideas that people have about who Jesus is. Can you give me just a few more minutes to explain who I think He is?"

Joe shook his head yes.

"Sure Franky. Not much else to do on a rainy day but sit here and talk at a good friend. Go on now."

Franklin's dad had obviously shared with Joe before who Jesus is and what He did for mankind. But because Jordan could never get Joe to attend church, Franklin knew the old man hadn't been schooled properly on the identity of Jesus. Joe was correct in saying that Jesus was the Son of God. Still, Franklin was quite sure that his buddy had no idea what it meant to call Jesus God's Son.

"Joe, when people call Jesus the Son of God, I often wonder if they know who the Son of God is?"

With his open palms raised upward, Franklin peered directly into Joe's eyes as he spoke. The blank stare that bounced back to the would-be preacher let him know that the old man's mind was hollow in response to his question.

"I mean," Franklin continued, "some think being the Son of God means that Jesus was more than a man, but less than God. Kind of like a superhero, you know. He was smart, kind and could perform superhuman feats like walking on water. But they don't think Jesus was all-powerful and all-knowing like God."

Joe quickly interrupted Franklin's monologue.

"But Franky, I never said He's Superman."

Franklin quipped back apologetically.

"Oh, I know Joe. I'm just saying that people generally have misconceptions about who God's Son really is. He is not some sort of sub-God. That little baby who was born in a manger two thousand years ago is God."

Joe tilted his head and wiped his brow with a handkerchief as he pondered Franklin's statement.

"Yeah, that God as a baby stuff has always kinda spun my brain a bit."

"You're right Joe," Franklin nodded in agreement. "It really is mind-boggling when you think about it. That the eternal God of heaven would take on a human body and walk among us is a staggering notion. But that's exactly what He did. And, you know what else Jesus did for us Joe?"

"What?"

"That perfect little baby was born so He could grow up to die on a cross to pay the penalty for our sins. And in doing so, He purchased a place in Heaven for us. That's why I said at the beginning of our conversation that Heaven is a free gift. God himself did all the work for us. We've done nothing to earn this gift."

"But again Franky, how do I get this gift?"

Franklin smiled at his anxious friend and took a deep breath.

"There's only one way Joe. You have to trust that God will give it to you. And you do that by having faith in his Son...."

Bang!! A loud slam of Joe's office door brought an abrupt end to Franklin's reflections of that drizzly Saturday morning the week before.

"Damn!" Joe exclaimed as he slowly shuffled back over toward the van. "I'm sorry Franky. I need to be fixin' that there door pump. Did I startle ya? Ya looked like ya was in some deep thought there partner."

Franklin turned toward the old man and grinned.

"Oh I was just thinking about our conversation last week at the graveyard Joe," said Franklin, who remembered that their dialogue about faith was abruptly stopped at that time by a sudden clap of thunder. "Have you given any thought to what we were talking about?"

"Yep, lots."

"Great. Maybe we can continue it on our way over to the school?"

The old man's eyes widened.

"I'd like that Franky."

Joe gave Franklin a fatherly squeeze on the shoulder as he opened up the passenger door of the beat-up old pickup truck for his friend. Once they were both inside Franklin glanced over to the back of the garage where he noticed a familiar sight.

"Isn't that Troy's Corvette over there?"

Joe looked at the car, which had a caved in right rear corner panel.

"Yep," he said, shaking his head in mild frustration. "That yung un ain't got no respect fer his daddy's money."

"What happened to it?"

"Don't rightly know. I just found it here this morning."

Joe started the pick-up truck and revved the gas pedal a couple times while waiting for the garage door to creep open.

"The boy probably spun it in some street race. He's got a wild hair up his, well, ya know Troy Franky."

"Yes, I know him all too well," said Franklin, recalling their many head to head confrontations. "He's a bright kid, but kind of cocky. Someone needs to take him down a few notches."

"He needs a good butt-whooping, but his rich daddy ain't bout to give him one," Joe said as he maneuvered the pick-up out of the garage. "I tell ya what, sometimes I believe them Battles think they own this town."

Franklin knew that Joe was correct in his assertion, but Richard Battles had also been very generous to Good Shepherd over the years. In fact, Troy's father had recently donated a huge sum of money to help the school construct the new gymnasium that was about to break ground on campus.

"Rich is a good man Joe. He's just spoiled his only son too much. We all love our children."

Joe paused before answering, realizing that Franklin worked at the school and saw the benefits of the Battles wealth.

"Oh, I know he loves his boy, Franky. I jest wish he'd discipline the yung un before he hurts himself or someone else that's all."

Joe pulled out briskly onto the busy highway in front of the shop, pretty much cutting off the traffic that was just getting up to speed after waiting at the stoplight less than a block from the garage. Franklin didn't say anything to his buddy about the dangerous turn.

"I wonder," Franklin mumbled to himself.

"What's that Franky?"

"I saw Troy and Gretchen arguing about something at the beach yesterday. Troy was talking to some young Spanish guy and Gretchen looked upset about it. I bet Troy was setting up a race with the guy. He had a really sharp five-point-o."

Joe quickly followed Franklin's lead.

"I'd bet the barn he was racin.' It would explain the damage to the 'vette."

"Maybe I should have a little talk with Troy," Franklin said, pulling on his chin with his left thumb and finger.

"Be careful what ya say Franky," Joe warned. "I don't reckon he cares much fer ya after all them times ya licked him on the race track recently."

Franklin looked over at Joe with a sheepish grin before responding.

"My dad taught me well."

"I know he did boy," said Joe, who had witnessed Jordan's schooling of then-teenage Franklin's driving skills. "I doubt Troy's daddy taught him much 'bout racin' cars."

"Joe, I think if Rich knew Troy was racing that Corvette, he'd take it away from him. Do you think I should tell him?"

"Naw. Not much sense in stirrin' up more trouble I reckon."

Franklin nodded in agreement.

"Yeah, I guess you're right. I'm just glad he didn't wreck the car racing against me a couple weeks ago."

"That's fer sure. That boy already had steam comin' out his ears when ya whooped 'em. He sure was pissed off I tell ya. Whew!"

Franklin laughed. He remembered seeing Troy pounding on the Corvette's roof after losing their quarter-mile drag race by a full two car lengths. Gretchen tried to consol her boyfriend with a hug, but he rudely pushed her away. Sara was right, Franklin thought, why did the sweet, delicate beauty stay with such a spoiled brat? Did Troy have something on Gretchen, or her family, which would make her tolerate his often-boorish behavior? Franklin just shook his head in wonder.

"So I guess Troy expects you to fix the car for him, huh Joe?"

"Oh no Franky," Joe answered. "That's one thang 'bout Troy. He likes messin' with his own car. He takes pride in fixin' it. I'll give that to him. He don't really like anybody touchin' it, ya know."

"Joe you're a great mechanic. I can't believe Troy won't let you help him. Why does he bring it to your shop?"

Joe smiled wryly.

"Don't know. Maybe so his daddy don't see the car broke down, I reckon."

Franklin frowned and shook his head.

"Yeah, that's true. Rich wouldn't like seeing his son act so irresponsibly. He's very demanding with Troy. He's always pushing him hard. It must be difficult for Troy to live up to his father's expectations."

"Maybe that's why the boy likes racin'," said Joe, who often noticed that Troy seemed to be most happy when he was alone working on the Corvette at the garage. "He needs to work off some them frustratin' times. That's why I gave him a key to the shop. He loves toyin' with that car more than anythin', seems like."

"You're a good guy Joe," Franklin said as he patted his buddy on the shoulder. "It's nice of you to let him use your garage. You're right, it must be like a sanctuary to Troy. A place where he can get away from the pressures of being Richard Battles' son. It's good for him."

"He spends a lot of time there, mostly at night when I'm not around though," said Joe, who didn't tell Franklin about the loan Troy gave him when the shop had dire financial difficulties a few months back. "I reckon the boy ain't so bad. Jest a little troubled that's all."

⥽❖⥼

Sara and the girls were approaching their exit on I-595.

Sara saw a small break in the heavy morning traffic and turned on her right blinker. She pulled the Camaro into the exit lane and headed up the elevated off ramp. But when she pushed her foot on the brake, the pedal went all the way to the floor. She let her foot back up and pushed down the pedal again. Still nothing. She frantically pumped the pedal up and down, but to no avail. The brakes were gone!

Panic set in! Sara, desperate now to halt the speeding car, pulled up on the parking brake set in between the gray bucket seats. That maneuver turned out to be disastrous. The Camaro immediately began to swerve out of control on the rain-slickened roadway. Sara yanked the steering wheel with all her might to the left, causing the car's rear end to slam into the concrete guardrail. It began to flip over onto the roof when she suddenly heard a load bang!

Still bracing the steering wheel, she quickly glanced back over her right shoulder. To her horror, Sara saw the word "Mack.' She belted out a shriek of terror as the grill of the fully-loaded dump truck plowed into the back corner of the car. The force of the impact easily lifted the Camaro a good ten feet into the air. After a couple of airborne revolutions, the car came crashing down roof-first atop the guardrail.

But the destructive episode, which seemed to linger like eternity yet lasted only about fifteen seconds, still wasn't finished.

The Camaro didn't rest on the guardrail for long. It slid backward on its rooftop down the hundred-foot grassy embankment. After a few seconds, the rear of the car smashed onto the highway's asphalt emergency lane below. The violent crash caused the Camano's fuel tank to rupture. A roaring explosion followed. Within an instant, the car was totally engulfed in flames.

Sara slowly opened her eyes. Fully aware of the calamity that just happened, it seemed strange to her that she felt not a touch of pain. In fact, Sara had no feeling in her what-so-ever. *What a surreal sensation,* she thought.

She looked left, then right. Up, then down. Trying to get her bearings in order, Sara placed both hands to her face. She still felt nothing.

Am I paralyzed? Sara wondered. *Can't be because I'm moving my arms. What's going on?*

After a few more curious moments, Sara found hers eyes affixed to three tiny specs of white light off in the murky distance. They floated slowly, but quite surely toward her. As the objects came into view, she had no difficulty understanding what they were -- angels.

Their magnificent beauty was enthralling to Sara. Though stunning in appearance, they were not really all that similar to humans. In fact, neither did they look like the traditional image of angels that Sara had dreamed about as a little girl.

There was an almost god-like aura about these creatures. They wore what appeared to be long, flowing, white, hooded robes, which covered up most of their defining features. Their somewhat human-looking faces were highlighted by brilliant eyes colored in a hue Sara never remembered seeing before. Their perfectly sloped noses seemed a flawless complement to their pursed ruby lips. The angels' mouths never opened, nor did they speak.

Suddenly, two of the angels swiftly departed, leaving just the one who had been floating in the middle of the trio.

The remaining angel pulled one of its arms out from under its robe and extended a hand toward Sara. She smiled at the angel, who smiled back in a highly-comforting manner. She placed her hand in the angel's, but did not feel a grip. Although Sara knew she was now in a different realm, she still was not anxious or nervous about her circumstance. There was a calm peace about her that pierced to the very essence of her being.

Seemingly as quickly as they had left, the other two angels

returned. Each one held in its arms a little child.

Even in her dreamlike state, Sara immediately recognized the children. Unspeakable joy overwhelmed her. The angel on Sara's left gently cradled Brianna. The one on her right seemed to delicately rock Ashley. The girls looked toward their mother and smiled. The angels, who carried God's precious cargo in their arms, also smiled at Sara. The tranquility of the moment was glorious.

But the harmony was promptly broken by a white light raining down from above. Yet, although the serenity of the scene had been disturbed by the heaven's glare, the calm still remained in the souls of the saintly trio.

The angels escorted the mother and her beloved girls toward the Eternal Light. Sara knew her steadfast faith had served her well.

Chapter IV

Joe's beat-up old pickup truck whipped a hard right turn into Good Shepherd's faculty parking lot. The aged country racer never noticed that he cut off one of Franklin's co-workers with the maneuver. Joe's driving skills were still sharp, but his vision had dulled greatly over the years. Franklin didn't bother saying a word to his buddy about the near fender-bender, figuring he would just apologize for the incident later if it came up. Besides, Franklin might be partially responsible for Joe's bad driving.

During the previous ten minutes, Joe and Franklin had been in a deep evangelistic conversation concerning what it means to truly have faith in Jesus Christ. Franklin wanted to be sure that Joe had a clear grasp of their discourse's main points before exiting the truck.

"So you see Joe," Franklin said as he shoved open the pickup's creaky passenger door, "having saving faith means more than just raising your hand and saying I believe."

Joe nodded his head in agreement.

"You need to not only have heard the story of Jesus," Franklin continued, "and also believe it is true. But you have to trust in Christ's work alone to be saved. That's the primary difference between Christianity and all other religions. God himself saves us."

Franklin stepped out of the truck and dropped his right foot into a puddle, completely soaking his shoe and sock.

"Ah!" he exclaimed.

Joe chuckled at his friend's misstep.

"Looks like He didn't save ya from that there puddle."

Franklin rolled his eyes and shook his head.

"Thanks for the ride Joe."

"Not a bother. Can ya find someone to give ya a ride to my shop later?"

Franklin nodded yes while shaking the excess water from his shoe.

"If I can't get somebody from here to give me a ride, I'll call Sara. Hey, thanks again for looking at the van on such short notice. I really appreciate it."

"Not a bother Franky. I'm sure it's jest the thermostat or sumthin'. Ya want me to call ya when I find out?"

"Oh no Joe, just go ahead and fix it," said Franklin, waving his hand. "You always treat me right."

"Awright then," Joe responded. "I'll see ya tonight. Have yaself a good day now."

Franklin shut the door and waved to his buddy. Joe slammed the truck into gear and spun the tires as he headed toward the exit gate.

"What a crazy old coot," Franklin giggled to himself after watching Joe's sophomoric antics.

As he walked up the steps to the school's gymnasium for the day's assembly, Franklin wondered if Joe was really absorbing the eternal significance of their gospel discussions over the last few weeks. He certainly had grown to love Joe and hoped God would soften his friend's heart, as well as, plant the seeds of salvation. Franklin smiled as he imagined Joe tooling down the new Jerusalem's golden streets in the old hick's favorite hot rod: an antique, souped-up '57 Chevy. But Franklin rested in the fact that it was God's job to save his buddy's soul.

As he opened the gymnasium doors, a blast of vibrant praise music greeted Franklin. The kindergarten and first-grade classes were singing a rousing rendition of *Lord I Lift Your Name on High*. Franklin stopped for a few seconds and admired the show. The little kids were always the cutest performers at any of the school's functions, whether it is the Christmas pageants, talent shows or the current Spring Praisefest. Franklin thoroughly enjoyed watching his daughters sing for the church and school productions. They were talented tykes, but Ashley and Brianna's classes were not scheduled to sing that day. It gave Franklin a reason to skip out early on the assembly, although he knew it probably wasn't the right thing to do. Still, Franklin wanted to get a jump on the day's lessons, especially his theology class, so he sat in the upper level of bleachers near the back of the gym.

As he gazed over the crowd, Franklin saw Gretchen walk in with a group of girlfriends. He couldn't help but notice how beautiful the eighteen-year-old was even when wearing a school uniform. The standard dark green polo and tan khakis may have hid her girlish figure, yet Gretchen still managed to stand out in the clique with her long golden blond hair. Franklin could see why Troy had always been dazzled by Gretchen's loveliness. He just wished Battles would attend to her as the delicate flower she was instead of acting like she was but another hunting trophy to hang above his family's mantel. Gretchen always stayed with Troy no matter how badly he treated her. Franklin didn't understand it, but figured young love always has its flaws. Even he and Sara endured some troubled moments when they were getting started.

The children finished their song to warm applause from the crowd. Franklin sat through a humorous skit about "senioritis" by the drama club and a ripping number by the middle school jazz band before exiting the assembly.

He dodged in and out of a tiny rain shower as he made his way back to the high school building. Franklin offered a morning greeting to Jose the janitor as he walked upstairs to his classroom. The young man responded ""Buenos Dias" and nodded respectfully. Jose, a smallish dark-haired fellow who spoke no English, was well-liked by the administrative staff because of his stout work ethic. He seemed to be on campus at all times. Franklin would have thought Jose lived at the school if he hadn't already met the lad's family.

The eight-member Hortese clan made a daring escape from Cuba by small boat the previous summer in the middle of hurricane season. The previously wealthy family by Cuban standards, fled the island to avoid being shot by government police, who thought they had helped finance a failed plot to assassinate Fidel Castro. Jose witnessed his grandmother and one of his sisters drown during the stormy sixty-mile voyage, which ended in Marathon. He and the rest of his family settled in a tiny two-bedroom house in Fort Lauderdale. Despite the trying endeavor, Jose was always quick to flash anyone his bright, white smile.

Franklin opened the door to his classroom and settled down at his old wooden desk, which had seen its better days. He found himself wondering when the school was going to get him some new furniture, but quickly stopped after thinking about Jose's story. Franklin was laying out the exams he was to give his theology students that morning when the buzzer sounded.

The pupils entered the classroom and took their seats. Franklin gave them a few seconds to finish their chit-chat before he ordered silence. He passed out the tests, barked some final instructions and told the students to commence.

Franklin took out some history term papers from another class to grade while his students did their exams. After about twenty minutes of pleasing silence, the school's headmaster, Herman Steponophlitz, cracked open the door and motioned for Franklin to come over. He noticed Herman had quite the distraught look on his face.

Since first coming to Good Shepherd a little more than a year before, Herman always seemed highly intense to Franklin. It was like he could never relax and enjoy the moment. Herman was usually running around putting out one fire or another at the eleven-hundred-plus student school. Franklin often thought the job might be too challenging for his boss. Even at faculty social functions, Herman was difficult to loosen up. Franklin was accustomed to Herman's distressed expressions, but the look being cast at that moment was unusual.

"I need you to come down to my office Franklin," said Herman, with tears welling in his eyes.

Franklin felt a knot forming in his own gut.

"Oh my God, what's wrong Herm?"

Herman put his arm around Franklin's shoulders.

"Please just come with me, okay," Herman said softly so Franklin's class wouldn't hear. "I've asked Debbie to keep an eye on your students. I know they're taking an exam. She'll make sure all goes well."

Franklin gave Herman a puzzled look as Mrs. Turner exited the teacher's lounge and walked over toward them. The high school algebra teacher smiled uneasily at Franklin as she entered the class-room and quietly closed the door. Herman hadn't told Debbie why she was to watch Franklin's class; she was just being dutiful in fol-lowing the headmaster's orders.

Franklin also wondered why a math teacher was taking over his theology class, especially during an important exam.

"Am I in trouble or something?"

"Oh no Franklin," Herman answered, choking back the tears. "I just have something to tell you in private."

Franklin was beginning to get tremendously nervous, almost to the point of feeling ill. *What could be wrong?* he thought to himself. *Am I going to be fired or something? What did I do? He can't be mad at me for leaving the assembly early.*

Franklin tried to calm himself by praying silently. *Lord, I don't know what's going on here, but you do. It seems serious. Please be with me.*

Herman opened the clouded glass door of the headmaster's of-fice for Franklin. Alice, Herman's secretary, was sitting at her desk. Franklin was so nervous that he didn't even notice her. If he had, he would have seen that frail, old Alice was clutching a box of tissues and dabbing the tears rolling down her wrinkled face.

Herman sat down on the dark green leather couch and pat-ted on the cushion for Franklin to sit next to him. As Franklin sat down, Herman began to shake his head and cry.

"Herm, what's going on?!" Franklin blurted out. "You're scar-ing me!"

Herman paused to regain his composure.

"I don't know how to tell you this Franklin."

"What?!" Franklin pleaded.

"A chaplain from the Sheriff's office wants to speak with you. There's been an accident."

The butterflies darting about in Franklin's stomach began to feel more like bats.

Alice opened the door to let in a portly, older gentleman with a graying crew cut. His all-black garb with white collar made the man appear to Franklin as some sort of Catholic grim reaper. He directed an empathetic smile toward Franklin as he walked over to the couch. The priest sat down on the other side of Franklin and folded his hands across his belly.

"Hello, my name is Father Thomas O'Malley," the priest said to Franklin in a gentle, comforting tone. "I work with the Broward County Sheriff's Office and I'm afraid I have some awful news to tell you. It's about your wife and daughters..."

"What? What?" Franklin interrupted frantically. "Herm said there was an accident. Are they okay?"

O'Malley placed his hand on Franklin's shoulder and began to rub it sympathetically. Franklin glared straight into the priest's moist brown eyes.

"I'm so sorry sir."

Franklin dropped his head back and stared up at the popcorn ceiling.

"They passed away in a traffic accident earlier this morning on the interstate," O'Malley continued. "The roadway was very slick from the rain and......"

Although he listened, Franklin didn't hear another word the priest uttered. He just fixed his eyes on the ceiling. His body felt paralyzed. He didn't weep. He didn't scream. He didn't do anything at all, just stared at the ceiling.

Through his own tears, Herman noticed Franklin's reaction to the horrible information. He thought Franklin might have gone into shock upon hearing of the deaths of his wife and daughters. He nodded for the priest to walk outside the office with him.

Alice came over to the couch and put her arm around Franklin, who still kept staring at the ceiling. It was as if he was looking straight into heaven and trying to coax God into waking him from a terrible nightmare. Alice just sat quietly with Franklin, the silence broken only by her sniffles.

Herman, in the meantime, told O'Malley that he would take care of the stunned teacher.

"He's with people who love him here," Herman said as he shook the priest's hand.

O'Malley nodded and smiled slightly.

"Just in case that poor soul needs to speak with someone else," the priest said as he handed Herman a business card from Saint Theresa Catholic Church. "I'll continue to pray for him."

"Thank you Father," Herman said to the priest, who turned and walked down the hallway.

In all his forty-plus years, Herman had never been directly involved in such a horrific tragedy. Not one of his close family members had even passed away to that point. In fact, both sets of his grandparents were still alive well into their eighties.

Herman didn't know what to do as he opened the door to his office. He and Franklin weren't really that close. How would he comfort someone he hardly knew? What would he say?

When Herman looked over toward the couch, he saw Franklin still looking up at the ceiling.

"He hasn't moved yet?" Herman asked Alice.

"Not at all," she responded with deep concern.

Herman motioned for Alice to come to her desk.

"I'm worried Alice," he whispered in her ear. "It's like he's in a coma or something."

"I know Herm. He hasn't cried or done anything since you left with the priest."

"I think he's in shock."

"Do you want me to call nine one one?"

Herman paused for a moment to gather his thoughts.

"No. Why don't you call Sam?"

"Dr. Simmons?" Alice asked.

"Yes, he's Franklin's best friend," Herman answered. "Sam will know how to comfort him."

Alice quickly thumbed through her rolodex and found Sam's number. As she dialed the phone, Herman went over and sat down with Franklin again.

"Are you okay Franklin?" Herman asked as he placed his arm around the still-stunned teacher. "I'm having Alice call Sam over for you. Can I do anything for you until he comes?"

But Franklin didn't respond. In fact, he didn't move a muscle. Herman didn't say another word. He just sat silently with Franklin and waited for Sam.

<hr />

The doctor's office was just a few blocks away from the school, so it only took Sam about fifteen minutes to drive his Porsche over to the campus. The wait seemed like hours to Herman.

Although she didn't yet know all the grisly details of the accident, Alice quietly informed Sam of the tragic deaths of Sara and the two little girls. Sam was obviously stunned by the news. He didn't even say goodbye to Alice as he clicked off his cell phone. His eyes began to mist while he waited at a stoplight just down the road from the school. Sam's stomach started to turn and his nerves began to frazzle. If he would have had any hair left on his shiny bald head, it probably would have been standing straight up. The hair on his arms certainly was.

Sam hadn't received such shocking news since his younger brother Bill was killed by a drunk driver five years earlier. Maybe going through that tragedy would help him comfort Franklin, Sam thought. But he really didn't know what he would say to his best friend. Franklin and Sam had become very close over the past two decades.

Sam was a fishing buddy of Franklin's father after having met one another in church when Jordan first moved to South Florida in the 1960's. After Jordan and Gracie gave birth to their only child in the fall of 1970, they honored Sam and his wife Sandy as Franklin's godparents. But Sam became more than just a spiritual father figure to his godson. He was sort of like that favorite uncle you could confide in when you feared telling mom or dad about something you did wrong. Sam wouldn't tattle on Franklin's youthful misdeeds, but he did correct the high-strung lad with insightful tidbits of wisdom.

Franklin's mentor was hoping he could conjure up a few comforting words once he arrived at the school. Sam went to the Lord in prayer. He knew only God could help him console his friend.

Sam's mind was so focused on Franklin when he arrived at Good Shepherd, he didn't notice that he parked the Porsche in the student lot. It blended in well the many Mercedes and BMW's. He ran up the stairs to Herman's office, not even saying hello to the receptionist in the lobby. When he opened the door, Sam saw Herman and Alice sitting on the couch with Franklin. His eyes still fixed on the ceiling; Franklin didn't see Sam enter the office. Herman motioned for Sam to come to them.

Sam walked over and crouched down in front Franklin, who sat with his hands clasped in his lap. He reached out and placed both his hands on top of Franklin's. His touch broke Franklin out of his trance-like state. He lowered his head and looked straight into Sam's sorrowful blue eyes. After a few seconds, Franklin's lips began to quiver slightly and a few teardrops rolled down his pale cheeks. Franklin dropped his head onto Sam's shoulder and finally started to weep. He was sobbing more loudly as Sam tightened his hug and placed a hand on top of his now-despondent friend's head. Sam let Franklin sob for a few minutes before uttering a word.

"Oh Franklin, my son," Sam finally said as he held the widower. "Just let it out. I'm here for you. Just let it out."

Franklin pulled back and wiped away the tears with his left hand. Alice handed him a couple of tissues. Franklin dabbed his eyes, then cupped his right hand over his mouth and slowly shook his head before speaking.

"I can't believe they're gone Sam, I can't believe it," Franklin wailed. "What am I going to do?"

Sam swallowed hard and nervously ran his fingers around his goateed chin. His tears began to flow profusely as well.

"I don't know Franklin, I don't know," Sam answered. "I'll tell you what. Why don't we get out of here? Let me take you to our house, okay?"

Franklin nodded yes. He knew the Simmons' house was always a place of refuge for the hurting. At that point, the Simmons seemed like the only family Franklin had left. Sam put his arm around Franklin's shoulder and led him to the door. Franklin continued to cry as they left the building. None of the teachers or staff said anything to them. No one had yet heard what had transpired, but they all certainly knew something was going on.

As Franklin and Sam drove off, Herman notified the faculty of the accident. Meanwhile, Alice put the news on the prayer chain. The tragedy cast a dreary pall over the entire campus. Pastor Reynard called a candlelight payer service for that evening in the sanctuary.

Sam and Franklin didn't say much to each other during the five-minute drive to the house. Sam tried to be strong for his friend, but his own sorrow over Sara and the two precious little girls made that extremely difficult. He would just look over at Franklin every so often and say sympathetically "I know." Sam silently prayed that God would help him provide better solace to his wounded brother in the faith.

Sandy was standing on the front porch of the massive two-story brick mansion as Sam pulled the car into the long circular driveway. He had phoned his wife on the way to the school and told her about the accident. After the Porsche stopped, she walked briskly over and opened the passenger door. Franklin got out and immediately threw his arms around his godmother. The petite blond lady could almost feel the barrenness of Franklin's heart as she held him tightly. His sobs audibly described the anguish in his soul.

After a few minutes passed, Sandy and Sam escorted Franklin into the house.

The three of them sat down on the antique French sofa in the front parlor. On a small, wooden table in front of them was a pot of coffee that Consuelo, the Simmons' housekeeper, had prepared. Sandy poured each of them a cup.

"I think this is how you like it dear," Sandy said as she passed a cup to Franklin.

"Thank you," he whispered, managing to crack a slight smile. "You both are always so good to me."

"That's the way family should be," Sam responded while flipping to Psalm number one hundred sixteen in his Bible. "Can I read you just one verse son?"

"Sure," Franklin answered.

Sandy reached over and held Franklin's hand as Sam read verse fifteen.

"Precious in the sight of the Lord is the death of his saints."

With tears running down his cheeks, Sam looked directly into Franklin's bloodshot eyes after reading those words.

"Franklin, I know nothing I or Sandy say right now will take away your pain. But you know how much we love you. We will be here to help you through this, anything you need."

Sam hugged Franklin, who started to weep again. Sandy looked at her husband and both began to cry. Franklin regained his composure after a minute or so.

"Sam, I feel like this is my fault," Franklin said with a bit of anger in his tone.

"How so?" Sam responded with surprise.

Franklin breathed a deep sigh. "Sara always hated to drive my car. I switched with her this morning to get the van checked out. If I just waited until after school, this wouldn't have happened."

He began to sob again. Sandy quickly reached over and grabbed both of his hands.

"Oh honey, no," she said. "You had no way of knowing what would happen. Only God knows these things. It's not your fault."

Sam backed up his wife. "Franklin, Franklin. You know God's will is perfect. Please don't blame yourself. Please."

Franklin slowly rubbed his now-weary eyes and reluctantly nodded in agreement. Although his sorrow was rapidly turning toward anger at God, he knew his dear friends were right. Sara and the kids were gone and there was nothing he could do about it. Franklin had always preached that God is sovereign and he was living that dreadful reality firsthand.

He glanced over at the Simmons' grandfather clock in the living room across the hall. But he could not make out the time. Franklin had forgotten his glasses at school and his eyes were sore from all the crying he had done.

"Sam, what time is it?"

Sam looked down at his gold Rolex. "It's almost two."

"Two-o-clock!" Franklin exclaimed. "Wow! I've got a lot of stuff to do."

Franklin started to get up from the couch.

"Whoa," Sandy said, reaching up and holding onto Franklin's arm. "You just try to relax."

"I can't Sandy. I need to get to the hospital. I don't even know where they took them."

Sam patted Franklin on the shoulder and got him to sit back down.

"Easy now," Sam said. "They're not at the hospital."

"Where are they?"

Sam looked down somberly at the floor.

"I saw a sheriff's car leaving the campus. Didn't they tell you anything Franklin?"

"I don't remember anything after the priest said they died. Maybe I passed out or something."

Franklin started to cry again. Sandy hugged him. The five hours since Franklin arrived at school seemed like five minutes. He was still hoping the whole episode was some sort of bad dream. That Sara and the girls would walk through the front door and wake him up. Franklin rested his head on Sandy's shoulder.

"I called your mother, dear," Sandy said as she gently stroked the top of Franklin's hair. "She will be here in the morning."

Franklin sat up.

"Oh, how did she take the news?"

"Well, she was obviously very upset," Sandy answered. "But Gracie is a strong woman. She'll be okay. She was more worried about you. I told her Sam was going to pick you up and bring you to our house."

Franklin seemed relieved that his mom was flying in from Kansas. He hadn't seen her since the family visited there last summer.

"Who's going to pick her up from the airport?" Franklin asked, feeling like he needed to do something all of a sudden. "What time is she coming in?"

"I'm going to get her around nine," Sam answered.

"I want to go with you," Franklin anxiously blurted out.

"Of course son," Sam said. "Why don't you sleep here tonight?"

"Huh," Franklin sighed. "I'm drained, but I know I won't sleep tonight."

Sam got up and walked over to his medical bag that he had tossed on a chair in the corner. He reached in and took out a small bottle of tranquilizers.

"Franklin, I'd like for you to take a couple of these," he said, handing two pills to his friend.

"Sam, you know I hate pills."

"I know. But this is going to be a difficult time ahead and you will need your rest. Please."

Franklin agreed and took the tranquilizers from Sam. He downed them with his coffee.

"Do you need a glass of water?" Sandy asked.

"No, this is fine. I guess I could lie down for a while."

"Absolutely," Sandy said. "I'll get Consuelo to prepare a bedroom for you."

Sandy got up, kissed Franklin on the forehead and left the room to find her housekeeper.

Sam patted Franklin on the knee.

"I know its hard now, but it will be okay son."

Franklin smiled and nodded at his best friend. He knew he was blessed to have Sam and Sandy caring for him. He loved them deeply.

"Franklin, don't worry about anything. Sandy and I will take care of all the arrangements. I'm concerned about you and I want you to let us handle this, okay?"

"Alright," Franklin said softly.

"Very well then. When Consuelo gets the room ready, why don't you go upstairs and rest until dinner. We'll order in something."

"I'm not really hungry Sam."

Not wanting to push food on Franklin, Sam agreed.

"That's fine. But do get some sleep okay. Those pills should take effect in about twenty minutes."

Franklin nodded yes.

"Oh, Sandy asked the small group to come over and pray later this evening. Is that alright?"

"Sure," Franklin said. "I could use a lot of prayer."

"Can I pray for you now?"

"Please pray for all of us Sam."

Sam folded his hands and bowed his head. Franklin did the same.

"Most gracious Father in Heaven. You are everywhere and You see everything. You are surely in the midst of the tragedy that has fallen onto my dear brother Franklin. I lift him up to You right now Father. Please let him know that You are with him Father. Show him your tender mercies. Give him strength during this terrible time Lord...I think of the promises of your Word now Father. That though you bring grief, You will show compassion, so great is your unfailing love. Please Lord, help Franklin to know that truth and feel it. Father also help Sandy and me, and all of us who love him, to comfort Franklin now. He is a child of yours Father, so we are all one family. Please comfort your family Father. We lost a sister and two covenant children today. We know they are in your home now Father, but we all will miss them deeply...Lord, I pray now that You will help Franklin get some rest and prepare for the long days ahead. Give him the peace that passes all understanding. Send you Holy Spirit to be with him every step of the way. Continue to show him your love Father...I humbly ask this in the precious name of Jesus, our Lord and Savior. Amen."

Sam wiped the tears from his eyes as he looked over at Franklin. Neither said another word. There seemed like nothing else to say. Both knew the days ahead would be tough and that they would have to rely on God for their strength. Sam again hugged his bother in Christ to physically let him know that he was not trapped in the mess alone.

Sandy came downstairs to tell Franklin his room was ready. Even though it was not the best of times, she always looked for opportunities to serve the Lord.

"Come with me dear," Sandy said, taking Franklin by the hand. "This is the best guest bedroom in the house. Consuelo just cleaned it. I think you'll be very comfortable."

Franklin smiled appreciatively for her hospitality.

"I'm so grateful that God placed you two in my life," Franklin said as he began to cry again. "I love you both so much. I couldn't go through this alone."

Sandy put her arms around Franklin and began to cry as well.

"Oh, and you won't have to honey. Sam and I will be with you the whole way. And God is here with us, I just know it."

"I know He is too," Franklin replied as he pulled away from Sandy and sat down at the foot of the big, brass, queen-sized bed.

Sandy gave Franklin another kiss on the forehead before she walked toward the door.

"Try to get some rest dear."

"I will. Those pills Sam gave me are making me sleepy."

"Well, good," Sandy said while offering one of her famous sweet southern belle smiles. "Oh, just use the intercom by the bed if you need anything at all. The group is coming over to pray tonight, but I don't want you to come down unless you feel up to it okay?"

"I'll see," Franklin answered.

Sandy waved as she gently closed the door. Franklin took off his shoes and fell back on the bed. Within in a matter of seconds, he was fast asleep. The group came to the house that night as planned, but Franklin didn't wake up. Sandy went up to check on him a couple of times. She found Franklin snoring away. The soundness of his sleep made her wonder if God was the one forcing his weary soul to rest.

✧

Franklin awoke the next morning at quarter till six. Consuelo quickly whipped up a light breakfast for Sam and Franklin before they headed out the door together. They went to the Edwards house so Franklin could shower and change clothes. It was good that Sam was with him at the house, Franklin thought, because it seemed so quiet there without Sara and the girls. He wanted to get out of the now hollow home as fast as he could.

Sam practically raced the Porsche through rush-hour traffic in getting them to the airport. When they checked the board in the terminal, they saw that Gracie's plane was scheduled to arrive right on time. Franklin could hardly wait to see his mother.

As the Boeing 747 from Kansas City pulled slowly up to the terminal, he thought about what to say. Franklin didn't want to break down in front of Gracie. Although no one would blame him if the tears began to flow again, he hoped to at least appear to be holding it together. Franklin knew his mother worried deeply about her only son and she wasn't in the best of health. Gracie underwent a triple bypass two years before and the open-heart surgery greatly sapped her strength. She was fully recovered, but still wasn't the same spry retiree Franklin and his family had become accustomed to seeing.

Gracie moved back to her native Kansas shortly after Jordan's passing. A down-home farm girl, she never really cared for the big-city life of South Florida. When the building boom hit the region in the 1980's and 90's, Gracie yearned even more for the slower pace of the Midwest. But Jordan had grown to love the ocean and warm climate. He also thought Franklin would receive better educational and career opportunities in Florida. Always submissive, Gracie respected her husband's wishes.

The passengers emerged from the chute leading into the terminal. Gracie was in the middle of the first pack, but Franklin didn't see her walking behind a tall Muslim man in a turban. It was Sam who spotted Franklin's mom.

"There she is," he said, pointing to the slender brunette with glasses.

Franklin ran over to his mother and threw his arms around her. Gracie held her son ever so tightly and began to gently weep.

"Oh honey," she cried. "I'm so, so sorry."

Although his eyes started to mist, Franklin surprisingly didn't sob at all. He just firmly held on to his mother like he used to do when he would injure himself as a young boy. To that day, Franklin always felt secure in his mother's embrace.

"I know mama, I know," he said.

After a minute or so, Franklin let go of Gracie. As he pulled away, he noticed a small patch just under the left collar of her silk white blouse.

"What's that?" he asked pointing to the patch.

"Oh, it's just some medicine I'm taking for my heart," she said. "Don't you bother with that right now."

"Are you okay mama? How's your health?"

Gracie smiled sweetly. "I'm fine dear, really. I'm more concerned about you. I just feel awful about Sara and the girls. I've haven't stopped crying since last night."

A tiny tear rolled down Franklin's cheek, but he remained relatively strong. He began to wonder if the initial shock of his family's terrible demise had waned so much that it had mostly dulled his emotions. Had the despair he felt last night turned to acceptance so quickly? Maybe it was the pills Sam had given him? All he knew was that seeing his mother brought him a great deal of comfort. Franklin was thankful she had come so quickly to be with him.

"I feel better now that you're here mama," Franklin said as he hugged her again. "Sam and Sandy have been great, but I need you."

Gracie stepped back and wiped the tears from his face with a tissue. "I'm here as long as you need me honey, you know that.

With God's help, we'll get through this. I promise."

"I know we will mama. I know we will."

Sam walked over and held out his hand to Gracie. She quickly grabbed it and pulled him toward her. Gracie hugged her dear, old friend for a moment or two.

"Thank you for always being there for our family Sam. You and Sandy are the best."

"We take care of our own Gracie. That's what God's children do. You know how Sandy and me feel about you."

"I know Sam. I love you both."

Sam looked into Gracie's bloodshot eyes and nodded in agreement.

"Let's grab your bags and get out of here," he said. "I hate airports."

Franklin held his mother's hand and the three of them walked over to the baggage carousel.

❧❖❧

For the next three days until the funeral, Franklin and Gracie spent time with their church family at the somber Edwards house. The home was so empty without Sara, Brianna and Ashley. Sam and Sandy took care of all the arrangements for the memorial service. That gave Franklin and Gracie time to reflect and mourn together. Though totally melancholic, it was also a sweet bonding time for mother and son.

Franklin and Gracie both hoped that Friday's funeral would bring some closure to the terrible episode. They were secure in the fact that Sara and the two children were living in bliss with their precious Jesus. Each tried to remind the other that for God's saints death is really a time of celebration. Gone are the troubles and pain of this world for those who are with the Lord. The Bible promises as much after all. Yet, living without their dear loved ones was still heart-wrenching for both of them.

Franklin did want to try to bring some good from the sudden death of his wife and kids. He told Pastor Reynard to make sure the funeral's message was evangelistic. Franklin also agreed to do a short eulogy.

Sara had only one close member from her side of the family still alive, her younger sister Jenna. But Franklin had no idea where the girl was living. She ran away from the family years before as a troubled teenager. Last Sara had heard, Jenna was living somewhere in Arizona. At least, that's where the postmark was from on a postcard Sara received a couple of years back. Sara always blamed Jenna's wild youth as a primary cause for her parents' early deaths just before Brianna was born more than a decade before.

The sanctuary was packed with faculty, students and friends for the mid-morning service. While Franklin was overwhelmed with the show of support, he wondered why it always seemed to take tragedy to fill the place. *How come more of you don't come for regular Sunday service?* he thought to himself.

Franklin took a quick scan of the crowd as he led Gracie by the hand to their seats in the front row. He was pleased to see that most of his students were in attendance, along with almost all the teachers and church staff. As expected, the mood was somber and many were mourning. But Franklin wanted a lot of them to leave the service with a newfound sense of hope. He knew the way he handled his own emotions would go a long way toward fulfilling that task. As he sat down with his mother, Franklin said a silent prayer asking his heavenly Father for the strength to get through the memorial.

A pianist and guitar player from Good Shepherd's praise band opened the service with Sara's favorite hymn, *I Will Praise Him Still.* The crowd sang along, most probably not knowing Franklin chose the song to show God glory in the depths of his sorrow. Pastor Reynard followed with a sympathetic prayer.

Sam then got up and read from the Bible. "This is Jesus speaking in John fourteen, verses one through four," he told the gathering firmly, yet gently. "Do not let your hearts be troubled. Trust in God: trust also in me. In my Father's house are many rooms; if it were not so, I would have told you. I am going to prepare a place for you. And if I go and prepare a place for you, I will come back and take you to be with me that you also may be where I am. You know the way to the place where I am going."

Sam returned to his seat next to Franklin and put his arm around him. Franklin smiled at his teary-eyed friend.

The praise duo then asked the crowd to sing *In Christ Alone* with them. The tune was one that Franklin and his wife requested the church play at each of their daughters' baptism. Memories from the christenings caused both Gracie and Franklin to weep during the song.

Pastor Reynard was the next one to lead the service. After a truly eloquent prayer, he presented a short, to the point message, about how he knew Sara's final resting place was now in heaven. He preached that Sara displayed how she was a child of God and that her home was with the Lord, by the fruit she produced during her life. "That fruit," he said, "was the faith of her two lovely daughters." Pastor Reynard finished the message by praying that all in attendance would come to know Jesus the way Sara and her daughters knew Him.

After the hymn *Holy, Holy, Holy* was sung, it was Franklin's turn to speak. Usually the pastor would end the funeral service with his message, but Franklin wanted to put his eulogy at the end to make a point. Chris graciously agreed to let his brother in the faith finish the memorial to his wife and children.

Franklin kissed his mother on the forehead before walking up on the stage. Strangely, he found himself not at all nervous speaking to such a large crowd on a sad occasion. He felt the Holy Spirit with him as he cleared his throat and began to speak.

"Dear brothers and sisters in Christ," Franklin said, as he gazed his moist brown eyes out over the gathering of more than two hundred. "I want to first thank you from the bottom of my heart for all your prayers and concern this awful week. I know my despair would be so much deeper if I didn't have you all to lean on."

Franklin paused to wipe away a few tears rolling down his pale cheeks and took a deep breath before continuing.

"Since Monday, I have pondered what I would say to you about Sara and the girls. I know you are hurting like I am. And I wanted to comfort you the way you are comforting me right now with your presence here today."

Franklin stopped again briefly, gazing down at his mother, who was rubbing her eyes. She sensed his glare and looked up. He cast a sympathetic smile at Gracie to tell her he was going to be okay. She returned the smile. Franklin sighed deeply.

"So, while this might seem strange to say, today is really a time for celebration. That's because I know that Sara, Ashley and Brianna are certainly in a wonderful place at this moment. I can say that with confidence because the Bible tells me so."

Franklin again paused for a moment and slowly circled the room with his eyes. He folded his arms across his chest and then began to run his index finger gently across his lips. Sam looked quizzically at Franklin, wondering if his dear friend was about to break down.

"You know, I've never done a eulogy before," he said, shaking his head from side to side. "I don't even know how to do one. I mean, all of you who knew Sara and my little girls, love them just like I do. So, if you wouldn't mind, I would just like to read you a couple of passages from God's Word that I have found very comforting this week."

Franklin opened up his Bible, which he had already marked by its silk black ribbon.

"There are two verses in Psalm twenty-three which are helping me a lot right now. I know many of you have heard both of them. But just in case there are some here today who don't regularly read the Bible, I'd like to read them for you."

He placed his right index finger on the Bible and guided it down to verse four.

"Even though I walk through the valley of the shadow of death, I will fear no evil, for You are with me, Your rod and Your staff, they comfort me," Franklin read from the text before gazing out at the crowd. "You see, I know King David is saying here that he can face death without fear. Why? Because he knows that God will always be with him, even at life's bleakest point, which is death. My wife knew that as well."

Franklin looked quickly at a few of his students, mainly the ones of whom he often wondered if they had entered into a saving relationship with Jesus.

"Sara was certain that God would always be with her. She always told me she wasn't afraid to die because she took God at his word. She knew her destiny because God himself told her what it was."

Franklin scanned down to verse six. "Surely goodness and mercy shall follow me all the days of my life; and I will dwell in the house of the Lord forever." He looked back at his students, who were all seated together in the pews about five rows back. "I take solace in the fact that Sara is in the Lord's house at this very moment. Sure, I grieve because she is no longer with me. But I also rejoice that Sara is with Jesus forever and that some day I will join her, and the children."

He choked up when he thought of Brianna and Ashley. Why did God have to take them too? He suddenly felt so alone again. But one look at his mother and Sam helped Franklin regain his composure. God may have taken his family, but Franklin remembered he still had brothers and sisters who loved him. He really wasn't alone after all.

"You know," he sighed. "Those of you who have children, remember to love them as the Lord wants you to love them. Hold them and hug them. Spend time with them...It may be a while before I can hug my two little girls again, but I know that I will. God promised me as much."

Franklin turned in his Bible to Acts chapter two, verse thirty-nine and read it aloud. "The promise is for you and your children and for all who are far off; for all whom the Lord our God will call." Franklin quoted the verse with a touch of extra vigor in his voice. "My dear friends. I know you all are saddened by their deaths. Obviously I am too. But again, I take comfort that God can't break his promises. He said in his Word that children of believers belong to Him. I know that my children, God's children, are with him in heaven. I will see them again!"

Franklin abruptly pounded his fist on the podium one time. The action startled the audience. After a few seconds, Franklin addressed the gathering again.

"Am I angry at God right now? You bet I am. But I'll tell you what. I'm also extremely grateful to Him. Yes I am." Franklin nodded his head as a slight scowl began to creep out from the corners of his mouth. He ran his fingers through his short brown hair a couple of times in an effort to calm himself. After a few seconds, Franklin scanned his misting eyes over the captive audience, which was now intensely focused on him. The Simmons, as well as his mother, stared intently at Franklin, wondering if he was about to lose it.

"I am thankful," he said, "because God chose to make my family part of his kingdom. He didn't give us the punishment we deserve for our sins, which is to spend eternity in hell."

Franklin again paused, this time for emphasis.

"No, our Heavenly Father, in his infinite mercy, chose to punish his Son on the cross instead. I deserve death, He gave me life. Sara deserved death, she received life." Franklin choked up slightly before continuing. "My precious Brianna and Ashley each deserved death, but God graciously gives them eternal life!"

The tears began to flow more profusely as Franklin covered his eyes and tried to collect his emotions. He knew he had to keep going. His point wasn't yet made. He pleaded inside for God to give him the strength to press on. Most of the audience began to weep, some rather loudly. Pastor Reynard walked up on the stage and put his arm around Franklin. The loving touch of a dear friend appeared to put Franklin back on track. He took a sip of bottled water that he brought with him to the podium. He winked at the pastor to let him know he was still in control.

"I'm okay Chris," Franklin whispered.

Pastor Reynard flashed an affirming smile and returned to his seat in the front row.

Franklin gently shook his head from side to side as his bloodshot eyes began to pierce the crowd. He sighed deeply before managing to flash a resigned grin.

"Dear friends," Franklin spoke softly into the microphone, "we know that even when things go badly, God is still glorified. He can, and often does, bring good blessings out of bad circumstances. May this be one of those times...I know my wife and children are gone from me for now. But I rest in the knowledge that they are with my Lord and Savior, Jesus Christ."

Franklin began to straighten the yellow legal papers he had brought with him to the podium. He had long since left his notes. In fact, he really hadn't used them much at all. It was a time to speak from the heart.

"I no longer worry about Sara, Ashley or Brianna. They are in God's care now. But I am worried about some of you here today. I worry that some here do not know Jesus. I think some of you know of Jesus, but you really don't know him...If I've been reminded of one thing this week it's this: our time here is fleeting. Every moment is precious. Not a second should be spent frivolously. How are you all spending your time? Remember, eternity beckons. It calls each and every one of us. When your days here are up, where will you be spending eternity? Will you be with Jesus, like Sara and my children? Or will you be forever cast from his presence? The time to think of such things is now. Please, I beg of you, use your time wisely."

Franklin turned and smiled at Pastor Reynard. The two hugged for a few seconds before Franklin returned to his seat between Gracie and Sam. They each put an arm around him as he bowed his head. Pastor Reynard led the gathering in reciting the Lord's Prayer.

Franklin wept gently as the crowd sang *Amazing Grace*. His thoughts turned to the future. What would he do now? What would his life be like without Sara and the kids? Would his heart ever stop aching so deeply?

He knew the journey would be long and arduous. But its final destination was being echoed as the congregation sang a line from the memorial's last song:

When we've been here ten-thousand years,
bright shining as the sun.
We've no less days to sing God's praise,
than when we've first begun.

Chapter V

O ne by one, the vehicles pulled up to the Simmons estate. The wide variety accurately reflected either the style or opulence of the various owners. Pickups were parked next to Porches, compacts alongside Cadillacs. Yet social status didn't seem to matter much that day.

Many who attended the reception after the Edwards memorial service were still just trying to make sense of the dizzying events from the past week. Students had to suddenly confront their own mortality as they were thrust into the reality of watching a beloved teacher mourn. Faculty and staff tried hard to keep their own emotions on an even keel as they dealt with the stunned student body. Dear old friends ardently consoled a brother reeling in deep despair.

No one could ever recall such a trying time at Good Shepherd. Sure, there had been dozens of people who passed on at both the school and the church over the years. But few, if any, present at the Simmons' house, could remember when death's sting had been felt so dramatically by so many.

The mourners entering the front door of the two-story mansion were drawn to a display on a large table in the parlor that was equally heartwarming and heartbreaking. Silver-framed portraits of Sara, Brianna and Ashley were placed directly behind what appeared to be three Oriental vases. But upon closer inspection, the smiling faces of the mother and daughters marked a stark contrast to the round blue vessels. There were no flowers in the vases. They were really urns containing the ashes of the departed family members. The small shrine served as a grim reminder of how sudden and cruel death can be, even for the Lord's saints.

A few dozen people had already gathered at the home when Franklin, Gracie and Sam arrived in Sandy's gold Lexus. The trio passed through the parlor, stopping for a moment to gaze at the display. Franklin smiled at the portraits, which used to sit above the fireplace in his home. He didn't say a word. He just put his arm around his mother and walked inside the living room to greet the guests.

Sandy was the first to come over to them, throwing her arms around Franklin and Gracie. She held them tightly for a couple of tender moments.

"Franklin, that was the sweetest eulogy I've ever heard," Sandy said as she gently rubbed her hand down Franklin's back. "Your faith shined brightly today. I'm sure Sara would have been proud."

"Thank you," he responded.

Sandy turned to Gracie and held both of her hands firmly. "And how are you holding up now honey?"

"I'll be okay," Gracie answered. "Franky and I just have to take it one day at a time, huh?"

"I know," Sandy said in a soft murmur before hugging Gracie again.

Franklin and Gracie walked around opposite sides of the large room, each receiving condolences and comforting hugs from their friends. After about ten minutes, Sam said a short prayer before the caterers brought in some finger foods and served the gathering.

Just before the wake was about to end, a small, chauffer-driven limousine pulled up in the circular driveway. Four people dressed in all black exited the vehicle. Franklin had no doubt who they were. Only Richard Battles would make such a grand entrance on such a somber occasion. His third wife Claudette was with him, along with Troy and Gretchen.

Sam had never cared much for Richard, especially after a few business deals between the two went sour. But Sandy always reminded her husband that Richard was a professing Christian who had bestowed many blessings on Good Shepherd. The elder Battles just required "a little extra grace" she'd always say. Sam noticed Richard come through the parlor and began to walk over to him. Sandy quickly stopped her husband and whispered in his ear.

"You be nice now dear," she said placing her hand on Sam's shoulder.

Sam smiled and nodded to his wife then walked over and shook Richard's hand.

"It's so nice of you to come today Rich, I'm sure Franklin will be glad to see you."

"I wish it were under better circumstances Sam, I truly do," responded the tall, distinguished gentleman in his late fifties, whose platinum-blonde, much-younger wife had her arm securely locked into his. Troy held Gretchen's hand as he stood one step behind his father and stepmother.

Franklin was talking with Joe Beacon when the Battles clan arrived. He hugged his racing buddy and excused himself before walking over to greet Richard and the others.

Richard unleashed his wife's arm and embraced Franklin. Although many people, including Sam, often thought of Richard as brash and arrogant, Franklin had seen the softer side of Troy's father during a men's Bible study they participated in a couple of years ago. He liked Richard's theological insight during the class discussions and knew the wealthy entrepreneur had a heart for the less fortunate. Franklin also saw these as qualities Richard was trying hard to instill in Troy.

"How are you brother?" Richard said with genuine tears in his eyes. "I've prayed so hard for you ever since I heard the news. I'm so sorry."

"I appreciate it Rich," Franklin said as he pulled back slightly. "I'm going to be okay. It will just take some time."

"Anything I can do for you, please don't hesitate to ask. You have my cell number right?"

"I do Rich. I do."

"Good. I'll keep praying for you as well."

"Please do. I covet all your prayers right now. Thank you."

Richard smiled at Franklin and shook his head affirmingly as he directed his wife toward some friends inside the living room. Gretchen hugged Franklin and began to sob slightly.

"I feel so bad for you Mr. Edwards," she said.

Franklin patted her on the shoulder and looked over at Troy, who had an unusually benign expression on his face; not really unsympathetic, but not overly caring either. It was almost like he didn't know how to react.

"Oh Gretchen, I'm going to be alright really," Franklin said to his weeping student. "Try not to cry. Remember what I said in the church today. All three of my girls are with Jesus now."

"I know," she said with a sniffle. Troy handed his girlfriend a handkerchief. "Your words were truly inspirational today." She dabbed her blue eyes. "They meant a lot to all the kids we were sitting with. Thank you so much Mr. Edwards."

"You're very welcome. Why don't you two join the others and have something to eat. I really appreciate you all coming today. It means a lot to me."

Gretchen wiped her eyes again and flashed her beautiful smile at Franklin as she walked with Troy into the living room.

Knowing his words had touched the hearts of some of his students brought comfort to Franklin. Maybe out of this tragedy, God could really bring some good, he thought. Franklin would not take the day lightly as he pondered his future in the coming weeks.

Gracie and her son spent the difficult next weekend beginning to sort through Sara and the kids' personal items. But every time they began the task, the sentimental strain was too intense. How do you pack up a decade's worth of memories without constantly weeping?

After a full week of emotional toil, Franklin realized he would be in no shape to return to his teaching duties any time soon. He didn't even feel the strength to get out of bed for church Sunday morning. So first thing Monday, Franklin called Herman to tell him he obviously needed the rest of the school year and summer off. The headmaster agreed wholeheartedly.

Gracie decided to stay with her boy for as long as he needed her. They were the only immediate family either had left at that point. She was very doting in her care and Franklin appreciated her Christ-like love. Although he had learned to enjoy Sara's cooking, it was good to have mom's homemade dishes again. Gracie also kept a nearly-immaculate house. She told Franklin that cleaning felt therapeutic in some way. There were times over the next couple of months that he seemed like he was reliving part of his childhood once more. Franklin loved having mom around.

Sam, Sandy and some friends from the weekly small group Bible study checked in on Franklin and Gracie quite a bit. They brought food, prayer and fellowship on their visits, all of which seemed to temporarily sooth Franklin's soul.

But there was still a huge hole in his aching heart. Franklin missed his children terribly, but the biggest void in his life was caused by Sara's absence. He didn't know how he would go on without her. She was his first true love. Irreplaceable he thought. Could he, or would he, even want to find another? He resigned to let God decide.

Franklin spent many evenings that summer reminiscing about his sweetheart. One particularly steamy June night brought back memories of their honeymoon in the Caribbean.

He recalled the southwestern trade winds swaying the coconut palms at a decent clip that summer evening in 1990. The tropical breeze which often swept over the St. John's resort offered a refreshing respite to the afternoon sun's blistering rays. Franklin soaked in the ocean view from the patio of the beachfront honeymoon villa. He and his bride had spent two glorious nights locked up in the villa getting to know one another as newlyweds should. Unlike many of their college friends, Franklin and Sara were one of the few couples they had known who made it to their wedding night as virgins. So they used the first three days of their marriage making up for lost time.

A romantic notion came to Franklin as he looked out at the crystal blue lagoon. He told Sara the idea as she was drying off from her late afternoon shower.

"Sweetheart, I was thinking," he said as his eyes quickly scanned his wife's nude body.

"Uh oh," she answered with a sheepish grin.

Franklin chuckled as he wrapped his arms tightly around Sara and kissed her.

"How bout we do something a little different for dinner tonight?"

"What do you have in mind dear?" Sara asked as she sat down on the bed and dried her hair with the same white bath towel she had been using.

"Well, we've been so busy in here, which I've thoroughly enjoyed by the way," Franklin kissed Sara again before continuing. "I thought it might be nice to watch the sun set over the ocean tonight while we ate dinner. Maybe we could order some food and a bottle of wine from room service and have a picnic by the lagoon."

"Ooh, that sounds very enticing," Sara said as she gazed into Franklin's eyes.

"Then it's a date?"

"Absolutely!"

The newlyweds spent a minute or so locked in a passionate embrace. "Uh, we better not get started again," Franklin said with a deep sigh.

"Yeah, you're right dear," Sara answered with a twinkle in her hazel eyes. "We might want to save something for later."

She got up and phoned in their order with room service. Franklin jumped in the shower as Sara put on her makeup. About forty five minutes later, one of the young kitchen workers knocked on the door. Franklin tipped the small Latin boy ten dollars for the basket of shrimp, crab legs and French fries, along with a modestly priced bottle of Cabernet.

The ocean breeze had let up significantly as Franklin and Sara strolled hand-in-hand down the wooden boardwalk that led to the lagoon. They slipped off their sandals to let their toes mix with the soft white sugar sand. They walked about a quarter mile down the beach to a place where they knew they would see the sun slip unobscured into the ocean. The couple were surprised none of the resort's other guests had come down to see the spectacle that was about to take place in thirty minutes or so.

"I guess we have the beach all to ourselves," Franklin remarked.

"Perfect. This is so romantic. I love it. Just my man and me and God's beautiful creation."

Sara planted a heavy kiss on Franklin's lips before laying out the blanket just a few feet from the water's edge. The tiny waves gently lapped on the shoreline as a few small birds searched for their supper in the surf.

Sara and Franklin wined and dined as the sun set slowly into the ocean.

"Listen, can you hear it?" Franklin asked Sara.

"What?"

"Shhhh,'" Franklin placed his index finger over his mouth as the sun dipped over the horizon.

"I don't hear anything."

Franklin closed his eyes and lifted his left index finger in the air. Sara closed her eyes as well.

"Sssssss," Franklin sounded a mock hiss.

Sara punched him in the shoulder and laughed. Franklin giggled like a schoolboy and put his arm around his wife shoulder. Sara nestled her head against Franklin's as the couple watched the bright orange ball's final decent.

The effects of a couple glasses of wine gave Sara an idea of her own on how to spend the twilight.

"Do you want to do something a little naughty?" she asked coyly.

Franklin raised his eyebrows in anticipation of his wife's suggestion. "I'm game."

Sara unbuttoned her flowery Hawaiian blouse and let it fall off her shoulders. Franklin quickly discovered she hadn't been wearing a bra. Then Sara stood up and slipped off her white board shorts. No panties either. Sara giggled as she turned and ran into the lagoon. Franklin was amazed at his wife's actions and greatly turned on. "What the heck," he said to himself as he hurriedly took off his T-shirt and shorts, "it's not like there's any one else on the beach." Franklin ran into the water and dove under. Sara laughed as her husband came up from the sea grabbed her in a bear hug.

Their playfulness quickly turned into lovemaking as a rising moon took the sun's place in the sky.

"It seems so long ago," Franklin said to himself as his mind raced back to the present. The brief glee brought on by thoughts of his honeymoon turned quickly to sorrow. Tears rolled down his face as he made himself another rum and coke at the bar by the pool. He remembered one of the reasons Sara loved this house was that it had a beautiful screened-in pool and patio. The girls spent most of their summers splashing around in the pool. They were already beginning to seem like distant memories to Franklin.

"Why? God. Why?" Franklin cried to himself before his guzzled down the rum and coke. He took the half-full bottle in hand and stumbled over to a lounge chair next to the kidney-shaped pool. He collapsed into the chair and stared up at the stars. It was only half-past nine, but the rum was already taking its toll. He had never been much of a drinking man, so a couple of cocktails were all it took to get him smashed.

After a couple more minutes of sobbing, Franklin stopped and began to direct his thoughts toward God. The joy of reminiscing about Sara quickly turned to anger at God. Franklin was mad and he wanted God to know it. He shook his fist in the air and shouted toward the stars "how could you do this to me?"

Tears once again began to roll down his cheeks as he glared into the heavens. "What did I do to deserve this?" Franklin cried out, this time in a much-softer tone. "I've always tried to do my best to serve you...Father, you say I'm your son, yet you take away my family. And in a fiery death no less."

Franklin coughed a couple of times. He twisted of the cap of the rum, leaned forward and placed

the bottle on his lips. Tilting his head back, Franklin chugged down four hard swallows. He placed the bottle on the patio and wiped his lips. Looking back up at the sky, he shook his head from side to side. The motion began to make him a little dizzy, but also relaxed him.

"Lord, you've got to help me," Franklin said as he closed his eyes and folded his hands across his bare stomach. "I'm losing it here. I know I told people at the funeral to be happy, but I'm miserable. Please make the pain go away. Please."

Franklin rubbed his eyes and turned his head to the side. He slowly began to doze off. A couple of minutes passed and the previously-despondent widower was sound asleep. It was almost as if God placed a hand over Franklin's eyes and forced him into a period of deep rest.

The slumber didn't last long, however.

Less than an hour later, Franklin felt his stomach begin to turn. When he sat up, he began to feel queasy. He got up and started to walk around a little bit. Big mistake! Abruptly, Franklin began to project the rum like a volcano spewing lava. He fell to his knees. In an ugly episode that seemed to take place in slow motion, he proceeded to empty the entire contents of his stomach all over the pool deck.

Gracie, who had been lying down on the couch in the back den, finally heard the commotion. She walked over to the sliding glass door and peered outside. Squinting into the darkness, she saw her son crouched down on his knees, coughing. Gracie quickly slid the door open.

"Honey, what's wrong?" the worried mother called out.

Franklin didn't answer.

Gracie hurried over to her son as fast as her feeble legs would carry her. When she got to him, she caught a whiff of the pungent smell of liquor in the warm night air. She winced at the reeking odor.

"Oh Franklin," she said. "Have you been drinking?"

He put his hand over his mouth and stared at the ground. Gracie placed her arm around her sick boy.

"Come on, let's clean you up and get you to bed now," she said as she lovingly rubbed his shoulder.

"I'm sorry mama."

Gracie smiled. "That's okay honey. You're probably not gonna feel too good tomorrow."

"I don't feel so good right now." Franklin kneeled down and tried to vomit again. Nothing came out this time.

Gracie helped Franklin into the house. After showering and brushing his teeth, Franklin felt a little better. He popped a few aspirin and lay down in bed. There seemed to be too much room in the bed with Sara gone. It was one of the reasons he had dreaded going to sleep the past few nights. He missed his mate so much. The lack of sleep the past week was really catching up to him. Exhausted, he rolled over and slept like a weary child that night.

※❖※

When Franklin awoke around nine-thirty the next morning, he felt the consequences of the previous night's misstep. His head was pounding, as expected, but he was also extremely thirsty. Franklin drudgingly made his way down the staircase to the kitchen. He remembered all the times Sara would yell at the children to not slide down the winding banister. The thought caused him to smile briefly. "Another memory that will quickly fade," he sighed to himself.

Franklin walked into the kitchen where he saw Gracie sitting at the table reading the newspaper. He poured himself a glass of orange juice and sat down across from her.

"So, how you feeling this morning?" she asked, peering over the top of her paper with a wry grin on her face.

Franklin felt embarrassed when he looked at his mother. "I'll never drink again," he said as he soothingly ran his finger through his matted brown hair.

"That demon liquor," Gracie said before lowering her eyes below the paper again. "Just try to get some rest and take it easy today honey."

Franklin took a sip of his orange juice and got up from the table. "Yeah, maybe I'll just lie down on the couch for a while." He walked over to his mother and kissed her on top of the head. "I love you mom."

Gracie smile and nodded. "I know you do honey."

As Franklin was leaving the room, Gracie remembered she had made plans that day.

"Oh, Sandy asked me to go to the mall today," she said. "Would that be alright?"

"Of course mama," Franklin answered. "It would do you good to get out of here for a while."

Gracie paused for a second before speaking again.

"Are you sure you're going to be okay by yourself here today?"

"Why? Because of last night mama?" he answered with a touch of indignation in his voice.

"Franky, that's not what I meant."

"We'll, I'm a big boy mama. I just made a mistake."

"I know honey," she responded, a bit defensively. "I just want to make sure you feel alright and don't need any help with anything today."

Franklin realized he was letting his hangover get the best of him. "I'm sorry mama. You go and have a good time with Sandy today. I'll be fine, really."

"Very well then," she said, directing a loving smile toward her son. "I'll have my cell phone on me if you need me to pick up anything for you, okay?"

Franklin nodded affirmingly before walking into the den and sitting down on the couch. About an hour later Sandy picked up Gracie and they headed to the mall. Franklin loved having his mom staying with him, but he was looking forward to spending a day by himself.

He noticed the family Bible centered on the coffee table. Sara often took refuge in the den when she wanted some peace and quiet. It was the place she came to read God's Word. Franklin picked up the gold-binded Bible and read the inscription on the front cover. It was written to Franklin and Sara by Jordan, who gave the Bible to the couple on their wedding day.

"My dear son and daughter-in-law, as you embark on this life-long journey together, I wanted to give you some loving advice from the Lord's Word. It is the creed Gracie and I have tried to pattern our marriage after. It is found in the book of Ephesians, chapter five, verses twenty-two through thirty-three. I have found this passage so helpful over the past twenty years and I know you will as well. I love you both very much. May God, who loves you even more than I do, grant you many blessed years together. By the Lord's grace, Dad."

Franklin started to choke up. He wished his dad was still here to help him. But a sudden and massive heart attack claimed Jordan five years before. The passing was strange to Franklin because his father seemed to be in fine health for a man in his mid fifties. He ate well, exercised often and didn't appear to let stressful circumstances bother him. Franklin always figured his mom, a well-known worry wart who secretly smoked cigarettes up until three years ago, would go first. But for some reason, God took Jordan home early. There were many times over the past weeks, Franklin wished the Lord would call him home.

After a few more moments reflecting on his dad's life, Franklin flipped to the passage Jordan wrote down. He already knew what the words said, but still read them again.

"Wives submit to your husbands as to the Lord. For the husband is the head of the wife as Christ is the head of the church, his body, of which he is the Savior. Now as the church submits to Christ, so also wives should submit to their husbands as in everything. Husbands, love your wives, just as Christ loved the church and gave himself up for her to make her holy, cleansing her by the washing with water through the Word, and to present her to himself as a radiant church, without stain or wrinkle or any other blemish, but holy and blameless. In this same way, husbands ought to love their wives as their own bodies. He who loves his wife loves himself. After all, no one ever hated his own body, but he feeds and cares for it, just as Christ does the church -- for we are members of his body. "For this reason a man will leave his father and mother and be united to his wife, and the two will become one flesh.' This is a profound mystery -- but I am talking about Christ and the church. However, each one of you also must love his wife as he loves himself, and the wife must respect her husband."

As Franklin read through the passage, he thought of Sara. She was a submissive wife, who did most anything to please him. At least, she always tried to do so. But had he loved her the way Christ loved the church? Was Saint Paul's command to the Ephesians really even possible to accomplish?

Franklin did love Sara as much as his own body. In fact, right then he thought he would have sacrificed his body for Sara and the two girls' lives. But he realized God's will for them was different than his. They were currently living in paradise with their Savior. He was still stuck in a fallen world. The previous night's drunken episode proved how sinful he could be.

What would Sara have thought of his behavior? He knew she certainly wouldn't have been pleased. Of course, Franklin wouldn't have been drinking like that if Sara was still with him. If only he could have one more chance to tell her how much he loved her. The next opportunity would now have to wait until he entered into eternity himself.

⚜

The more Franklin thought about Sara and the children over the next month, the more depressed he became. Everywhere he gazed in the house there were reminders of his departed spouse and kids. On the walls, hung dozens of snapshots of blissful times together. The smiles in the photos would bring Franklin to tears each time he looked at them. It was almost as if their joy was haunting him. He thought about taking down the pictures, but that would just be a temporary remedy for his sorrow.

Franklin knew he needed to make a more permanent change in his life if he was to get past the tragedy. He made a decision one evening while praying by the pool. This time, though, he was sober.

Gracie was drinking coffee while sitting in an antique wooden rocking chair on the front porch the next morning when Franklin decided to inform her of his potential life-changing choice. She was in deep thought when her son approached. Her mind had drifted back to her beloved Kansas. Harvest time was just a couple months away on the small farm where Gracie helped care for her chronically ill sister Ethel. The place had been in the family for many generations. Because Gracie lived in Florida when her father Seth died more than twenty years ago, Ethel and her husband Junior inherited the hundred-acre farm. The corn crop grown there barely supported the couple and their two sons, so Ethel worked in the cafeteria at the local school before contracting tuberculosis four years ago. Her forced retirement nearly coincided with Junior's untimely death in a car crash. Gracie moved back home to nurse Ethel while the boys worked the farm. How strange it was, Gracie thought, to be dealing with the tragic consequences of an auto accident again so soon.

Franklin startled his mom when he placed his hand on her shoulder. She looked up and put her hand on top of her son's.

"I'm sorry, I didn't mean to disturb you mama," he said before kissing her on the top of the head.

"That's okay dear," she responded, "I was just daydreaming."

"About what?"

Gracie smiled at her son as he pulled up a white plastic chair and sat next to her. "Oh, I was thinking about home. Jack and Joseph will be getting ready to harvest the fields pretty soon. I wonder what price the crop will bring this year."

"You miss the place don't you mama?"

Gracie sighed and then frowned slightly. "I do. But I'm very happy to be here with you Franky. I've loved spending time with you again even if..."

Her voice began to fade as she choked back a few tears. Franklin reached out and held both his mom's hands.

"I know mama. It's been tough. But having you here has helped me so much."

"I hope so dear," Gracie said with a sniffle, "I've tried to do what I can."

The tender moment was broken by a car honking its horn as it swiftly passed another on the street in front of the house. The kid pulling off the maneuver in a red convertible yelled back an obscenity at the older couple in a white sedan.

"I bet you don't see much of that in Kansas do ya mama?"

Gracie shook her head in disgust. "No Franky, people are much nicer out there. That's one thing I don't miss about this area, the lack of respect for other people."

"I know. It's sad mama. It wasn't always that way around here either. At least when I was a kid, it wasn't."

"Well," Gracie replied, "it wasn't as bad as now, but it was never great. I used to tell your father as much. But he loved it here and I know you do as well, don't you?"

Franklin paused for a moment before answering. His view of South Florida was rapidly changing since Sara and the girls' deaths.

"There's something I want to talk to you about mama."

"What's that dear?"

Franklin took a deep breath. "Well, I've been doing a lot of thinking and praying since that horrible day, and I've come to a decision about my life."

Gracie looked at her son curiously. She was glad he was seeking the Lord's council through prayer, but she wondered whether his mind had settled enough yet to make what appeared to a serious determination about his future.

"Okay," Gracie said hesitantly. "What's on your mind?"

Franklin looked down at the green outdoor carpet covering the porch before returning his gaze directly into his mother's concerned eyes.

"We'll mama," he said, "I'm glad you've been thinking about the farm, because I think it's time for you to go back home and take care of Aunt Ethel. I know she must miss you."

Gracie affirmed Franklin's remark. "I talked to my sister last night and she sounded a little depressed. But I think she's alright. With her condition, she has good days and bad days. She asked how you were holding up and I told her you were muddling through."

"That's just it mama," Franklin interjected. "I'm tired of just muddling through. I need to get my life in order."

"How so?" Gracie responded, her tone reflecting a bit more worry.

Franklin shuffled his feet.

"I need a change of scenery. I feel like I'm going mad around here."

"Oh Franky, why don't you stay at the farm with me for a little while? The country air and slow pace will do wonders for you. I just know it."

That was not the scenario Franklin had in mind at all.

"Mama," he said, shaking his head with his eyes closed. "Like I said, having you here with me has been wonderful for these many weeks. I don't know how I could have gotten through it without you."

The teary-eyed son reached over and hugged his mother tightly before continuing. "It's just that I feel like I need to start my life over again in a new place. I don't know where yet, but it's not in Kansas."

Gracie was surprised at her son's thinking, but not totally against it.

"What about this house?" she said. "There are so many memories here for you?"

"That's the main problem," he said. "It's not like I don't think of Sara, Brianna and Ashley nearly every minute of the day, I do. I will never forget them, ever! But I don't think I can go on living here any more without driving myself crazy. It's almost as if I feel this house is haunted in some way."

Franklin began to cry. Gracie held him. After a few moments of sobbing, Franklin rubbed his eyes and gathered his emotions.

"I really feel like I need to get out of here," he said. "Do you understand mama?"

"I do honey, I do. I'm you mother and I'll support you no matter what you decide to do with your life. You know that."

After a minute or two, Franklin enlightened Gracie about his plans.

≈≈≈❖≈≈

Franklin resigned his position at Good Shepherd. Although he thoroughly loved teaching young people, he thought it about time to shore up his own education. He wanted to learn more about his country and what better way than to hit the road. To do so, however, he would need funds. Franklin listed the house with a realtor from the church and within about three weeks during the red-hot 2001 South Florida market, it sold.

Every piece of his plan seemed to be falling into place so perfectly. Franklin figured his decision to move must be in God's will. His friends, though, especially Sam, were not as certain. They echoed Gracie's concerns about Franklin's course of action to get his life in order.

Sam drove to Franklin's house about a week before the widower's departure on the cross-country journey. By that time, it had been almost three months since the deaths of Sara and the two little girls. Sam, as well as many of Franklin's friends from Good Shepherd, had shown a great deal of love for their fallen brother since that desolate May day. Some brought meals over for Franklin and Gracie. Others stopped by to just chit-chat and pray. Franklin felt no lack of fellowship from his Christian family. But they didn't want to smother him either, so they also gave him some much-needed breathing room. The announcement of Franklin's upcoming move, however, shocked many at both the church and school, including Sam.

As he wheeled his Porsche into the driveway of the Edwards' residence that Sunday afternoon, Sam saw that many of the drapes were already removed from the windows. He could see right into the house. The living and dining rooms were completely bare. The only furnishings were cardboard boxes stacked neatly up against the walls.

"I guess he really is leaving," Sam mumbled to himself as he rang the doorbell.

A few moments later, Gracie opened the door.

"Sam, how good to see you," she said before hugging her old friend. It was almost as if Gracie thought she might never see him again. Their embrace lasted a minute or so. "Come on inside."

Gracie walked over to the staircase and yelled up to Franklin. "Franky dear, Sam's here to see you."

Sam looked around the living room as he waited for Franklin to come down. It seemed as if all the life had fled the once-vibrant home. Sam remembered many of the joyful occasions when he and Sandy visited for dinner. Ashley and Brianna were almost like grandchildren for Sam and his wife. Thoughts of the girls caused Sam's eyes to mist.

"Can I get you something to drink Sam?" said Gracie, breaking his recollection.

"A bottle of water would be nice if you have one?"

"Coming right up," Gracie said as she turned and slowly shuffled her way into the kitchen.

As Sam watched her leave the room, he wondered if Gracie was feeling ill. She didn't seem to be moving too well. He hoped her heart condition wasn't getting worse. *Or maybe her heart is just still hurting from all the grief of the past few months,* Sam thought.

Franklin held a box in his arms as he called down the stairs to Sam.

"Hey buddy, what's up?"

Sam looked up at Franklin and grinned. "I was just about to ask you the same thing. Come on down here."

Franklin placed the box on the floor and gleefully slid down the banister, jumping off just a few feet from his best friend.

"Sara used to hate when I did that," Franklin said with a slight twinkle in his eye.

Sam was surprised by Franklin's giddy mood. "My, aren't we chipper today," he said.

Franklin reached out and shook Sam's hand and patted his shoulder a couple of times.

"You know Sam, for the first time in months I feel alright."

"That's great son."

"Yes it is Sam, yes it is."

Gracie walked back into the living room with two bottles of spring water, handing one to each of them.

"Thanks mama."

"Yeah, thank you Gracie," Sam said, twisting off the cap and taking a swig.

"You're welcome," she answered and began to walk up the stairs.

"Do you need some help mama?"

Gracie turned her head around quickly. "I'll be fine Franky. I may be seventy-one, but I can still walk up a flight of stairs you know."

"I know mama," Franklin said somewhat apologetically as he watched Gracie leisurely ascend the seventeen steps to the top. "Why don't we go sit out by the pool Sam?"

"Is your mom okay?" Sam whispered to Franklin, making sure Gracie didn't hear him. "She looks kind of frail."

"Oh, she'll be fine," Franklin responded with a sigh, "especially when she gets back to her beloved Kansas. She's never really liked Florida much you know."

Sam nodded affirmingly. "That's what I wanted to talk to you about. It doesn't seem as if you like it here much anymore either?"

Franklin sat down at the glass patio table next to the pool. Sam plopped into a lounge chair across from him. "Sam, can you blame me?"

"No, can't say that I do. I know the last few months have been extremely difficult for you."

Franklin stared down at the clouded glass table and began to nervously tap his fingers. His joyful mood turned somber. He tried not to seem angry at Sam, but he didn't really feel like explaining himself to his friend. He did so anyway. He owed Sam that much for all he had done to help him through this devastating time.

"I've done a lot of deep thinking since they died Sam," Franklin said as he wiped a single tear from his right eye. "And I just can't stay here anymore. If I'm ever really going to get back on my feet again, I feel I truly need a fresh start. This house, the school, everything, is just too full of painful memories. I feel like a dead man around here anymore, Sam. I need to enter the land of the living again and I just can't do that here."

Franklin put his hands to his face and began to weep steadily. Sam got up, walked behind his dear friend and placed his hands on his shoulders. He didn't say anything to Franklin. He just let him cry.

After about five minutes, Sam took a seat at the table across from Franklin.

"Sam, you probably think I'm crazy for doing this don't you."

Sam shook his head no. "Brother, I don't know if moving is the right thing to do. But you know I will be supportive of you any way I can be. I don't think you're crazy. I love you."

Franklin managed a slight smile and tried to wipe his eyes with his hands. Sam handed him the handkerchief he always carried in his back pocket.

"Franklin, son, I came over here to try and talk you out of moving away. I know you've already sold the house, but I was hoping you could get a condo or something. I don't know if it's wise for you to leave those who love you behind so soon after losing Sara and the girls. We all just want to help you."

"And you all have been a great help to me," Franklin interrupted. "That's not what this is about. I just need to start over. Try something new, you know?"

Sam looked straight into Franklin's dreary brown eyes. His stare made Franklin a bit uncomfortable. Did Sam think he had another motive for leaving? Did he think he was running away from his troubles? Franklin did his best to answer Sam's interrogative glare.

"Sam, I know you're worried about me."

"I am."

"And I appreciate your concern. But I feel this is something I have to do. I've prayed a lot about it."

"And you think this is God's will for you?" Sam quickly responded.

Franklin paused for a moment. "Honestly, I don't really know. I hope it is. I think it is. But my discernment is not all that great right now. I do know this though. Life here is too short for me to sit around and wallow in misery. I want the chance to do something different in my life. Maybe make a difference in someone else's life. I just want a new direction. And I plan to hit the road and see where God takes me."

Sam exerted a resigned sigh and slumped back in his chair. He knew he wasn't going to change Franklin's mind.

"I'm going to miss you," he said, his eyes beginning to water.

Franklin leaned forward and smiled. "Sam, Sam. I promise I will keep in touch with you and Sandy. I love you both so much.

I will never let any distance come between our friendship. Please believe me."

"I do," Sam said. "Do you know where you'll go first? When are you leaving?"

"Next week," Franklin answered. "I think I'll head to the Smokey Mountains first and spread Sara and the girls ashes."

Franklin choked up again with the thought of dispersing his beloved's remains to the winds. After a few seconds, he regained his composure.

"Mama's flying back home this weekend. I'll probably leave next Tuesday or Wednesday after I put the rest of this stuff in storage. I'm really looking forward to seeing this beautiful country of ours Sam, I really am."

Sam noticed the excitement return to Franklin's face as he spoke of his upcoming itinerary. He was happy to see his friend looking joyfully toward the journey.

"I wish you well brother," Sam said as he tightly hugged Franklin. "Let me pray for you now that God will grant you travel mercies and help you find that peace in Him that you are seeking."

Sam reached out and held both of Franklin's hands as he began to pray. Gracie looked down at the touching scene from her bedroom window. Then a thought came to her mind. She went over to her small jewelry box and took out a family heirloom that she knew Franklin would treasure. She had been meaning to give it to him and now seemed to be the perfect time.

"So we'll see you for dinner next Saturday night?" Sam said as he was getting into his car, trying to confirm plans for Franklin's send-off.

"Absolutely," Franklin answered. "I'd love to break bread with you and Sandy again before I leave. That would be wonderful."

"Great, I'll call you with the time," Sam said as he revved up the Porsche.

Franklin waved to his dear friend as he drove off. He thought Sam took the news of his move fairly well. Better than he expected at least.

When Franklin opened the front door of his house, Gracie was waiting there with her hands behind her back and a broad grin on her face.

"I've got a present for you," she said.

His eyes lit up. "Really, what is it mama?"

"Close your eyes and hold out your hand."

Franklin promptly followed his mother's order. He loved receiving gifts and mom's were always extra special. Gracie dropped the heirloom into her son's palm and closed his fist.

He opened his eyes and looked at the present. A rush of joy flooded his heart when he saw it.

"Oh mama. It's daddy's gold pocket watch." Franklin's eyes began to moisten once more. "I'd almost forgotten about this."

He opened the cover and looked at the locket-sized photograph inside. It was a small picture of Gracie, taken just after she and Jordan were married.

"Your father told me that was his favorite photo of me," she said.

Franklin continued to stare at the tiny picture. "I know. Daddy used to say that whenever he checked the time, your picture would remind him to cherish every minute he spent with his beautiful bride. And you still are beautiful mama."

Franklin hugged his mother and kissed her on the cheek.

"I miss him mama."

"Oh Franky, so do I. But I know Jordan and I will be together again one day." Gracie squeezed her son tightly. "Franklin, don't ever forget that the love you receive here goes with you when you pass on. Jordan will never forget his love for me, just like Sara will never forget her love for you. I truly believe that from the bottom of my heart."

Franklin nodded his head in agreement and gazed at the watch once again. It was a little larger than a silver dollar and made of fourteen-karate gold. Not one bit of it was tarnished. Tiny diamond chips encircled the black Roman numerals set against the white background. The hands on the expensive Swiss timepiece were gold-painted arrows. Franklin pulled out the knob on the side and set the time according to his well-worn Timex wristwatch. He wound up Jordan's watch and placed it to his ear.

"Wow, after all these years, it still works," he marveled.

Gracie was pleased that Franklin admired the master craftsmanship. "Take good care of it now, won't you dear?" she said. "Your father really loved that watch and he always wanted you to have it. It was just so hard for me to part with it."

Franklin hugged his mother again. He felt like a child at Christmas. "Thank you so much. I will cherish it mama. I will."

Gracie shut the door and put her arm around her son's waist. Franklin continued to stare at the watch as they walked out toward the pool area that evening. He knew it would probably be one of the last special mother-son moments the two would share for a while. Franklin had promised he would visit Gracie at the farm sometime during his travels, but he didn't know when. He could hear the road calling his name, though he had no idea where the way would lead.

Chapter VI

T he old man's eyes began to moisten as he squeezed Franklin tightly. The widowers hugged for just a few seconds, no longer. But during that brief moment, it was almost as if two torn hearts pressed together to offer mutual sympathy.

While it had been many years since Joe's wife passed on, he had not forgotten the bitter despair her death carried deep into his still-stinging soul. He had really never fully recovered from her passing, so he knew Franklin would need time to try and regain some semblance of normalcy. Joe felt so empty when Tess died that he didn't leave his house for months. That's why he was actually quite pleased Franklin was trying to get his life in order so quickly. He would miss his buddy, but unlike Franklin's other friends, Joe's joy over the decision to move on outweighed his reservations.

"I've heard it said the open highway can soothe a man's sorrows Franky," Joe said as he patted Jordan's boy on the shoulder a couple times. "I reckon leavin' here jest might do ya some good."

Franklin nodded in agreement. "I know it will Joe. I just know it."

Joe let go of Franklin and walked across the garage toward the Edwards' family minivan. With some of the fifty-thousand dollar profit he made from the sale of his house, Franklin paid off the last six months he owed on the 1998 Dodge Caravan. Now before departing on his trek, he had Joe inspect the van from bumper to bumper. Franklin was always very prudent when it came to servicing his vehicles. It was a responsibility both his father and Joe had instilled in him. That's why it was such a surprise to him when he read the police report from Sara's fatal accident in his beloved Camaro.

Because the car was burned so badly, the Highway Patrol could only determine from the charred wreckage that the vehicle suffered some kind of major mechanical failure. And although no primary cause for the tragedy was given in the report, witnesses at the scene said that Sara appeared not to brake at all while skidding out of control. During the past four months, Franklin had been trying to figure out what went wrong that fateful day.

While he knew that Sara wasn't a great driver, she wasn't terrible either. So how could she have wrecked so badly? Was she distracted by the girls for some reason? Did she overcompensate on the rain-slickened road and cross directly into the dump truck's path? What happened to her brakes? These and many other questions were still running through Franklin's mind. He didn't have the answers. And at this point in time, he wasn't trying to seek them anymore. He just wanted to put the whole ordeal behind him before it drove him mad. Besides, he thought, doesn't the entirety of life fall under God's sovereign will?

Joe interrupted Franklin's thoughts by letting the hood drop hard on the hunter green van.

"Sorry boy, didn't mean to startle ya now," Joe said with his hardy country chuckle.

Franklin rolled his eyes and shook his head. "I guess I'm a little jumpy today Joe."

"Nervous 'bout leavin' us folk behind?"

"No, just anxious to hit the road I guess."

"Yep...Can't say I blame ya fer wantin' to get out of here. Really gonna miss ya though boy. That's fer certain."

"I'm really going to miss you too Joe. You are a dear friend. Thank you for all you've done for me all these years. I really appreciate you."

Joe smiled at Franklin and shook his hand. "It's been my pleasure son. Yur family's meant a lot to me." Joe was beginning to choke up. "Anyway, she seems to be in tip-top shape," Joe said as he patted on the hood. "Purrin' like a kitten."

Franklin reached into his back pocket and took out his checkbook. "So how much do I owe you for getting the van running so well?"

Joe frowned at Franklin. "Yur money's no good here now. Jest consider it a goin'-away present from a good friend. Awright?"

Franklin smiled and nodded affirmingly. He knew there wasn't any sense insisting Joe take payment for the work. In fact, the old country boy just might consider that an insult.

"Thank you very much Joe," Franklin said as he tugged on his buddy's shoulder a couple of times.

Joe opened the driver's-side door like a valet and Franklin hopped inside. He turned the key and started it up. He was amazed at how quiet the engine was running.

"Wow Joe, this thing sounds like it is brand new."

"I told ya. Purrs like a kitten."

"It sure does," Franklin remarked as he revved the motor a couple times. "You've still got the touch with an engine Joe. Best mechanic I've ever known."

Joe began to blush a bit. "Aw, get on now."

Franklin's eyes began to mist as Joe shut the door. He gave the old man a salute, put the van in drive and maneuvered out of the garage. Joe tipped his Miami Dolphins ball cap at Franklin as he turned on to the street. Franklin wondered if he would ever see the old man again. He certainly hoped so, because Joe wasn't in the best of health, either physically or spiritually. But just like his own journey ahead, Franklin knew his buddy's future was in the Lord's hands.

❧❖❧

It was still only half-past eight that Saturday morning when Franklin arrived back at the Simmons' house to load his suitcases into the van. Sam and Sandy were in the Bahamas on business that first week of September. Franklin had been staying at the house since Thursday when his closing became final. He had said his goodbyes to his two best friends Sunday evening before they departed. He wished they were still home for his sendoff. Although Franklin knew he could phone them any time he wanted to, their fellowship wouldn't be quite the same.

It only took Franklin about a half-hour to load the rest of his belongings. He wanted to travel as light as possible, so whatever personal items he hadn't sold or given away, Franklin placed in the storage unit he had paid up for a year in advance.

At that point in time, Franklin couldn't wait to blow out of town and see what adventures lay ahead.

He said goodbye to Consuelo and thanked her for the hospitality she had shown him during the past few months. She'd been the Simmons' maid for about a decade and Franklin could see why Sandy valued the Cuban lady's services so much. For a rather slight woman well into her sixties, Consuelo kept the large dwelling nearly spotless practically all by herself. Her work ethic was impressive to say the least.

Franklin said a short prayer before leaving the Simmons' driveway. He asked God for directions, but not concerning his travel plans. Franklin had already mapped out the route he wanted to take. His first stop would be the mountains of Tennessee like he told Sam. Then he would journey west, taking the slow route to California, mostly by way of the older scenic highways instead of the interstate system. He wanted to meet the real folk of this vast country. Franklin asked the Lord to show him a new spiritual direction in life. He wanted an adventure, but he also wanted to make sure God went with him. He was certain the coming journey was in God's will.

Franklin knew one thing as he pulled out onto the street in front of the Simmons' house; he was determined never to take I-595 again. He couldn't bear to drive the same road on which his beloved wife and children had lost their lives. No way! So Franklin took the long way from Plantation to the Florida Turnpike. He moseyed along the ten or so miles on Nob Hill Road to Sample Road, where he picked up the Turnpike. It would really be the only long stretch of interstate Franklin traveled for most of his cross-country tour.

He drove for nearly eleven hours straight the first day. Franklin credited adrenaline and caffeine for helping him make it quickly through that first six hundred miles. But deep down, he knew it was his overwhelming desire to put the past behind that pushed him. He truly thought his life would begin anew once he left Florida. But no matter how he looked at it, Franklin really was running away from his sorrow. It remained a mindset that would soon enough prove troublesome.

He spent the night at a modest motel just off Interstate-75

in southern Georgia. After a late supper at the motel restaurant, Franklin passed on taking a swim in the indoor pool and went straight to bed. Although many young people seemed to be having a good time at the poolside bar that evening, he wanted to get an early start the next day. Besides, the day-long drive had worn heavy on his eyes. He fell fast asleep.

⪼⬦⪻

While Franklin slept that night, he dreamt of a vacation his now-departed family had taken in the Great Smokey Mountains three years prior.

Because of her northern New England upbringing, Sara always loved to get back to nature, especially in the fall when the leaves were changing colors. The temperatures were crisp, but not too cold during that October excursion. The foliage featured a broad array of spectacular red and yellow hues. Franklin pictured in his mind one particular afternoon when his wife and girls frolicked on a leaf-covered hill next to their campsite. Sara chased little Ashley and Brianna about the quickly-wintering trees, tossing leaves in the air as they ran from her. The girls giggled with delight as they managed to stay one step ahead of their mother in the merry game of tag. Sara motioned for Franklin to come join the fun. He dropped the small bundle of wood he was carrying for that evening's campfire. He dashed over to Ashley and quickly swooped up the five-year-old in his arms. She squealed with glee as he lifted her high above his head. Meanwhile, Sara grabbed Brianna by the arms and slowly flung her round and round. It was a game mother and daughter used to play in the backyard at home all the time. The playful action was even more fun in the cool mountain air. Franklin knew blessed times like that with his family were certainly a gift from God himself.

He was truly savoring the moment when the alarm clock sounded in the motel room. Franklin slapped his hand down on top of the clock to silence the buzzer that halted his blissful vision and abruptly ushered his consciousness back into the present. As he lay in the bed just before dawn that morning, Franklin started to feel the sorrow of his current circumstances. He bitterly realized he would no longer be able to share times like that with his family. At least not in this world anyway. He felt himself beginning to slowly drift back into the depths of his months-long despair. But he was not going to embark down that path again, no way!

"Enough!" Franklin barked to himself as he hopped out of bed and hurried to the bathroom. As he showered, he focused on the day ahead in an effort to deflect his grief. The attempt met with mixed results, probably because the day's itinerary included a task Franklin knew would bring both agony and closure to his awful ordeal.

With still about an eight-hour drive to Great Smokey Mountains National Park, Franklin hit the road by six. He listened to the Book of Psalms on C.D. as he drove that day. He was hoping the disc would bring him some comfort and inspiration as he headed toward the mountains. The Psalms, especially those written by King David, always seemed to bring a sense of peace to Franklin. He definitely knew he would need to feel the comfort of the Holy Spirit as he spread his family's ashes.

The weather was splendid that early September day, partly cloudy and still fairly warm. Autumn was nearly two weeks away, so Franklin knew the trees in the mountains would still be summertime green. But that was okay with him. The closer he got to the park, the more he just wanted to get his one-man requiem over with. He hoped the ceremony would somehow allow him to move on with his life.

Franklin pulled into Pigeon Forge Tennessee around two in the afternoon. The town had changed greatly over the years, thanks mostly to the opening of Dollywood. He found lodging at a motel just outside Dolly Parton's countrified theme park. He had wanted to take the girls to the amusement center on their previous vacation, but Sara was beginning to come down with a cold, so the family trip ended a couple days early. Franklin definitely was not in the mood for Dollywood on this solo journey.

After quickly checking into the motel, Franklin hopped back into the van and hightailed it to the mountains.

The Smokies were as beautiful as ever as he drove through the park late that afternoon. The tops of the tree-covered peaks were just beginning to turn color, though the weather was not quite cool enough yet to usher in the coming brilliance. As the sun drifted toward the horizon of the vivid blue sky, Franklin likened it to a slowly-dimming lamp gently closing out another chapter of God's eternal epic. The widower realized he was just a mile or two from the location where he would play his somber role during another act in the lengthy and sorrowful saga. He hadn't prepared anything to say before he cast his loved ones ashes to the wind. What was the point of doing so? The occasion wouldn't be like the funeral service. Only he and God would be present for the ceremony.

The van's tires squeaked slightly as Franklin rounded a curve on the steep and winding mountain road. But then, just up ahead, he spotted the place he was looking for. He braked and pulled the van off the road to a small rest area and got out. He and Sara had snapped nearly a whole role of film three years earlier at the very same place. They loved the view there, thinking it could possibly be the prettiest locale in the entire park. The panorama was truly spectacular.

A trio of tall peaks stood elegantly above a deep valley. They were accented on each side by progressively smaller hills that seemed to step down to the valley floor. The sun lit up the three peaks from the left, but its angle of descent behind a mountain cast a shadow on the side of the valley where the viewing area was located. The setting seemed eerily appropriate to Franklin.

It was almost as if the Lord had made a special reservation for Franklin because there were no other people there that day. After taking a deep breath and inhaling the fresh mountain air, he reached into the van and removed a small plastic box containing the three urns. He set the box on the ground and grabbed his Bible from the front passenger seat. He placed it on top of the box and carried the items over to the railing that guarded the mountainside.

The steady breeze that had been blowing all day was beginning to pick up a little bit as Franklin removed the urns from the plastic box. He carefully tore off the bubble wrap that had been protecting each urn and set them on top of the container. Franklin's eyes began to tear as he stared at the blue oriental-looking urns. He wondered if scattering the ashes would really release the anguish over losing his family. The act was really nothing more than ceremonial, he thought. In fact, he and Sara had planned on being buried side-by-side when they died, although they had not yet purchased a family funeral plot. But cremation seemed only logical after the manner in which Sara and the girls had departed this life. And what did it matter, really? It was the soul that passed on, not the body, Franklin reminded himself.

As he gazed out at the beauty of the mountains surrounding him, Franklin tried to imagine how the scene before his eyes compared to what Sara and the girls were witnessing at that very moment. But heaven was too difficult for him to visualize from this side of eternity. How he longed to already be living in God's realm. But his time had not yet come. So Franklin opened his Bible and found a passage in Paul's second letter to the Corinthians that he knew would settle his soul:

"Now we know that if the earthly tent we live in is destroyed, we have a building from God, an eternal house in heaven, not built by human hands. Meanwhile, we groan, longing to be clothed with our heavenly dwelling, because when we are clothed, we will not be found naked. For while we are in this tent, we groan and are burdened, because we do not wish to be unclothed but to be clothed with our heavenly dwelling, so that what is mortal may be swallowed up by life. Now it is God who has made us for this very purpose and has given us the Spirit as a deposit, guaranteeing what is to come. Therefore we are always confident and know that as long as we are at home in the body we are away from the Lord. We live by faith, not by sight. We are confident, I say, and would prefer to be away from the body and at home with the Lord."

The sound of a couple of birds squawking while flying overhead interrupted Franklin's reading before he finished the passage from chapter five. But the point had already been made to him. He should be happy that Sara and the girls were with the Lord because they were truly enjoying infinite bliss. And God had promised that his own sorrow would only be temporary. Though he would indeed suffer while in this earthly tent, he should find joy in the fact that his eternal home was guaranteed. The thought brought a smile to Franklin's face and comfort for his heart.

After praying to thank God for the mercy he had been shown at that time, Franklin reached down and took the urn with the Sara's name labeled on it. He removed the tape that held the lid on and then poured out the ashes into a gold bowl that he had placed next to the urns in the plastic box. He held the bowl over the metal guardrail and turned it upside down. As the wind softly picked up the ashes and floated them through the valley below, Franklin whispered "My dear Sara, this act reminds me that you now dwell in the house of the Lord forever."

After he watched Sara's ashes drift from sight, Franklin repeated the same process and spoke the same words for each of his daughters. As he saw the last of Ashley's remains carried away by the wind, Franklin began to sob. But he noticed something a little different about himself. His tears of sorrow were beginning to flow into tears of joy. Though still not exactly filled with glee, he did feel his emotional load begin to lighten somewhat. He believed the healing of his heart had begun.

❦❧❧

Franklin slept well that night. In fact, it was the soundest slumber he had enjoyed in months. He felt thoroughly refreshed when he awoke just after dawn that Tuesday morning. Over the last nine hours, it was almost as if the Lord had forcibly shut down any sensation of consciousness Franklin was supposed to have. His sleep was so deep that he didn't even remember a single dream during the night. The recurring nightmares of the accident were also silenced. As he stared up at the dingy popcorn ceiling of his motel room, he wondered aloud: "Could this be the start of the new life I'm searching for?"

Franklin pondered the question for a few moments. He knew he had no reason to dwell in the past. The final remnants of his old life had been scattered to the winds the day before. Sara would always tell him to live out his days for the glory of God. Just because she was gone didn't mean the moral obligation to do so was no longer required of him. He vowed he would try to diligently follow the Lord's will, beginning today. Franklin was invigorated as he sat up on the side of the bed. He wanted to make a mental note of the date. He reached over and grabbed his father's gold watch off the nightstand. He opened the cover and looked at the date: 9-11.

"September eleventh," Franklin mumbled to himself. "Very well. September eleventh, two thousand one, will be the day I begin anew. It all starts over now."

He decided to spend the first day of his new life in Gatlinburg. Although the quaint hamlet nestled in the heart of the Smokies was a bit of a tourist trap, Franklin loved the Tennessee town's charm. It reminded him of a small Swiss village, kind of like the one in *The Sound of Music*.

Franklin checked out of the motel around seven-thirty and made the hour-long trek through the mountains. It was another spectacular morning in the Smokies. There was a slight chill in the air, but the scenery was nearly a carbon copy of the previous day. He said a prayer as he drove, especially thanking God for the beauty in that part of the nation.

As he pulled into Gatlinburg, Franklin noticed there weren't many people walking the streets. Even on a weekday, the small town was usually bustling with activity. But that day, it was very quiet. He parked the van in front of a little restaurant and went inside for some breakfast. There was no one at the hostess station to greet him, so Franklin wondered if the place was really open. He walked around a small partition and looked toward the back of the dinning room. He saw a group of people, about a half-dozen or so, staring intently up at a small television in the corner.

Franklin walked over and tapped a waitress on the shoulder. "What's going on?" he said.

The short, blond girl turned around. She wore a look of deep concern. "A jet crashed into the World Trade Center," she answered, her voice cracking slightly

"Really," Franklin replied and quickly fixed his eyes on the TV.

The screen showed heavy smoke billowing from the tower on the left. The tower on the right appeared to have no damage. Franklin listened to the TV report in silence along with the rest of the group. The reporters were busy speculating about the incident when another plane came into the picture. It flew behind the other tower and exploded.

"Oh my God," shrieked a female TV reporter. "Another jet has just crashed into the building."

A loud gasp echoed through the stunned crowd at the restaurant. The waitress, who had just spoken to Franklin, covered her mouth with both hands. An older couple stared at one another with eyes wide open and jaws agape.

"What the hell is happening?" said a tall, black man with a white apron, obviously the cook at the diner.

"Man, I wonder if we're under attack," replied a young busboy, who was still holding onto his plastic dishpan. "Maybe its terrorism or something."

Franklin abruptly placed his index finger to his mouth and glared at the teenage boy. "Shhh. Listen to the TV."

The busboy raised his eyebrows and nodded in agreement.

No one in the restaurant said much for the next hour. They mostly just pulled up chairs in front of the TV and watched the horrific events unfold in front of them.

Although the news reports were somewhat chaotic for a while, once the viewers were informed about another jet crashing into the Pentagon, the busboy's earlier assertion was fast becoming alarmingly accurate. The United States was under attack by someone.

Franklin suddenly wasn't hungry anymore. He left the diner and walked across the street to an old, brick hotel. The streets of Gatlinburg had become a lot noisier as people rushed back to the various places they were staying. Franklin entered the hotel and walked up to the clerk at the desk. She was talking on the phone and didn't notice him at first.

"I don't know how long I'll have to stay here mama," the brown-haired lady said quite sternly. "I'll get home as soon as I can. Oh, I have a customer. I have to go now. I'll call ya back okay...Alright mama, I love ya too. Bye bye."

The clerk hung up the phone and began to wait on Franklin.

"May I help ya," the forty-something woman said, her overbite accenting a feigned smile.

"Ah, yeah, I need to get a room please," Franklin said, trying not to stare at the rather homely, but seemingly pleasant lady. "Do you have any available?"

"Why certainly we do," she said as she slid over to her computer. "Anything in particular?"

"What to you mean?" Franklin asked quizzically.

"Well, we have single or double occupancy, many with great views of the mountains. What's to yur likin'?"

Franklin paused for a moment. He was a little befuddled by the woman's quirky mannerisms, especially the nervous tapping of her fingers on the keyboard. Was she always like this? Or maybe the morning's stunning events had gotten to her. They had certainly made him feel a bit uneasy.

"Um, I'll just take a single room. The best you have available will be fine."

"Very well then. I'll just need yur driver's license and a

major credit card please."

Franklin took out his wallet and handed them to her. She moved back to her computer and began feverishly striking the keys. He was doing his best not to break out in laughter at the tiny woman's mousy way.

"Jest terrible 'bout them planes crashing into that building this morning ain't it?" the clerk asked Franklin as she entered his information into the computer.

"Oh, I know. I still can't believe it," he replied.

"They think its terrorism ya know."

"Yeah, I know. I was over at the diner across the street watching it on TV. Everybody over there was shocked by what they saw. Man!"

The clerk stopped typing and began to shake her head. Franklin wondered if she was about to cry.

"Are you okay?" he asked.

The woman looked up at him and put on her fake smile again.

"Oh, I'll be fine I reckon. Good Lord willing. Better I suppose, than those folk on them planes."

Franklin nodded in agreement.

The clerk tore a piece of paper of the printer and handed it to Franklin.

"The room is fifty-nine dollars a night plus tax fer as long as ya want it. Ya planning on staying here fer a while are ya Mr. Edwards?"

"Probably just a few nights if that's alright?"

"Fine with me, it's kind of quiet around here right now," the clerk said. "We try to be hospitable folk, so just ring the desk right here and let us know if ya need something alright?"

"I'll do that," Franklin said, taking his room key from the lady.

"What's your name anyway?"

The lady quickly placed her hand over her mouth and widened her eyes. "Oh my. Where's my manners? My name is Sally. Right fine to meet ya."

She held out her hand for Franklin to shake.

"Pleasure to meet you Sally," he said, shaking her hand. "Nice place you have here."

"Why thank ya," she replied. "Hope ya enjoy yur stay."

Franklin smiled and turned to go back to the front door. He noticed Sally quickly return to the telephone. He figured she was calling her mother back. It was the kind of day to check in with your relatives. Franklin reminded himself to call Gracie once he settled into his hotel room. He drove the van around the back of the rustic two-story building. He grabbed just one of his three suitcases from the van and walked inside the hotel through the rear entrance. As he entered the elevator, he looked back and saw Sally still on the phone. She saw him and flashed a wide grin at him again. Franklin thought maybe her smile wasn't fake after all, just a little peculiar.

Ditzy Sally had forgotten to tell him where room two-fifteen was, but Franklin figured it must be somewhere the second floor. Turns out, it was straight down the end of the hall from the elevator. The room was small, but quite charming actually. The single bed was covered with an old-fashioned country quilt and two lase-covered pillow cases. A peppermint was placed atop each pillow. The wooden furniture had an antique look about it, although Franklin knew it was probably just purchased from a second-hand store. He placed his suitcase on the small table and draped his flannel coat over the back of the chair. After slipping off his shoes, he sat down on the bed and turned on the TV in front of him.

Franklin was beginning to get hungry, but once he starting

watching the news he couldn't turn it off. Every channel seemed to be covering the day's tragic events and he continually flipped through the remote for different perspectives of the breaking story. He became almost mesmerized by what he was seeing, especially the pictures of the towers falling. Franklin was shocked by those images. He didn't know the towers had collapsed because he was checking into the hotel at the time.

Like most Americans that fateful day, Franklin's emotions ran the entire gamut. His initial shock and fear eventually evolved into anger and outrage. He couldn't believe that even the most brazen of terrorist groups would have the audacity to attack the United States' homeland directly. But the actions that really inflamed Franklin the most were the pictures of the celebrations by the Muslims in Palestine.

"What kind of religion finds joy in the deaths of innocent people?" he kept muttering to himself while gritting his teeth.

After a couple of hours, Franklin couldn't bare to watch anymore. What had started out as a day of recovery for him had turned into another day of mental anguish. He decided to phone Gracie before finally heading out for a bite to eat. She didn't answer, so he left her a message and asked her to call him back later that evening.

Franklin decided to return to the diner across the street. He was pleased the place was still open. But the mood was understandably somber, so he hurried through his meal, walked over to a convenience store and bought some beer and returned to his room for the night. He talked to his mother for a good hour about the day's events, and when he was certain she was okay, he went to sleep.

❦

Franklin spent the next three days in Gatlinburg, but the town wasn't much fun. In fact, during the entire first week after the horrible attacks, most of the nation was still in an ugly mood. That fact was readily evident to Franklin when he stopped for a couple days in Oak Ridge.

A point could be made that the mid-sized town located in the northeastern foothills of Tennessee was probably not the safest place to be following the attacks of September 11. Being the site of one of the country's most important nuclear facilities, some town folk wondered if Oak Ridge could also be a potential target of terrorist rage. Despite the area being on high alert and access to the nuclear laboratories severely limited, tension and anxiety were running strong among many residents.

Franklin noticed the aura as soon as he drove into town late that Saturday morning. The clerk who checked him into a motel downtown requested three different forms of identification. And the old guy certainly wasn't as friendly as Sally had been in Gatlinburg. But Franklin tried not to let the ornery clerk bother him. After quickly dropping his luggage off in his room, he decided to drive around and find a place to eat lunch.

Many thoughts were running through his mind as he drove through town. Like most people, he wondered where the nation was heading in the next few weeks and months. Was war a possibility? Those responsible for the reprehensible acts five days prior would definitely have to be punished, Franklin reasoned. Unbridled patriotism was running rampant for the first time in years, especially there in the South. It seemed like every car Franklin passed flew some kind of American flag from its antenna or had a decal or sticker affixed to its windshield or bumper. It amazed him how quickly the wide variety of patriotic slogans were already flooding the American marketplace.

One maxim in particular caught Franklin's eye. The sticker was attached to the rear windshield of a slick, red F-150 pickup truck, its breadth not quite concealing the gun rack on the inside of the cab. A cross and the Christian symbol of a fish served as parenthesis for the sticker's message, which read:

No Matter What The Wicked Do,
God Still Loves Red, White & Blue

As Franklin was contemplating the theological meaning of the message while parked behind the truck at a stoplight, his attention was quickly diverted to the driver. He could only see her face as it reflected back from the side-view mirror. The image was pleasantly striking. Her golden blond hair elegantly framed a delicate teenage face. But it was the girl's stunning blue eyes that captured Franklin's attention. They were quite enthralling. He knew he shouldn't stare, but he couldn't stop himself. Then, as if she felt his gaze upon her, the gorgeous young girl glanced into the mirror and spotted her anonymous admirer. She flashed Franklin a comely smile and quick wink. It was obvious the teenager was accustomed to men marveling at her loveliness. Franklin blushed and quickly looked away.

The traffic signal turned green and the pickup moved on. Franklin hung back in the van and made sure there was another car between him and the truck when he approached the next stoplight. It was certainly too soon after Sara's death for him to be looking at other women. But although he was displeased with himself, Franklin knew he would have trouble allowing the girl's alluring beauty to escape his mind. In fact, he found himself not really wanting to let go of her image.

Franklin saw a restaurant up ahead on the right and pulled into the parking lot. The growling of his stomach helped him to change his focus. Although the aroma emanating from the establishment was pleasing, the place was the typical Southern greasy spoon. Franklin walked in and sat down at the counter of the crowded diner.

A short, motherly-looking waitress immediately greeted him.

"Hello sir, how are you today?" the slightly-graying woman asked.

"Very well, thank you," Franklin answered, noticing the lady didn't feature the twangy, country accent, he'd been growing accustomed to.

"May I get you a cup of coffee or another beverage?" she said as she handed Franklin a menu from underneath the counter.

"Coffee would be great Midge," Franklin replied, responding to the gold nametag which was pinned just below the collar of her standard black and white uniform, complete with visor.

Midge walked away to get fetch the coffee while Franklin browsed the menu. As he was looking over the choices, his concentration was interrupted by a stout man on the stool to his right. The guy was making slurping noises while finishing a cup of soup. Franklin felt like correcting the man's poor manners, but didn't say anything. When the guy had finally lapped up every last drop of the creamy broth, Franklin turned his head and hurled a disparaging smirk at the slovenly fellow. He tipped his filthy, orange UT cap to Franklin.

"Howdy," said the man, his yellowed teeth barely slipping through his crooked grin.

Midge came back with Franklin's coffee. "See anything you like?" she asked. "Our lunch special today is country fried steak with mashed potatoes, green beans and desert for five ninety-five."

"Wow, that sounds real good," Franklin answered. "I'll give it a try. Thank you. Oh, may I have a coke with my meal please?"

"Certainly," Midge said with a courteous smile and then left to place Franklin's order.

As he unwrapped his silverware from the confines of the paper napkin, Franklin could sense the stare of the soup-slurper. *Why didn't I get a booth?* Franklin thought to himself before exchanging pleasantries with the disheveled man in dingy blue overalls and mud-crusted brown work boots.

"Hello, my name's Franklin how are you?" he said, reaching over to shake the middle-aged man's still somewhat grimy hand.

"We'll, ya surely are a polite fella ain't ya now?" the man said as he reciprocated the handshake, though somewhat awkwardly.

"Always try to be," Franklin responded, wondering if he offended the stranger with a judgmental survey of the guy's dingy dress.

Then, as if a switch suddenly turned on in his brain, the man's demeanor changed. He flashed a broad grin at Franklin like they were lifelong buddies or something.

"Well, real glad to know ya Franklin. I'm Justin P. Tremly." He continued to clutch Franklin's hand so hard that it was beginning to get a little sore. "Ya ain't from round here are ya?"

"No, I'm from South Florida actually."

"Oh, down by them Everglades."

"Well, kind of. Really near Fort Lauderdale."

"Oh, I know that area real good," Justin said with a confirming nod. "Used to go gater hunting there way back when with my daddy. Kinda hot. Lots a misquitters."

Franklin coughed out a slight laugh. He was beginning to wonder if the guy was a distant cousin of Joe's. "Yeah there are in the summer. It's real nice in the winter, though."

Justin nodded. "So what brings ya to these parts?"

Franklin paused for a moment before answering. He definitely wasn't going to go into personal details with a stranger.

"Oh, I'm just passing through really. I'm on my way to Kansas to visit my mother."

"That's real nice," Justin said with his broad grin now displaying a desperate need for intense dental care.

Franklin felt a little sorry for the guy. It seemed like Justin was really happy someone would take the time to chat with him. They continued the small talk until Midge brought Franklin his meal. After politely thanking the waitress, Franklin bowed his head and silently said grace.

The gesture caught Justin's notice.

"Ya religious man Franklin?"

"I'm a Christian," he answered in between bites of his tasty, but greasy, breaded steak. "But unfortunately I haven't had much of a chance to go to church during my travels over the last few weeks. I'd really like to go somewhere tomorrow morning, especially with what's been happening during this past week."

Justin squinted his eyes at Franklin ever so slightly, as if he were trying to figure out whether to tell him something or not. Franklin took a sip of his coke before continuing the conversation.

"You know man, sometimes I don't know what to think about this world anymore. It's just crazy what's been going on."

"Oh yeah," Justin quickly responded. "Folk ain't got no respect, that's the problem, especially them damn Mooslims. We ought to jest nuke all of 'em. I'll tell ya."

Franklin almost choked on his food at the logic of Justin's backwoods philosophy on world politics. "Shoot first and ask questions later, huh Justin? That's not going to solve the problem."

Justin's smile turned into a frown when even with his challenged intellect he realized that violence only begets more violence. "Aw, I know. We should try an help them poor folk know the truth about the Good Lord."

Franklin nodded in agreement. "Do you go to church Justin?"

"Yep, sure do. Every Saturday night."

"Really?" Franklin said in a surprised tone.

"Ah uh. Plannin' on goin' tonight. Wanna come? All are welcome where I go to praise."

Franklin pondered the unexpected invitation for a moment. He was already caught off guard by the fact Justin appeared to be a believer. And he has always been interested in how other denominations' worship styles were different from his distinct reformed Presbyterian upbringing. *Hey, why not?* he thought. He didn't know any of the other churches in the area and he really felt the need to worship Christ.

"I usually go on Sunday mornings, but okay," Franklin said.

Justin's eyes lit up. "Great!" he said. "I'm sure ya'll love our church. It's different than some others."

"Okay, well where is it?" Franklin asked as he finished up his lunch. "How do I get there?"

"Jest meet me here at six' clock. I'll show ya. Ya got a car? I ain't drivin' right now. No license."

Franklin didn't bother asking Justin why he didn't have a driver's license. In fact, he thought it might be better if he didn't know why. "I have a green minivan out front. I'll drive."

Justin shook Franklin's hand with enthusiasm. "Awright. I'll see ya later then. Can't wait!"

"Looking forward to it," Franklin said.

Justin smiled, tipped his hat and left the diner without paying for his soup.

"Did he leave?" Midge sternly asked Franklin a few minutes

later. "He skipped out on me again?"

Franklin didn't have an answer for the perturbed waitress, but offered to pay for Justin's meal. He figured the man was just so overly-excited about having someone to take him to church that paying must have slipped his mind.

⌘

Franklin went back to his motel room and napped for a couple hours before getting ready for the evening's service. Although he'd packed a couple of suits for his cross-country journey, he figured casual attire was probably appropriate for a small-town church. Back home, he always dressed up when going to see his King, but a pair of slacks and a button-down shirt seemed to suit the occasion. After all, Franklin didn't want to show up Justin, who he figured would probably be wearing jeans and some sort of T-shirt.

When Franklin arrived at the diner at the set time, Justin was waiting out front for him. And he was dressed just the way Franklin thought. A slight drizzle was starting to fall as Franklin pulled the van up to the front of the restaurant and opened the passenger door for Justin.

"Howdy partner, ya ready to roll?" Justin said with a broad grin on his face.

"Absolutely," Franklin answered. "How far away is this place? I might have to get some gas. I've got about a quarter tank."

"Aw, it's only about two miles down the road. Ya'll be fine."

Franklin followed Justin's directions, which took them to a small dirt road on the outskirts of town. The rain was coming down harder, opening up a few potholes on the gravel. A couple claps of thunder rumbled off in the distance. They traveled about a half mile down the dirt road until they came upon a decrepit old building set in a clearing among some trees. It was a shack really, and it didn't look much like a church. There didn't appear to be any windows on the wooded building, just a double door in the front. Franklin was beginning to feel uneasy about the place, but he kept his concerns to himself.

Justin directed Franklin to a grassy area around the back of the shack. There were a half-dozen vehicles parked back there, including a familiar pickup truck, which Franklin pulled up next to.

"Hey, I saw that red pickup today," Franklin said to Justin, upon verifying the sticker in the back window. "There was a pretty blond girl driving it."

"Yep,'" Justin replied. "That would be the preacher's daughter, Violet. She helps him a lot with the service."

Franklin thought the name was appropriate, considering the how dazzling he found the eyes gazing back at him in the mirror earlier that afternoon. The two men hustled through the rain to the tiny foyer awkwardly sloping over the double doors. They went inside. The room that served as the sanctuary was only about fifteen feet wide by twenty feet long. Each side was lined with four rows of metal folding chairs with six in each row. A single light bulb hung down from the raftered ceiling over what appeared to be a makeshift alter. On it was a shiny silver crucifix, about the size of a desk lamp. Next to the cross were a Bible and two gold communion plates. Franklin also noticed a small wooden box on the back of the lace-covered card table that made up the altar.

Justin led Franklin to the second row on the right. There were less than twenty people in attendance, but not one of them came over to greet the two men. Franklin assumed a small country church like that would be full of friendly worshipers, but these folks just sat quietly in their seats, some with their heads bowed in prayer. Justin looked over at Franklin and smiled.

"This will probably be different than yur used to," he whispered to an increasingly bewildered Franklin. "I think ya'll like it though."

Franklin nodded uncomfortably. Something just didn't feel quite right to him. And he didn't sense the Lord's presence like he normally would in church.

As Franklin was contemplating the aura of the place, Violet emerged from a back room. Barefoot, she was wearing a long white robe, accented by a purple cloth belt around her waist. A pink carnation was tucked into her silken, blond hair. Her stunning blue eyes appeared somewhat glassy, as if she was medicated. She clutched an acoustic guitar in her right hand.

The congregation rose in unison as Violet walked in front of the altar, turned with her back to the crowd and bowed in reverence. Violet then turned back toward the gathering, strapped on her guitar and began to strum a few chords. The people started to sing a hymn that Franklin didn't know, so he just stood and observed in silence. Violet sang beautifully and the congregation followed her lead well. In fact, it seemed choreographed.

About halfway trough the opening number, a tall, gawky, gray-haired man dressed in all black came out of the back room, belting out the hymn at the top of his lungs. He walked behind Violet, kneeled in front of the altar with his hands raised high and continued to sing to his heart's content.

When the song was over, Violet joined the congregation in the front row. The preacher rose from his knees, bowed before the altar just like his daughter had done and turned to face the people. He lowered his hands signaling the crowd to sit.

"Please join me in prayer," he said, closing his cloudy, blue eyes and once again raising his hands high above his head. "Oh great god, your people turn to you in their time of need. Here them now."

"Yes hear us lord," the congregation responded in unison.

The preacher continued. "Oh mighty ruler of the universe, your subjects humbly ask for your presence. Join them now."

"Yes join us lord," they chanted.

The charismatic leader began to tremble, his still-raised arms twitching feverishly. "Oh sovereign of sinners, your flock begs forgiveness. Have mercy now."

"Yes have mercy," they cried loudly. One middle-aged woman in the front row even fell onto the floor weeping. Violet walked over and hugged the sobbing lady. Franklin wondered what the woman had done to feel such apparent remorse. Her actions were either a sign of heartfelt repentance or cult-like insanity. Franklin couldn't determine which it was, so he nervously just continued to witness the proceedings.

After Violet led the group in a couple more rousing praise songs, the preacher delivered a short message about how the world was still under control despite the past week's horrible terrorist attacks. The message appeared to bring comfort to the congregation, although Franklin didn't find the preacher's riveting words to be very theologically sound. But he reminded himself that he was just a guest at the church and he should remain respectful.

Then the service turned downright freaky.

The preacher snatched the Bible from the altar, opened it up to a premarked spot and read aloud to the congregation.

"Oh my people, hear the voice of god himself in Mark sixteen, verses seventeen and eighteen," the old man cried dramatically, his right hand outstretched above his head and left hand holding the Bible. "And these signs shall follow them that believe. In my name shall they cast out devils. They shall speak with new tongues. They shall take up serpents and if they drink any deadly thing, it shall not hurt them. They shall lay hands on the sick, and they shall recover."

He abruptly slammed the book shut, startling Franklin, and slowly scanned the mesmerized crowd with his piercing eyes for a few seconds. "Do you believe?" he growled, both hands raised high now.

"Yeah, we believe," the followers quickly chanted back, not quite in harmony.

Their zeal was apparently not frenzied enough for the now-profusely sweating madman. "I said, do, you, believe!" he screamed at the top of his lungs, his fierce blue eyes about to burst from their sockets.

Most of the gathering, including Justin, erupted at that point. Some began to weep, others fell to their knees. Franklin had never witnessed such a spectacle and it was beginning to frighten him tremendously.

"Oh yes, we believe!" they wailed like a collection of mourners in agony over a fallen relative.

The preacher suddenly dropped both his arms, slammed them across his chest and cast his eyes toward the cob-webbed ridden rafters. After a few seconds, he slowly lowered his head and sternly glared out at the congregation. "Then you must," he exclaimed, pausing like an angry father would do for emphasis, "prove your faith!"

Franklin felt like bolting for the door at that point, but he couldn't resist seeing what was going to happen next. The scene reminded him of the times when his father would take him to one of the traveling carnivals that often came through town during his youth. Although Gracie didn't care for them one bit, she still allowed Jordan to take the pre-teen boy to the midway madness. They especially marveled at the sideshows like the bearded lady and the two-headed goat. Franklin knew he never would forget the freak show he was now witnessing.

The preacher walked over to the wooden box on the makeshift altar. He bowed his head and said a silent prayer. The now-hushed crowd did the same. When he was finished, the old man lifted off the box's cover and carefully reached inside. Franklin nearly fainted when he saw what the preacher pulled out of the box and held in his outstretched arms: a diamondback rattlesnake, about five feet in length.

Justin winked at Franklin and patted him on the shoulder a couple times without saying a word.

The preacher held his left hand just behind rattler's head and turned the snake toward his face so that he could look it directly in the eyes. He smiled at the rattler as its tongue slithered out of its mouth a couple times. He looked directly into the serpent's eyes and nodded a few times, almost as if paying homage to the beast. Franklin was stunned by the man's calmness, but chilled by what came next.

The lovely Violet got up and stood next to her father. She held out her arms, palms raised. The preacher gently placed the rattler across his daughter's arms. Before he let go of the snake, Violet put her right hand behind the reptile's head. She then followed the same ritual as her father: directly looking into the snake's eyes and smiling, almost lovingly.

Justin nodded and grinned at Franklin before walking up and standing next to Violet. He didn't even break a sweat when the girl handed off the serpent to him. Three more followers joined the cult-like procession before the preacher thankfully put the rattler back into its box.

The entire ceremony made Franklin queasy, so much so, that he passed on the communion plates when they were handed to him. Besides, there was no way he was going to partake of the Lord's Supper with a sect of snake worshipers.

As the service ended, Violet and her father left the so-called sanctuary through the same door they had entered. It could have been the gateway to hell for all Franklin cared. He just wanted to get out of there as quickly as possible.

"I need to go," Franklin said as he firmly grabbed Justin's arm and pulled him toward the doors before anyone could stop and talk to them.

Justin could tell Franklin was upset and followed his ride home to the van.

As they pulled out of the parking lot, Franklin's nerves began to settle. He was happy to be free of the whole scene that was for sure.

"Kinda freaked ya out a little didn't it?" Justin asked.

Franklin tossed an angry glare at the hick. "I don't want to talk about it okay."

Justin responded with a demented giggle. Franklin immediately felt like punching him, but he held back, knowing better than to get in a tussle with a lunatic.

"Aw man, ya jest need some more faith that's all," Justin said snidely.

"I guess so," Franklin quipped.

Justin just shook his head and looked out the window. Neither man said another word until Franklin dropped off Justin at the diner.

"Thanks fer the ride," Justin said as he closed the passenger door. "I'll pray for ya."

Franklin sighed deeply and smirked at the crazy snake worshiper. "You do that."

Justin flipped a quick wave at Franklin before turning and walking into the diner. Franklin made sure he took a different route back to his motel. He was afraid Justin, or maybe one of the other lunatics he met that night, might follow him. He knew he was probably being a little paranoid, but after all he had witnessed that evening, better to be safe he thought.

As Franklin lay down in the bed, he knew he wouldn't sleep much, if at all. How could he? Why did he let his curiosity get the better of him? He started out just wanting a place to worship. He should have told Justin no and found a safe old Baptist church to visit. Franklin said a prayer, asking God to clear his mind of the events he saw. But it was no use. He kept on thinking about what Justin had said to him on the way back to the diner; he just needed more faith.

Although he knew Justin was probably insane, Franklin was beginning to wonder if the cult follower was correct in some ways After all, Franklin's faith had been severely tested over the past six months. Maybe his faith was weakened somewhat by all that he'd been through. He did take solace in the fact that no matter what happened to him, he could never completely lose his faith. He would persevere because God had promised to preserve him. The Lord said so in his Holy Word.

Maybe tonight was a lesson for him, Franklin thought. The old preacher at the shack was proof that anybody could turn God's truth into falsehood, especially by taking the Word out of context. Being a theology teacher for years, Franklin knew that many cults had developed over the centuries since Christ's ascension by twisting the meaning of sacred scripture. He then remembered a saying father had told him when he was a boy: "False faith can make fools of many."

Franklin knew they were words that still rang true.

Chapter VII

The screaming of gunfire resounded through the chilly autumn evening with the frenzy of a forlorn beast. Franklin covered his head with both arms as he squeezed beneath the steering wheel of his van. He was safe for the moment. But people were dying inside Trudy's Old Town Tavern, Franklin just knew it.

As he bid his time waiting for a ceasefire and a chance to escape the melee, Franklin pondered if he was somewhat at fault for the rage of the madman shooting up the rundown bar.

All he wanted was a quiet drink before heading back to the motel. Franklin's two-day stay in St. Joseph had been quite uneventful to that point. He'd visited the Pony Express Museum and played a couple of slot machines on the riverboat casino the day before; nothing too thrilling, just the time-killing ways of a tourist with no better place to go at the moment.

After getting a haircut and window shopping at the mall, Franklin stopped off at Trudy's. He'd noticed the place a week earlier on his way across the Missouri River to visit Gracie in Kansas. He wanted to keep his promise to drop in on his mother while traveling through the Midwest. But Franklin could only handle a couple of days on the farm before he began to get bored. Gracie knew her son wanted some excitement, so she graciously suggested he go to St. Joe and have a little fun. After all, they had spent plenty of quality time together just a few months before.

It was barely a month into his cross-country trek and Franklin was starting to drink more heavily. He found that he liked the smaller saloons better than the bigger tourist-centered bars. The people who frequented the hole-in-the-walls were real folk with real problems. And at that point in his life, Franklin could certainly relate to the abundance of hardship he'd heard while perched on a barstool. He was listening to the woes of a downtrodden woman that afternoon when all hell broke loose.

Lucille was a mildly attractive gal in her mid-thirties. Franklin was sipping his second rum and coke when she sat down next to him at the bar. She was wearing light blue hospital scrubs that covered up most of her womanly features. By her dress, Franklin figured she was a nurse or worked at a dental office. She flashed him a brief smile as she removed a flowered wrap that bound her thick red hair. The color of her long locks wasn't as shiny as Sara's, but it did bring back unsolicited thoughts of his deceased wife. Franklin quickly washed those away by guzzling the rest of his cocktail.

"Can I have a scotch on the rocks Jimmy?" the anxious woman called out to the bartender while fumbling through her purse like she was looking for some loose change to pay for the drink.

The bartender frowned and nodded his head reluctantly. The woman shrugged her shoulders at him and offered a crooked grin. Franklin lifted his glass to Jimmy, signaling for another drink.

"Put hers on mine alright?" he stated as Jimmy winked back to affirm the order.

The lady looked over at Franklin after pulling a pack of cigarettes and a lighter from her well-worn handbag.

"Why thank you sir," she said, extending her hand to shake Franklin's. "My name's Lucille, but my friend's call me Lucy."

"Nice to meet you Lucy, I'm Franklin," he answered with a smirk.

The redhead laughed slightly while packing her cigarette on the bar a couple of times. "I guess your friends call you Frank?"

"No most call me Franklin, although some people call me Franky, especially my mother."

Jimmy brought over their drinks. Franklin raised his glass and Lucy tapped hers against his.

"Mind if I smoke?" she asked

"No, go right ahead."

Lucy lit up her cigarette and took in a few small puffs. Franklin noticed she wasn't wearing a wedding band. She tilted her head back and closed her eyes for a couple seconds as if to make herself relax. She looked back at Franklin and grinned as she ran her hands somewhat nervously through her curly hair.

"Been a long day, you know," Lucy sighed, before taking another deep drag off her cigarette. "I haven't seen you in here before. You live in town?"

"No, just visiting," Franklin answered, swirling his finger around in his drink.

"Visiting Trudy's?"

"No," he chuckled. "My mom lives on a farm across the river in Kansas. I just stopped in for a couple of drinks. It's a nice place."

"It's a dump!" she exclaimed before downing almost all her drink in one swallow. "Good scotch, though."

Lucy started to sway slightly to the twangy country song blaring from the jukebox. Although she was kind of brash, Franklin found her manner charming for some reason. Her green eyes were quite bewitching, or maybe that was just the rum's effect on him. He spent the next ten minutes or so watching her chair dance to the beat of a couple more country crooners. Her movements were kind of sexy in a trashy sort of way.

"Need another drink?" he asked.

"Why sure, thank you Franky," Lucy answered, batting her eyes and pulling her stool a little closer to his.

He ordered another round. She squelched another smoke in the ashtray. "You seem like a nice guy Franky. Kinda cute too."

Franklin blushed like a schoolboy. It had been a long time since anybody but Sara complimented his looks. He liked it.

The joint was beginning to get crowded, so it took a little longer to get their drinks. They continued the small talk to pass the time. All the while, Franklin wondered why Lucy made the "cute" remark. Was she hitting on him? Or was it just her way of acting thankful? More importantly at that moment, was he ready to pursue the answer? Lucy provided the opportunity.

"You hitched to anyone Franky?" she asked, while boldly placing her hand on his thigh.

"I was," he answered, staring glumly down at the bar.

"Divorced huh?"

"No widowed," he replied somewhat somberly.

"Oh, I'm sorry," she said, quickly removing her hand from his thigh.

Jimmy arrived just in time with their cocktails. Lucy lit up another cigarette and offered Franklin one. He declined. They tapped glasses once again, before each took a hard swig.

"I didn't mean to bring up a sad moment," Lucy said apologetically.

"Oh that's okay, you didn't know," Franklin responded. "I'm

starting to heal now."

He finished off the drink. Lucy downed hers as well. They continued to talk as Jimmy made another round. After a few minutes, Lucy's green eyes began to water as though she was going to cry.

"I didn't mean to make you feel bad," Franklin said.

"Oh, you didn't," she replied with a sniffle while lighting another cigarette with the one she already had going. "I've been having a rough time myself. I broke up with my boyfriend last week. We were going to be married until he started treating me like crap. I just hope he...Oh, I'm sorry. I'm sure you don't want to hear about my pathetic life."

"That's okay, I don't mind," Franklin said sympathetically. "I've been told I'm a good listener."

Lucy wiped her eyes with her index fingers and smiled delicately at him. "You're such a nice guy."

Franklin smiled gently back at her. She seemed a little desperate, but he still couldn't fully assess why. Another bartender arrived with their drinks.

Then, just as they were about to toast again, a large, burley man clad in leather barged through the front door and headed straight for them. He looked very perturbed to say the least. His steaming scowl appeared hot enough to singe the whiskers of his scraggly graying beard. His bloodshot blue eyes were aflame with anger. He focused his rage on Lucy as he closed in.

"You scheming whore!" the incensed man screamed as he pulled Lucy off the barstool by her hair. He slapped her severely across the face as she fell hard to the concrete floor.

Franklin jumped off his stool and grabbed the guy by the back of his collar. "Hey, what the hell are you doing?" Franklin yelled as he tried to pull the brute away from Lucy. But the man elbowed

Franklin in the gut, doubling him over. A right uppercut then connected with Franklin's chin, sending him flying backward about six feet into another couple seated next to the wooden dance floor. The force of the punch didn't knock Franklin out, but left him dazed and dizzy.

The rampage continued as the maniac began to pummel poor Lucy unmercifully with both fists flying. A couple of young construction workers jumped on the man, but he flung both of them off his back like a bucking bronco. About thirty seconds into the melee, the bar's bulky bouncer finally made his way into the mix. He was able to pull the enraged man off Lucy, who was now bleeding profusely from her mouth and nose. The bouncer punched the man in the face, sending him to the floor.

That's when the scene turned dire.

The lunatic reached into his boot and pulled out a small, snub-nosed revolver. He pointed the weapon directly at the bouncer now hovering over him. The bouncer jumped back.

"Hey now, don't do anything stupid!" the bouncer screamed at the gun-wielding man. But before the he could say another word, the psychopath took aim and pulled the trigger. The bullet tore through the bouncer's forehead, sending him crumpling to the ground.

As the madman struggled to his feet, the patrons ran for cover under tables or behind the bar. Once on his feet, the man began to again scream loudly at the barely-conscious Lucy. Franklin took the opportunity to make a beeline for the front door.

He heard a few more shots ring out as he pulled open the driver's-side door and dove into the relative safety of his minivan. Franklin wondered about Lucy as he was tucked tightly under the steering column. Did the gunshots he had just heard snuff out the pitiful girl? What could she have done to incur such wrath?

The gunfire stopped. Maybe the guy killed himself? Franklin thought. Maybe he was reloading? Franklin wasn't about to wait around and find out. He slid from under his hiding place and peeked above the dashboard. People were fleeing the tavern as Franklin started the ignition. He almost hit one lady while he was backing out of the parking space. Gravel started to fly as he peeled out of the lot and drove off. The buzz he had acquired from the cocktails he drank was long gone. He thought he heard police sirens when he sped away, but he didn't see the cars. Franklin was sure someone had dialed 911 during the incident, but there was no way he wanted to be further involved. He just wanted to get out of St. Joe as fast as possible.

Franklin drove to the motel where was staying, gathered the few belongings he had left in his room and quickly checked out. If the authorities wanted to question him about the trouble, they would have to track him down. Although he hadn't done anything wrong, Franklin wanted to put the whole mess behind him. It did occur to him that he didn't get the chance to pay his tab because of the violence that erupted so suddenly. But Skipping out on his bill was of little consequence at that point anyway.

❧❖❧

Adrenalin drove Franklin through the night and all the next day, arriving in Denver the following evening. The only two stops he made were for fuel. He was tired, hungry and very sore from the punch the madman delivered to his jaw. The first thing he did when he checked into a hotel for the night was purchase a newspaper. He perused the entire paper as he ate dinner that night in the hotel restaurant. Franklin finally found an article about the shooting buried in the national news section deep inside the paper. He was thankful it wasn't on the front page.

As he read the story, Franklin was saddened to find out that Lucy had been killed in the melee, along with the bouncer. Like Franklin had suspected, the shooter was Lucy's estranged fiancée. He tried to flee when the police arrived on the scene and was gunned down himself when he began to fire at the authorities. No motive for the incident was given in the story, as the investigation was still in the opening stages. Franklin was relieved that so far there was no mention of the police looking for another man involved in the bloody episode, especially someone driving a green minivan.

Franklin figured it might be a good idea to get as far away from Missouri as possible. California seemed highly appealing at the point. But a stopover in Las Vegas first sounded like a good way to relieve some tension as well. So after a good night's sleep, Franklin set out for "Sin City."

⚬⚭⚬

It was a full day's drive to Vegas from Denver and the sun was beginning to set behind the neon city as Franklin arrived. He felt the rush of excitement the casinos and hotels seemed to exude while he drove down the strip. It was almost as if the flashing lights and glittery signs were screaming out for the folly of wayward folk, whose wallets often left town terribly lighter than when they had first made the scene. It was painfully obvious to Franklin that gambling was king in Vegas. But the lure of making quick cash at a roulette wheel or card table didn't hold much appeal to him. In fact, the only reason he had played the slot machines in St. Joe was for kicks. Franklin figured he just didn't possess the betting bone that hampered many visitors to Vegas. He still had about forty-thousand dollars left and he wanted to hang on to it.

He nearly drove the entire length of the strip, before settling on a moderately-priced hotel to spend the night. It turned out that there were plenty of good rooms available at the Silver Nugget, so he decided to take advantage of a special rate to rent a small suite for the week. Although it was a Sunday, the city was still hopping. If Franklin hadn't been so dog tired from his day-long drive, he might have gone out on the town that first night. But instead he ordered room service and crashed before midnight. As it turned out, that would be the last night of fruitful sleep he would enjoy for a while.

For the next two days, he visited many of the most-frequented tourist traps, especially the lavish casinos and stylish shows. Although he was still drinking more than he was accustomed, Franklin managed to keep his behavior in check. But his conduct changed radically for the worst on Wednesday.

Franklin woke up that morning with a splitting headache, most assuredly brought on by the last cocktail he downed at a sports bar the night before. He'd spent the evening gabbing with a couple of guys from Wisconsin about the current college football season. They kept buying him "one more" drink to keep him there. After about five "one-more's," Franklin left the establishment at half-past midnight, fully loaded. His bar buddies had offered to take him with them to a nudie bar, but he had declined. He was too drunk. As he was contemplating the previous night, Franklin wished he had gone with them. The thought of attending a risqué show had never even crossed his mind while he was married to Sara. Oh, he would sometimes have lustful thoughts like most men do, but Franklin would not consider acting on them in respect to his wife. But Sara was long gone and he was suddenly becoming intrigued by the seedier side of humanity.

This was the point during his journey where Franklin's life began to spin totally out of control.

He remembered it was Halloween as he showered and readied himself for another night out. For generations, the Edwards clan never celebrated Halloween, believing it to be the devil's day. There were no ghoulish costumes for Franklin as a child, always firemen or policemen or some other noble outfit. Nor would his parents let him go trick-or-treating. The church had always held a fall harvest festival for the children instead. Franklin never felt deprived because his haul of candy was usually as full as any kid in the neighborhood. He and Sara continued the tradition with Ashley and Brianna, who were always cutely dressed up as fairies or princesses.

Franklin quickly ushered from his mind the thoughts of his deceased children, pouring himself a glass of rum from a bottle he now always kept close to him in his hotel room. His conscience told him he shouldn't continually try to wash away the still-lingering sorrow in his soul, but the evil elixir did act as a soothing remedy many times. The better cure would have been God's Word, but it seemed the further west Franklin headed, the more he began to drift from the Lord's way of controlling circumstances.

So that night, Franklin would find himself enthralled with a world he'd never witnessed before. Even in his college days at UF, he had avoided frat parties and other wild times. In fact, he had met his beloved Sara at a sorority tea for crying out loud! She seemed so distant from him now.

❧❖❧

The hard rock music was blaring when jittery Franklin pulled open the door of The Wild Side, a small cabaret-style establishment, tucked cleverly behind one of the older casinos just off the strip. His hand was almost shaking when he forked over the twenty-dollar cover to the muscular man just inside the door. The smoky place was packed full of guys hooting and hollering over a bevy of barely-clad beauties slowly stripping off their scant holiday costumes.

Franklin located a place to sit at a two-person table just off the runway-style stage. The view was excellent. So were the sights he was soaking in. There were naughty nurses, cutesy French maids and blushing brides among the sultry group, along with hardcore biker chicks, vampires, devils and every other fantasy a hot-blooded male would long to bed down with for one evening. As the fancy rum drinks began to delude his mind the most unholy of nights, Franklin grew more and more bold. He slipped money into the garter belts of each of the girls as they made their rounds of the outer tables after finishing their routines on stage. They were highly appreciative of his generous tips. Money didn't matter to him that night and he was totally willing to part with some of it. After all, he had never seen so many gorgeous women in one place at one time. And they were completely naked to boot! Franklin was amazed, and also intoxicated.

He took a particular liking to a beautiful blond featured dancer going by the moniker Davilla D'Vine.

She cast a deceivingly gracious presence upon the stage when her angelic apparel, halo and wings included, made its grand entrance. Her enchanting white chiffon did little to hide her curvaceous figure. Of course that was the point. And Franklin quickly became entranced by her seductive three-song act.

The consummate professional, Davilla made sure to make direct eye contact with each patron captively sitting stage-side. Her beguiling baby blues enticed the boys to relinquish their cash while she demurely removed her top to the soft cries of a classy pop standard. The next number was a bit more up-tempo and ended with lovely Miss D'Vine sporting nothing but a white-lace G-string that left her fans breathless. The transformation came full circle when the steamy siren scorched the stage to the driving rage of an 80's glam-metal anthem. Her entire performance was different than the usual tawdry striptease. It was more like some kind of religious metamorphosis catered to a horde of idolatrous devotees. They devoured every delight Davilla dished out while changing from virgin to vixen during the spicy spectacle. Franklin savored every morsel, mesmerized by the wanton woman.

Like the other girls, Davilla made the rounds after her show. Although she was collecting a decent appearance fee for her performance, thanks to a few dozen pictorials in select men's magazines, Davilla had no problem making bank off her star-struck admirers. And lust-driven labor paid very well in Vegas. While waiting backstage before her show, Davilla heard some of the girls buzzing about a big-spender sitting in the audience. Although at first she didn't know who he was, it didn't take her long to sniff out the cash burning a hole through Franklin's wallet.

Once again wearing her see-through chiffon and g-string due to club rules, Davilla approached Franklin from behind. She coyly reached around and placed both her hands gently over his eyes. Franklin was startled to say the least.

"Guess who?" Davilla whispered into his right ear, as Franklin caught a whiff of her delectable perfume giving off its jasmine-like aroma.

Franklin smiled, but didn't move a muscle. He liked the ploy taking place. "I don't know," he said. "But I bet it's a beautiful woman."

Davilla released her hands from Franklin's eyes and walked

around in front of him. "You're right, the most beautiful," she said boldly with a wink. "Did you enjoy my performance?"

"Very much so," he responded, his eyes widening greatly. He quickly reached into his wallet and took out a crisp one-hundred dollar bill. His hand began to again shake slightly as he nervously placed the money between the silken white garter hugging her soft pale left thigh. Davilla found his timidness endearing in a boyish sort of way.

She also noticed the wad of cash bulging from his tightly-packed wallet. Over the past couple of weeks, Franklin had become somewhat nonchalant with his money, carrying much more cash with him than was wise. He should have known better, especially in a town where many a man can be quickly separated from his funds. His carelessness would indeed prove costly.

"Mind if I sit down for a while?" Davilla asked.

"By all means," Franklin answered quickly. "Can I buy you a drink or something?"

Davilla laughed slyly at her jittery mark. "Or something," she paused for a second. "A glass of champagne would be wonderful. Thank you."

Franklin nodded in agreement and summoned a waitress over to the table. The cute redhead handed back some change to another patron and promptly walked over to Franklin's table.

"Could we have a bottle of your best champagne please?" he ordered before the waitress could even ask.

"Our best costs about two-hundred dollars sir," she stated while glancing over at Davilla, who flashed her winsome smile at both the waitress and Franklin.

"That's quite alright dear," he responded with a somewhat perturbed grin. "I have the money."

The waitress raised her left hand in a defensive manner, hoping she hadn't offended her customer. "Oh, I'm sorry. It's just that I have to make sure our patrons know the expense of their orders. Some of these guys, well you know, they have a few drinks and they go overboard a little."

"I understand," Franklin said. "I assure you I'm good for it."

The redhead was beginning to feel a little embarrassed at that point. "Coming right up," she said, before quickly walking over to the bar and placing the order.

Franklin rolled his eyes at Davilla, who reacted with a girlish giggle. She began to sway in rhythm to the erotic love song playing over the sound system. Within a minute, the redhead returned with a bottle of champagne in an ice bucket and two glasses. The waitress uncorked the bottle and poured a glass for Franklin and his newfound muse. They each raised their glasses and toasted each other.

"Here's to lovely dancers," Franklin said with a wink.

"And to their adoring fans," Davilla responded with a snicker.

As they intently observed a sensuous short-haired brunette slip out of the last stitch of her jungle warrior costume, Davilla slyly placed her hand on Franklin's left thigh. At first, he didn't understand the meaning of the brazen move. He had only met her five minutes before. How could she be coming on to him so quickly? Although he was enjoying her forwardness, it made him feel a little uneasy. What was her angle? Then it occurred to his rapidly-inebriating mind that a huge tip and an expensive bottle of wine go a long way toward turning complete strangers into fast friends. Franklin coyly reacted to her move by placing his left hand on top of hers. Davilla responded with a playful grin while gazing her glistening blue eyes into his glazed browns.

"Do you know they have these VIP rooms in the back?" she offered with a whisper into his ear.

There's the pitch, Franklin thought to himself. But he didn't mind one bit. For the first time in many months, someone made him feel special. He loved the attention he was receiving and he didn't care that it was coming from an exotic dancer. Davilla was buxom, beautiful and bold. He was sleek, soused and newly single.

"What are they for?" Franklin inquired, but he kind of already knew the answer.

"Very important people," Davilla answered, batting her baby blues.

"Am I one of those?" he asked.

"You are to me."

Franklin threw his head back and let out a hardy laugh

"What?" Davilla said with a smirk, feigning slight offense at Franklin's short cackle.

"You're good," he responded with a crooked grin. "You haven't even asked me my name yet."

Davilla placed her hand over her mouth, somewhat embarrassed. "Oh I'm sorry. How rude of me."

"That's okay," he said, reaching over to shake her hand. "My name's Franklin."

"Very nice to meet you," she said, still a bit unnerved by her stupid mistake. "I'm Leah, I mean Davilla."

Franklin chuckled at the girl's cute cover-up.

"Anyway," Davilla said, trying to quickly get back on track. "Want to find out how good a dancer I really am Franklin?"

He took a deep breath. He knew their dialogue had taken a tempting turn. His head was spinning. His heart was racing. His hormones were surging. He should have listened to that little voice inside him pleading for some common sense to emerge. But his conscience gave way to sinful will. It was no use. He was bound to serve his own master that night: unabashed desire.

"I'd love to," Franklin said, gently biting his lower lip.

Davilla didn't say a word. She nodded her head cunningly as she took Franklin by the hand and walked him over about twenty feet toward a burly guy standing by a black-curtained doorway. The leather-clad dude with a red bandana wrapped around his head whispered into Davilla's ear and then held up two fingers.

"They charge two-hundred dollars an hour for the room," she said to Franklin. "But it includes another bottle of champagne. Is that too much?"

That was Franklin's final chance to back out of the deal. He could gather his wits and gracefully walk away. Davilla would probably be disappointed, but he was quite sure it wouldn't have been the first time. Or, just ten feet away, he reasoned, was a chance to experience a carnal dalliance that might never happen again. He considered his choices for but a few seconds. Option number two fatefully won out.

Franklin took out his wallet and handed the man four fifties. The bearded biker quickly counted the cash and pulled back the curtain. Davilla hugged Franklin and gave him a peck on the cheek. She seemed overjoyed by the transaction. Franklin was antsy to get the show started.

Davilla led him to the second room on the right of a dimly lit hallway. The reddish glow in the small corridor seemed appropriate to Franklin for the action about to commence. She opened the door and he followed her inside. The tiny wood-paneled room was actually quite nice. There was a small black loveseat surrounded by plush red carpeting, accented by a little antique-looking end table.

There was a bottle of champagne in a gold ice bucket on top of it. Davilla handed Franklin one of the crystal glasses from the table and began to uncork the bottle.

"I'll do that for you my dear," he said.

"Why you're such a gentleman, thank you," she answered and held up the other glass.

Franklin smiled at the succulent stripper and uncorked the bottle. The cork broke in two as he tried to wrestle it out of the bottle with the inadequate corkscrew provided by the club. No bother, he just forced the other half back inside the bottle and poured each of them a glass. The champagne was much lighter than the bottle they had drank in the main club, but it was strong enough to keep Franklin's buzz going. He certainly didn't want to come down from his high.

They sat on the couch and toasted each other while offering sensuous glances. Davilla took a couple of sips from her glass and stood up. She walked over by the door and dimmed the overhead florescent lights just enough to soften the mood. She turned another switch and a jazzy style of music began to play.

"Just sit back now Franklin and relax. Don't say anything okay? Just listen to the music and feed your passion."

Davilla's performance was astounding! She displayed a unique ability to weave elegance with eroticism in her dance, kind of like a bawdy ballerina. Franklin was nearly hypnotized by her half-hour routine. It was almost like he was in a trance. But the dance moves were just part of Davilla's alluring plan.

When she was done displaying her wares, she offered Franklin the chance to sample the delicacy she had been so shrewdly showing off.

Wearing nothing but a lascivious look on her immaculate face,

Davilla swaggered over to the loveseat and sat on his lap. She slipped both her arms around the back of his neck and intently focused her primal gaze directly into his idolatrous eyes. She could feel that she was absolutely the object of his undivided attention at that moment. The mesmerism was complete when she delivered a potent kiss that must have drawn the last bit of righteousness from her willing prey. The once-virtuous Franklin was helplessly trapped by that befaller of many a man: unmitigated lust.

Never letting his mouth part from hers, Davilla had her mark's head spinning as she brought him to the zenith of their carnal escapade. She then gently rested her head on Franklin's shoulder and allowed him to catch his breath. The enticing fragrance emitting from her neck continued to compel him. At that point, he felt neither guilt nor remorse. All he desired was to cling to the utter bliss that consumed him. He was determined not to let it flee his grasp.

"May I speak now?" Franklin finally sighed, as he allowed his head to fall back against the soft fabric of the loveseat.

"If you must," she answered with a devilish expression on her face.

"You certainly live up to your name," he said, swallowing hard. "I've never in my life experienced anything like that."

"I'm pleased that you enjoyed it. I love bringing pleasure to people. It's my calling."

"It's a gift!" Franklin exclaimed. "Whew!...You are so beautiful."

The stripper nearly blushed for the first time since they met just an hour before. She tenderly kissed Franklin in response to his flattery. Most of the time when Davilla danced for any man besides her boyfriend, she took a devil-may-care attitude. Her tawdry talent was just a means to make money and men never had a problem relinquishing their cash when she waltzed her voluptuous figure through any door. They were always willing to give and she was happy to accept.

But Franklin appeared different in some way. She couldn't put her finger on the reason why, but she felt kind of guilty taking his money. He seemed so vulnerable, which strangely, was a quality that she had always found highly attractive. Davilla's current squeeze was a drugged-out ex-con when she met him two years back. She fell madly in love with Derek while helping him recover from a near-fatal heroin overdose. But once Derek was back on his feet their relationship began to strain. He was a user, but of more than just drugs. He had his own sort of devious charm and was capable of getting Davilla to do anything he wanted. Derek used Davilla's devotion to him to force her into some highly-unscrupulous schemes. Her exotic dancing was just one means of their profitable chicanery.

Although Davilla liked Franklin, she couldn't stop herself from continuing the ruse at which she had become so adept.

"You know," she said, placing her right index finger to her mouth after breaking her kiss with Franklin, "we could continue this somewhere else if you'd like."

He smiled and nodded his head eagerly. His mind was totally captivated at that point by the wily fox. Common sense had orphaned him to his sole whim: to completely satiate his long pent-up sexual yearnings. No one, not even his beloved Sara, could bring him to such absurd heights of ecstasy. He followed his lust for Davilla in an almost lock-step march.

The hotel where Franklin was staying was just about a half-mile down the strip, so he suggested they go there. Davilla wholeheartedly agreed, realizing that very seldom does the prey foolishly offer the predator no resistance into the nest. Usually she at least had to allow her cunning to slowly seep into a man's self-control before he would take her into his residence. It often took a few meetings before Davilla would gain the complete confidence from the targets of her fleecing. After all, she wasn't some prostitute who provided sexual favors for a set price. No Davilla, under Derek's deft tutelage, had learned to set her sights on a mark's entire cache. Greed was her creed and Franklin was recklessly bowing down at her altar.

Davilla politely excused herself and went to her dressing room to retrieve her street clothes. Even in Vegas, she couldn't walk around in her dance attire. Franklin waited by the door for a few minutes while she gathered her things. Davilla phoned Derek while putting on some fresh makeup. He was quite pleased she had found the opportunity that evening to secure for them what appeared to be a big score. Derek was such a dirt bag that it didn't bother him one bit his girlfriend was forced to sell her body to appropriate their lavish lifestyle. He had always been a slave to excess and it was Davilla who toiled to provide for their exquisite tastes. It was often a tough road to hoe, but she did so out of her twisted love for a conniving deviate.

She was willing to lie in the bed she had made for herself. But that night, Davilla felt a bit unnerved at the thought of lying in Franklin's. Oh sure, she found Franklin attractive. Most of the guys she had to sleep with were swine; overbearing brutes with bulging bellies, big mouths and balding heads. Franklin, on the other hand, was physically fit, with a boyish face and a sweet, passionate demeanor. She sensed that he normally would be the kind of fellow a girl would be proud to take home to her mother. She noticed he wore no wedding ring. She wondered what he was doing at a place like The Wild Side. Was he a lonely divorcee just kicking it out in an effort to forget a busted marriage? Or maybe he was the victim of unrequited romance trying to somehow put a healing salve on his wounded heart?

Davilla abruptly halted her train of thought and quickly refocused on the task at hand. Oh how she hated to think of it that way, a task. But really that's what it was after all. She slept with men for financial gain. Derek had indeed turned her into a hooker even though they never referred to her role in their scams as such. Her eyes began to mist a little as she thought about how much she had changed since leaving small-town Ohio just five years earlier. Still just twenty-three years old, she realized lovely Leah had completely transformed into dastardly Davilla. It was a role that she had learned to play all too well. And that night, another pathetic soul would succumb to her amorous wiles. It was destined to be that way. She just knew it somehow.

A tap on the door summoned Davilla's attention. She bushed her hair back and opened the door. It was Franklin standing there with a single red rose he had purchased from a flower girl who had been selling them in the bar.

"I was beginning to think you forgot about me," he said with a cute frown on his face as he handed her the rose. "Are you ready to go yet?"

Davilla loved the gesture and beamed a wide smile at her unwitting suitor.

"I most certainly am," she said, locking her arm with Franklin's. "I'm going to show you a night that you will never forget. I promise."

"Awesome!" he exclaimed. "I can't wait. I just need to stop at the ATM machine by the door first if you don't mind. This place took a lot of my cash."

"Oh, I know," she said, faking a bit of concern. "It can be expensive to come here and have a good time. Are you okay?"

"Oh sure," he responded. "It's just that I used up all the cash I had on me and I don't want to wait until tomorrow and end up short if I need some more."

Davilla nodded her head in agreement. She knew he would need some more cash alright after this night. Although she didn't specifically ask for payment for her services, she never left a man with a full wallet.

Davilla still had her arm locked in Franklin's as he made his withdrawal. His carelessness continued as he entered his Personal Identification Number into the machine. She took advantage of his sloppiness and made a mental note of the number: 7272. The numerals corresponded to the letters SARA on his cell phone. Franklin thought it a good way to remember his PIN. Too bad his dead wife's name didn't flash into his mind during that moment. But Sara had faded from his memory for the time being. His focus had taken a debaucherous detour that would soon leave him destitute.

✎❖✎

It was around one in the morning when Franklin drove the minivan into the parking lot of the Silver Nugget. He was fortunate not to get pulled over during the half-mile jaunt to the hotel. His alcohol intake that evening was surely over the legal limit and it never occurred to him that he was ripe for a DUI arrest. Franklin also bypassed the hotel's valet parking service, which would later prove to be another mistake.

After parking in one of the guest spots, Franklin turned off the ignition and revved up his hormones again. He boldly leaned over to Davilla and kissed her passionately like she was a high school sweetheart. She happily returned the affection. She liked the way she felt when Franklin kissed her. The softness of his lips reminded her of a woman's tender touch, a sensation that she had also experienced many times. In fact, Davilla had just parted ways with one of her girlfriends the night she first met Derek.

He was trying to stay clean at a mutual friend's house after wrapping up two-month stint at a drug rehabilitation center in the desert just outside the city limits. Davilla was returning a car she had borrowed while hers was being repaired, but the guy wasn't home and Derek answered the door in his workout attire. She was immediately attracted to his buffed-up physique, which he acquired by substituting long hours of weight training to offset the wasteful months of drug abuse. He offered to drive her back to her apartment. She accepted. The love affair commenced that night and two years later, they were still together. However, their relationship at that point was highlighted more by business than pleasure.

Derek's kisses also used to cause her heart to flutter. But it had been a long time since he had done that to her. She missed the romance. Their sexual appetites for each other had waned a while back also. Although she thought she still loved the guy, Davilla wasn't as sure as she once was. In fact, she would often wonder why they were still together. The only thing they had in common anymore was their desire for easy money.

Franklin was the object of that desire at the moment. Davilla felt her heart sink slightly as their lips parted. Guilt began to sow her conscience again. He was such a kind man she thought. How could she bring herself to carry out the ploy in which she and Derek had become so proficient? She knew more alcohol would certainly help her cause.

"Franklin, would you mind if we bought some more wine?" she

asked while slowly caressing his chest through his half-opened blue dress shirt.

"If you'd like my dear," he said. "There's a little market right around the corner. They're open all night."

Davilla smiled. "Mind if I wait here in the van for you? I don't care to walk much in these stilettos. They hurt my feet."

"I don't know how women walk in high heels at all," Franklin remarked. "It must take a special talent or something."

"It does. In fact, I have many special talents to show you tonight."

Davilla leaned over and kissed him firmly, yet tenderly. She didn't do it teasingly like she would to most of her clients. Her lips exuded her growing affection for Franklin. She was eagerly longing to spend the night with him.

"Go quickly," she sighed, as she pulled away from him and wiped a few beads of sweat from her brow.

Franklin promptly opened the door and began to walk away. He then turned, came back to the van and opened the door again.

"What kind?" he asked.

"Huh?" she answered.

"What kind of wine would you like? Anything special?"

Davilla placed her right index finger to her mouth and thought for a few seconds.

"Nothing too strong," she said. "A blush or white zinfandel would be nice."

Franklin smiled and nodded approvingly, although he was so full of lust that he didn't even recall that white zinfandel was the last wine he and Sara had enjoyed together the night before she died. "Good choice," he said. "A sweet wine for a sweet woman."

He shut the door and started to walk behind the back of the hotel where the store was located. Davilla began to get nervous while he was gone. She knew there was really very little sweetness in her soul. Her heart had become so bitter that she felt it was almost as if there was poison flowing through her veins. She was starting to hate herself for who she had become. Her thoughts brought forth tears. But she didn't want Franklin to see her that way. She dried her eyes and regained her composure. Good thing too, because he returned in less than five minutes.

They walked hand-in-hand past the desk in the hotel lobby, but the night clerk didn't bother to raise his eyes from his paperwork to notice them. The elevator door opened. There was no one inside. Franklin considered briefly about pausing the elevator before it reached the tenth floor. Love in an elevator might make a kinky diversion, he thought. He was sure it happened all the time in the carefree town. But he passed on the idea, figuring it better not to chance interrupting the interlude he was anxious to begin.

Davilla put her arms around Franklin's shoulders as he opened his hotel room door. She enjoyed hugging him. It brought her warmth on a night that would end up leaving her ice cold on the inside.

"Wow, this is a pretty room," Davilla remarked after Franklin flipped the switch on and then dimmed the light to conjure up just the right mood. "Ooh, you even have a lovely view of the city."

She walked over to the sliding glass door and stepped out on to the small balcony. The neon lights on the strip were beaming in full dazzle as she watched the crescent moon creeping toward the horizon. A chilly desert breeze ushered in the first morning of November. Davilla tilted her head back and drew in the refreshing air. It seemed to reinvigorate her.

Franklin opened the bottle of wine and brought over a full glass for each of them. He kissed Davilla on the side of the neck. With delight, she laid her head up against his.

"Mmm, this is so nice," she cooed, gently running her fingers through his hair.

Franklin handed her a glass. She turned toward him and gazed into his eager eyes. He smiled sweetly at her.

"I wish I could find the words to tell you how unbelievable this evening has been for me," he said, holding up his glass as if preparing a toast. "I honestly have never done anything like this before."

"I could tell," Davilla said with a sheepish grin.

"Really?" he answered, somewhat timidly, casting his eyes away from hers.

She leaned forward and kissed him on the cheek.

"I think you're charming. You're not like most of the guys I meet. That's what I, well, let's just say it's very endearing to have a man treat me like a lady."

Franklin looked back at Davilla and tapped his glass against hers. "It would be difficult for me to treat you any other way."

"I know," she said demurely before taking a sip of her wine, as if to halt any feelings of remorse that were again beginning to creep up inside her.

Franklin drank half his glass of wine and set it down on a small table on the balcony. He then took Davilla into his arms and kissed her deeply. They made out for a couple of minutes before heading back inside the room. Their passion became intense as they continued to kiss while undressing one another. Their actions quickened to a frenzied pace as the heat building inside each of them feverishly sought a path of release. They fell onto the sprawling king-sized bed, exploring each other in every imaginable way.

Surprisingly, the whole erotic encounter seemed to whisk by

swiftly. It had been so long since either of them had experienced such ecstasy. Franklin liberated tension that had been pent up since making love to Sara the night before she departed this life. For Davilla, it took only a flash to be freed from countless nights of frustration, languishing in the arms of self-serving lovers. That night, each one bestowed a favor the other so earnestly craved. Utter gratification was the payoff.

They caressed intimately as the bliss began to wane. Complete satisfaction deserved such a moment. There was a need to cling closely for as long as possible, because both knew the afterglow of the precious liaison would inevitably flame out. It had to, though neither wanted their time together to end. Two desperate souls had somehow found refuge that evening.

Franklin was the first to break the bond, having needed to use the restroom. Davilla knew the time had come to finish the job for which she was fiendishly called to do. How hard it would be to crush so soft a man. But she realized Derek would certainly take her to task if she failed to carry out their long-running scheme. She was getting so tired of it all that contempt for her boyfriend was beginning to possess her. But so was her fear of him, and his increasingly violent temper. She set their devious plans in motion once again.

"Would you like a nightcap dear?" she called out to Franklin. "I'm going to have another glass."

"Sure," he replied through the closed bathroom door. "I'll just be a couple of minutes."

That was ample time for Davilla. She reached into her purse beside the bed and pulled out a small capsule wrapped in foil that she had hidden inside a pack of cigarettes. She poured some wine in Franklin's glass and then twisted open the capsule. She tapped together both ends of the capsule and released the fine white powder into his drink. She mixed the powerful sedative into the wine with her index finger, being careful to wipe off the excess on the bed sheets. She then filled up her own glass with wine only.

Franklin exited the bathroom and comically pranced his still-nude body back to the bed. Davilla laughed at his antic and handed him his wine glass. She kissed him passionately once more, like a black widow ready to poison her lowly prey.

"To a wonderful lover," she said, tapping her glass against his and then taking a sip.

Franklin didn't say a word. He raised the glass to his mouth and drank the entire concoction.

They cuddled for a few more minutes before Franklin fell fast asleep. Davilla strongly considered just falling asleep herself and blowing off the entire con. But she couldn't. The devious side of her being always won out. There was no way that night was going to be different.

She dressed quickly and spruced up her make-up and hair in the bathroom. As she looked at herself in the mirror, the image staring back was that of a tawdry tramp. Davilla knew that truly was what she had become. Her conscience tickled her one more time, but it was no use. Money always trumped morals in her fractured mind. She managed to convince herself this game was just like all the others. It didn't matter deep down that she liked Franklin. She had to take him. That was the rule her and Derek had committed to when they began play a year before.

As Franklin snored loudly, Davilla removed his wallet from the trousers that were so hastily thrown over a chair. It held about five hundred bucks. But more important than the cash, was his social security, credit and debit cards. Davilla had memorized the PIN number and Derek was a whiz at computer theft. She knew when

Franklin woke up, he would eventually find himself without an identity. It was destined to be his lot.

Davilla's final chore was always to leave her hapless victims with no dignity. She took all the clothing from the dresser and closet, and placed them inside two pillow cases from the bed. After she left the room, she would make sure to send the pillow cases down the hotel garbage chute. It would be hard for Franklin to catch up with her if he was completely naked.

But as Davilla opened the door to leave the room, she looked at Franklin sleeping so soundly. She suddenly felt a touch of compassion for him. She bent over and pulled out the black pants and blue shirt he had been wearing that evening and placed them on a chair next to the bed.

Tears began to roll down her face. He didn't deserve such treatment. All he had done was shower her with kindness. Sure Franklin had received a bounty of pleasure in return, but the trade-off was to be unmercifully brutal.

Davilla knelt down and kissed Franklin on the forehead. It would be her last chance to go straight and back off of the rotten deal she was doling out. But once more, the demons who so thoroughly ruled her heart convinced her to do otherwise. Time after time, she had heeded their lurid call. On this occasion though, their cry left her soul reeling. She despised the very essence of her being.

Chapter VIII

A tormented heart most often seeks refuge in the lair of the wicked. A haunt where misguided hope of restoration easily falls victim to extreme acrimony. It is a den for the desperate. A haven for those woeful souls who long for renewed zest in their pitiful existence, only to find themselves so totally ensnared that willful escape proves futile. The only chance for survival rests singularly on Divine intervention.

Franklin found himself in such a predicament the moment he tried to arouse his beleaguered body. Not a muscle seemed to want to answer his call to action. His arms felt as if they were being weighted down by two fifty-pound sacks of cement. His legs were also of no use at the time, as if disabled by running back-to-back, full-distance marathons. The pounding in his head inferred that an entire marching band had sounded off constantly for two days in the confines of his ransacked hotel suite. He was conscious, but just barely.

His left eye twitched a couple of times as he lay face down on his saliva-drenched pillow. He strained hard to coax open the eye, but to no avail. It just wasn't ready to cooperate. So Franklin laid there for a few more minutes, trying purposely to gather his wits.

He was nearly helpless, having nary a clue about where he was or what had happened to him over the past twelve hours. It was like his memory had been wiped clean, and his mind and body were existing on two separate planes. The sensation was surreal.

Then, ever so slowly, Franklin started to come around. It was as if God had sent one of the heavenly hosts to directly minister to a fallen son. After forcibly prying open his encrusted eyelids with his fingertips, he tried to focus his vision, intently peering at a thin stream of sunlight slipping through a slit in the curtains covering the sliding glass door. But even that sliver of light caused pain, like a needle piercing into his eyeballs straight through to the back of his skull. He winced and slammed shut his eyes again. He realized just getting out of bed would be an excruciating endeavor.

Franklin rolled over and looked away from the light, an action highly consistent with his behavior the past couple of weeks. After a couple more minutes, he tried to arise again. He managed to hoist himself up to the edge of the bed. The thin stream of sunlight illuminated the room just enough for Franklin to get his bearings somewhat in line. He was dizzy and his head was throbbing like someone had squeezed his skull in a vice and then shook it back and forth. The feeling worsened when he tried to stand up. He fell back onto the bed. He suddenly felt nauseous. Franklin knew he somehow had to drag himself to the bathroom or there was going to be a tremendous mess to clean up.

He slithered his still-nude body off the bed and crawled on his hands and knees the few yards to the bathroom. He felt around the cold tile floor until he found his mark. He flipped up the toilet seat and hugged the bowl with all the strength he could still muster. A couple seconds later, he violently spewed forth every ounce of the previous night's debauchery.

Despite the putrid smell, Franklin made sure to stay put until he was certain his stomach was completely void of its intolerable contents. He managed to wash off his face in the dark, daring not to turn on the light. He staggered back to the bed and collapsed face down on the mattress. The episode sapped him so much he fell back to sleep for another three hours.

It was dusk when Franklin woke up again. This time the sun-beam that had been sneaking through the curtain was replaced by a green neon glow, courtesy of a neighboring casino marquee. He was a whole lot more stable when he regained consciousness the second time. The pounding in his head had subsided greatly and his stomach was not nearly as queasy.

As he lay in bed, Franklin began to recall Halloween night in his mind. It didn't take long before his recollections drifted toward Davilla. Thoughts of her stunning beauty brought a brief smile to his face. It was an experience he knew he'd never forget. He reached his right arm over to where she should be lying. He knew before-hand, however, it was a wasted motion. Women like Davilla would rarely be found snuggling closely in the morning. It just wasn't done in her trade. Passion always came with a price, and not just in monetary terms. The bitter sting of loneliness was often the debt due to both parties in such transactions. It was an outlay that had to be met.

The longer Franklin allowed his thoughts to linger on Davilla, the more disturbed he became. His improprieties the night before were dreadfully unusual for a man of his supposed moral standing. The demons that clutch the reigns of guilt began to brutally as-sault him. How could a good Christian man slide to such depths? Hardcore sex with a stripper, no matter how enticing, was a sin he should never have permitted to consume him. And where was she now? Why did he still wish she was lying next to him? After all, didn't he harbor a longing for her at that very moment?

Franklin grasped his still-pounding head tightly with both hands. He pulled on his matted brown hair until it brought him a punishing pain. "Stop! Stop!" he cried, rolling on the bed from one side to the other in an almost convulsive manner.

Charge upon charge was being hurled at him by the great accuser and his minions. Franklin could not mask his guilt. He knew the hellions' tormenting taunts were accurate. *Look what you've done,* they screamed through his conscience. *God can't possibly still love you. One of his children would never act out so immorally. Are you sure you're one of his children?*

On and on it went. Insult after insult. Crime after crime. The assault was draining. Franklin sought a means of escape. He found none. All he could do was lay there and endure the pummeling.

Nearly broken, he began to weep profusely. But even his bawling was shallow. There were few tears of remorse, just insincere whimpering, like that of a puppy being punished for soiling the carpet one too many times. Franklin felt the consequences of his actions, both physically and emotionally, but true repentance had not yet touched his heart. In fact, he had fallen so badly it didn't even occur to him to cry out to the Lord for mercy. He wanted the torment to cease, but didn't even think to use the most basic means of grace: prayer. It was like he didn't even know God at that point. He was battered and circumstances were about to get worse.

There was a firm knock on the hotel room door. Franklin didn't hear it. The party outside the room knocked again, more forcibly the second time. Again, no response from Franklin. He was still wallowing in his misery. The sound of a card key slipping quickly in and out of the lock finally did catch Franklin's attention. He rolled over onto his back and pulled the bed sheet up to his shoulders. The door slowly crept open, allowing a flood of light to rush in from the hallway. Franklin trembled, a belated symptom of paranoia brought on by the powerful narcotic Davilla used to spike his drink the night before.

A man peeked his head inside the room.

"Are you alright Mr. Edwards?"

His eyes still wincing from the light, Franklin didn't recognize the man at first.

"It's me Gerald, from the front desk. I'm sorry to disturb you, but no one has seen you for a couple of days. You had the sign on the doorknob, so housekeeping wouldn't go in. The girl heard some crying and the sound of glass breaking inside the room. She got worried and called me."

Franklin didn't respond. He found himself unable to speak. He wanted to answer, but his vocal cords didn't react when summoned by his brain. He just cast a wide-eyed blank stare at the uniformed night clerk.

Gerald entered the room and turned on the light. Franklin quickly shielded his eyes with both hands.

"What's wrong Mr. Edwards?" the highly-concerned clerk asked as he started to walk over to the bed. "Are you ill? Should I call an ambulance?"

Franklin coughed a couple of times. The action appeared to bring him up to speed for some reason. Gerald picked up the phone by nightstand and began to dial 911. But Franklin suddenly pressed down on his hand to stop him.

"Don't call anybody, I'll be alright," Franklin said in a moderately perturbed tone.

Gerald pulled his hand away and hung up the receiver.

"You don't look so good sir," Gerald responded as his eyes left Franklin for a few seconds to quickly scan the room. He noticed a broken wine bottle on the floor next to the bed. The smell of vomit also permeated the air. "What went on in here? This place is a wreck."

Franklin looked around the room. He was amazed at what he saw. The room looked as if it had been ransacked. The bureau drawers were cast about the floor as though somebody had been intently searching for something of value. The coverings were missing from the bed pillows. A lamp had fallen off the table by the slider and shattered. It looked as though Davilla had begun to trash the hotel room before she left.

The damage changed Gerald's demeanor from one of concern to outright anger.

"Look," he said rather sternly. "I don't know what's been going on up here, but you're going to have to pay for this. I suggest you get your things together and come downstairs with me right now."

Franklin, still suffering from a stiff headache, didn't appreciate Gerald's candor. "Hey man, give me a few minutes to get dressed alright?"

He started to get out of the bed before it dawned on him that he was still completely naked. "Do you mind?" Franklin yelled while quickly yanking the sheets over himself again.

Gerald folded his arms across his chest and hurled a stinging scowl at the disheveled guest. "I'll give you an hour. If you're not downstairs by then, I'll call the police and have you removed."

The tall, lanky clerk shut the door quietly behind him as to not rouse the other guests. Franklin sat on the edge of the bed for a few moments trying to recall the last several hours. But his memory was pretty much void of detail. He remembered drinking at the strip club and of course, lovely Davilla, but specifics were a blur. He walked over to the shower and turned up the hot water. The steam seemed to help him wake up a little more. He washed in about ten minutes and toweled off. As he rubbed his scruffy chin, he looked for his shaving kit on the counter. It wasn't there. He looked in the drawers in the vanity and under the sink, but couldn't find it there either.

Franklin walked into the bedroom and pulled out the two dresser drawers that hadn't been tossed on the floor. But they were empty. He began to panic a little, realizing something was amiss. He searched all over the hotel room, not only for his shaving kit, but for his entire wardrobe as well. Everything was missing.

"What the heck?" Franklin mumbled to himself, as he frantically scurried about the room. But the only pieces of clothing he found were the slacks and shirt he had been wearing the night before, tossed carelessly over a chair. He couldn't even find his underwear. His docksiders were under the bed, but his socks were missing. Franklin was stupefied.

He reached into his pants pocket, but his wallet was gone. A sudden burst of despair consumed him. Davilla had ripped him off!

Franklin slumped into the chair next to the bed. He closed his eyes and shook his head from side to side. What a fool he had been; totally duped by a devious dame. He felt so stupid that all he could do was begin to giggle snidely to himself. He deserved what was happening to him and he knew it.

He dressed himself in the wrinkled outfit he had left and went down to the lobby to face the music.

Gerald had an extremely stern look on his face as Franklin approached the desk.

"We seem to have a big problem here Mr. Edwards?" the clerk said with a snarl.

Franklin thought *great, what's wrong now?*

Gerald began to explain to Franklin that the credit card he had presented when he checked into The Silver Nugget was now being declined by the hotel computer.

"You apparently went over your credit limit when you were out partying," Gerald said sarcastically. The heavy-set, young female clerk at the next computer terminal quickly drew her eyes toward her partner and then at Franklin in response to the snide comment. But she didn't say a word at that point, instead returning to her own duties.

"I haven't used my credit card all week, except when I checked in here," Franklin snapped back. "I've been using my ATM card or paying with cash."

"Okay," Gerald responded, "let my try running your bankcard."

Franklin paused for a moment, trying to think of the right way to tell Gerald that his wallet, as well as most all of the other personal belongings in his room, had been stolen.

"Well?" Gerald asked anxiously. "Are you going to give it to me, so we can wrap this up?"

Franklin sighed and shook his head.

"After you left the room, I discovered my wallet was missing."

"Hey now," Gerald answered defensively. "I barely entered your room. You were there. Your not trying to say I took it are you?"

"No," Franklin said with a touch of resignation in his voice. "Not unless you also stole my shaving kit and all my clothes. No, I know who ripped me off."

"What? Who? Did you get mugged? Your room looked trashed."

In a matter of just a few seconds, Franklin saw that he might have a way to wiggle out of his predicament. Maybe he could tell Gerald that someone forced their way into his room, beat him up and stole everything he had. But that wouldn't explain his clothes being gone, or him being found stark naked in his bed. But if he were drugged, that might help account for his circumstances, Franklin reasoned. Yet how would he prove that somebody forcibly slipped him a Mickey. As he quickly worked over the deceptive scenario in his mind, Franklin figured there was no way to plausibly script such a plot. He'd never been good at lying or even telling half-truths. Fessing up to his plight looked to be the best option.

"Well?" Gerald asked impatiently. "What happened?"

The other clerk again glanced over at the discourse that was unraveling.

"Look," Franklin said, casting his eyes downward. "I met a lady friend Halloween night. Hmm, some friend. Anyway, we went up to the room for some drinks. We were both pretty drunk. I guess she put something in my wine, because I passed out. I really don't remember much about the night. I didn't wake up until this afternoon. I got very sick and fell back to sleep again until you came knocking on my door."

Gerald was thankful to be getting at least some explanation.

"Who was this lady? Did anybody see you with her?"

"I do remember you were working at the desk that night when we came in. You didn't see us?"

"No. I didn't notice you coming into the lobby."

Franklin shrugged his shoulders.

"Well, I don't suppose you know where she is, do you?" Gerald asked, his sarcasm beginning to return.

"No. I don't really know her that well. I only met her that night."

"Where did you pick her up?"

Franklin smirked. "A strip club."

Gerald sighed, ran both hands along his balding scalp and looked up at the ceiling. The other clerk snickered. Franklin felt his embarrassment begin to overcome him. If only he could slither away and find some rock to crawl under.

Gerald smiled at the girl next to him and shook his head. He turned and looked right into Franklin's bloodshot eyes.

"You're screwed. The girls who work at those places live loose and easy. You'll never find her."

"Maybe if we call the police, they can help track her down," Franklin responded anxiously.

Gerald paused a moment before answering the pathetic man. He felt a little sorry for Franklin, but not too much. He refocused his empathy back on himself. How was he going to explain to his bosses that he forgot to tabulate Franklin's bill daily as per hotel policy? He also remembered spending his time Halloween night playing Free Cell on his computer, which was probably the reason he didn't see Franklin and Davilla come into the hotel. He'd already been reprimanded earlier in the week for dereliction of duty. As an Assistant Manager, Gerald knew he would be called into account for not following up on his guests, especially one whose room was in shambles and couldn't pay his bill. He took his frustration out on Franklin.

"You know," Gerald said with a disgusted frown, "this really isn't my problem Mr. Edwards. It's yours. I feel like calling the police alright, but on you."

Gerald's attitude triggered Franklin's ire.

"Hey man," he said, his voice rising in irritation. "I'm telling you the truth. What do you want from me? I don't live in this town. I don't know anybody here. I'm trying to find a way out of this mess."

"Where do you live? Can you call someone there?"

Franklin thought about phoning his mother or Sam, but his brain began to throb again. He couldn't remember their phone numbers at all. Besides, he didn't want to involve them, at least not yet. He felt they would be ashamed of him and his actions. Pride got the better of him once again.

"My whole family's dead," Franklin said angrily with his eyes beginning to tear up. "And my friends won't help me. I left everything behind a while back. I'm on my own now. Completely on my own!"

Gerald didn't appreciate Franklin's tone and other guests were beginning to stare. Confrontation is always bad for business. Gerald was already in enough trouble, so he figured it best to resolve the situation quickly.

"Hey, keep your voice down," Gerald said, almost pleading. "I'll tell you what I'm going to do. If you leave here within the next five seconds, I'll forget the whole incident. Just get out of here. Now!"

"But I need somebody to help me. I don't know where..."

"Five!" Gerald exclaimed.

"But..."

"Four!"

Franklin knew it was of no use to argue anymore. He had used up any common sympathy due him. He turned and headed for the revolving glass door.

"Three!" he heard Gerald cry, almost mockingly, as if to make Franklin run for the street. But he wasn't about to give Gerald the satisfaction. Just a week earlier he had to flee another scene, the one that occurred at Trudy's. He wouldn't let it happen again.

Franklin pushed open the door and exited briskly, almost knocking over an elderly couple coming inside.

As Franklin was leaving the hotel, the female clerk gave Gerald a piece of her mind.

"You handled that guy like a real jerk, you know," she said bluntly.

"Mind your own business and get back to work," Gerald retorted.

The girl just shook her head in disgust. She'd seen his public relations skills many times before.

❧❈❧

Franklin reached into his pocket for the keys to the van, but naturally they weren't to be found either. Why should they be? The way things were going, he figured Davilla probably stole the van as well. His suspicions were confirmed when he met up with the valet by the curb.

"Sure, I remember a green van," the smallish young Mexican said to Franklin. "A pretty blonde lady drove away with it last night."

"Why didn't you stop her?" Franklin cried.

The valet was taken aback. "Why would I man? I don't ask no questions."

Franklin just looked at the smug valet with a wry grin that displayed his seeping mood. "Perfect. That's perfect."

Franklin walked away from the hotel, wishing he had never stepped foot in Vegas. He tried to flag down a cop walking his beat. But like all the other folk in the city at that moment, he was no help at all. Franklin had never seen such frigidness toward the desperate. And that's what he truly was at that point, desperate. In fact, the cop took one look at the destitute widower and threatened to arrest him for vagrancy if he didn't move along quickly.

Franklin planned to do just that, move along. He needed to get out of the city as fast as he could. That was his only hope for survival. But how? He didn't have any money. And even if he wanted to call his mother or Sam, which he didn't, they would only tell him to hustle back home, where the memories were just as terrible. No, it would be better to keep pushing forward somehow. He just needed to get a hold of some cash.

Providentially for Franklin, he found a surprise when he reached into his back pocket. Apparently in her hasty retreat, Davilla had missed stealing the only remaining item of value, his father's gold watch. Franklin knew the heirloom should fetch a fairly decent price. But did he have the audacity to pawn such an endearing family treasure? He had promised his mother he would take good care of Jordan's timepiece. And it was the last memento of his precious dad he still had left, save for his fond recollections.

Franklin sat down on a bus-stop bench and stared at the watch. He opened up the locket and gazed at the photo of Gracie inside. How beautiful his mother was back then, he thought. No wonder Jordan loved her so. Her outer radiance perfectly reflected the inner beauty of her heart. Franklin realized he grew up in a nearly idyllic family. There was rarely conflict in the Edwards household. Franklin couldn't recall ever seeing his parents fight. And even their disagreements were almost comically cordial. If either were to render a cross word at the other, repentance would always quickly follow with an outpouring of affection. Hugs and kisses provided the perfect salve for tears and injured feelings. Gracie and Jordan resolved on their wedding night to never let an argument simmer while they slept. Ill will was to be squelched before the lights went out.

His parents did their best to instill the same ideals in Franklin. Respecting the marriage bed by never falling asleep angry was one way to a long and happy union. He and Sara had followed that model with moderate success for more than a decade. Yet there were times when each would unintentionally let their emotions lead to callous remarks. They didn't cuss at each other, but a harsh word or stinging stare occasionally left a wound nonetheless. Franklin suddenly realized that the last time he saw his wife's face the morning of the fatal accident; she was hurling just such a look toward him. The thought neither had the opportunity to apologize for the mildly angry moment that morning brought a gnawing distress to Franklin's gut.

As he looked at his mother's photo again, he began to feel guilt overcome him. Both Gracie and Sara would be so disappointed if they had seen his actions over the past week. He was glad neither knew the circumstances in which he found himself. The more he stared at the gold watch, the more unworthy he felt about having it in his possession. Franklin began to cry bitterly as a brisk wind blew in from the desert. He clutched the watch firmly in his hand and was about to toss it into the traffic bustling along the strip. As he cocked his arm back to hurl the timepiece, and with it a host of haunting memories, Franklin noticed a pawn shop across the street.

His arms drooped to his sides. His head bowed down toward

his chest. He began to laugh. But it certainly wasn't like a sudden burst of giddiness. It was more akin to the disconcerted cackle of a chicken headed for slaughter. The disillusioned soul stepped off the curb and strode uncaringly through four lanes of traffic toward the pawn shop. Many of the cars came to a screeching halt in order not to strike Franklin. A few of the drivers hurled expletive-laden insults at him, but he didn't hear a word. He wasn't trying to take his own life, but Franklin acted like he had fallen into a trance as he walked.

Once inside, he looked around the shop for a few moments, trying to muster up the courage to part with the watch. The place was fairly typical of what you'd expect in a town that had been built on the misfortune of others. Walls lined with musical instruments, antique clocks, firearms of various sorts and hordes of other merchandise, echoed the folly of gamblers who had cashed in their lives for the foolish hope of a lucrative strike at the casinos. Franklin saw an old, bearded man sitting in the corner behind a glass counter containing a wide assortment of jewelry. The gentleman peered over the newspaper he was reading and saw Franklin coming toward him.

"Can I help you with something?" he said, removing his black-framed granny glasses.

Franklin opened his right hand, in which he had been clutching the gold watch. He took one last look at the timepiece before handing it to the man. "I was wondering how much I could get for this?"

The old guy put his glasses back on and took the watch from Franklin. He looked it over for a few seconds before handing it back to him.

"I'm not really wanting to buy any more jewelry right now. I'm trying to sell what I already have in stock first."

Franklin was surprised by the man's lack of interest in purchasing his father's prized watch.

"I thought that's what you do in here," Franklin said as he tossed a puzzled expression at the frail old man. "Don't you buy stuff that people want to sell?"

"Well, kinda," the man answered. "If somebody wants to sell something really valuable or unique at a low price, I'll buy it. But what I mostly do is loan folks money against the value of their items. Then I give them thirty days to pay off the loan and give them their stuff back."

Franklin cocked his head to one side, trying to understand the concept of the pawn game. The old guy quickly gathered that Franklin had never been to a pawn shop before.

"Let me see your watch again."

Franklin handed it to him. The man removed his glasses and placed a small magnifying glass up to his right eye. As he inspected the watch more closely, he realized it was a well-made piece of jewelry. He noticed the fond inscription on the back and the photo on the inside.

"Who's the lady?"

"My mother," Franklin answered. "She gave it to my father when they were first married."

The old man nodded and glanced at the photo again. "So I guess her name was Gracie. Fine-looking woman, your mom."

"Yes she is," Franklin responded. ""She's still alive. Lives in Kansas. My dad's dead though."

He began to choke up a little, especially when thinking how upset his dad would be knowing that he was about to pawn the watch.

"Jordan was your father then."

"Yep."

"Why do you want to get rid of it?"

Franklin quickly looked down and shook his head. "I don't, but I really need the money."

The old man smirked. "Lost a lot at the casino, huh?"

"No. It's not like that. Somebody ripped me off and I have to get some cash quick."

Franklin didn't feel like explaining his desperate circumstances to a total stranger.

"Look, can't you just tell me what you think its worth?"

The old man had heard many stories over the years, so his heart was cold to sympathy. But he saw the desperation on Franklin's face.

"Well, I would have to get it properly assessed in order to tell you how valuable it is. Can you come back in a few days?"

"No!" Franklin exclaimed. "I need money right now!"

The guy frowned and glared intently at Franklin. "I could loan you a hundred dollars against it."

"What? I know the watch has to be worth more than that."

"Oh, I'm sure it is. But I can't loan you full value. What if you don't come back for it? I'll be stuck with a watch that I can't sell. See most of the stuff in here? It is mostly from people in the same boat as you. They never came back for their stuff, and now I have to sell it to make my money back."

Franklin's head was beginning to throb again. "Why do you think you couldn't sell it?"

"Because of the inscription on the back: 'To Jordan, Love always, Gracie.' What are the odds of someone named Gracie coming in here to look for a watch for a Jordan? Pretty slim, I'll bet."

Franklin frowned and nodded. "I guess I see your point."

The old man sighed. He felt a twinge of compassion come over him. "I'll tell you what. I'll give you a hundred-fifty for the watch. But that's the best I can do."

A hunger pain growled in Franklin's stomach. Or maybe it was just queasiness, kind of like a reminder he was selling out his father's memory for a mere pittance.

"Alright," he said reluctantly.

The old man reached under the counter and pulled out a pad of paper. He told Franklin of a local statute requiring him to catalogue all items coming into the shop, in an effort to hinder the laundering of stolen goods. The document also informed Franklin of the twenty percent surcharge the pawn shop assessed for making the loan. Franklin signed the form, put the cash in his pocket and shook the old man's hand.

"Don't feel bad son," the pawn dealer said. "If you come back in thirty days with a hundred-eighty dollars, you can get the watch back. I'm required to hold it for that long. But like I said before, if you don't come back, it probably won't sell anyway."

"Thank you," Franklin said as he turned and headed for the door. He doubted very much that he would ever again step foot in Las Vegas if at all possible.

⌘

Franklin received directions to the bus depot from a cab driver, who offered to take him there. But he decided to walk the twelve blocks and try and clear his guilty conscience of the feeble transaction he'd just made. He realized it was just one of many falterings he'd endured over the past week. The more Franklin thought about his many mistakes, the angrier he became at himself. He felt rage begin to inflame his insides. He wanted to punch somebody he was so mad.

The anger didn't subside until Franklin was approaching the bus station. He made note of a small strip mall next to the station, with a liquor store and a Salvation Army thrift shop side by side. Franklin found the juxstapositioning both amusing and convenient. He purchased a one-way ticket to Los Angeles, but the midnight bus wasn't scheduled to depart for about two hours. Franklin bought a couple hot dogs from a vendor on the street to try and quell his stomach. He found a cheap second-hand coat at the thrift store and spent all but three dollars of his remaining funds on a liter-sized flask of rum.

Franklin parked himself on a cold, metal bench at the bus station and killed the final forty-five minutes downing more than half the flask. He was pretty well lit when he boarded the bus and took a seat in the rear.

The bus wasn't even one-third full for the six-hour trip to L.A., so Franklin was able to take a whole seat for himself. He was thankful for that because he was in no mood to socialize with anyone. The other passengers must have sensed his despair, maintaining at least a two-row distance from him. And he was happy to be left alone and wallow in his own misery.

❧❖❧

The full moon seemed to light the way to Los Angeles, illuminating the dessert as the bus crept toward its destination. Franklin inconspicuously took a couple more swigs from his flask and looked out the window. His heart felt as barren as the wasteland around him. He closed his eyes and fell into a deep sleep.

Whether it was the effects of the alcohol or just extreme fatigue, Franklin fell under the scrutiny of the dream demons. His mind was barraged by nightmares that felt so real it was like he was still awake. They ran the gamut from satanic creatures stalking to wild beasts attacking to hideous sirens shrieking. But the vision that proved most disturbing was the last.

Franklin was looking down upon a scene that made him shudder. He saw a Camaro rolling over and over as it descended a steep hill at a brutally endless pace. When the car finally hit bottom, it burst into flames. A crowd of onlookers rushed to the burning vehicle, but the flames were too intense to allow them to pull out the victims. They stood by helplessly and watched the car scorched to the frame. Then suddenly, the dozen or so witnesses to the fiery episode did something truly bizarre. They held hands, formed a line and began to ascend the hill toward Franklin. They hurled accusations at him as they climbed, assaulting both his fortitude and his faith. The closer they got to the top, the more Franklin felt the fierceness of their insults. Although their words were barely audible at first, they made it known that he was entirely at fault for the accident. Franklin tried to run, but his legs would not move. They were coming closer and closer. One man held a noose in his hands. A woman shouted obscenities. Another just featured a face filled with so much rage Franklin trembled at the very sight of her. It wasn't until they were about to overtake him that he began to recognize many of the people who made up the mob. They were his family, friends and students, including Gracie, Jordan, Sam, Sandy, Joe, Gretchen and Troy. Franklin could not tolerate the anger in their eyes, so he covered his own and began to weep uncontrollably. Death would be the only desirable option at this point. He pleaded to God for the privilege.

An abrupt shake on his left shoulder thrust Franklin back to bittersweet comfort of reality. He looked up gingerly from the confines of the bus seat where he had been laying in an appropriate fetal position. He saw a slender, old black man towering above him. Franklin was startled at first.

"Sir. Come on now sir. Time to move along now," the man said gently to Franklin, who was awkwardly trying to right himself. "You looked like you was having yourself quite the rousing there now. You'll be alright."

Franklin rubbed both his eyes. He tried to stare intently at the man, but his vision was still blurred. After a few more seconds, he was able to focus. "Who are you?"

"Why I'm Freeman Watson. I drive this fine piece of machinery. Yes sir, I do."

Franklin ran his hands through his hair, trying to urge the cobwebs to clear. Nightmares can seem so real at times that they almost cause the ordinary to appear foreign. At first, Franklin thought the man he was speaking to was still a figment of his imagination. A deep sigh ushered him back to normalcy.

"I guess I fell asleep for a while."

"I'll say you did," Mr. Watson noted, his bright white smile offering an unsolicited touch of friendship toward his wayward fare. "Probably about six hours I figure. You was the quietest passenger I had until a few minutes ago."

"I had a terrible nightmare. Scared the hell out of me."

"It looks that way," Mr. Watson said, noticing the wetness seeping through the front of Franklin's trousers. Franklin touched the dampness and quickly pulled his long coat around to cover the spot.

"Wow, that hasn't happened since I was a little boy," he said, the embarrassment causing him to look away from the kindly bus driver. "Where am I?"

"Why, you in the City of Angels now son, yes sir."

Franklin cast a confused look at the man. For a split second, he wondered if he was really still sleeping. What angels? Am I dead? Is this heaven? I should be so lucky, he thought.

Watson was amused by Franklin's expression.

"No man," he said giggling. "Los Angeles. It's called the City of Angels. Boy, you did have quite the stirrin' didn't cha?"

Franklin smiled and nodded his head. Watson's laugh had brought him back to full consciousness.

The bus driver helped Franklin to his feet and led him to the door.

"You know where you headed son?"

Franklin couldn't offer an answer because he had no clue where to go next. He just shrugged his shoulders uncaringly.

"Best be careful round this part of town, pretty rough folk," Watson warned.

"I can handle myself," Franklin answered sarcastically as he stepped out of the bus.

The bus driver winced a little when he heard the response. He'd known of many a fare who had left Las Vegas hopeless and wound up dead in Los Angeles.

"Thanks for the ride," Franklin said, his tone putting forth only a slight hint of apology for his shortness toward the sympathetic man.

Watson again flashed a wide smile. "My pleasure sir, always my pleasure."

He closed the door and began to drive the bus toward the back of the station for refueling. He watched Franklin walk inside the station and head straight for the restroom. "Lord, I pray that you take care of that fella. He ain't right now. He just ain't right, poor soul."

❧❖❧

Franklin washed himself up the best he could in the men's room before heading out into the early light. The sun had just risen on that cool November morning. The day possessed all the promise of a Southern California postcard. Clear skies fought back a thin veil of smog, extremely acceptable by L.A. standards. The air was dry and crisp, not a drop of rain would have the chance to quench the always-thirsty vegetation. It was amazing that the landscape managed to remain lush and green in a city that usually found itself in near-drought conditions.

As the morning progressed, Franklin found himself wandering aimlessly. He had no place to go. He reached into his coat pocket and pulled out the flask of rum. It was still half full. He sat down on a bus stop bench near a vacant lot about a mile west of the bus station. Franklin was still thinking about the nightmare he had endured. It was so disturbing. He was aware he had witnessed the crash that took the lives of Sara and the girls six months prior. The accident scene was depressing enough, but the part of the drama that really troubled him was the reaction of his friends. In his dream, they seemed like demons. He pondered whether God was somehow holding him responsible for the tragedy. After all, it was he who had suggested Sara drive his Camaro that fateful day. Maybe it was his fault that they were all dead. He was certainly to blame for his own state of mind right now, wasn't he? The guilt drove him back to the bottle.

Franklin slugged down a few hard swigs. The liquor hitting his empty stomach caused an almost immediate buzz. The feeling was so refreshing to him. He finished off the rest of the flask promptly. Franklin was starting to feel much better about himself. He decided to find his way to the beach. He wondered if the Pacific Ocean was as pretty as the Atlantic. He quickly found out as he started to walk west. As it turned out, the bus station where he had been dropped off was less than a mile from the ocean.

Franklin was still buzzing fairly well as he touched his toes to the cold water. It was certainly not like the seas off the Florida coast. In fact, the contrast was striking. The icy Pacific drove its chill right up the center of his spine in a matter of seconds. Not even a nippy January day in South Florida incurred such a hostile reaction to submerging a small part of one's body into sub-tropical waters. The ocean even looked different. The Pacific appeared dark and foreboding, even with bright sunshine beaming down upon the wind-churned water. On just such a morning, the Atlantic would glisten as the sun cast an inviting luster through similar-sized breakers.

The chilly reception of the sea clouded Franklin's mood even more. He wondered greatly if he would ever tilt his life back on some sort of an even kilter. He'd been in a downward spiral ever since the accident six months before. Sure, early on, he had covered his emotional deficiencies well, even courageously to some he knew. But it was all a shaded guise really. Sam, Sandy, and even his mother, were fooled by Franklin's apparent reliance on God's sovereign mercy. He had convinced them that he believed it was the Lord's will for him to seek a new start elsewhere. The blessings were sure to come if he just blindly followed the Spirit's call in his heart to hit the road. But in truth, there was no such call. Franklin had surrendered his conviction for the sake of his own freedom. At this point, it was most probable he was adhering to Satan's volition more than any other. The misguided means of escaping his sorrow had only led him into a more miserable entrapment.

He downed the rest of the flask with the hope that drunkenness would allow for a brief respite from his newfound wretchedness. The reprieve didn't last long, however.

After spending the entire day wandering the seashore in an alcohol-induced stupor, Franklin finally hit the proverbial wall. His head began to pound again. His stomach felt queasy. He desperately needed a place to crash. Franklin sought refuge under a fishing pier as the sun finished its day-long march toward the sea. But there were too many other forgotten men who had beaten him to the spot. He moseyed over to a tiny beachside park across the street from the pier.

The park was under repair and only one bench was available. Franklin was so dizzy as he began to sit down that he didn't notice a decrepit old bum already sleeping there. He heard a deep groan as he plunked his one-hundred-ninety-pound body right down on the poor guy's chest. Franklin quickly stumbled to his feet. The bum looked up at him with distain in his one bloodshot eye. Franklin's disposition turned uncharacteristically combative. He pulled up the slight-framed man by the collar of his grungy flannel shirt and tossed him to the ground. The bum's eye now only featured terror as he stared at Franklin. The scowl on Franklin's face warned the bandana-clad bum of his chances to reclaim the bench. Not a word needed to be uttered. He hopped to his feet and scurried off like a startled mouse suddenly roused by a mean old ally cat.

Franklin felt no guilt whatsoever as laid down on the bench and slipped off to sleep. The tragedy of his actions was perverse. He used to minister to bums like that during school-sponsored mercy trips to inner-city Fort Lauderdale. At this point, he was fighting the homeless for the comfort of a wooden park bench. And he didn't possess even a hint of remorse for his actions. Franklin had truly sunk to the depths of his depravity at last.

⨁

The consequences of his thuggery caught up to him shortly thereafter. He was abruptly awakened about an hour later by a swift kick in the abdomen. That was followed by a tug on his hair and a punch across the face. Franklin rolled off the bench and looked up to find half-dozen angry bums yelling obscenities at him. They started kicking and stomping on him. They were like rabid animals in their ferocity.

"Ya think ya can beat up our buddy do ya?" Franklin heard one of them scream as he tried to cover his head with his arms and protect himself somewhat. "Ya ain't one of us. We'll kill ya."

Franklin figured they were well on their way to doing just that when a siren sounded from a nearby police patrol car. The group of bums scattered as the glow of flashing blue lights swirled through the park. Franklin lifted his head, expecting to see the squad car pulling onto the scene. But the sirens and lights began to fade as the car sped down the street, apparently headed to another call.

Franklin struggled to his knees and braced himself on the wooden bench. A large splinter pierced his right arm and broke off under his bloodied skin, like a final reminder of the punishment he knew he deserved. Mercifully, the bums didn't return. Unwittingly, the police had broken up the melee and Franklin was grateful for that. He knew he had to get out of the area quickly or the angry mob might return. The incident seemed like a painful climax to the nightmare Franklin endured earlier on the bus. He felt the bruises of the encounter, but managed to make his way to the street.

He reached into his pants pockets, looking for the three dollars in cash he still had left. But it was gone. He reasoned the bums had taken it while they were beating him. It was a shame because Franklin was hoping to use the money for a cheap meal later on. Despite the pummeling, he was hungry for some odd reason.

Franklin slowly wobbled down the sidewalk, but instead of offering help, the nightly throng on the boulevard parted as he passed by. Franklin thought he might try to find a hospital or clinic to seek treatment for his wounds, but he couldn't even get anybody to stop and give him directions. Then, in increasing pain, he fell up against a storefront window. The sign painted on the plate glass brought precious relief to Franklin's weary body: "New Hope Church."

He turned the knob on the front door. It was locked. Franklin knocked a few times, but no one answered. The lights were off inside, so he thought he might be out of luck. The building stood alone on a small lot, so Franklin walked around to the back. He found the rear entrance unlocked. He opened the door and went inside.

The only light available was being cast by a red exit sign. Franklin felt along the textured plaster wall to guide his way through the place. He touched a door knob, but the room was locked. A few paces later, another knob, but the same result. Franklin continued down the corridor about another fifteen feet before running smack dab into a swinging door. The weight of his body and the disorientation brought on by the darkness, as well as the throbbing pain in his head, caused Franklin to push through the door and fall hard to the floor.

He laid there for a minute or so and tried to gather his wits. When he opened his eyes, Franklin could vaguely see a soft light glowing from the opposite end of the room. The lighting was just bright enough to allow him to get his bearings straight. He looked around the room and noticed five rows of benches separated down the middle by a narrow path leading to a small counter at the other end from where the light was emanating. As he refocused, Franklin was able to make out the light source. It was an illuminated white cross hanging on the back wall of the room. He had stumbled into the sanctuary of the storefront church.

Franklin made his way to the front row and plopped his weary body down on the wooden pew. He laid on his side and stared at the cross. Its light shone down on what appeared to be a small alter. On one side of the altar was a set of gold communion plates and on the other side were a couple of wicker baskets, probably used to collect the offering, Franklin figured. His mind immediately raced back to the last time he had entered a church. It was the harrowing encounter with the snake-handlers a couple months back. Was this place some sort of cult as well?

But with the predicament he was in at the moment, Franklin really didn't care too much. He knew he desperately needed help and maybe this church would be kind enough to do so. Because there was nobody there at the time, all Franklin could do was try to rest up a little.

He found himself continuing to stare at the glowing white cross. The light was not bright enough to strain his eyes. In fact, it strangely had a sort of soothing effect on his tired pupils. Every time he tried to close his eyes and fall asleep, he would quickly open them again and stare back into the light. It was beginning to have a mesmerizing effect on him.

As he continued to gaze at the cross, Franklin recounted the last six months in his mind. A swarm of emotions overcame him as he did so.

Thoughts of his dead wife and children immediately brought on a stinging sadness. Thoughts of his dear friends back home bought on miserable loneliness. Thoughts of his loving mother brought on a childish longing. Thoughts of the events of September eleventh brought on intense rage. Thoughts of Trudy's bought on ashen fear. Thoughts of Davilla brought on shameful desire. Thoughts of alcohol abuse brought on gripping nausea.

Franklin's whole body began to tremble as awareness delved further into his depravity. His downward spiral was prompted mainly by pride and he knew it. He'd always been able to maintain a rigid control over his behavior. But he was not nearly the same man as when Sara was alive. She had always helped him not to stray too far from God's way. But where was the Gospel at that moment he wondered? Had he fallen too far? Did God still love him at all? How could He?

Oh how Franklin had forgotten so much over the past six months. The theology he so eagerly taught his students had abandoned him suddenly. Just who was God, he bitterly lamented?

Despair crushed Franklin to the very core of his soul. Tears began to cloud his vision of the lighted cross as he tried to focus on it. His weeping turned into a wail. He started to bang his fists on the wooden pews, hard enough to draw blood. He wanted to tear his clothes and don sackcloth. Death would have been a tremendous blessing, more of a blessing than he deserved. He could not have felt more dreadful.

"Father!" he cried aloud. "Father!"

And that's when he finally realized the poignancy of the cross at which he had been staring.

It wasn't about him at all. It was everything about Jesus. Every sin that Franklin had committed over this painful season had been nailed to the precious cross. That's what it meant to have the Savior. That's what it had always meant. The cross and the cross alone!

Franklin took a deep breath and closed his eyes. His angst was replaced by calm. The fury of the storm inside him had suddenly passed away in the presence of the beloved cross.

Chapter IX

It's been said that crosses are ladders that lead to heaven. For centuries, the faithful have been called to personally bear their burden in the shadow cast so passionately from the salvation tree atop the hill of Calvary. Even before that fateful Friday, Jesus had warned his followers: "If anyone would come after me, he must deny himself and take up his cross and follow me." These sharp words spoken by the Savior are not optional for believers. The command is expected to be dutifully obeyed. Some do so joyfully, others not so much.

As Franklin lay asleep on the hard, wooden pew, the true sentiment behind the passage in Matthew became vividly engrossed in his consciousness. He saw old Pastor Thomas vehemently spewing forth Christ's message from his oversized Bible: "For whoever wants to save his life will lose it, but whoever loses his life for me will find it." In his always riveting manner, Pastor Thomas' stern blue gaze found its mark, blasting straight into Franklin's preadolescent eyes.

"What good is it for a man if he gains the whole world, yet forfeits his soul?" he bellowed. "Or what can a man give in exchange for his soul?"

Franklin clutched his mother's hand and leaned his head up against her comforting shoulder.

"For the Son of Man is going to come in his Father's glory with his angels!" exclaimed the raging pastor, his right index finger pointing high above his head, "and he will reward each person according to what he has done!"

Franklin knew he was doomed. "Mama, save me!" he cried.

Gracie looked helplessly at her son. "I can't," she mouthed softly. Franklin noticed her eyes held little lament. In fact, they appeared almost joyful.

Franklin was confused. He couldn't understand how his mother could find glee in his dreadful circumstance. Didn't she realize her boy was headed straight for hell? Where was her heart? Where was her love? He dropped his face into his hands and started to sob.

As the desperate drama reached its peak, Gracie exhibited the ultimate act of a mother's love. She placed her hand under Franklin's chin. She kissed his forehead. She turned his head and directed his eyes beyond the Pastor's dooming glare. She re-aimed his anguish toward the symbol of salvation fastened firmly to the back wall of the church.

"Look at it dear," Gracie said, her smile beaming with tender love. "That is your only hope. The cross. Place all your fear upon the cross. Comfort is found there, only there."

As he looked up, he felt warmth. The kind of warmth you experience when the shivers of a bitterly cold night are abruptly calmed by diving under a soft quilted blanket in front of a crackling fireplace. Franklin sensed all of his trepidation pass away when he beheld the glorious cross. Mother was right, like always.

The early morning sunlight began to peak through the tiny stain glass windows that lined the top of the church's thick metal doors. The rays beamed straight onto Franklin's right cheek, adding an appropriate rosy glow to his pale skin. He turned over onto his back and opened his eyes.

He was greeted that morning by a highly-pleasing image. A raven-haired beauty was peering down at him. Her piercing, yet calming black eyes gazed intently into his as he tried to gain his focus. Her appearance was so angelic that for a split second he figured he must still be dreaming.

Her radiant smile alone told Franklin he had found a welcoming refuge.

Cassie, the twenty-two-year-old daughter of Pastor Ramon Ramirez, was always the first one to arrive each morning at the missionary church plant. Since graduating from the University of Southern California the past spring with a degree in social work, Cassie had been helping her widower father minister to the poor and homeless minorities in the hood where New Hope was located. In addition to her secretarial and bookkeeping duties, she reflected her deep love of the Lord Jesus with daily acts of compassion toward the needy and downtrodden.

Franklin was in desperate need of Christ's love at that moment. Yet Cassie sensed that the scraggily man lying on the pew was not like most of the drunken bums who often stumbled into the church looking for a place to crash.

As she looked down into his glassy eyes, Cassie noticed a certain depth to his gaze. She perceived a soul whose serenity had been unjustly ruffled. Whatever misfortune had befallen him was not entirely of his own doing, she gathered. And Cassie was usually correct with her impromptu diagnosis of a person's spiritual state.

Finally fully awake, Franklin tried to crack a slight smile at the slender, young woman standing above him. But his lips were so dry and his throat so parched. The rum he had consumed left him severely dehydrated. The beating he endured from the other bums had thoroughly sapped his strength. He managed to sit up on the pew.

"Good morning," Cassie said, her smile casting a glow that seemed to light up her captivating face.

"Good morning," Franklin responded in a barely audible tone.

Cassie sat down beside Franklin.

"Are you okay?" she asked with a touch of concern. "You seem like you're not feeling too well. Can I get you something for you?"

"I could use a glass of water," he answered in a raspy voice.

Cassie nodded her head and promptly walked outside the room to a water cooler down the hallway. The sun was really beginning to lighten up the small sanctuary. Franklin saw that the place was actually quite charming. The wood-paneled walls were lined with a few evenly-spaced, hanging cloth banners quoting various evangelical Bible verses. The pews were old, but the wood was well-kept and appeared to have been recently lacquered over. A wooden pulpit fronted the red, cloth-covered altar. The lighted cross was affixed to the wall behind it. Gold-platted candelabras accented either side of the altar. The room had a highly-comfortable feel to it, Franklin thought to himself as Cassie returned with a cup of water.

She handed the cup to Franklin and he took a few sips to clear his throat.

"Thank you,'" he said.

Cassie offered up another delightful smile. Gosh, she seemed so cheerful. Franklin hadn't been looked on with such favor by a stranger since leaving home nearly three months before.

"How did you find your way in here?" she asked.

Franklin took another drink of water and swallowed hard. "The back door was open, so I just walked in."

Cassie frowned and sighed. "I must have forgotten to lock it again when I left last night. I do that all the time. Papa won't be happy with me, I'm afraid."

"I hope I didn't get you in trouble," Franklin quickly responded.

The girl smiled at him again. "Oh, no. I suppose he's used to my forgetfulness after all these years. Besides, I think we should always maintain an open door policy."

"I'm glad you did," Franklin said as his headache began to return. "I had nowhere else to go."

"We'll you're certainly welcome here," she said, holding out here hand for Franklin to shake. "I'm Cassie. What's your name?"

"Franklin."

"Pleasure to meet you."

Franklin continued to shake her delicate hand as he began to stand up. Her skin was soft as a child's, kind of like little Ashley's. The thought of his sweet angel brought him a tiny burst of cheer.

"I guess I should be going," he said, before becoming dizzy and slipping back down toward the pew.

Cassie grabbed onto his shoulder to steady him into the seat.

"Whoa! You look like you're about to faint or something. Sit here for a second."

Franklin placed his hands over his eyebrows and began to rub his forehead. His skull began to throb intensely again. He thought he might pass out.

"What happened to you?" Cassie asked, her concern deepening.

Franklin continued to message his head with his fingers, hoping to ease the pain.

"I got beat up pretty good last night. Probably deserved it I guess."

Cassie noticed a few lacerations on his arms and some blood stains on his shirt. As the room began to take in more sunlight, the bruises on his face became more apparent.

"You might have a concussion. Let me call an ambulance."

"I'll be alright. I just need a couple minutes to get my wits back."

"No!" she protested. "You're not alright. Just lay there and I call them. I'd feel terrible if I let you leave and something happened."

Just as Cassie got up to make the phone call, her father walked in.

"Cassie, are you in here?" the short, stocky bald man said.

"Up front here papa."

Ramon walked over to the pew and saw his daughter with her left arm around Franklin's shoulder.

'This poor man stayed here last night. He's hurt. I think he might have a concussion."

Cassie's father kneeled down in front of Franklin, whose eyes were now totally glassed over.

"You do not look so good amigo," the pastor said. "Why do not you lie down in the back room for a little bit? Here, we will help you."

Franklin nodded his head in agreement. He really was in no shape to argue with anybody right then. Besides, it was about time he responded humbly to the kindness of strangers.

Ramon and Cassie escorted Franklin to a room in the back of the building. It was about the size of a small den. There was a single bed, a dresser with a thirteen-inch T.V. on top, a small wooden table and chair, and a little closet bolted to the back wall. They laid Franklin down on the bed. His dizziness began to abate.

"Is that better amigo?" Ramon asked, his deep, brown eyes showing concern.

Franklin opened his eyes wide and let out a deep sigh. "Much better, thank you."

The pastor smiled as he carefully scanned the bum. Like his daughter, Ramon thought the man seemed different from the usual street clientele they dealt with at New Hope. Franklin was more polite for one thing.

"You are the first people who've been nice to me since I arrived in this town," he said. "Who are you and what kind of church is this?"

The pastor looked at Franklin quizzically. "What do you mean?"

"Oh, I assumed this was a Christian church because of the cross, but I've had bad experiences with churches recently."

"How so?"

"Well, the last church I went to was some sort of cult that handled snakes. Scared me silly."

The pastor laughed boisterously. "Oh no sir, I assure you we do not do that here. I hate snakes myself."

He glanced over to his daughter, who flashed her snowy smile once again.

"My name is Ramon Ramirez, and you have already met my daughter Cassie."

Franklin smiled at Cassie. "Yes, she's been very gracious."

"I know. I call her my little Angel of Mercy."

Cassie rolled her eyes and began to blush. "Oh papa...Maybe I should go get a wash cloth and towel for our guest. Would you like another glass of water Franklin?"

"Yes, that would be great. Thank you."

Cassie nodded her head and turned and left the room. During the five minutes or so that she was gone, Ramon began to inquire about Franklin's current circumstances.

"I hope you do not mind me asking, what happened to you? What brought you our little church this morning?"

Franklin closed his eyes and ran his fingers through his hair a few times, trying to massage his still-throbbing head. He didn't feel like going through a long, drawn-out explanation of his plight. But the pastor and his daughter had been so kind; he felt he owed them some reason for stumbling into their house of worship.

"I've had a rough go of it lately. Somebody stole everything I had. I was sleeping on a park bench last night when a group of guys started punching me and kicking me..."

His ribs suddenly began to sting a little as he talked. He coughed a couple of times. Ramon put his arm under Franklin's back and helped him to sit up in the bed in an effort to relieve the pain and help him catch his breath better.

"We probably better get you to a doctor."

Franklin winced as he swung his legs around and dropped them to the floor. "I just can't get comfortable."

Cassie returned with a bowl of soapy water, a washcloth and a towel. She lightly tapped the cloth around his face and forehead, wiping off some of the dried-on blood. Ramon helped Franklin remove his shirt so that Cassie could wash his chest and back. That's when they noticed the bruises covering his torso.

"It looks to me that you might have some cracked ribs," Ramon said. "Do they hurt?"

"Yeah, but I'll be alright."

Ramon shook his head in disagreement. "Mmm, we need to get you to a doctor. Cassie, call the clinic down the street and tell them we are bringing someone over."

"I don't have any money!" Franklin pleaded, and again winced as he turned up his hands in dismay.

"That is okay," Ramon said. "They know us over there. We bring people to them all the time. We will work it out. Go now Cassie."

The daughter set down the washcloth and handed her father the towel before dutifully leaving the room to phone the clinic.

Ramon helped Franklin on with his shirt. "It will be fine really," he said. "Let us help you. That is why we are here."

Franklin nodded reluctantly. What else could he do? He was in no position to help himself at that point.

"While we wait for Cassie to come back, do you mind if we talk a little bit. If you are up to it."

"No I don't mind," Franklin said. "I actually feel a little better now that I'm sitting up. I guess I'm lucky those guys didn't kill me last night."

Ramon saw the opportunity to present the gospel to the troubled man.

"You know, most of the people who come through the doors here are in some kind of desperate situation. They are lost and they need to find their way again. They have nowhere to turn and I truly believe that God sends them here to guide them back on the right path. Now, it is not like we are some kind of miracle workers here or anything like that, we just try to let God use us to help him fulfill his mission in this fallen world."

Franklin liked what he was hearing so far. Maybe it was the physical pain he was enduring that drew his attention deeper into Ramon's words.

"And Franklin, son, do you know what we believe God's mission for us is?"

"No, why don't you tell me. I'd like to hear it."

Ramon offered a pleased reaction. Franklin could see where Cassie got her lovely smile from.

"I believe He uses this little mission church to gather his children, especially those who have been hurt by the woes of this world. Are you following me so far?"

Franklin nodded affirmatively.

"Good," Ramon said before clearing his throat. "Now, you said you were lucky those men who beat you up last night did not kill you, right?"

"Oh yes."

"Well, I do not think luck has anything to do with it. I believe that God has a purpose and a time for everything that happens in this world. But before I go on, may I ask you a question?"

"Sure, go ahead." Despite his pounding head, Franklin was enjoying the pastor's loving witness.

"Okay, suppose those men would have beaten you to death last night. Do you know where your final resting place would be? Do you think you would have gone to be with God in heaven or maybe someplace else?"

Franklin grinned and looked straight into Ramon's questioning eyes. "Heaven," he said boldly for someone in his condition.

Ramon was somewhat taken aback by Franklin's boldness.

"You sound pretty confident. I wonder if I could ask you why you think you would go to heaven. I mean, I do not want to make you feel like you are worthy or something. I am just curious."

Franklin lowered his head in shame and gazed at the faded white tiled floor.

"Well, I certainly don't deserve to go to heaven," he confessed, his eyes beginning to mist a little. "I deserve hell. My recent behavior has bluntly pointed that out to me. But I believe in Jesus' work on the cross. And I believe that He has saved me despite myself. He loves me, man. Me."

Franklin put his face in cupped hands and started to cry. The flowing tears made his head throb all the more. His short breaths brought sharp pains to his aching ribs. His remorse was self-evident.

Ramon sat next to Franklin on the bed and placed his arm around him. The pastor was delighted in Franklin's confession of faith, but also puzzled why an apparent believer had fallen so far. He allowed the weeping man finish his spiritual letting before continuing their conversation.

Meanwhile, Cassie returned from calling the clinic. She was about to enter the room until she heard Franklin crying. She stopped short of entering.

Franklin took the towel and wiped away his tears. He began to enlighten Ramon with some of the tragic details of the past months. Confessing his tale seemed to comfort Franklin, while touching Ramon's heart as well.

Although she knew it was eavesdropping, Cassie stood quietly behind the closed door and listened to Franklin's testimony. The account also brought her to tears. She stifled her sniffles well. She was glad that her previous notion was correct. He wasn't a bum, just a desperate soul whose life had been turned upside down. Right then, she made a vow to herself and God, to help him work through his troubles. He seemed well worth it.

Ramon was helping Franklin to his feet as Cassie came into the room.

"The nurse at the clinic said for us to come right over papa."

Cassie stayed behind at the church while Ramon drove Franklin to the clinic. The urgent care center was only about a half-mile down the boulevard, so Ramon didn't get the opportunity to quiz Franklin much further. He was anxious to find out more about the stranger's past, but knew physical repair was more of a priority at that point than spiritual healing. The pastor and his daughter had come to realize over the years that mercy ministry often means sharing the gospel through practical provision.

At first, the doctor who tended to Franklin considered sending him off to the emergency room at the county hospital. Franklin obviously had no proof of insurance and his injuries were fairly severe. But after Ramon guaranteed payment for the medical procedures, Franklin was treated at the clinic. X-rays showed a couple of cracked ribs, but no other broken bones. Dr. Parlhak, a young-looking internist from Pakistan, judged Franklin to have a mild concussion, but thought it would be safe to release his patient into Ramon's care. One of the nurses took Franklin to a triage room to bandage his cuts and scrapes.

"I think he will be fine after a few days," Dr. Parlhak told the pastor, who had brought many patients to the clinic over the last two years. "He will be sore, but just give him this prescription for pain. I will have a nurse call you tomorrow to see how he is feeling."

Ramon nodded in agreement. "Thank you Hamed."

"Very well," the doctor replied in his thick Arabic accent. "It is good to see you again Ramon. You are a fine man. May god bless you for your work."

The pastor smiled appreciatively for the compliment. Ever the evangelist, he wished the Lord would bless him further with an opportunity to share the good news with his Muslin acquaintance. He had developed a soft spot for the lost souls entangled in Islam's web of false hope. Perhaps God would use him or his daughter, or even one of the injured folk he frequently brought to the clinic, to convert Dr. Parlhak. Ramon remained hopeful.

～❖～

It was late in the afternoon when Franklin and Ramon arrived back at New Hope. Cassie had spent most of that Saturday cleaning up the sanctuary in order to prepare for the worship service in the morning. She was pleased that her father brought Franklin back with him. She greeted Ramon with her usual hug and warm kiss on the cheek before helping him assist their wounded brother in Christ.

"How are you doing Franklin?" she asked, rubbing him softly on the shoulder.

"Not too bad I guess. Still kinda sore, though."

"Oh I'm sorry," Cassie said, quickly pulling her hand off his shoulder and clasping her other hand.

Franklin knew he had winced a little when she touched him, but didn't want to make her feel bad about her compassion. "You and your father have been so kind to me. It makes me feel blessed to receive such sincere Christian love. It's been so long. Not since, well..." His voice faded as he began to choke up.

Ramon stepped forward with a suggestion.

"Franklin, I told the doctor we would look after you. He was going to send you to the county hospital to convalesce, but I thought it might be better for you here. There is a shelter down the road, but it can be a very nasty place."

It quickly dawned on Franklin that he didn't have much choice. He didn't want to impose further, but he was homeless after all. He thought maybe he should phone his mother or Sam for help. He knew they truly loved him and would be quick to offer any assistance he needed. Yet, for some reason, that option still didn't hold much appeal for him. He reasoned pride was to blame. Or maybe it was embarrassment for his woeful failing. He wasn't quite ready to deal with his shame at this point.

"We'd love to have you stay for a while Franklin," said Cassie demurely.

Franklin could not resist her gracious sensibility. Her glistening onyx eyes beckoned comfort and stability. Her serene smile sealed the deal.

"Thank you so much," said Franklin, his humility bringing forth tears.

"Then, you will stay?" Ramon said excitedly, putting his arm around him.

Franklin nodded yes.

"Great. Cassie, could you make sure the spare room is cleaned up for our guest. You know, change the sheets on the bed, vacuum."

Cassie tried to reign in her father's enthusiasm a little. She knew how joyful it always made him to serve a Christian brother in need.

"I've done this before papa."

Ramon realized he was being overassertive and hugged his daughter. "I know honey. I just need to brush up on my sermon for tomorrow. Franklin, we will all eat dinner together tonight, no?"

Franklin smiled and nodded yes.

"Good," Ramon said as he clasped Franklin's hand. "Cassie will take good care of you. Oh honey, I am sure we have some clean clothes in the locker that would fit our guest."

"I will get them papa. Now you just go and get your message ready so we can eat supper at a decent hour, okay?"

Ramon kissed his daughter on the forehead and headed for his office in the back of the church. Cassie walked Franklin over to the room where he had been laying down before.

Like a doting sister anxiously longing for a favorite brother to return to the family roost, Cassie had already prepared the berth Franklin would call home for the time being. The white tile floor sparkled from the scrubbing it had been given. The bed was neatly made, with linens that smelt clothesline fresh. The old wood furniture was so finely dusted that a white glove would have a difficult time picking up just the slightest piece of lint. Cassie even set out a vase of freshly cut flowers, a pleasing mix of carnations, which added a feminine vibrancy to the tiny ten-by-ten refuge. Many of the hotel rooms Franklin had stayed in over the past two months were certainly not nearly as homey.

"I hope you will be comfortable here," Cassie said, placing her index finger shyly on her slightly-quivering bottom lip.

Franklin was touched by her girlish nervousness.

"It's lovely. Thank you. I sure could use a comfortable place to rest right now. I'm very tired."

"Oh okay. You lay down now. I'll run upstairs and get supper ready for us."

Something compelled Franklin to reach out and gently grab hold of Cassie's forearm as she turned to leave.

"No stay," he said with an almost pleading look in his eyes. "I mean, would you mind sitting and talking with me for a few minutes?"

Cassie smiled at Franklin. She was glad he had requested her to stay. It wasn't often she spent time by herself with a man. Her father was always the one who ministered to the wayward guys who came through the church's doors. Cassie's charge was to the women, as was proper. But she felt strangely comfortable and safe with Franklin.

"Alright," she said, taking a seat at the small table while Franklin sat himself down on the edge of the bed. He rubbed his eyes and yawned before smiling at Cassie.

"I can't wait for this headache to go away. My head seems like it's been throbbing forever."

"You've been through a lot."

"If you only knew," Franklin sighed and shook his head.

"Want to tell me about it? Sometimes it's good to vent you troubles."

Although she had heard much of his tragic tale earlier with her eavesdropping, Cassie was curious if Franklin would share the same information with her as he had so selflessly divulged before to Ramon.

"Wow, where to start?" Franklin paused for a moment to gather his thoughts. She stared intently into his eyes. *Was her gaze a means of judgment?* He thought briefly. He didn't feel she was sizing up his worth as a human being. After all, he was pretty sure Ramon had told his daughter that their guest is a Christian. And brothers and sisters in the faith deserved the benefit of any doubt. Jesus himself had said so many times. Besides, she had been nothing but kind to him since the first second he laid eyes on her delicate face that morning. He reasoned it wouldn't be fair to not tell her the truth about his steady decline the past six months. But he also figured it would be wise to leave out some of the more lurid details, at least for the time being. He hadn't even told those to Ramon.

"Well, last spring I lost my wife and two young children in

an auto accident back home in Florida." Franklin closed his eyes tightly to fight back the swelling tears. "I've been in a progressively downward spiral ever since. I've made so many mistakes since then Cassie. Many of my problems I've caused myself."

Franklin sniffled a couple of times, but didn't burst forth into the full sob that was so common recently. Cassie was becoming misty-eyed herself as she listened to his tender confession. The heartfelt sympathy that shone in her placid dark eyes allowed Franklin to continue with less encumbered effort.

"I wasn't always a bum, you know."

"You're not a bum," Cassie sternly interjected.

Franklin sighed. "No, I guess not. But I've acted terribly lately. I've treated people with little or no respect. The reason I got beat up last night was because I forced a poor, old bum from his park bench so I would have a place to sleep. His buddies came along and gave me the beating I deserved. At least they showed some respect for their fellow bum...Me on the other hand; I've lost all respect for people, including myself. I've become a drunk, a bully, a lowlife."

Franklin couldn't hold back any longer. The dam broke. His tears flooded out like a raging torrent, even stronger than before with Ramon. Cassie got up from her chair and sat next to Franklin on the bed. She put both her arms around him while he wept uncontrollably onto her neck and shoulder. She didn't say a word. She just let him release all his remorse. She was pleased to do so.

About five minutes elapsed. While still hugging Franklin, Cassie reached over to the nightstand and grabbed a few tissues. She gave them to him to wipe away his sorrow.

"Franklin," she said, pausing to wipe away her own tears, "the Lord places us through trials, but He still loves us. You know that right?"

"I do."

"I don't know why He allows bad things to happen to us, but I do believe that He does it to make us stronger. It is not easy for you right now, but I promise that me and papa will help you if you will let us. Will you?"

Franklin nodded his head yes. It felt so good to confide in another Christian. He was already beginning to feel like trying to live life again.

"The Lord, our loving Savior Jesus, is with us. He will always be. He led you to us Franklin. That's why you came here last night. He drew you here in order to draw you back to himself. So please, stay with him, and us, until you find out where He wants to send you next. Okay?"

Franklin smiled at Cassie. He wanted to hug her again. He felt so secure in her embrace. But instead, he ran his fingers through his hair a couple of times and bowed his head.

"I would be very grateful to stay here for a while," he said.

"Very well," Cassie replied, gently rubbing his shoulder a couple of times. "May I pray for you now before I go and make supper?"

"Please do. I covet all the prayer I can get right now."

Cassie held both his hands in hers and went before the Lord.

❧❀❦

Franklin awoke the next morning to the sweet murmur of an ancient hymn resonating through the thin paneled walls of his room. He couldn't hear the lyrics clearly, the singing somewhat muffled by the distance between the sanctuary and his bed. But the distinct timbre of the organ brought a soothing massage to his now-healing soul. He had slept well that night. Better than any in the past week, maybe even the last month. Though still sore from the pummeling two days prior, Franklin felt surprisingly refreshed and upbeat. He knew God had fully begun the restoration process in his life under the guidance of a church family who truly lived up to its name: New Hope.

In just one day, Ramon and his daughter had renewed Franklin's faith in humanity's ability to reflect the tender mercies the Creator bestows on the ones He loves.

For the first time in a long while, Franklin felt truly thankful. He looked forward to what the Lord had in store for him in the future. He again welcomed his destiny.

After quickly washing up in the bathroom, Franklin walked over to his bed and began to put on the slightly oversized blue jeans and red polo shirt Cassie had loaned him from the donations closet the night before. But as he looked over toward the dresser, he noticed two small boxes placed neatly on top. They were the kind department stores use to gift wrap clothing. There was also a tiny card on top. Franklin picked up the card and read it: "The King would be pleased by you presence this morning if you feel up to it, Cassie."

Franklin smiled and opened one of the boxes. Inside was a neatly folded pair of new dark-blue slacks in just his size, thirty-two inch waist, and thirty-six length. The other box contained a large, light-blue, long-sleeved dress shirt. A tear came to his eye. He glanced down at the floor. By the foot of the bed was a pair of brown loafers. A plastic bag next to the shoes contained a pair of dark-blue socks and a black belt.

"How thoughtful," he muttered to himself. Cassie must have slipped out and went shopping for him after supper and then placed the items in his room while he was sleeping. Franklin thought she must truly be an angel. What a sweet show of kindness. He felt like a new man as he donned the outfit. That was probably Cassie's aim with her charitable act, he figured. Compassion for the destitute obviously flowed through her veins.

The sanctuary was nearly full when Franklin opened the doors and went inside. He found a seat in the right front pew. Like he'd always noticed in most churches, the faithful tended to shy away from the front row if at all possible. A young Mexican couple in the same row nodded respectfully at him as they continued to joyfully sing another hymn, which Franklin still didn't recognize.

Cassie was deftly playing the organ while singing along with the boisterous congregation. She saw Franklin and smiled pleasingly at him dressed in his new outfit. When the song was finished, Cassie walked down of the slightly elevated stage and stood next to him.

"You look very nice," she whispered, obviously impressed with the selection of clothes she had picked out.

"Thank you so much," he responded with an appreciative smile.

Cassie, dressed in a classy, sky-blue pants suit, patted him on the shoulder a couple of times. "You're welcome."

Ramon, fully attired in a black robe with a gold cross stitched neatly across the breast, left his place in the left front row and walked up to the pulpit. He motioned for the congregation to be seated.

"Let us pray," he asked. "Most gracious Father in heaven, we, your blessed children, love you so much. We confess that we, like sheep, so easily go astray from the pasture of our Good Shepherd. Each of us has truly turned our own way. But we thank you Father that you laid upon your own Son, the sins of us all. In response to your grace and mercy Father, may each of us seek to be obedient to your will out of the love we now feel because of your forgiveness. We ask that your Holy Spirit guide us down the long and narrow path toward the righteousness that only you can grant us. We ask this in the holy name of Jesus, the Christ, our Lord. Amen."

Ramon turned his back to the crowd and bowed respectively three times before the lighted cross above the altar. The service took on more of a high church order than Franklin was accustomed to in South Florida, but he found himself really enjoying the surroundings. Ramon motioned the congregation to again rise while singing the doxology in acapella as a prelude to his message. This pastor's sermon was a far cry from the heretical wailings Franklin had listened to the last time he darkened a church's doors two months back. But the snake-handlers were more of a cult than anything else. The message Franklin heard then had nothing to do with the Gospel. It was all show and no glow. Fear and darkness suppressed grace and light.

Ramon's preaching, on the other hand, once again revealed the glory found in the church's name.

The sermon told all about the undeserved grace that each believer receives daily while walking with Christ. Like a good under-shepherd, Ramon pleaded with his followers to rely only on their Heavenly Shepherd for their course in life, through both the good times and the bad. He pleaded with the flock to take joy in the fact that with Christ there truly is new hope every day. The scripture-laced sermon stirred Franklin's heart so much he began to weep. But this time, the tears were joy-filled, not swollen in sorrow. It was a relief to receive such an abundant dose of grace in one half-hour message. Franklin was thoroughly thankful.

Cassie led the congregation in a rousing rendition of *Great Is Thy Faithfulness* before Ramon ended the service with the benediction. No offering was taken. There were just a couple of baskets placed by the exit doors as the faithful left the church. They were full when the last of the sheep exited the sanctuary.

Rosie's Streetside Cafe was bustling with activity that Sunday afternoon. The usual delightful fall weather in L.A. drove the masses onto the boulevard to enjoy the wide array of outdoor activities for which Californians need little excuse to indulge. Shoppers, rollerbladers, curbside musicians and the like, were all out in force as the sun's warm rays offset the cool ocean breeze.

Franklin pulled out a chair for Cassie, who sat down next to her father at the tiny glass table. Rosie's was one of the preferred eateries for the Ramirez family to dine after church services. They would often bring a guest with them to enjoy a Sabbath meal consisting of typical deep-fried American cuisine. Although proud of their Mexican heritage, both Ramon and Cassie favored American style and taste. That day, each felt a sense of pride because God had used them to bring a lost family member back into the fold. They knew Franklin would become a blessing to them. They could feel it.

"It is so nice to see that chivalry is not dead," Ramon said as he watched Cassie sit down on the cushioned metal chair.

Franklin winked at the pastor. He hadn't been so full of joy since Sara and the girls were alive. It was amazing how a little dose of kindness and one solid helping of God's word could feed a soul.

"My mama taught me manners," he said.

Cassie grinned and nodded. "She taught you well. Is she still alive Franklin? My mother died when I was a little girl."

"Oh, I'm sorry Cassie."

"That's alright. She's with the Lord now, right papa?"

Cassie reached out and lovingly rubbed the top of her father's hand. Ramon's face cast a look of content toward his daughter. Their hearts had long since tempered from the loss.

"I guess we are both widowers," Ramon said, as he looked sympathetically at his newfound friend, reminding himself that Franklin's bereavement was even greater. "The pain does soften some, my son. It just takes time. The Lord is faithful in our sorrow too."

"I know," Franklin replied wistfully.

A tall, lanky, acne-faced, young waiter came over from the bar to take their order of chicken wings, fries and soft drinks. While they waited for their food to arrive, Cassie and Ramon continued their ministry to Franklin.

"Papa, will you ask him?" Cassie said to her father with an almost-pleading expression.

"What is that my dear?"

"Oh papa, you know. What we were discussing last night after supper. Don't tell me you've forgotten already, have you?"

"No. I have not."

Franklin whisked his eyes between the two of them, pondering the gist of their discourse.

"Is there a problem?"

Ramon smiled gleefully toward the concerned brother. "No. Not at all. Well, maybe we do have a bit of a problem that you might be able to help us with. At least something to consider."

Franklin had no clue toward the idea at which Ramon was hinting. He could tell the preacher was an honest man who appeared to sincerely love the Lord and his flock, especially his loyal daughter.

"What's on your mind Ramon?"

The waiter arrived with their drinks. Cassie flashed him her delightful smile. His eyes told that he enjoyed the attention. Cassie's aura seemed to have that effect on people. Franklin was certainly taken by it.

"Well, amigo. We have been looking for a man to help us out around here. We employed a gentleman, a handyman, a few months ago, but Immigration sent him back to Mexico. Turns out he showed us a false green card. We did not know. He was a good worker."

"A Christian too, no papa?" Cassie interjected.

"Maybe. I was still trying to figure that out."

"I think Jorge is a believer."

"He might be Cassie, I do not know for sure...Anyway. Since he has been gone, we have been trying to find someone to take his place."

Franklin's smirk told Ramon to be specific. "And?"

The pastor began to lightly laugh. "Well I, we, were wondering if you might be interested in the job. Both of us have really taken a liking to you these past two days brother."

Franklin was touched. "And I you."

"The job is mostly custodial," Ramon continued, slightly rambling. "You know, washing the windows, waxing the floors, a few minor repairs here and there, that kind of thing. The pay is not much, about eight dollars an hour, but you could stay in the room you are in now for free. I thought it might be a good way for you to get back on your feet and it would help us out a lot."

Franklin didn't say anything at first. Cassie waited eagerly for some kind of response. Then his eyes began to well up once more. He couldn't believe what he was hearing. Ramon and Cassie were the epitome of Christian love. They were the gospel of grace lived out in the flesh. He was sold. He loved them.

"I have never seen such a reflection of Christ. I don't know what to say."

"Say yes," Cassie implored, her eyes moistening.

Franklin paused a couple of seconds. "Yes."

On impulse, she leaned over and hugged him. She felt compelled to do so. Her father took notice of her action, and was pleased.

"We are very happy to have you with us," Ramon said before realizing he hadn't inquired about Franklin's previous employment history. "Is this work really okay with you? I never asked you what you did before."

Franklin figured it might be a good time to fess up. He was glad to have a new task in life and didn't mind doing janitorial duties at all. He thought working menial labor might in some way be good for him. Actually help him to heal, both physically and spiritually. After all, working around the house or on his sports car used to have a soothing effect on him. But he felt holding back his former vocation from Ramon and his daughter would be deceiving. It was time to share more about himself. And surprisingly, he felt more comfortable doing so.

"I have another confession to make," Franklin said, waiting a moment to gather their expressions, which were rather casual. "Well, first of all. I was going to tell you this in the church today after your sermon, but I didn't get the chance. Oh, by the way, that was some of the finest preaching on the depth of God's grace that I have ever heard brother. It really touched my heart, amigo."

Ramon giggled at Franklin's false Mexican dialect. "Thank you," he said. Cassie wiped a teardrop that had dripped through her thinly-painted mascara.

"I will love to help you in any way I can. I am so grateful for all you've done for me." Franklin paused again to dry his tears with a napkin. "Anyway, you wanted to know what my former job was. I'm a teacher. I was head of the theology and history department at a Christian school in Fort Lauderdale, Florida."

"Really?" said Cassie, thoroughly impressed.

Ramon nodded. "I knew there was something more to you when I tried to present the gospel yesterday in your room. You had the correct answers to the questions I usually ask."

"That's because they were similar to the way I try to share the good news with people," Franklin responded.

"The Lord really does have his hand in every aspect of our lives, doesn't He?" Cassie wondered aloud.

"He does," Franklin said. "I am a witness to that firsthand. He has never left me over these last six months since my wife and kids died, even though I did my darndest to flee him. His unfailing love tracked me down. Like it says in *Amazing Grace*, "I was lost, but now I'm found."

Ramon broke in to correct Franklin slightly.

"But the first time you were found, you were never truly lost again," he said, his right finger raised in the air in a highly-pastoral gesture. "We may stumble at times, in fact we all do. But we can never fully fall from grace. Remember, once saved, always saved."

Franklin grinned and lightly bit down on his bottom lip as two female servers brought out lunch. He was going to enjoy discussing his reformed views with Ramon.

"John Calvin couldn't have said it better himself."

Ramon smiled at Franklin's statement and nodded affirming-ly. "Cassie, my dear, would you mind saying the blessing for the food?"

Cassie folded her hands together and took a deep breath. The joy in her heart was bottomless. She couldn't remember a time when she had felt so blessed. Her father had found a new confidant, another man he could talk to who thought like he did. A man who harbored the love of Christ in his soul. A man who had been deeply wounded, but knew he still needed the healing that only the Lord could give. She prayed for a blessing on the food, as well as for new opportunities for the three of them to minister to the community.

But Cassie Ramirez also secretly thanked God for sending her a soul mate. In her heart, she knew Franklin Edwards was the one for whom she had been praying.

Chapter X

P ossibly the most stunning expression of fresh romance is the sensation of suddenness. The moment when the mind and heart align in union to confirm the inevitability of endearment. An instant realization the ownership of one's affection has been ceded voluntarily and eagerly. The beneficiary of such fondness might still need to be made aware of the role so providentially cast, but that crucial act in the performance must be scripted later. Because for the time being, the premier player is often found gleeful, yet guarded. Gloriously in love, yet maybe not loved. Hopeful, yet helpless. Emotionally, there's no turning back. The drama reaches a point where just a singular scene takes precedence. What to do next?

⚜

Cassie had always struggled with her passion. Like most young women, she longed for intimacy. But over the years, a little girl's dreams of being gallantly swept off her feet by a dashing suitor had morphed into utter distaste for the natural coupling of the sexes. Such an outcome often plagues good girls and adolescence was exceptionally trying. Boys would swoon at the sight of her unadorned beauty, and then just as quickly balk at her virtue. Chastity was more than just an outdated ideal, however, it was biblical truth for Cassie, straight from the mouth of God himself. In a world that lived for the moment, she always held firm to the future, as the Word commanded.

Strict adherence to scripture came at cost, though. Saving herself for God's perfect choice often left Cassie lonely and depressed. She spent many a night flooding her pillow with tears, drawn out by reliving the almost-daily taunts of her teenage schoolmates. "Goody Two Shoes," "The Little Virgin Mary," and "Halo Head" were a few of the nicer jabs that she endured, and those were hurled by her so-called girlfriends.

The boys' ridicule bore an even nastier sting, their venom inflicted out of retribution. Their misguided hormones refused to allow them to understand why Cassie would happily befriend them, but then hold out when amorous desires arrived as a matter of course. Frustration brought on futility which begat ferocity. They called her a tease. After all, what good was her beauty if it didn't satisfy their needs? They abused her, most often just verbally, but sometimes physically as well.

Circumstances got to the point where Cassie no longer wanted to attend high school at all. Dating became a discarded activity. She enjoyed no close friends, just the casual company of a few acquaintances from whatever church her father was rotating through, as basically a preacher for hire during those lean days. In fact, for a time, papa was the only person she could cling to at all. Cassie loved her father dearly, but she sure could have used her mother to confide in back then. Oh sure, Cassie and Ramon meant everything to each other as she hobbled through her awkward teenage years. But her mother's passing when Cassie was ten, left a void that Ramon could only partially fill. As Cassie matured into womanhood, not having mom around made growing up more difficult. There are certain discussions, after all, for which mothers seem more adept.

Ramon would only caution his daughter to be wary of boys. He figured the further Cassie stayed away from them, the safer she would be. He had watched her grow into a lovely young woman, much too fine for any of the guys who courted her. He was all too sure of the prize they were ultimately after, and they weren't going to get it from his daughter if he had any say in the matter. He protected Cassie as best he could, but knew there were situations for which his wife would have been better suited to handle.

After finishing lunch at Rosie's with her father and Franklin that first Sunday afternoon, Cassie was alone in the living room of their apartment on the second floor of the run-down building that housed New Hope Church. She glanced over at the oil painting of her mother hanging on the paneled wall. The gold-plated frame perfectly outlined the portrait it hosted. Cassie's smile beamed as she looked upon her mother's delicate face. Ilianna's image always brought ease to her daughter whenever it drew her gaze. It somehow made Cassie feel that her mother was still with her. A mirror would also have the same effect at times. Many had said that Cassie distinctly resembled her mother. Ramon noted as much.

❧❀❧

"I know Cassie sure will appreciate you taking over some of the housekeeping duties around here," Ramon said to Franklin as they walked through the hallway leading into the sanctuary.

"It's my pleasure, really," Franklin responded, holding the door open for his newfound friend. "Again, I feel so blessed to have met both of you."

Ramon smiled appreciatively. "We have all been blessed."

They entered the sanctuary and began tidying up the place a bit, first picking up handouts that were left behind by the sixty or so attendees from that morning's worship service. As they were returning some of the hymnals to their rightful places on the back of the pews, Ramon suggested they sit and talk for a few minutes. He had wanted to discover if Franklin had intentions concerning Cassie. At lunch, papa had gleaned his girl seemed to be taking a fancy toward the stranger from Florida. Ramon didn't mind Cassie's interest in Franklin, in fact, he approved. But he knew how strong-willed his daughter was when she set her sights on a project. He didn't think Franklin would want to hurt Cassie. Ramon usually possessed pretty good discernment when judging character. But still, after just two days, neither he nor his daughter knew very much about the troubled man.

"Franklin, I hope you will enjoy working with us. It can be pretty hectic around here sometimes, believe it or not."

Franklin turned over a hymnal that had been mistakenly placed upside down in its holder. "Oh, I bet it can be. You had quite a few people in here today."

"Yes, this was pretty much a typical Sunday. But we also do a lot of other ministry during the week, especially mercy. There are a lot of poor people living in this neighborhood, you know."

"I'm one of them," Franklin said with a slight smirk and a sigh.

"Yes but you are rich in here," Ramon replied, tapping his own chest with his right index finger. "I could tell the first time I spoke to you."

Franklin nodded. "I know."

"I think Cassie saw that in you as well, no?"

"I hope so Ramon. I do. She's a very sweet girl."

The pastor looked away from Franklin and cast his moistening eyes on the cross. "So was her mother."

Franklin patted his brother on the back a couple of times. "You still miss her don't you?"

Ramon looked back at Franklin with a resigned smile. "Yes, even after all these years. I still miss her. We were each other's first and only loves."

"I know how you feel," Franklin said as he watched Ramon gaze down at the concrete floor while nervously twiddling his thumbs in a circular motion. "It was the same for me and Sara."

Franklin didn't want to go into further detail at that time. He knew talking about his deceased wife would only bring forth more sorrow. He had promised himself while standing next to Cassie in worship that morning he would try to only focus on thoughts that would bring joy. He believed it was his best hope for recovery. "What did she look like Ramon?"

"Who?"

"Your wife. You haven't told me her name?"

"Ilianna," Ramon quickly answered back. "I used to call her Lana though. She was very beautiful Franklin. Cassie looks just like her, especially in the eyes. I see Lana every time I look at my daughter. In a different way though."

Franklin smiled and nodded. Ramon would be very sheltering of Cassie, which was plain to see. He should be too, Franklin thought. The young lady possessed all the qualities a man might long for: great looks, warm personality and strong morals.

"You should be very proud of you daughter Ramon. She's a fine girl."

"Oh, I am. She has brought me so much pleasure since Lana passed into the arms of our loving Savior."

Franklin wondered how Lana died. He didn't know if he should ask Ramon. Whether or not it would be appropriate to try and pry out particulars he might not be entitled to after knowing the man for just a couple of days. Although, he remembered he had briefly shared with Ramon a broad view of the details surrounding Sara's untimely death. Franklin decided to inquire anyway.

"How did your wife die?"

Ramon removed a handkerchief from his back pocket and patted his teary eyes a few times. "Cancer," he said. "Leukemia. She went very fast. Really surprised me and Cassie. One month she was sick, the next month she was gone. They didn't have the treatments back then that they have now."

His voice began to fade as he choked up. Franklin could certainly sympathize with how it felt to lose a family member so suddenly. He had lived the feeling three times over. He put his arm around Ramon. He knew what it was to be a firsthand witness to the adage misery loves company. In fact, anguish and fellowship often seem to balance one another, tempering false hope while seeding veritable truth.

❦

Ilianna's lucid midnight eyes seemed to peer straight into Cassie lonesome heart. Mama's countenance was gripping. Cassie could feel it ever so sharply as she stared intently at her likeness. The bond had not been severed despite the dozen years since Illiana's passing. Cassie had always felt her mother was still with the family, at least spiritually. Not in some sort of ghostly form, haunting them from beyond the grave. That would be ludicrous, of course, and certainly not biblical, as Cassie was well aware. Still, she knew she could draw affection from afar whenever she sought counsel from

Ilianna's image. Cassie had always believed that love was the one emotion a person carried with them into the next life. She still felt mother's tenderness.

"Mama, I've met a man," Cassie said as she looked up at the painting while reclining on the black leather couch. "I know, I know, I've said that before. But this time I feel he's the one I've been praying for."

Cassie paused, as if waiting for affirmation that she knew could not be verbalized. Yet Ilianna's eyes seem to sense her girl's longing, at least from Cassie's perspective.

"He's hurting badly, mama." Cassie's eyes began to moisten. "Papa and I are trying to help him get his life back in order. Franklin, that's his name, has a wonderful heart mama, I can sense it. He just needs to feel the Lord's love again. I hope we can show him that love."

Cassie started to weep softly. Her soul ached when she thought of the hardship Franklin had endured over the past year. She knew what it was like to long for a loved one who would not be present again until eternity rushed in.

"Oh how I wish you were still here mama," Cassie whispered, the tears blurring Ilianna's face a bit. "I miss you so much... I think you'd like Franklin mama. He's sensitive, polite, smart... handsome."

Cassie smirked modestly, placing two fingers on her lips as she turned her eyes away from the painting in a bashful fashion. For some reason, she always had been one to feel embarrassment when sharing that she found a man attractive. Ramon used to gently tease her when she told of the boys in school who had caught her eye. She was hopeful he would not do the same to her with Franklin. For the time being, she would make sure to keep her feelings securely to herself. Neither her father, nor especially Franklin, could yet be privy to such tender information.

Cassie knew mama wouldn't tell.

～✦～

Ramon was giving Franklin a complete tour of the two-story building. Just a glance at the punch list outlining his janitorial duties showed Franklin that his employment would definitely be a full-time job. He didn't mind one bit though. It had been a while since he had worked manual labor, probably college, Franklin figured. He was good with his hands, as he had shown while employed part-time by the University of Florida's maintenance staff. But teaching had allowed Franklin to skirt "real work" over the years, though he did enjoy fixing up the house with Sara and tinkering with his Camaro.

"Just do the best you can," Ramon told Franklin as they looked at the old fuse box together. "Whatever you can not fix, we will subcontract to an electrician."

Franklin looked over the fuses. Some of them had burned out. Lights would often flicker during the services at New Hope, frustrating Ramon as he presented his sermons. During that morning's service, the hallway leading into the sanctuary went pitch black.

"Well, it seems like a very old building," Franklin said, putting a burnt fuse back into the box. "Might need to replace the box or some of the wiring in the walls, or both."

Ramon nodded in agreement. He knew it should be the landlord's responsibility to fix the electrical problems, but realized that Jesus would probably return before the work would be finished by the landlord. The owners of the building were basically slumlords, who exchanged cheap rent for little service. They rented out dozens of dilapidated buildings around the city and didn't feel much need to attend to their poverty-stricken tenants.

"I think it was built in the forties," Ramon said.

"The eighteen-hundreds or nineteen-hundreds," Franklin quipped.

Ramon belted out a hardy laugh. "That is a good question. Could be either one I guess. Its home though. We like it here."

Franklin smiled and closed the door to the fuse panel. "Well, maybe we can just replace all the fuses first. It would definitely be cheaper."

"Yes, we always try to do whatever we can to keep costs down," Ramon replied. "Being a church plant, we only get so much money from the mother church each year. I try to use as much of that as I can for the people in the neighborhood. The rest comes from donations."

Throughout the afternoon Ramon had been explaining the history of the mission church to Franklin. New Hope's fifth birthday celebration was slated for the upcoming spring. Franklin hoped he would still be working there when the event took place. He was looking forward to his new adventure in ministry and was willing to serve in any capacity he could. Ramon admired Franklin's eagerness.

"I like your zeal amigo," he said, rubbing Franklin's shoulder a couple of times.

"Ain't nothing wrong with a little hard work. My daddy instilled that in me when I was young. We Edwards have never been very fond of lazy people."

Ramon laughed. "The Ramirez family as well. Although, many of my people think God owes them something for their work."

"I was wondering about that," Franklin interjected. "Not to

generalize, but I was surprised that you aren't Catholic. I figure most Hispanic people are."

"I used to be," Ramon responded. "My whole family still is. But I was converted in college."

Franklin wiped some dust off his hands with his handkerchief and sat down on a stool in the small kitchen behind the sanctuary. "Mmm, I still think a lot of Catholics are Christians. I mean, they do believe in Jesus as their Lord and Savior. Their theology is a mess though."

Ramon frowned and nodded his head reluctantly. His mind quickly flashed back to his college days when his evangelical witness to Ilianna not only won him a soul for Christ, but also a wife.

"The family of Lana was not happy with us when we walked away from the Roman Catholic Church," Ramon said, shaking his head from side to side. "In fact, they shunned us for the longest time."

"Really?"

"Yes. Did not even come to our wedding. Only my side of the family did."

"Wow!"

"Oh yes. They figured we were headed straight for hell. Or purgatory at least."

Franklin raised his eyebrows in disbelief. "Well, what about their daughter? Or Cassie? How could they not want to see their grandbaby?"

Ramon's frown turned upside down. "That is what brought them back to us I guess. I mean, they still did not like our religious differences, but they didn't want to miss out on their grandchild growing up. Children are often the great equalizer."

Franklin began to grow a little sullen in response to that truth.

He obviously still missed his two little girls greatly. Ramon saw his friend's change in disposition.

"I am sorry. I did not mean to bring back bad memories for you."

Franklin sighed. "That's okay. They're really not bad memories. They're actually pleasant. It's still a struggle though."

Ramon got up and walked over and put his arm around Franklin's shoulder. "I know it is. But remember, me and Cassie are here now to help you through it."

"I believe that brother. I do."

Ramon went back and sat down on the other stool opposite Franklin.

"So, did they finally come around?" Franklin asked. "I mean, did Lana's mom and dad finally give up their Catholic ways when they saw Cassie?"

Ramon shook his head adamantly. "Oh no. In fact, they tried to convince Cassie that we were wrong every chance they got. You see, they are devout Catholics. They believe in works, the veneration of Mary, the whole deal. It was rough, still is sometimes when they visit us."

"How so?" Franklin asked.

Ramon rolled his eyes and grinned. "Well, I believe they think I am responsible for sending Lana into purgatory. They would not say that around Cassie of course. But I am sure they pray for the soul of my Lana every day. Though I can not prove it, I even think they snuck a priest into the hospital to perform last rites on her in those final days. Cassie told me she saw a priest leaving the hospital room the day before she died."

Franklin shook his head in disbelief.

"But you know, God is still sovereign," Ramon said. "It is still his world and anything that happens is under his providence. All I can do is pray her parents will someday know the truth. That is what I am called to do."

Franklin realized Ramon was correct.

❧❀☙

Continuing to seek guidance from Ilianna's portrait, Cassie queried her conscience on the subject of virtue. Was her blooming affection for Franklin pure in its nature? Did she entertain honorable motives toward the man she believed God had sent her? Was it even the Lord's will she was following? Could it be only untouched loneliness that had so captured her heart?

From what Cassie was able to remember, her mother had always displayed a picture of piety for those who knew her. Through her daughter's eyes, Ilianna was righteous, commendable, practically a saint right up until the very end of her life. Cassie had done her best to meet the lofty standard she saw in her mom, even going so far as contemplating living in a convent. Before marrying Ramon, Ilianna's family had been trying to direct her toward the solemn way of life. Becoming a Protestant quickly sacked that notion. So Cassie's grandma strongly pressed the issue on the young child, until Ramon caught wind of the subtle scheme and dashed any hope his mother-in-law had of his daughter becoming a nun.

The entire episode left Cassie confused and dismayed about her sexuality as she blossomed into womanhood. Her mindset had not changed.

"Oh what should I do mama?" Cassie pleaded to the painting. "I know I must be patient and wait on the Lord. All things in life are set through his timing, I know that. It's just that I've never felt this way before. Will it pass? What if Franklin never feels the same way? I couldn't bear it. I just couldn't."

Cassie started to sob, the disconcertment in her tears yet tempered by the joy filling her heart. How could happiness be so frustrating, she wondered? She needed so much to share her emotions with some one. Feelings of love must be heralded somehow. She wanted to go up to the roof and shout her merriment across the neighborhood, to anyone who might listen. But such an action wouldn't be rational at all. Franklin might hear her cry and laugh at such foolishness. He would certainly run away then and she would be crushed.

Cassie again focused on Ilianna, smearing her thin black mascara as she cleared the tears from her vision. Mama's dignified smile offered enough resolve to steer her lovesick daughter's sentiments back onto the appropriate course of action. Cassie knew if she wanted to align her process with her feelings, she must seek guidance from the only sure source of hope: the Bible.

She walked over to the thin, wooden bookshelf and pulled out her mother's well-worn black Bible. Not being a fan of the King James Version, Cassie hadn't read mother's Bible in years. She dusted off the binding and opened the front cover. Inside was a handwritten inscription from Ilianna's parents to their daughter. She read the message dated March 3rd, 1969: "To Our Sweet Angel on the day of your first communion, may the Father of our Lord and the Holy Virgin keep you in his loving embrace always, may his blessings continually flow to you and hold you firmly in his good graces. With tender love, Mama and Papa."

Cassie sniffled a couple of times and smiled. Grandma and grandpa had always been so sweet to their grandbaby, even if they didn't approve of their daughter and her husband's differing faith. Cassie continued to pray for her mother's parents. She asked the

Lord to enlighten them into the true meaning of his sacrifice on the cross. Cassie didn't know if they really understood the eternal gospel announced by the Savior. She hoped so.

Noticing the silk ribbon nestled between the sheer, browning pages, Cassie flipped to the marked passage. It was centered in the book of Second Corinthians. Her eyes found the first verse of chapter seven: "Having therefore these promises, dearly beloved, let us cleanse ourselves from all filthiness of the flesh and spirit, perfecting holiness in the fear of God."

Even in its outdated language, Cassie immediately understood the full meaning of the Lord's direction through his Word. As a believer, she must keep herself pure, in thought and deed, out of reverence to God.

Cassie put the Bible down on the couch. That one verse was all she needed to guide her. She folded her hands and bowed her head. She prayed for patience and perseverance in her quest for Franklin's love. She couldn't push the issue; God would have to bring Franklin's heart to hers. It was His will to be done, not hers. Cassie found herself grateful to the Lord as she looked up and cast her eyes upon her mother's portrait.

"Thank you as well," she whispered.

❦

A capacity crowd filled the sanctuary the spectacular Easter morning. Celebrating Christ's triumphant resurrection was the primary aim for the more than one-hundred in attendance. Their rousing voices resonated the glee in their hearts as they sang hymn after glorious hymn. Ramon elected to do a sermon cleverly playing off the letters of the church's name. The congregation was especially touched by the last letter in New Hope: E for eternity. Ramon explained how Jesus won eternal bliss for all his followers with his conquering of the final consequence of sin: death. The empty tomb proved Christ's victory over evil was secure. Ramon preached that those who placed their faith in Jesus should be "confident of their final destination and therefore free to live a life bearing fruit for their Savior."

Cassie and Franklin smiled at each other upon hearing those last words from Ramon's message. Over the past five months, they had both witnessed the fruits of their faithful labor for Christ. God had truly blessed their ministry to the poverty-stricken community where they lived and worked. It seemed the Holy Spirit was adding to their fold daily. One joyous example of the Spirit's work had occurred just the other night, during New Hope's week-long, fifth-anniversary celebration.

The pastor's daughter and his new best friend decided to forgo their normal Thursday night Bible study during Holy Week, opting instead to combine jubilee with reverence. They hosted sort of a special thanksgiving dinner for the dozen or so usual attendees to their mid-week small group. While Cassie spent most of the day preparing a meal centered on lamb as the main dish, Franklin set up a large table in the sanctuary and readied his devotional.

The group ate, laughed and thoroughly enjoyed one another's company that evening while celebrating their version of the Last Supper. Then Franklin stood at the head of the table and gave a short scripture reading from the book of John. He read from the thirteenth chapter, verses one through seventeen, which describes Jesus washing his disciple's feet. When he was finished reading, Franklin winked at Cassie, who was sitting at the opposite end of the long banquet table. She smiled and got up from her seat. She walked into the adjacent kitchen and Franklin followed behind her.

The rest of the party quizzically stared at each other and whispered among themselves.

A couple of minutes later, Franklin and Cassie returned from the kitchen, each holding a plastic bowl of water and a small white towel draped over their forearms. They knelt down before each person at the gathering, removed their shoes and proceeded to wash everyone's feet. Cassie took care of the women while Franklin catered to the men. Some were reluctant at first, but conceded to the honorable act. Others giggled and went along more easily with their hosts' servitude.

Just as they were wrapping up the biblical representation, Franklin noticed a haggardly man in a red bandana walking through the door. The bum looked strangely familiar, but Franklin couldn't place him at first. He walked over and greeted the one-eyed man, inviting him to join the party. The guy was a bit skittish when he saw Cassie finishing up washing an old lady's feet, but finally he came over to the table and sat down.

"Have I met you before?" Franklin asked the man, as Cassie prepared a plate of food for the scrawny, old beggar.

"Don't think so," the man responded, tearing into his portion like he hadn't eaten in days.

"Well, we're glad to have you here," Franklin said. "Enjoy your meal."

"Thank you," the man mumbled through a mouth full of meat and potatoes.

Franklin left the man alone to eat for a few minutes as the other guests put their shoes back on and got ready to go home. Cassie began to clean off the table and bring the dirty dishes to the kitchen.

The bum was still eating when the last person left. As Franklin helped Cassie clean up, he glanced back at the guy. He was sure he'd seen him before, but he couldn't place the location. Then it dawned on him.

"I got it," Franklin said as he handed a stack of plates to Cassie, who was washing the dishes in the sink.

"What?" she replied, blowing a wisp of hair from her eye.

"I know where I've seen that guy before," he said.

"Who?"

"The old guy out there who wandered into the party."

Cassie took the plates from Franklin and rinsed them off. "He seemed very hungry, that's for sure. I'm glad we had some food left over."

Franklin nodded and let out a big sigh. "Will you excuse me for a moment? There's something I've got to do."

"Sure," Cassie said as Franklin rushed from the kitchen.

"I hope he hasn't left yet."

When Franklin went back into the sanctuary, he found the man nearly asleep at the table, his head resting on his arms. Franklin tapped him on the shoulder.

"What?" the startled man said, nearly jumping from his sit. "Oh, okay, I'm leaving."

Franklin smiled at the poor guy, whose gray beard managed to catch the pieces his meal that missed his mouth. "I know where I've seen you before."

"I didn't do it, I swear! You've got the wrong guy!"

The man's defensive antics caused Franklin to laugh. The old guy was obviously accustomed to be accosted by suspicious characters. Franklin tried to quickly alleviate his concern.

"Whoa there buddy," said Franklin, as he patted the man on the back a couple of times. "I just want to talk to you for a minute. In fact, I think I may owe you an apology."

The bum was bewildered by Franklin's statement. "Uh? I don't think I know ya."

"Yeah, you do. You probably just don't remember."

The man didn't say a word, just shrugged his shoulders.

"Sure, it was about six months ago when I first came to this town."

The man drank a few sips of water from a cup on the table, not knowing who had drunk from it previously. In his world, such aspects of cleanliness were of no matter anyway.

"I had just gotten off the bus at the station by the beach," Franklin continued. "I was extremely drunk and in a very bad way. You were sleeping on a bench in the park. I remember your red bandana."

"Okay, so," the man responded, pulling on his unkempt beard.

"Well, I'm afraid I did something to you that I'm ashamed of."

"Oh yeah, what?" The bum's one bloodshot brown eye intently focused on the stranger who seemed to tower above him.

Franklin took a deep breath, feeling a touch of remorse come over him. "I pulled you off the bench by your collar and threw you to the ground. I wanted the bench for myself to sleep on."

"What did I do?"

"Nothing, you just ran away."

The man squinted his eye and stared at Franklin. "I don't remember it."

Franklin sat down in a chair next to the old guy.

"Look, I'm very sorry for doing that to you. I don't usually act that way. Like I said, I was in a bad way. But that's no excuse. Really, I'm sorry."

The old man offered a slight grin. "Ah, don't worry about it." The dozens of gallons of beer and wine he had consumed since that night had so soused the old man's brain that he didn't recall anything about the incident. Anyway, it certainly wasn't the first time he'd been roused from a drunken stupor and lost his perch in the park.

Franklin didn't remind the man about the retaliation that night. It was a time for repentance and to ask for forgiveness. Besides, the beating the bum's buddies had unleashed upon Franklin is what God used to steer him to the place he was at that point. Franklin was actually thankful and wanted to return the grace he himself had been shown by the Lord through Ramon and Cassie. They had become like family to him.

"You know, it's still kind of cool outside tonight," Franklin commented to the old guy. "Why don't you crash on one of the pews here? I'll get you a pillow and blanket from the back."

The bum's eye lit up. "That would be great! Thanks!"

Franklin smiled at the man. It felt good to serve someone in need. "Not a problem. There's a restroom in the back if you want to use it."

The old guy grinned and took another drink of water. Franklin left to retrieve a pillow and blanket from his own bed.

Cassie had been listening in on the whole episode from behind the hallway door. She rushed back into the kitchen as Franklin approached. She did want him to know she had been eavesdropping again. Nosiness was one of her secret sins. Franklin stopped into the kitchen and told Cassie of his plans to let the man stay the night. She agreed and continued to wipe clean the sink for a second time, having already finished her kitchen duties. Franklin went to his room.

Cassie was so proud of Franklin's actions. His kindness to the old bum was a sign of true repentance. She also noticed Franklin didn't remind the bum of the beating his cronies had dished out in reprisal. Franklin had confirmed to her a fact she already knew. He lived out the gospel in both word and deed. He forgave because he had been forgiven himself. Franklin displayed he truly loved his neighbor even if he was still relearning how to love himself. And for that, Cassie found her love for Franklin deepening more with each passing day.

⚜

On an unusually hot spring evening about six weeks later, Cassie walked in on Franklin sniffling with his head lowered in prayer. She wondered if he had caught a cold or just come down with the flu. But as she approached him while he sat in the front pew, she quickly saw that his sniffles were accompanied by tears.

"Oh Franklin, what's the matter?" Cassie asked as she sat next to him and placed her right hand on his knee. "Are you not feeling well?"

Franklin looked up, his glassy, brown eyes meeting Cassie's concerned gaze. He immediately broke down, sobbing profusely as he laid his head on top of her hand. She reached over and wrapped her free arm around his slumping shoulder. Her own eyes began to swell as he unleashed a torrent of sorrow, his tears flowing freely from his cheeks down her wrist.

Cassie made sure to let the bawling abate before saying another word. She was certain Franklin would share with her the reason for being upset. They had grown so much closer through the months, though not as near as Cassie would have liked. Still, she had learned to rely on the patience for which she'd been praying.

A couple of minutes passed before Franklin raised his head and started to wipe the tears from his eyes. Cassie brushed away a few tears of her own and smiled sympathetically at him. He managed a snicker, somewhat embarrassed at his breakdown.

"Where did that come from?" she softly asked.

Franklin looked up at the lighted cross and sighed deeply. He closed his eyes and shook his head, as if trying to urge the distress to flee his mind. Cassie misunderstood his action.

"Oh Franklin," she said almost despondently, "I wish you could learn to forgive yourself. God has."

"It's not that," Franklin quickly responded, staring up at the cross again.

"Then what honey?" Cassie asked. "What's wrong?"

Franklin looked back at her and smiled, realizing the endearing term she had just said to him. The tone wasn't quite the same as when his mother called him honey. The inflection in Cassie's voice was steeper, like it was delivered unwittingly from the inner reaches of her heart. There was passion, as well as compassion, in her query.

"A bitter reality struck me today when I woke up and I've been fighting it all day," he said.

Cassie didn't follow. "How so?"

Franklin took another deep breath before continuing.

"I realized it was one year ago today when I lost Sara, Ashley and Brianna," he said, staring straight ahead like that would help him hold back further tears. It helped, but not completely, He blinked a few times before covering his eyes.

Cassie wrapped both arms around him and placed her head against his neck. It was a forward move, but she didn't care. She immediately felt his pain as he sobbed for about five minutes.

"I am so sorry," she said.

Franklin leaned his head against hers. The embrace brought

instant comfort and eased his sorrow greatly. Then he heard Cassie sniffle twice.

"I didn't mean to make you cry also," he whispered.

"When you hurt, I hurt," she replied, still holding him tightly as if fearing he would escape from her.

Franklin's mood changed suddenly. His grief transformed to glee in a matter of seconds. What was going on? How could his feelings have progressed so quickly? One minute his insides were wretched from missing Sara and the girls. The next, he felt an unexpected urge to kiss Cassie. Was he that shallow?

Thankfully, Cassie broke the awkward silence they both sensed.

"Franklin, you know how much I care for you, don't you?" she asked, still clinging to him.

"Yes I do," he replied humbly.

"And you know I will do anything I can for you right?"

An anxious smile displayed the building elation brewing inside his heart. "I know that. You're such a loving girl. I didn't think I would ever meet anybody like you again."

Cassie finally released her grasp on Franklin. She sat up and looked him straight in the eyes. Her nerve was fading fast, so she knew she must spill her soul as quickly as possible.

"I'm in love with you," she blurted out before courage failed her. "I've known it since the first day I met you." Cassie's eyes began to mist. "I don't know if it's appropriate to tell you at this time. But I can't hold it in any longer. I can't."

Cassie started to weep. The relief over finally telling Franklin her feelings was tainted by the rising discomfort in her gut. Now that her emotions were laid bare for him to see, she longed desperately for his response. Time seemed to stand still at that point.

Franklin rubbed Cassie's shoulders as she wept. Her admission wasn't a shock to him. He had sensed the bond growing between them for months. But he'd suppressed his own sentiments out of deference to his departed wife. He didn't know if falling for another woman so soon after his Sara's death was proper. Being with Davilla was certainly not love, just sinful sex that had led him into big trouble. His feelings for Cassie were not at all the same. He was attracted to her, no denying that. But he also admired and respected her. That's where the difference lies.

Cassie had her face buried between both her hands. Franklin gently reached his hand under her chin and turned her face toward his. He smiled delicately at her. She sniffled a few times and smiled back. He didn't utter a single syllable. He leaned forward and passionately kissed her. The touching of their lips gave Cassie her answer.

⁂

After much fasting and prayer, Franklin and Cassie each discerned God was calling them to unite as one flesh. There was really not much point to dating; they already knew each other so well. For basically the sake of formality, they went out to dinner and the movies a few times. However, they always found themselves laughing at such ritual. The courtship had commenced, for all intent and purpose, the moment each laid eyes on the other that first day in the sanctuary. Betrothal was predestined, but neither one was fully aware of God's intentions until He had set his plan into action.

The Lord was working out all the details.

A few months after Franklin settled in at New Hope, Ramon convinced him to reconnect with his family back home. Franklin had been too ashamed of his foolish behavior since Sara's death to inform even his mother about his failings. The letters he wrote to

Gracie were short and sweet, always lacking the pertinent details of his situation. Sam had altogether no idea of Franklin's misfortune. Needless to say, both his mother and his best friend were shocked when Franklin fessed up to his problems.

Gracie was ready to hop the first jet to Los Angeles when she heard the news. But Franklin persuaded her to stay in Kansas and care for sickly Aunt Ethel, promising to telephone every week. Being the ever-doting mother, Gracie only agreed to stay put if her son would accept her monetary help. It was then Franklin fully realized the effects of Davilla's cunning.

Franklin Edwards no longer existed, at least according to every financial institution. His identity had been wiped clean. The first time he tried to cash his paycheck from the church, he was turned away by a check-cashing store because of no valid identification. Ramon gave Franklin cash instead, but insisted he touch base with his Florida roots. Cassie also pushed Franklin to face his past, knowing their future together would be influenced by his willingness to rearrange his life. One heartbreaking call to Sam was all it took to get Franklin back on track.

Thanks to Sam's friendship with a highly-placed government official, Franklin was able to obtain a social security number and acquire a California driver's license. Sam also deposited a few thousand dollars in a secured account under Franklin's name at a nationwide bank. The Simmons' were known as generous benefactors with their wealth, so bailing out a fallen son was just one of many loving acts by Franklin's father in the faith.

Repentance had led to blessing for Franklin, just like God's Word abundantly promised. Franklin vowed to put his blessing to faithful use for the Lord. He made the woman he loved a top priority.

About a month after confessing their love for each other,

Franklin proposed to Cassie.

A postcard-worthy sunset brilliantly etched across the Southern California sky that summer evening. Cassie held Franklin's hand has they strolled along the beach just as the bright city lights began to overcome the setting sun. Ironically, it was the very same stretch of sand that Franklin hopelessly meandered along the previous fall. How much life had improved since that time, Franklin thought. He prayed silent thanksgiving to the Lord for not allowing him to wallow forever in misery.

Cassie stopped walking. She reached down and picked up a shell that had just washed in from the cool surf.

"Wow honey, look at how white this is," she said, holding up the shell to the quickly-fading remnants of twilight. "It looks like it's been bleached clean. It's so pure. How beautiful."

Franklin smiled at Cassie and took the shell from her hand.

"Oh, don't drop it now; I want to keep it," she said.

Franklin rubbed the shell on his T-shirt, blew on it a couple of times and rubbed it some more. He held it up and inspected it.

"Not bad," he said.

Cassie punched him on the arm and pouted. "Hey. I think it's lovely. Pure as virgin snow. You agree, no?"

Franklin giggled. Cassie batted her eyes and tilted her head to one side.

"Come here you," Franklin said as he pulled Cassie into his arms. He kissed her deeply as he put the shell into the pocket of his shorts.

"What did you do with the shell?" Cassie asked after they broke their embrace.

A tear rolled down Franklin's cheek as he looked at Cassie's glistening eyes. This was to be a moment he wanted to cherish forever. The luster of the evening had already tapped his soul,

"I have it," he said. "But I would like to trade you something for it."

"Oh, for what?" she asked coyly. "That shell is one of the prettiest treasures of God's creation I've seen in a while."

Franklin nodded his head in agreement. He reached back into his pocket. "I believe you'll think this is even prettier."

He took Cassie's left hand and placed a small, felt-covered box in it. He closed her hand and smiled.

Cassie opened her hand and gasped. She slowly opened the box. The first sight of the tiny diamond shimmering in the glow of the streetlights that had just flicked on overhead brought forth an immediate stream of tears. She threw her arms around Franklin and kissed his neck.

"Yes!" she screamed, "yes!"

Franklin held her and kissed her until the last rays of sunlight flickered into the ocean.

Cassie laid her head on her fiancé's shoulder as they walked the four blocks back to the church. They both soaked in the glory of the moment. Nothing else needed to be said.

～❖～

Maintaining purity throughout their engagement would prove a formidable burden for the newly betrothed.

Cassie treasured her chastity, yet longed for ultimate intimacy with Franklin. With the planning of the nuptials still in the infant stages, she knew the challenge would be great. She found her willpower through prayer and scripture study.

Franklin, on the other hand, accepted that he was more easily susceptible to the desires of the flesh. His dalliance with Davilla readily proved that point. He tried to curb his lust for Cassie, reminding himself she was the daughter of one of his best friends. That thought alone was usually incentive enough to thwart any prospective yearning to deflower his beloved.   Still, despite each of their best efforts over the next couple of months, they were often barraged by the evil one's enticements. Hormones were sent raging like impatient teenagers by the most subtle of glances. An unsolicited glimpse of future amorous delicacy forced a nearly nauseous quenching of desire. Hearts would race and heads would spin by the most accidental brushing of bodies passing by too closely.

Satan's devices for sin were unrelenting, and he used most every weapon in his arsenal he could think of to try and trip them up. Cassie and Franklin fought back valiantly in their effort to remain sexually virtuous until wedlock. But they nearly lost their battle one evening, before God stepped in to help.

After finishing dinner with the happy couple, Ramon left for the monthly board meeting by the elders of New Hope's parent church downtown. Franklin was helping Cassie with the dishes, drying as she washed. He couldn't fend off his childish antics, snapping her bare leg with the wet end of the dishtowel.

"Ooh, you've done it now!" Cassie exclaimed, her terse expression tempered only by the slight smile trying to sneak out from between her pursed lips.

Two handfuls of soapy water found their mark, soaking Franklin's face and green Dolphins T-shirt. He retaliated with another crack, this time to her rump.

"Stop!" she cried.

Franklin laughed. "Make me."

Cassie grabbed the towel as Franklin tried for another crack. She managed to pull it from his grasp and spun it over a few times.

"You know what they say about paybacks, no?"

Franklin stuck out his tongue and giggled. "No."

"Well, you going to find out."

He turned and ran into the living room as she directed a couple of misguided snaps his way. Franklin jumped over the couch and rolled onto his back. He raised his arms and then covered up as Cassie snapped him a few more times with the towel. He reached up, snatched the other end of the towel and pulled his fiancé down on top of him. She giggled with delight before he put his arm around her head and brought her lips to his to mark a truce.

"Oooh, you're getting me all wet," Cassie said as she sat up.

"Well, you're the one who splashed," Franklin responded, as he removed the sopped shirt.

"Yes, but you started it," she replied, finding herself becoming excited at the sight of his muscular chest and broad shoulders.

Franklin held both ends of the dishtowel, brought it behind Cassie's neck and used it to once again pull her down to him. She didn't resist any further. Passion consumed them as they made out heavily.

They had always tried to make sure they were never left alone in the upstairs apartment. Franklin was steadfast about heading back down to his room before Ramon turned in for bed. Sometimes Cassie would walk him to the front door and kiss him goodnight, but they always wrapped up the evening there.

The intensity of her current affection would not let Cassie pull away from him as usual. She loved the feeling of his bare chest pressing up against her. She needed to feel her soft skin lying on top of his. She was unable to control her desire any longer.

Cassie broke her kiss from Franklin and sat up. She let out a deep sigh to relieve her nerves. Franklin noticed the blissful shine in her hungry eyes. She undid the top two buttons on her silky white blouse before deciding to pull the garment up over her head. She leaned down and kissed her man again while she unsnapped the back of her bra and pulled it out from between their bodies.

Flesh pressed against flesh. There was no turning back now. Their love had to be consummated!

Then the doorbell rang.

Cassie sat up quickly, startled back into the reality of staining her virtue as the ringer sounded off once more. She hopped off the couch and snatched her bra and blouse from off the floor, donning the clothing as briskly as she had removed it.

"Just a minute," she shouted toward the door. "I'll be right there."

Franklin got up and started to put back on his wet shirt.

"Honey, go into papa's room and put on one of his shirts for now," Cassie ordered.

Franklin let out a frustrated moan and hastily walked to Ramon's room. Cassie caught her breath, fixed her ruffled hair and answered the door.

She was greeted by a young couple whom Franklin would remember immediately.

Chapter XI

O nly God is able to truly discern intentions. His creatures must rely on supposition. Apply passion, and determining purpose often reaches a point where clear perception is tragically clouded. The free will the Divine also allows to every individual sometimes trumps sound reason. So, obscured comprehension can ultimately define the difficulty of the path one follows. For two couples, the road ahead would prove to be especially bumpy.

⤞◆⤜

Cassie was still trying to regain her composure as she greeted the dark-haired young man and the striking blond girl standing in her doorway. She wondered if there was any way they had seen or heard the lust-filled episode going on inside the apartment before ringing the doorbell. She didn't know either of them, but if they had sensed any hint of impropriety, she would have been mortified.

"Is this New Hope Church?" the blond girl demurely asked, appearing not to have noticed the previous indiscretion.

"Yes it is," Cassie quickly replied. "Well, downstairs."

Cassie smiled politely at the couple, who didn't immediately forward the reason they had come to the place that evening. "Can I help you with something?"

The girl cupped her hand to her mouth, seemingly embarrassed about the awkward silence. "Oh, I'm sorry. My name's Gretchen." She reached out and shook Cassie's hand. "This is Troy."

Troy shook Cassie's hand as well. "How do you do?" he said, noticing the top button on her blouse was missing. Cassie smiled at Troy, uncomfortably aware that his eyes were wandering the course of her body. Gretchen then realized Cassie had no idea about who they were.

"I phoned Pastor Ramirez this morning. He said that it would be alright if we stopped by tonight to talk about a ministry opportunity you might have available. Is he not here?"

Cassie shrugged her shoulders and rolled her eyes. "Oh papa," she sighed. "I'm his daughter Cassie. I'm sorry, but sometimes my father is forgetful. He didn't say a word to me...Won't you come inside."

Gretchen and Troy entered the apartment just as Franklin was leaving the back bedroom, wearing Ramon's dark blue New Hope polo shirt. He was understandably surprised to find two of his former students there to greet him.

"Oh my gosh!" he exclaimed, briskly walking over to greet them. "Troy. Gretchen. What are you doing here?"

Gretchen, always one to act on emotional impulse, immediately grasped her teacher in a bear hug.

"Mr. Edwards," she said, "Dr. Simmons told us you were working here. It's so good to see you again. How are you doing?"

"Just great Gretchen," Franklin replied, as he glanced over her shoulder toward Cassie, who looked bemused by the scene unfolding in her home. "I'm surprised to see you."

Franklin let go of Gretchen and shook Troy's hand. "How are you doing man?"

"Fine. Good to see you again, Mr. Edwards."

Troy noticed Franklin seemed to be fully recovered from the tragic loss in his past. It was kind of awkward for Troy to see Franklin smiling so freely. He wondered how the widower had bounced back so quickly. He'd heard rumors from Florida that Franklin had gone through a very rough time during the past year, but he didn't fully know the details.

"So what brings you to this part of the country?" Franklin asked.

"We're both going to college here Mr. Edwards," Gretchen answered, her crystal blue eyes beaming with joy over seeing Franklin again. "UCLA. Troy and I are just beginning our sophomore years. We love it out here. California's so beautiful."

"Yes, it really is," Franklin replied, still amazed he was standing in the middle of the living room talking to some old friends from Florida. He really didn't miss his former state much, but still harbored a longing for the faithful back home.

Troy remained unusually silent while Gretchen did most of the talking. She explained that she and Troy had hooked up with the denomination's national mission's team and were looking for a place to serve the poor in Los Angeles. They were advised by the mission's agency to call New Hope. Franklin was delighted to see two of his former students still doing the Lord's work since graduating high school. Theirs was a success story for Good Shepherd Christian School, or so Franklin thought.

As they continued to get reacquainted, Franklin directed Troy and Gretchen to the couch while Cassie fetched two chairs from the kitchen. She placed the chairs directly across from their guests and sat down next to Franklin.

"Thank you dear," Franklin said to Cassie, suddenly realizing in the excitement of the moment that he failed to introduce her as his fiancé. "Oh! I've got some news for you guys."

Franklin winked at Cassie and took her hand in his. "This is my lovely bride to be," he announced, as Cassie turned and cast a loving glance toward her future husband and placed her hand on top of his.

Gretchen immediately jumped up from the couch and raced over to squeeze Cassie tightly.

"Congratulations," she said, a joyful tear managing to find its way down her face. "I'm so happy for you Mr. Edwards."

"Please call me Franklin, Gretchen," he interrupted. "We are no longer in the classroom."

Gretchen smiled brightly. "Okay, Franklin."

She reached down and touched Cassie's left hand. "Can I see the ring?"

Cassie proudly displayed the small diamond Franklin had given her months before at the beach. He hoped to bestow upon her a much larger token of his love when they were married. At the time, the tiny diamond was all he could afford. The size of the ring didn't matter at all to Cassie. It was the symbolism that counted for her.

"Oh, it's lovely," Gretchen said, smiling delicately at Cassie. Gretchen, herself, had been longing for more than a year for Troy to ask her hand in marriage. She'd dreamed of marrying Troy since she was a little girl. But the fantasy had not yet materialized, despite Gretchen's best efforts. She had even forsaken her virginity for him. Still, Troy always told her the timing for marriage wasn't quite right yet. He would know when they were ready and insisted that she be patient. Selfishness always had been a trait passed down through generations of Battles men. The self-centered gene was firmly imbedded in Troy's DNA.

Cassie immediately sensed Gretchen's yearning. The hunger shone deeply in the pretty girl's eyes, the brilliant sparkle of which still failed to cover her hidden hurt. Cassie could relate. She'd often felt the same as Gretchen, until becoming engaged to Franklin. Maybe she could encourage the young lady if they became friends? Although she had just met Gretchen, Cassie already felt a certain kinship toward her, at least from the perspective of Christian sisterhood.

The two women talked liked they'd known each other for years as Cassie brewed a pot of coffee in the small kitchen. They discussed topics like faith, fashion and college life, even joking about the intense cross-town rivalry between USC and UCLA. They laughed loudly as they shook hands and agreed not to let the contentiousness of their two schools hamper possible friendship.

"I guess Christ loves Trojans and Bruins equally," Cassie noted as she playfully patted Gretchen on the back a couple of times.

"He does... He just created Bruins first," Gretchen replied with a sly wink.

Cassie rolled her eyes and pursed her lips, feigning offense. "Hey now, watch it. We agreed."

Gretchen burst out in a rolling giggle. "Just kidding."

Cassie brought a tray of coffee and cookies into the living room, where Franklin and Troy were recalling some old times back in Florida. Their discussion had naturally proceeded on a predictable course toward a passion they both shared: auto racing.

Troy wasn't about to bring up the topic, considering his bitter feelings toward Franklin when the two competed against one another on the track. He also didn't think Franklin would want to be reminded about the tragic fate of his race car, and it occupants, on that rain-slickened stretch of Florida interstate more than a year before. But it was Franklin who touched on the subject when he asked Troy about Joe Beacon's health. Franklin had heard that the old mechanic was having some recurring heart problems.

"Honestly, he didn't look so good when I saw him over the summer," Troy said of Joe.

"Really?" Franklin replied with a frown, realizing that he might not see his dear friend again. "I hope he gets better. Troy, I really miss that old hick."

Troy nodded in agreement. "He's a great guy. Best mechanic I've ever seen. He helped both of us a lot, I know that."

Franklin couldn't resist needling Troy a little bit. "Maybe me more than you, huh?" Franklin said with a shrewd grin.

Troy smirked snidely. He knew Franklin was just messing with him about the dusting teacher gave pupil during their last head-to-head encounter on the track. But Troy was never one to let even the slightest dig at his ego not bother him. For some reason, when the barb came from Franklin, whether in jest or not, it pierced even deeper. But it wasn't the time for a sarcastic comeback, although the remark made him seethe inside.

Knowing her man well, Gretchen saw Troy had taken offense.

"Now boys," she said, placing her hands on her hips and batting her eyes, "let's not go down that road again. You know how racing churns the blood in both of you the wrong way sometimes. Behave."

Franklin started to chuckle. "I'm sorry Troy," he said somewhat apologetically. "I was only having some fun with you. Gretchen's right. I guess we take our racing too seriously sometimes."

Troy responded with a fake laugh that barely hid his long, deeply-rooted resentment of Franklin. Jealousy of his former teacher's many talents had built up a growing animosity in the past that easily manufactured discontent, the results of which most often proved harmful.

"No problem," Troy said, holding up both arms in false surrender, smirking as he looked away. "Don't get the chance to do much racing out here that's for sure. She won't let me."

Gretchen stuck her tongue out at her boyfriend.

"Don't stick that thing out unless you're gonna use it," Troy responded with a curt wink.

Gretchen put her arms over Troy's shoulders and gave him a slight peck on the cheek.

Cassie smiled and stared at the curious couple. She knew there was something peculiar about their bond. She wondered what kept them together. Outwardly, they paired up beautifully. But there was something about the match that wasn't quite uniform inside. Over the coming months, she would find ample opportunity to discover the reason for her concern.

❧❖❧

"Follow my lead and let me do the talking, will ya?" Troy told Gretchen rather sternly before they knocked on the door to Ramon's office that steamy Saturday morning in late August.

He had been irritated with his girlfriend since their impromptu meeting with Franklin and Cassie two nights earlier. Troy was always one who wanted plans to follow the path of his choice and he felt Gretchen had taken over too much of the conversation with their former teacher and his fiancé. But she couldn't help herself. The bubbly personality God had given her was so infectious it was quick to permeate most all who met her. Nearly everybody they encountered loved Gretchen. It was hard not to do, after all. Her delicate beauty immediately captured the attention of men while her elegant charm easily found the good graces of women. Sometimes, she was just too nice for Troy's liking.

"Okay dear," Gretchen replied smartly, perturbed at Troy's usual domineering attitude.

He rolled his eyes and shook his head. "Well, this is an important interview for my future," he said, knocking on the door.

"You mean our future, don't you?" she responded.

Troy sighed deeply. "Whatever."

Ramon opened the door and welcomed in the couple, who were surprised to find Cassie and Franklin sitting side-by-side at a conference table in the office. Gretchen immediately walked over to Cassie and gave her a friendly hug. It was clear a sisterly connection had been made the first time they met. Troy shook Franklin's hand and sat down across the table from him. Gretchen took the seat next to her boyfriend.

Cassie prayed to open the meeting before Ramon explained the various aspects of the two volunteer intern positions available at New Hope that fall. He also apologized again for his absent-mindedness in missing their appointment two nights earlier. Cassie smiled at her father, who looked away sheepishly. He knew his daughter had been hounding him to find a better way to keep track of his time. Ramon again promised Cassie he would try to remember to write his appointments down in the spiral calendar book she had bought him. Ramon didn't know his forgetfulness the other night had almost provided a highly-embarrassing moment for his daughter, as well as Franklin, who threw a quick wink Cassie's way. She grinned shyly as she looked away from her man, remembering once more just how close they had come to prematurely indulging in a blessing not supposed to be shared until their wedding night.

"So tell me a little about yourselves," Ramon said to Troy and

Gretchen. "I have read the letter you wrote me when inquiring about the ministry. But I would like to get to know you better personally. Maybe you could each give your testimony on how you came to believe in Jesus as you Lord and Savior. Would you like go first Gretchen?"

Gretchen's eyes lit up. She loved to talk about her personal walk with God. It was easy for her to tell of her deep love for Christ. She had always loved him, ever since she could remember. In fact, she had never known any differently. She explained Christ had always lived in her heart and was profoundly aware that she was a child in his sight, just like one of the children Jesus spoke of in the Bible. Whenever she shared about the love God held for her, Gretchen couldn't help but feel tearfully humbled by the covenant He had made with her. He was her Lord, her Savior, her reason for living.

"You see," Gretchen said, wiping away a couple of rolling teardrops with her index fingers, "how could I not want to serve him? He's given me life itself, eternal life in fact. I owe him everything I am. I can't pay him back for what He did for me on the cross, nor do I want to. It's a debt I could never repay, I know that. My sins are and will always be too great. But I do want to serve him in any way I can to show him how much I love him."

Cassie passed Gretchen a small box of tissues that were always kept close at hand in the office.

"Thank you," Gretchen said, slightly embarrassed by her sniffles. Cassie nodded and smiled at her sister in the faith. Franklin had long ago witnessed Gretchen's belief in the Lord's grace. He had seen her faith bear much fruit while serving in the youth groups at Good Shepherd. He knew she was a fine, young Christian woman.

"So you think you might be happy serving our Lord here in the inner city?" Ramon asked.

Gretchen dabbed her eyes once more with a tissue. "Yes I do sir, if you'll have me?"

Ramon was surely pleased by Gretchen's humility. He moved his eyes quickly to Franklin and Cassie. Their broad grins displayed their concurrence. "It would be our pleasure for you to join us in this mission," Ramon stated.

Cassie got up from her seat and walked over to hug Gretchen. She gently kissed her new partner on the cheek after letting go and returning to her dingy brown folding chair.

"What about you Troy?" Franklin asked. "Why do you want to serve with us?"

Rarely did Troy, or any male member of the Battles clan for that matter, ever find need to explain his intentions to any one. But on that occasion, he was aware that he had a multitude of reasons for needing to do God's work at the mission. His primary motive for doing anything, however, was always self-serving, always had been, and always would be. And over the scant twenty years of his young life, Troy Battles learned to excel at covering up his true intentions in any situation. He had become quite adept at deception, especially when it served his selfish purpose. Even his childhood sweetheart Gretchen was fooled time and again by his narcissistic ploys. Troy figured he would have little problem deceiving his former teacher and the others about his main incentive for wanting to volunteer at New Hope. His act wouldn't even require his best performance.

"I'm always touched and humbled by her testimony," Troy mumbled, as he cast his eyes down toward his folded hands in his lap. "It is one reason I love her."

Gretchen placed one of her hands in Troy's and softly ran her fingers over them a couple of times.

"I too want to serve our Lord," he continued. "I know I've

been truly blessed in my life. First of all, the cross changed my life. It changed all of our lives. Without salvation, nothing else really matters does it?"

Franklin looked at Troy and nodded yes in response to his question. Franklin had lived out that fact firsthand over the course of the last year or so.

"I come from a wealthy family. I've never really had to struggle for anything in my life, especially the basic necessities. You know, driving over here this morning, Gretchen and I were both saddened by what we saw in this run-down neighborhood. Not just the trash all over the place or the squalor in which people live here. But what got to me the most was the destitute looks on their faces. You can easily see that most of them have no reason for hope at all." Troy swallowed hard and looked into Ramon's inquisitive eyes. "When I read the Bible, I can't help but notice how intensely Jesus was drawn to the poor. He lived among them. He served them."

"He loved them," Cassie interjected.

"That's exactly right," Troy responded. "And that's what I want to do also. Loving the poor is something I realize I'm going to have to learn how to do. I know I've been spoiled in my life. I've had most everything handed to me. Nice clothes, beautiful house, cars, private school."

Franklin smiled at the level of anxiousness in Troy's voice. He was glad to see that Troy realized his blessings.

"Look, I don't want to sound preachy, but I've, actually we've," Troy pointed at Gretchen and then himself, "had it too good. We're spoiled, and in many ways been sheltered from life's hardships. I know that. I know I need to get some real-life experience after living in high society so long. It's one of the reason's we didn't attend a private Christian college. To be blunt, I know I need to see how the other half lives. After all, Jesus didn't come to live here with all the trappings of his kingdom. He came and lived here as a pauper even though He was a king."

"He still is," Ramon added.

Troy agreed. "You're absolutely right. He still is a king and I need to learn to live as less of one."

Gretchen reached over and hugged her boyfriend. She loved it when he got up on his soapbox for all the right reasons, not for his usual selfish motives. She saw that he could be sweet during the times when his intentions were noble, even if others didn't see him in the same light as she did. But her undying love for Troy had always been Gretchen's undoing. She did tend to overlook his dire shortcomings, which would often exact a severe toll on her heart. She never understood that her love for Troy was nowhere near as great as his love for himself. It never would be either.

Troy had easily won them over with his deceptive soliloquy. Neither Ramon, Franklin, Cassie, nor especially Gretchen, understood Troy had ulterior motives for wanting to serve at New Hope Church.

It wouldn't be until months later that any of them found out Troy was really just trying to impress his demanding father, who strongly urged him to do whatever was necessary to earn the required community service points needed to gain entry into a prestigious graduate school.

Later that afternoon, while reflecting on the meeting alone in her bedroom, Cassie realized Troy hadn't given a true statement of faith in Jesus Christ. She began to have doubts about the sincerity of his profession, about whether he had really made a profession of faith at all. She began to worry about his real reasons for showing up at New Hope. What was he up to, she wondered? Did he really believe in Jesus as his Lord and Savior? He had never actually said so.

Cassie decided it might be best for all involved to keep her concerns to herself for the time being. After all, she felt a growing love for Gretchen Bjorn. But as for Troy Battles, Cassie couldn't dispel her increasing mistrust. Her instincts told her to keep a close eye on him.

❦

The first commemoration for the infamous events of September 11, 2001 had just passed the day before, as Franklin sat down at the table. About a dozen or so members of New Hope's weekly small group Bible study were congregating in the sanctuary that Thursday evening, discussing the television coverage marking the anniversary of the tragedy. Conversation in the group turned to the subject of misguided faith.

An older Mexican woman wondered aloud why Americans quickly turn to God in times of calamity, like was the case when thousands of lives were lost as the twin towers fell, but then drop by the wayside when the adversity inevitably subsides.

"The people in this country only want God when they are in trouble," scolded the wrinkled, gray-haired lady, who had befriended Cassie just two weeks prior while shopping in the neighborhood market. "I don't understand you Americans. You are very forgetful people, no?"

Cassie smiled at the old lady. "Yes we are Migdalia. My grandmamma always says people in the old country appreciate what they have a lot more. And that includes their God. I just pray that we can regain some of the zeal for God that we had after that terrible day. But I'm afraid that most care more about the country they live in now than where they will reside for eternity. It's sad, but we still must pray. God is still in control. I do believe that is true."

Migdalia seemed satisfied with Cassie's answer and the group began to pray for renewed spiritual vigor in the hearts of all Americans. The nation would need as much prayer as possible as its leaders prepared to enact retribution against the terrorists responsible for the heinous acts. Full-scale war was just around the corner and everybody sensed as much.

It was Franklin's turn to lead the devotional that evening. He and Cassie would alternate weeks guiding the group, and both were hoping to get Gretchen and Troy more involved with such duties as well. Franklin asked the members of the gathering to turn in their Bibles to the book of Second Chronicles, chapter thirty-three. He read the entire chapter to them and then asked a question.

"Where do you think King Manasseh is now?"

The men and women, who were a wide variety of nationalities and walks, looked at Franklin in confusion. He noticed they didn't understand the gist of his question, so he asked more specifically.

"From what we just read, do you believe that King Manasseh went to heaven or hell when he died?" Franklin asked with a sly grin on his face. "All the passage tells us is that "Manasseh rested with his fathers and was buried in his palace.' It doesn't say whether he received eternal salvation or not, does it?"

Many in the crowd shook their heads no.

"Okay, so we can't know for sure whether Manasseh went to heaven or hell," Franklin continued. "Now, we do know from our reading that he was possibly the most evil king Judah ever had. In fact, Jewish tradition holds that he was such a wicked king that he even killed one of God's most righteous prophets, Isaiah. He ordered the prophet placed between two wooden planks and sawed in half." Franklin cringed at the thought. "King Manasseh obviously deserved eternal damnation for his wicked deeds, right?"

The group nodded yes.

"Well, you know what I think?" Franklin asked. "I think Manasseh most probably is enjoying the bliss of heaven with our Lord right now...Why is that?"

Troy didn't bother to raise his hand before quickly blurting out "he repented."

Franklin slowly rubbed the evening whiskers on his chin, pleased at Troy's response.

"Yep, that's correct. You see, despite his wickedness, it appears King Manasseh found his faith in God. The Lord forgave him and restored him when he repented. And Manasseh went on to do many great things for the Lord. It was an amazing turnabout."

Franklin paused for a moment to let the message sink in. Cassie smiled admiringly at her fiancé. She loved the zest he exuded when he presented a hope-filled devotional. She had witnessed his own amazing turnaround over the past months. She was so proud of the faithfulness he himself had regained.

"Now, yesterday we remembered the events of September eleventh," Franklin said. "We even held a memorial candlelight service in this very room, which many of you attended. You know, I see signs and stickers on cars all over this town saying 'We will never forget.' And it's true, that we should never forget what happened that day...But I think that just like were learned from the story of Manasseh, great good can come out of evil deeds."

Gretchen raised her hand.

"Yes Gretchen?" Franklin said.

"I think a lot of good as already come out of September eleventh," she replied. "I think a lot of people in this country have turned back to God. Tragedy often brings revival."

Franklin nodded his head in agreement. "Yes that's true. But does it bring about a lasting revival?"

"Sometimes, I suppose," she answered.

The rest of the group responded affirmingly, so Franklin posed another question to them.

"What do you think would be a great example of faith to come out of this tragedy? Think back to our Bible passage now."

Migdalia was the first to answer. "How about Osama Bin Laden being converted to Christianity?"

Many, including Troy, shuddered at such a thought. How could a just God bring such an evil man in among the faithful? But Franklin often wondered why Christians don't pray for the salvation of their enemies like Jesus had commanded them to do? It is a truly befuddling fact.

"If Osama Bin Laden repented and turned to Jesus as his Lord and Savior, would he not receive salvation as Manasseh probably did?" Franklin asked. "I say probably, because we can never know if somebody truly trusts in Jesus alone for their salvation. God judges a person's heart; we can only judge their actions. But still, the Bible says if they believe, we should love them like a brother."

Troy shook his head. "Can you imagine loving Osama Bin Laden like a brother?"

A few giggles broke out among the crowd.

"Why not?" Cassie asked. "It's God's choice to convert who he wants, not ours. He determines who will be saved or not. Salvation is all in his hands."

Many in the crowd shook their heads in agreement. Despite their differences in heritage, they were being trained well in the reformed perspective of faith taught at New Hope. Troy wasn't a fan of that school of thought. Calvinism had never made him happy. But despite his irritation, he remained quiet. Troy wasn't about to let a difference of opinion even slightly interfere with his future plans.

❧❖❧

All seemed well as Troy laid his weary head on the pillow two nights before Thanksgiving. When he woke up the next morning, he and Gretchen would be jetting back to Fort Lauderdale to spend the holiday with their families. The college sophomore figured his demanding father would have to be pleased with the progress he'd made that quarter. Troy had indeed accomplished a great deal over the past couple of months.

First off, his grades were stellar, as always. The Battles name once again lauded on the UCLA Dean's List showed that daddy's money was being properly spent. Plus, he'd served the Lord well since coming to New Hope, both Ramon and Franklin had told him so.

Troy still didn't fully know what Cassie thought about him. He often sensed her brewing suspicions whenever their paths crossed. He would usually just ignore her as best he could, though doing so was difficult because Gretchen and Cassie had become the best of friends, confidants in both thought and process. But Cassie wasn't really upsetting his predetermined course of action at this point, so he tolerated her friendship with his girlfriend. Franklin's fiancé was basically just an annoyance to him, nothing more.

Still, it became trying with her living right upstairs from him. Since taking up residence at the mission a few weeks back, Troy was always under Cassie's watchful eye. But the scrutiny was proving to be worth it. Richard Battles was ecstatic when his son informed him about living in a spare room at the church in order to truly minister to the downtrodden in the hood. The spoiled young boy was finally growing up, or so his father thought.

Richard didn't realize Troy's true motivation to serve the Lord in such capacity was drawn deceivingly from a hidden well of greed.

Convincing his father he was worthy of taking over the thriving family import business later on was the main thrust of Troy's seemingly admirable work. Richard had never felt Troy was capable, nor even desired, to run his empire when he passed on. The elder Battles reasoned he would just dismantle the company before he died and leave his only child a hefty inheritance, which he figured Troy, would blow through in record time. Racing cars and living the high life was all that seemed to matter to the bright, but troubled boy throughout his teenage years. In fact, dating Gretchen was really the only noble endeavor Troy had managed in his father's eyes. Richard loved his best friend's daughter as if she were his own child. He expected Troy to marry Gretchen one day, though Richard was willing to wait until the couple graduated from college. Troy planned to announce the engagement at Thanksgiving dinner, although he hadn't even formerly proposed to her. But he knew Gretchen wouldn't turn him down. She never could resist his beguiled charm. Nor did she ever want to. After all, she had already surrendered her virtue to him.

"Yes," Troy whispered as he drifted off to sleep, "the design for my destiny is truly taking shape."

But the confidence of the conceited can be easily confounded when Satan comes calling.

A sudden darkness consumed Troy's soul as he slept that night. The subtle voices which periodically haunted his dreams during the last year and a half progressively spoke in a more condemning tone.

Their inflection was especially spirited as they sounded off. It was evident the Evil One was not fully pleased with Troy Battles' current course of action. He uttered a stern reminder to his unwitting charge.

You are my seed, the voice cried in a frightening whisper that still pierced sharply though the young man's conscience.

I bore you Troy.

The scene became more vivid. A serpent slithered up a golden pole, wrapping its length evenly around the fixture. The skin molted and the serpent's head configured itself into the shape of a human skull. A new texture began to slowly cover the skull and hair started to grow out of the crown of its head. As the slumbering Troy fixed his gaze upon the metamorphosis, a face became more recognizable. Troy felt his eyes squinting tightly until he could make out the image he saw. The sight made him gasp. It was his own face. He tried to scream, but his voice didn't utter a peep through his silent sleep.

You are my seed, again the whisper sounded.

Troy covered his ears and turned his eyes away from the serpent. He looked down and another image caught his sight. It was a naked woman, long golden hair hiding her most intimate features. She was cradling a baby in her arms, cooing at the child like new mothers do. She then suddenly tossed the infant in the air, looking over at Troy and smiling with a certain calmness. Troy looked up and noticed a flurry of pure white sparkles cascading down. As the sparkles hit the ground, a concealing mist formed around them. When the mist cleared, the nude figure of a man emerged. Troy recognized the man immediately. It was Franklin!

A much lighter voice than the one of darkness sounded off.

Behold the seed of the woman.

Troy became confused. He longed to discover the meaning of the vision. The Darkness was eager to provide a few subtle clues.

You know what you have done my son.

Troy began to weep. He recognized the depth of the despair due his soul. He knew no earthly wealth could discharge such debt.

Your Christian works will do you no good, the whisper uttered disparagingly.

Troy lost all hope. Any resolve he may have had withered completely. He looked back for the woman, but she was gone. So was Franklin. Troy started to giggle slightly, like a man struggling to grip the last fragile strands of his sanity. The Darkness offered a foreboding comfort.

You are my seed.

Troy burst from his sleep. Sweat poured from his brow, stinging his eyes as the droplets rolled down his face. He took a few deep breaths to calm his nerves. As he regained his focus, realizing the episode was just a dream, Troy took stock of his current surroundings. He began to ask himself a few questions.

What was his purpose here?

What did the future ultimately hold in store for him?

Who did he really serve?

Tears began to slide down Troy's face as an insolent cackle arose from the inner reaches of his gut. He managed to choke back his conflicting emotions before they drew notice in the normal silence of the night. He didn't want Franklin to hear his turmoil from the bedroom the next door over. Troy wasn't ready to face the fact that his growing envy of Franklin during the last two months, and really for the past four years, had begun to fester into an infectious hate.

"Stick to your plan," he muttered to himself as he laid back down, already feeling comforted by the suggestion.

Troy slept well the remainder of the night. The Darkness had already spoken its tenuous peace to him.

The announcement came without warning. Gretchen was stunned by its suddenness.

The proclaiming of betrothal should have been a crowning highlight of her blessed young life. But there was callousness to Troy's declaration of their engagement to the families during the middle of Thanksgiving dinner. Gretchen was totally thrown off kilter by Troy's public proposal, which seemed more like a royal decree than an affectionate display of his boundless love. Kind of like: "Yes, we will be married in the near future, and now will you kindly pass the turkey father?"

Although they had discussed marriage often since they were teenagers, Gretchen hadn't accepted a proposal as of yet. In fact, one had not even been offered by the supposed man of her dreams. It was just assumed by Troy, and the rest of both families for that matter. Gretchen was bound to accept. After all, how could anybody turn down a Battles proposal of any kind, especially one of marriage?

As her heart continued its rapid barrage in her chest, Gretchen tried to compose herself from Troy's impromptu disclosure. Her eyes began to glisten dubiously, their radiance tempered by concern. Oh, she definitely loved him, always had. But his manner often left her perplexed. This time his actions had split her in two. The love of her life had selfishly stolen what should have been one of the most glorious moments in a girl's existence. And that moment could never again be captured. It was lost forever. She could never forgive him for that.

Yet Gretchen graciously accepted the congratulatory hugs and kisses of her relatives. Richard was especially touched, joyfully welcoming his soon-to-be daughter in-law into the fold. Gretchen was happy to please the teary-eyed patriarch. She understood Richard's love for her and the circumstances from which it arose. She would never do anything to hurt him, even if she felt like strangling his son at the moment.

While Gretchen hugged her own father, her eyes met Troy's as he casually bit off a piece of a drumstick. There was a conquering feel to his gaze, as if he knew she was a spoil in a victorious family power play. It didn't need to be that way. She had always desired to marry him, and was sure he knew as much. She just wanted to be properly asked. Their relationship would be forever tainted and her resentment toward him already grew more bitter by the moment.

Troy cleverly covered his planned misstep well, with a ploy that was sure to warm over Gretchen's frost-nipped heart. While the family looked on, he stood next to his fiancé and tenderly took hold of her left hand. With a manufactured tear gently streaming down his cheek, he placed her hand to his lips and kissed it delicately. Troy smiled at Gretchen, who returned a resigned grin. He then took a ring out of his shirt pocket and placed it on her finger. The engagement ring was rather small by Battles' standards, but its significance was exceptional. Gretchen immediately relished the sentiment, as did all who were in the room. The ring had belonged to her beloved, deceased mother Ingrid. Gretchen threw her arms around Troy and kissed him deeply. Her displeasure had been resolved by that single act.

Troy's charm managed to sway Gretchen's heart once more. He was truly her desperate weakness.

The luster of the moment quickly faded when the couple returned to Los Angeles. Reality struck Gretchen with a thud as Troy displayed his inner darkness again one day before a fellowship gathering at New Hope.

Cassie, Gretchen and Ramon had spent the day decorating the sanctuary for the Christmas season with a few other church members. They were enjoying some refreshments afterward as Gretchen proudly displayed her engagement ring to the ladies of the group. Cassie had been extremely delighted when her best friend shared the news. But she also was well aware of Gretchen's vulnerable nature, especially when it came to dealing with Troy. Cassie had been trying to mentor the younger woman as best she could, discipling her a great deal in the ways of gospel-based romance. So when the others had left that evening, she pulled Gretchen aside for a heart-to-heart talk.

"I couldn't help but notice that you seem, I don't know, maybe a little reserved about marrying Troy," Cassie said in the church kitchen while pouring a cup of coffee for each of them. "Do you want to talk about it?"

Gretchen chewed nervously on the nail of her ring finger, feeling a touch of shame needling her insides. "There is something I need to tell you, but I'm embarrassed." She placed her hand over her mouth and began to cry.

Cassie immediately put her arm around her friend's shoulder. "Oh, honey, what's wrong? Is it Troy? You can tell me."

Gretchen held back for a few seconds before speaking. "Troy expects so much of me." She sniffled a couple of times and wiped away her remorseful tears.

"How so?" Cassie asked with concern.

Gretchen hesitated a bit. Looking into Cassie's pure black eyes as she explained her dilemma, Gretchen felt the dread of her sin even more. She didn't know if Cassie would understand the firm grip Troy always held on her behavior. He could convince her almost any deed was honorable if done with the right intent, the act of fornication included. They had been engaging in premarital sex since high school, but had covered their tracks pretty well. And it wasn't that Gretchen didn't enjoy making love to Troy, but she would always feel terrible afterward, knowing she had broken one of the Lord's commandments. Gretchen wanted to repent, but Troy would artfully twist her love for him and somehow manage to convince her to physically succumb to his lustful cravings. Their engagement only raised the level of his expectations. She felt trapped between her willingness to fulfill the needs her of future husband and the desire to obey her Lord.

"I'm so confused Cassie," Gretchen moaned. "I guess I don't really know who I love more, do I?"

"Oh yes you do," Cassie sternly replied.

"Then why do I always fall?"

Cassie felt compassion for her desperate friend. She knew Gretchen was a good girl inside, but sin can slay even the purest of hearts. Cassie understood that fact deeply. She decided to confess her own shortcomings to Gretchen.

"Oh sweetie, you're not the only one," Cassie said softly, reaching out to clasp both of Gretchen's hands in hers. "The men we love can tempt us to do things we know we shouldn't do, even if they don't realize they're tempting us. I struggle with it just like you."

"You?" Gretchen asked, her eyes displaying surprise. "But I thought you were still a virgin. I thought you and Franklin were waiting until you're wedding night?"

Cassie smiled. She was amazed she didn't feel the slightest bit unnerved talking about her sexuality. It was so nice to have a girl-friend to confide in. She could never talk as such with her father, that fact was certain.

"Well, I still have my virginity," Cassie replied. "But that doesn't mean I don't have lustful desires for Franklin. I'm very normal in that regard."

Gretchen rolled her eyes. "It's not the same Cassie if you've never actually gone to bed with Franklin. I've slept with Troy so many times it's shameful." She began to cry more profusely now, her guilt spilling further with each falling teardrop.

Cassie didn't sway from her course of counsel, despite Gretchen's claim. Although she and Franklin had not carried their carnal cravings to the ultimate climax, they had dallied on a dangerous path at times. Cassie was well aware she could have easily stumbled into even greater sexual sin just like Gretchen. It was by God's grace alone she managed to maintain her chastity.

"Now, what you say is true," Cassie said as she handed Gretchen a tissue to dry her sorrowful eyes. "But God looks at our sin differently than we do. In his eyes, my lust is just as sinful as yours. Remember when Jesus said even lustful looks are adultery in the heart. Sin is sin in his book. Some sins have greater consequences than others, but they're all sin...You love Jesus right Gretchen?"

"Yes with all my heart."

"Do you believe He died for all your sins?"

"Of course I do."

Cassie rubbed Gretchen's shoulders consolingly. "Then accept his forgiveness honey. He loves you. He still wants you. He's changing you...A Christian's repentance lasts a lifetime. You know that."

A charming smile immediately broke across Gretchen's face. She reached over and hugged Cassie tightly to show gratitude for her advice. Cassie always had a way of making her understand the profound relief of hope.

"I love you," Gretchen whispered as she clutched her sister in the faith.

"Oh, I love you too," Cassie responded, kissing Gretchen on top of the head.

Gretchen pulled away and finished wiping the tears from her eyes. A couple seconds passed before she looked at Cassie with a sly grin.

"What?" Cassie asked with a slight smile, subtly gathering the thoughts twirling through Gretchen's mind.

"So, how close did you and Franklin come to doing it?"

"Gretchen!"

"Well, I was just curious. I mean, what stopped you?"

Cassie began to giggle, shyly but boldly. She shook her head, slightly embarrassed by the details she was about to confess.

"What's so funny?" Gretchen asked.

"If you only knew."

"Well, I will if you tell me. Come on, fess up girl."

Cassie smirked and looked squarely at her friend. "Alright, one evening Franklin and I were well on our way to having sex. We were truly in the throws of passion," Cassie mixed a little emphasis into her voice to teasingly add some drama to the scene she was beginning to describe.

"Okay yeah?" Gretchen asked anxiously.

Cassie began to giggle some more, even though looking back the scene was more intense than humorous. "We were in the midst of making out on the couch in the apartment. Clothing was even beginning to be removed."

"Really?"

"Oh yeah," Cassie replied. "But then it happened and I was stunned back into reality."

"What?" Gretchen exclaimed.

Cassie took a deep breath and sighed. "The door bell rang."

Gretchen covered her mouth and began to giggle also. "No!"

"Yep," Cassie said. "Thank the Lord for that doorbell or I would have followed through that night. I know it."

"Well who was at the door?" Gretchen asked, eagerly awaiting a response.

Cassie prolonged the moment just a bit longer before bursting out in unrestrained laughter.

"What?" Gretchen cried. "Who was at the door?"

It took a minute or so for Cassie to regain her composure before answering, frustrating Gretchen to no end. "It was you."

"Uh?" Gretchen said.

"Yes, it was you, and Troy. That first night we met you guys."

Gretchen covered her mouth with both hands. "Oh my gosh!"

"Mm uh," Cassie said, widening her eyes, falsely mocking Gretchen's shock.

"I'm so sorry!"

Cassie waved her hand across her face as she put down her coffee cup after taking a sip. "Oh, don't be. You saved me from making a huge mistake. I'm actually grateful to you."

Gretchen was a little embarrassed for her friend. It then dawned on her suddenly, that God was using Cassie's explanation to reaffirm his presence in any and all situations, including her own sinful dilemma. She was thankful for Cassie's openness and felt more comfortable sharing a deeper concern about Troy's dark side. Tears began to flow again when she thought about his recent treatment of her.

"Gretchen!" Cassie exclaimed. "Hey! I said I was happy you and Troy rang the bell that night. Don't cry!"

Gretchen dabbed the tissue on her face, smearing her perfectly-applied mascara. "No, it's not that."

"What then? What's wrong?"

Gretchen's lip began to quiver slightly. "Cassie, ever since I got engaged I've been afraid of him."

"Who?"

"Troy... He hit me today Cassie." Gretchen wept into her hands.

"What?" Cassie asked fervently, grabbing her friend tightly as the girl cried onto her shoulder. She let Gretchen spill her sorrow for a minute or so before asking any further details. Cassie's anger began to boil. She sensed from the first time they'd met Troy would be trouble. "What happened honey? Did he hurt you?"

Gretchen sniffled a couple of times. "No. It was more of a slap really. Kind of a reaction on his part, I guess."

"A reaction to what? There's never a reason for a man to hit a woman. Maybe I should have Franklin talk to him."

"No!" Gretchen exclaimed abruptly. "Don't tell anyone please! Promise you won't! Please!"

Cassie was startled by the near terror in Gretchen's eyes. There had to be more to the story. She knew Gretchen would only tell her so much. Cassie tried to pry further details from her, but Gretchen would only go so far before claming up tightly.

"Maybe it's my fault," Gretchen said, still sobbing, almost inconsolably. "You've warned me that I dress too provocatively some times. You're pretty Cassie, and you dress like a lady... Troy called me a tease."

Cassie was beginning to have difficulty understanding Gretchen's ramblings. "What do you mean? You said you've given him what he wants. How could he call you a tease?"

Gretchen looked up at Cassie, but barely opened her eyes. Her mind was spinning as she recalled the lurid details of her last encounter with Troy. Fear of him caused her to tremble, a symptom which did not escape Cassie's notice.

"Gretchen!" Cassie shrieked. "What did he do? Please honey, tell me!"

Gretchen grabbed hold of Cassie and squeezed her. Both were crying at that point.

"He forced himself on me this afternoon in my dorm room," Gretchen cried. "I tried to resist. I told him I didn't want to sleep with him again until we were married. But he wouldn't listen."

Cassie couldn't believe what she was hearing, but she didn't say a word. She wanted to let Gretchen finish. She gently stroked the blond girl's hair to comfort her.

"I told him no. That's when he slapped me...He said how dare I deny him after all he's done for me." Gretchen held back from Cassie the full nature of Troy's temper. It wasn't the first time he had abused her, but in the past the damage had only been applied verbally. That afternoon, it became physical. "I gave in Cassie. I let him have me again...I don't understand what's wrong with me."

Cassie lifted up Gretchen's head and stared straight into her bloodshot blue eyes. Cassie seethed with anger toward Troy, but was more concerned with Gretchen's unwarranted guilt.

"Oh no. Don't you blame yourself, you hear."

"But I always..."

"No Gretchen. Stop! Listen honey. He basically raped you..."

Gretchen shook her head and closed her eyes. "You don't get it Cassie."

"What? What don't I get? You said no."

"But that's the sick part," Gretchen protested, "even though he hit me, I still love him. I did say no, but my heart said yes...Oh Cassie don't you see...I wanted him to make love to me. He knows that. Troy knows I can't resist him. He knows I really don't want to."

Gretchen sank her head back onto Cassie's shoulder and wept aloud. Cassie just held the distraught girl and let her cry. They were still the only two people at the church that evening. She realized she couldn't help Gretchen any further right then, but she promised herself she would begin to tackle the problem in the morning. She drove Gretchen back to her dorm. Gretchen said Troy wouldn't be back that night; he was staying at a friend's apartment to watch a football game. Cassie figured her friend would be safe for the time being with her dorm mates. She had offered to let Gretchen stay with her that night, but the somber girl felt like being alone. Cassie was worried, but respected her dear friend's wishes.

As she drove back to New Hope, Cassie planned to get to the bottom of the whole episode. She knew Gretchen wasn't giving her the entire scoop. She was sure Gretchen was covering up something for somebody for some reason. Cassie didn't understand why, but she was determined to find out. The feeling in her gut told her that Gretchen's future would probably hinge on her discovery.

Cassie remembered that Troy kept a small, aluminum file box under the bed in his room at the church. He was very secretive about the information in the file, not even telling Gretchen what was in it. Troy told his fellow workers at the church the box just contained some family business papers that his father said he might need some day. Cassie's intuition told her differently.

Troy Battles was hiding something. Cassie had never trusted

him from the day she met him and Gretchen's struggles only confirmed her notions. Troy was an evil seed and Cassie had to find
out just how depraved he was. Early the next morning, before Troy
arrived for work, Cassie vowed to get a gander into those private
papers in his box. She hoped the answers to her questions about the
devious rich boy from Florida would be found among the papers.
Cassie figured at least it was a good place to start.

Chapter XII

*T*ap. Tap. Tap.

The subtle rap of knuckles on hollow wood gently nudged the eardrums of the soundly slumbering woman wanting to hoard for herself the last few seconds of precious sleep. But Cassie understood she could not ignore the persistent appeal for her awakening much longer.

Tap. Tap. Tap.

There it was again, this time followed by a familiar voice urging a reply.

"Are you in there dear?" Ramon asked in a tone just audible enough to be heard through the closed bedroom door.

Cassie rolled over onto her back and yawned, refusing to allow her weary eyes to catch their initial glimpse of the mid-morning rays slipping underneath the drawn pastel curtains.

"Yes papa," she groaned, like a little girl struggling to arise on the first day of school.

Ramon slowly turned the knob and eased the door open a crack.

"It is late honey. Are you okay?"

Cassie rubbed her eyes and sat up. "I'm fine. You can come in papa."

Ramon entered the room and walked over to his daughter's bed. He noticed she was still dressed in the same blue jeans and maroon USC tee shirt she'd worn while decorating the sanctuary the night before.   Cassie was out when he arrived home around midnight after visiting a church family with Franklin.

"You got in late last night huh?" he asked.

Cassie yawned again, not remembering what time she had gone to bed. "Yes, I had to drive Gretchen home. She wasn't feeling well."

Ramon sat down on the bed and smiled at his daughter. "What happened? You two did not spike the egg nog did you?"

Cassie giggled and rolled her eyes. "No papa. Nothing like that...Although, that probably would not have been a bad idea."

An expression of concern appeared on Ramon's face. "Is Gretchen sick or something?"

After taking a sip from a bottle of water on her nightstand, Cassie ran her finger through her matted black hair. "No, she's not physically ill. But she's emotionally troubled. Her and Troy are having some problems." Cassie nodded her head drearily a few times. "Oh my gosh, what time is it?"

Ramon looked at his watch. "It is nine fifty-five. What is wrong? Is something going on with those two?"

Cassie realized it was too late to sneak into Troy's room and look at the file. She should have done it the night before, but her comforting of Gretchen had left her drained. She didn't know when she would have another opportunity to investigate the personal papers of the dubious miscreant. That's really what he appeared to be, Cassie thought to herself. Troy's vicious behavior toward his fiancé confirmed that fact as far as Cassie was concerned. She felt rage quickly filling her heart again as she remembered Gretchen's desperate tears. Ramon sensed his daughter's building turmoil.

"Cassie, what is eating at you?"

There was no way she was ready to go into detail. She knew she had to get more facts before saying anything to her father. "Nothing papa."

"Oh, you can not fool me. Now what is wrong? I want to know. Is Gretchen in trouble?"

"Papa please!" Cassie pleaded. "I told Gretchen I would help her."

Ramon was becoming irritated at his daughter's reluctance to fill him in. He was worried about Gretchen, but he trusted Cassie's instincts. He believed she would minister biblically to Gretchen.

"Is there anything I can do?" Ramon asked, his tone less demanding. "I really like those kids. I want to help them if I can do so."

Cassie smiled and hugged her father. She had always recognized his undying love for those in difficult circumstances. Pastoring to troubled souls was the primary reason he founded New Hope Church in the first place. But Cassie was well aware Ramon's heart could overrule his head. He correctly showed grace when situations called for it, but often struggled with issues of discipline. Cassie knew her father was just too nice sometimes. She would have liked his perspective on the problem, yet she couldn't break her confidence with Gretchen until she had a better grasp on Troy's motives.

"I know you do," Cassie said, as she held him tightly. "Just let me care for them right now, okay? It's why you sent me to school. Let me try to love them like I was taught."

Ramon kissed his daughter on the cheek. He cherished her Christlike resolve. "My little girl is so grown up...I am so proud of you Cassie. You are just like..." His voice faded.

Cassie pulled back and gazed into her father's moistening, brown eyes. "I know papa. You miss her too. I often wonder what it would be like if mama was still alive."

Ramon looked toward the floor. He knew he would begin to cry if he didn't remove his eyes from Cassie's replicate face. Her image was always too striking at such tender moments.

"Lana was such a strong woman, just like her daughter," he said, resting his head on her shoulder.

Cassie put her arm around her father. "You know Gretchen lost her mother at a young age too."

"I know, she shared that with us."

"Oh that's right," Cassie replied, remembering Gretchen's testimony during a recent Bible study. "Maybe that's why I feel such a close bond with her."

"I am sure that has a lot to do with it. God is wonderful at placing similar hearts together to minister to one another."

"I love her papa. Gretchen has such a sweet spirit. I hate to see her hurting so."

Ramon placed his chin on his hand and stared straight ahead at the sunlight now radiating more fully through the thin curtains. He wished Cassie would give him more details about the couple's struggles. But he wanted to let his daughter do her work at her own pace.

"I do worry about Troy also," he said. "He seems so distant sometimes, no?"

Cassie nodded in agreement. She wanted to tell her father about Troy's actions the day before, but Gretchen had warned her not to. The warning left Cassie deeply disturbed. What was Troy capable of? Was Gretchen concerned about her own life? Would he take his abuse to a more violent end? Could he bring harm to her father,

Franklin or even herself? Such thoughts made Cassie shudder. She believed getting to the bottom of the matter was imperative. However, Cassie was also wise enough to understand she must follow God's timing in all circumstances. His sovereign will had to guide her course of action.

"Papa, would you pray for me now the way we used to when I was a little girl?"

Ramon clutched both of Cassie's hands. He was highly pleased by her request. Sweet memories flooded back to him, bringing tears to his eyes once more. "Sure. I would love to."

Father and daughter held hands and knelt beside her bed. They looked up at the shelves of stuffed animals that still lined her bedroom walls. They smiled at each other, closed their eyes and bowed their heads.

"Don't forget to pray for Gretchen, and Troy also," she whispered. "Oh, and of course Franklin."

⊰⊹⊱

It ended up Cassie would have to wait until after the Holidays to sneak a glimpse into Troy's personal file. Every time she thought she might get the opportunity to investigate further, Troy would appear at the last moment and spoil the chance. One evening, about a week before Christmas, just as she was opening the door to his room, Cassie heard Troy's corvette engine revving outside the back of the church. She thought it was safe when he had gone off to visit Gretchen at her dorm, but he returned suddenly after remembering his fiancé had to take a makeup exam that night. Cassie barely slipped into the sanctuary before Troy walked into the building and went to his room.

The close call left Cassie nervous about how Troy would have reacted if he caught her snooping through his personal belongings. She knew he had a violent temper, Gretchen told her so. Troy had slapped Gretchen at least the one time that Cassie knew of, and maybe also on other occasions, she couldn't be sure. But if Troy would strike the woman he supposedly loved, Cassie figured he might not think twice about belting her also. As she lay down on the front pew that night and stared at the lighted cross, Cassie felt a deep uneasiness in her gut. The sensation was more than just rattled nerves from nearly being caught by Troy. Her trepidation stemmed from the aura of iniquity that always seemed to drift toward her whenever Troy was nearby. She hated not being able to fight off the eerie vibe by herself. But the benefit of Cassie's helplessness was the blessing of being able to entrust her worries to the Spirit of God. Gazing at the lighted cross brought calm to her anxiety.

Gretchen had told Cassie that Troy apologized sincerely for his boorish behavior and she was satisfied by his repentance. Realizing Gretchen could often be deceived by Troy's hollow remorse, Cassie's perception wasn't so easily clouded. He wasn't fooling her, or more importantly God, a fact that put Cassie more at ease. She believed the Lord was always in control of all situations even if it didn't appear that way to her. His sovereignty reigns supreme and Cassie would just have to trust him.

She decided to let the matter rest for a while, at least until after Christmas. The entire staff at New Hope would all be together for the season of joy and peace that year. One of the main reason's Troy and Gretchen traveled back to Florida for Thanksgiving was because they knew they wouldn't be home for the Christmas holiday. Gretchen had convinced Troy to serve with Cassie, Franklin and Ramon at New Hope in an effort to help bring blessing to the poor during the advent season.

The decision pleased both families back home. The Battles and the Bjorns derived great joy from the Christlike servitude of their children. Yet, while Gretchen's service was born of a sacrificial heart, Troy's motivation, like usual, was drawn from self-centered desire for future reward. Long ago, he had made a promise to himself that nothing, or certainly nobody, would thwart his lofty plans. Troy silently vowed to crush anybody who tried. But he knew he had to maintain his best behavior to accomplish his goals, even if it meant temporarily satiating his lustful cravings.

That task was made much easier by the holiday sleeping arrangements. The college dormitories were closed for the nearly three-week vacation period, so Gretchen was forced to share Cassie's room. Like a couple of girlish teenagers, the two best friends thoroughly enjoyed their extended sleep-over. They grew closer in their walk with God, as well as each other. They became like the sisters that neither one had grown up with. They were nearly inseparable for the whole holiday season.

Cassie also realized a couple of added fringe benefits of the two interns staying at New Hope.

For one, Gretchen sharing a room with Cassie would greatly reduce the vulnerable girl's temptation to share a bed with her lascivious boyfriend. If Troy wanted to get to Gretchen, he would have to go through Cassie first. All involved understood that scenario wasn't going to happen.

Cassie also found sufficient time to delicately examine Troy's true character. Despite his apparent repentance, she still felt she needed to protect Gretchen. Because no matter how often Cassie prayed her concerns to the Lord, she couldn't resolve the fact she didn't trust Troy at all. She knew he would eventually hurt Gretchen. She could sense the inevitability of the heart-wrenching pain to come.

It was only a matter of time.

❧❖❧

The burden of Cassie's constant scrutiny began to wear on Troy as Christmas turned toward New Year's Day. He always felt the gaze of her piercing black eyes upon him, as if she were trying to inspect the very state of his soul. Oh sure, Cassie was outwardly pleasant to him, her snow white smile offered a purifying cover to the intense mental interrogation taking place. But Troy wasn't buying Cassie's still-evident ruse any more than she was tricked by his malicious cunning. The false faces appeared masked to only the other players in the rapidly-building drama.

Paranoia started to slowly creep into Troy's conscience. What was she up to he wondered? He knew Gretchen and Cassie were close as sisters, but he was pretty sure his girl had only divulged just a small sample of their contentious bond. Gretchen tearfully admitted she had told Cassie of his hitting her, a reactionary mistake he promised his fiancé, as well as himself, would not happen again. But Gretchen had forgiven him for that blunder and they had made up beautifully, save for the intimacy which would now have to wait until their wedding night. Troy was willing to tolerate that cost, though the price caused him to increasingly despise Cassie's counsel of Gretchen. But the payoff would be worth it once he and Gretchen exchanged wedding vows.

Troy had to make sure his father remained highly satisfied with his son's progression in life. Richard Battles was proud of Troy's supposed maturation over the past two years. Excellent scholastic aptitude, fine Christian service and sound stewardship of finances had sprung renewed confidence for Richard in Troy's ability to run Battles Trading Corp. in the future. But Troy knew marriage

to Gretchen would seal the deal. There could be no further slip-
ups. If Richard ever found out that he had abused Gretchen, Troy's
dreams would be finished. Gone would be the CEO position, the
company perks, maybe even his stake in the family fortune. That's
how much Richard loved Gretchen, possibly, Troy thought, even
more than his own son. It was a sad fact that the young man was
forced to live with throughout his childhood. Although he understood the reasons behind his father's affection for Gretchen, he still
felt resentment. But those emotions could be dealt with later. Troy
knew he had tougher trouble to contend with at the present. Cassie
couldn't be allowed to disrupt his plans in any way. He had to make
sure of that.

Troy figured maybe he could distract Cassie's attention toward
him by way of her own fiancé. After a couple of glasses of champagne during their private New Year's Eve celebration, Troy hoped
to persuade Franklin to get Cassie to back off a bit.

The New Hope family, plus a dozen or so close friends and
ministry associates, gathered in the church dinning room to ring in
the new year. The modest party was obviously much more reserved
than most of the revelry taking place in L.A. that night. Except
for a few bottles of bubbly, a couple platters of sandwiches and the
sound of adult contemporary pop music playing on Cassie's small
boom box; it would be hard to tell a party was even taking place.

Ramon and Franklin were discussing theology when Troy sat
down at their table about fifteen minutes before midnight. He was
happy Cassie and Gretchen had scurried upstairs to fix their hair
and makeup in advance of the New Year's countdown.

"You know Ramon, I recently read somewhere that there are
four kinds of people," Franklin commented as Troy cordially nodded
to his ministry cohorts while sliding into his metal folding chair.

"Just four?" Ramon replied, taking a sip from his wine glass.

"Yep, just four," Franklin answered, holding up his left index finger to signify the first type. "There are those who are saved and know they are saved."

Ramon nodded in agreement.

"There are those who are saved and don't know they are saved."

"Very true," Ramon responded. "We have been blessed to meet a lot of those people here at this mission."

Franklin smiled and looked up pleasingly as if to thank God for his gathering of the saints. Troy didn't say anything and just twirled his finger around the condensation that was sweating the outside of his glass. He hoped Franklin would quickly finish with his discourse. He had often witnessed how difficult it could be to curtail his former teacher once he became fully engaged in theological discussions. In fact, most often, it really irked him when Franklin espoused his highly-opinionated beliefs, even if they were being quoted from other sources. Troy knew the reformed ideology of the magazines to which Franklin both ascribed and subscribed. But that was a debate for another time. Troy had a bigger concern to deal with at the moment and it wouldn't be long before she returned to the party.

"The third type of people," Franklin continued, "are those who are not saved and know they are not saved. You know, pagans who have no desire whatsoever for Jesus and never will. And don't care that they never will."

Ramon frowned and sadly stared down at the floor. "There is really nothing we can do about them, I suppose."

"Well, we are still called to love them," Franklin interjected. "Even though they are enemies of God, Jesus told us to love our enemies."

Ramon agreed. "Yes, you are right. I guess we need to strive to do that better...Maybe it can be a resolution for all of us in this coming new year."

Ramon and Franklin gently tapped their glasses together as a sign they would vow to do just that in 2003. Troy raised his glass in the air in response, before downing the rest of the sparkling contents. He looked at his watch as his mind began to drift. He remembered the dream he had a few months back in which Satan claimed him as his own. He wondered if Franklin was referencing him as one of the third types of people. Troy began to feel increasingly uneasy about the current topic of discussion. It again dawned on him that Franklin always had a way of making him feel uncomfortable. It was almost like his old rival did so on purpose. Troy wished he had been able to successfully silence Franklin in the past. He knew that at times like these he strongly resented Franklin. Maybe even hated him.

Calm down, Troy thought to himself. *You have more important issues to deal with right now.*

"You know brother," Franklin said to Ramon. "I read that the fourth type of person is the saddest of all."

Ramon again frowned and nodded his head. He knew the direction in which Franklin was heading.

"I feel really bad for those people who think they are saved, but really are not saved. They are the ones on judgment day who will hear Jesus say "depart from me, I never knew you.' It doesn't get much sadder than that." Franklin shook his head, almost despondently.

Troy waited to see if Franklin would drop a tear. He knew Franklin was such a softy for the lost, especially those folks he deemed clueless about salvation matters. It was another trait about his former teacher that always touched a bitter nerve in Troy.

"Why are you talking about this stuff now man?" Troy asked with a deep sigh. "It's New Year's Eve. Chill out a little. Have another glass of champagne. Like you always say, God is in control."

Franklin started to respond with vehemence toward the sarcastic Battles boy, just like he used to do at Good Shepherd Christian School. But then he suddenly realized it was no longer his charge to steer a wayward pupil. Troy was a grown man now. Franklin softened his stance quickly.

"I guess you're right," Franklin said, pouring himself another glass of champagne. "God even directs those who follow Satan... We're probably all Christians here anyway, right?"

Ramon raised his glass in a mock toast. "Oh, there are the girls. Just in time for midnight."

Troy realized his plan to talk privately with Franklin about Cassie would now have to be put on hold. Once again, Franklin had disrupted his intentions, leaving him perturbed to no end.

Cassie and Gretchen walked over to the table, each decked out in matching royal blue evening dresses. Cassie kissed Ramon on the cheek and then Franklin on the mouth. Gretchen hugged Troy around the shoulders and kissed his neck.

"Wow, you girls look fantastic!" Franklin remarked. "I thought you were just going up to fix your hair. You certainly are showing us up, that's for sure."

Both woman batted their eyes and struck a glamorous pose at the men, who were all just wearing casual dress slacks and polo shirts. "We wanted to surprise ya and dress up a little tonight for New Year's," Gretchen said.

Their gowns were more classy than sexy, kind of like the old time movie stars used to wear. Just enough sparkle accented the silken material to cast an almost regal glow on each elegant young woman. The hemlines and necklines were perfectly placed, enchanting but not overtly enticing, a style modest Cassie had been trying to impress upon Gretchen since they'd first met. As a pampered blue-blood growing up in South Florida, the stunning blond had been schooled to fashion her look with boldness and maximum exposure. Being Christian did little to curb the societal influences courting her wardrobe selection. Troy certainly appreciated the appeal of his girl's choices, which unwittingly presented a challenge to his normal youthful cravings. But he noticed much had changed since Cassie began to broaden her sway on Gretchen. The inconvenient nuisance of the ever-growing influence by Franklin's fiancé inflamed his previously-restrained disaffection. It seemed his loathing intensified with each passing day.

"Do you like my dress baby?" Gretchen asked cutely before bestowing another kiss on him.

Troy realized she hadn't called him baby since the last time they made love nearly two months before. His whole body began to tingle at just the notion of lying with Gretchen again. "You look lovely," he responded, gently placing both arms around her waist as they drifted with the love song playing on the radio.

Right on time, Cassie cut short their moment by changing the channel to a local broadcast of the final countdown to midnight. Gretchen smiled demurely at Troy and laid her head on his shoulder.

"One minute to go," Cassie cried out to the crowd, standing on a chair like a barker at a traveling carnival. Franklin and Ramon hustled about the room filling everyone's champagne glasses for a midnight toast.

"Thirty, twenty-nine, twenty-eight," Cassie called to the gathering, encouraging all to join in with her chant. Gretchen followed suit, jumping up on a chair with her cohort. Troy just stood alone, not uttering a word.

"Ten, nine, eight," the group shouted. Gretchen swirled her arms in the air, urging Troy to join in. He finally did, reluctantly. He didn't appreciate Cassie's interruption to the prelude of possible intimacy for which he had so been longing.

"Three, two, one, Happy New Year!" they all screamed.

Cassie and Gretchen leaped down from the folding chairs and rushed to kiss their respective beaus as *Auld Lang Syne* sounded off from the radio.

After embracing Franklin for a minute or so, Cassie walked over to the wooden column Ramon was leaning against and kissed her father on the cheek. She always remembered how much he missed her mother at moments like this.

"Happy New Year papa, I love you," she whispered into his ear as she hugged him tightly.

Ramon gently rubbed the back of his daughter's head while a tear rolled down his face. He recognized there was another man in her life now. A fine, Christian brother who would take the hand of his beloved daughter during the rest of her walk with the Lord. Though it would be difficult to let go, Ramon was thankful to be releasing her into Franklin's capable hands. He knew neither of them would ever truly be walking toward glory alone.

"Go spend the rest of the time with your betrothed," Ramon said. "I will be fine...You kids enjoy yourselves."

Cassie gazed into her father's misty brown eyes. She understood his loneliness. She had often felt it herself until she met Franklin. But she knew her father was also so happy for her and the man he had grown to love as a son. Cassie saw how proud he was that Franklin would soon be part of their family. She kissed her father again and sought out her fiancé.

Ramon finished his glass of champagne and headed upstairs to the apartment. It was late, an hour for the young, not for the young at heart.

✦

Franklin could feel the rounded edges of the tiny diamond engagement ring he had given Cassie as he gently caressed her left hand with his interlocked fingers. It still troubled him that he thought the token of his affection for her was a woefully inadequate adornment to her ravishing beauty. Cassie looked especially captivating that night in her lovely New Year's attire. Her dress finely framed her hourglass figure, displaying a thinly-veiled allure without forsaking devoted virtue.

Temptation always proved a worthy adversary when they found themselves alone with one another. Franklin could still taste the sweetness of the champagne on her breath as they broke their kiss. Both knew not to linger closely for too long. Previous passion had taught them well.

Hands still clasped as one, they strolled barefoot along the ocean's edge, the surf unusually serene for a cool winter's night. The Pacific Ocean was normally raucous that time of year, often raging with storm swells sweeping down from the icy northern seas. Also surprising was the absence of people on the beach as the couple walked along the brightly moonlit way. There was always someone, at least a homeless person, moseying about the sands in the middle of the night. But for some reason on that extremely early New Year's morning, Franklin and Cassie had the ocean all to themselves. The mood would have been made for romance except for a certain concern distracting Cassie. The matter didn't escape Franklin's notice.

"Is something bothering you honey?" Franklin softly asked as he brushed aside a curly wisp of black hair draped delicately over Cassie's satiny cheek.

Her docile smile quickly shifted into a vexing frown. "Yes, there is," she answered, circling her toes in the wet sand. "Let's sit down a minute."

Franklin began to get worried. He wondered if he had done something to upset her. Cassie's tone bemoaned distress. In all the time he'd known her, they had not so much as argued over anything, not even once.

"Okay," Franklin asked cautiously, "what have I done?"

Cassie immediately realized Franklin's misinterpretation of her sudden mood change. "Oh no sweetie, it's not you," she responded, giggling slightly, before hugging him tightly and kissing the side of his face. "Nothing about you troubles me. I love you so much."

Franklin reached his hand under her chin and turned her face toward his. "You know I love you more than I can ever tell you." She nodded yes. He kissed her mouth and their tongues met once more. But again, they stopped after just a few moments, so as not to succumb to their sinful desires.

Cassie sighed deeply. Her eyes began to well up. She sniffled a couple of times and dropped her head sorrowfully into her hands. Franklin wrapped his arm around her shoulder.

"Hey, what's wrong baby?" he asked. "Tell me."

"I promised I wouldn't say anything," she answered, not looking up.

"Say anything about what?" he pleaded, now rubbing her back. "You know you can tell me anything." Cassie began to cry harder. "Oh please, what's wrong?" Franklin started to become upset. "Is something wrong with Ramon? Is he sick or something?"

"No, no, papa's fine," she quickly replied, wiping the tears from her eyes.

"Then what? You're scaring me."

He hated to see her cry. Whenever she was sad, her pain seemed to strike deep into his own heart. Over the passing months, each of their emotions had become so intimately entwined it was almost as if they were beginning to blend into one soul.

Cassie peered deep into Franklin's anxious eyes. The usual comfort she found in them told her she could confide in him.

"I'm worried greatly about Gretchen," Cassie said.

Franklin was surprised. "Gretchen? What's going on with her? She seemed very happy to me tonight."

Cassie gazed somberly down at the sand as a ripple of the ocean gently lapped over their feet. "I'm afraid circumstances are not what they seem."

"How so?"

"Well," Cassie looked back at Franklin, "I think she might be having second thoughts about marrying Troy."

Franklin looked at his fiancé quizzically. "I saw them kissing tonight. What did she say to you? I mean, they've been together since, I don't know, forever."

"That may be so, but Troy isn't always the sweet, young man he makes himself out to be. At least not to her. He can be downright mean to her sometimes."

Franklin knew that assessment was correct. He'd seen Troy's ugly side a few times in the past. But he thought the boy had grown up somewhat since high school.

"What has he done?"

Cassie sighed deeply again. She knew she had to tell Franklin now.

"Well, he's abusive."

"What?" Franklin quickly responded. "How do you mean?"

"I know he's hit her at least once, she told me he did."

Franklin couldn't believe what he was hearing. He knew Troy had a temper, he'd witnessed as much at the racetrack. But he didn't think the boy would strike his woman. How could anyone hit the lovely Gretchen? She probably had the sweetest disposition of anybody he'd ever met. Something was amiss.

"I can't imagine Troy hitting her. He practically worships her."

Cassie held her palms up and shrugged her shoulders. "Gretchen told me he did Franklin. Why would she lie honey?"

Franklin shook his head in disbelief, but he knew Gretchen would never make up such a charge and then tell Cassie. "But why? I know there is never any reason to hit a woman, but why would he do such a thing? Did she tell you?"

Cassie looked away. She felt ashamed for her best friend. She understood she had to tell Franklin everything.

"It's partly my fault," Cassie said.

Franklin didn't follow.

"I've been trying to disciple her honey. I've grown to love that girl so much. She's like a sister to me." Cassie began to sob again.

Franklin put his arm around her once more. "I know. It's so beautiful how close you two have become."

Cassie wiped her tears again. "One of the things I've been trying to counsel her about is sex...They had been sleeping together Franklin."

Franklin shrugged his shoulders. "I always figured as much. I mean, just because they're Christians doesn't mean they can't fall into the same traps as every one else...You know all about my past troubles in that area."

Cassie nodded empathetically. Both realized how easily they could fall also if they weren't constantly on guard. It was a battle they would wage until their own wedding night.

"Are they still having sex?" Franklin asked.

"Gretchen says they're not," Cassie answered.

"Do you believe her?"

"Of course I do honey...Don't you see? That's why he hit her. She began to feel guilty, so she cut him off. She said he tried to force himself on her."

"Force himself? What?" Franklin began to get angry.

"Well, she told him no, and I guess that's when he slapped her."

"When did all this happen?"

"A few weeks ago."

Franklin was livid. He knew he had to straighten Troy out once and for all.

"I gonna talk to that boy today!" Franklin exclaimed as he began to get up.

Cassie firmly grabbed his arm and pulled him back down. "You can't!"

"Why not?"

"Because I promised Gretchen I wouldn't say anything."

"But Cassie, he needs..."

"No way!" Cassie yelled. "She told me in confidence. I shouldn't have told you." She began to cry again. "I feel like I've already betrayed her."

Franklin didn't want him and his fiancé to have their first argument, so he consented to her wishes. But he vowed to keep close watch on Troy.

"Honey, tell me what you want me to do," he said. "I want to help."

Cassie laid her head on his shoulder. She loved his sensitivity toward her feelings.

"Just being able to talk to you about it has helped," she said. "You're such a wonderful man. I sensed that the first time I saw you." Cassie again kissed his cheek. "I don't know what to do about the situation. But I said I would leave it in God's hands. All I can do right now is be Gretchen's friend, I guess. At least she knows she can come to me any time she wants to."

Franklin stood up and grabbed Cassie's hand to lift her to her feet. "And you know I will always be there for you no matter what."

"I do," she replied. "I surely do."

They embraced and kissed one more time before walking arm-in-arm back to New Hope. Their faith in God was as important to them as their devotion to one another. Daily, they would continue to pray the same for Gretchen and Troy.

The tingle of anticipation stirred the deepest carnal cravings in Troy as he leaned over the center consol inside his corvette and kissed Gretchen. Making out in the cramped confines of his sports car was obviously not the most comfortable place, but at least they were alone in the darkest corner of the parking lot. It wasn't long after midnight when everybody at the small New Year's party went their separate ways. Troy was extremely pleased when Franklin informed him he was going to take Cassie for a walk down to the beach. Finally, he and Gretchen would have the opportunity to spend some time alone together.

It had been weeks since they had wandered out of what seemed like Cassie's constant inquisitive view. But while Gretchen thoroughly enjoyed the attentiveness of her best friend, Troy despised every moment. He saw how Cassie was protecting Gretchen like an overbearing chaperone, though the girls were barely two years apart in age. Sure, he had given Cassie good reason for concern, but he resented her influence on Gretchen nonetheless. He read the contempt in her leer every time Cassie's eyes found their way to him. But the pastor's daughter was not around at the moment, so Troy knew he had better make wise use of the occasion.

Gretchen found herself being drawn into Troy's passion as he caressed the back of her neck while kissing her deeply. He could be such a warm and giving lover when his motives matched his mood. She'd noticed his disposition toward her much improved since he'd begged for her forgiveness after the shameful episode in her UCLA dormitory room. His remorse seemed as genuine as the tears he'd shed when she pardoned his almost-criminal conduct. And although she still sensed a lack of completeness in his repentance, he acted as though he was trying his best. Maybe effort was all she could ask, for the time being. She knew it would always be difficult to suppress her love for him, no matter what he did to her.

"I love you so much baby," Troy whispered into Gretchen's ear as he kissed her neck.

"I love you," she cooed as she leaned in to further absorb his kisses. She felt her own yearnings rising steadily from the self-subdued depths of desire. Her resolve was waning fast. She wanted as much. She abruptly pulled his face to her lips and thrust her tongue into his mouth. Her heart was pounding. Her head was spinning. She couldn't control her exhilaration much longer. Troy placed a hand on her breast. She left it there. It felt good. It had been so long since he'd touched her like that. She'd forgotten how much she enjoyed the pleasure of his touch. She would have to let him take all of her that night.

Gretchen's submission gave Troy a newfound audacity. While he continued to love her with his roaming hands, he wished for his own needs to be met. He felt the engagement ring as he softly rubbed her left hand. The diamond signified to him that she would soon be his forever. With boldness, he placed her hand in his lap.

The move startled Gretchen. Reality suddenly came racing back. It was like her conscience had been hastily awakened from a coerced slumber. She quickly realized the desires of the flesh were overwhelming her capacity to resist his amorous actions.

"Troy stop," she moaned, pulling her hand away and folding it across her chest. Images of Cassie flashed through her mind. What would her friend say if she found out lust had consumed virtue once again? She had promised Cassie to immediately cry out to the Lord in prayer if temptation crossed her path. He would always provide a way out, Cassie had told her. Gretchen followed through on her pledge, closing her eyes and turning her face away from Troy.

Exasperated, Troy smacked both his palms against the steering wheel. He knew full well from where Gretchen's sudden apprehension had sprung. Rage quickly followed as a matter of course.

"What the hell's wrong?'" he yelled, his temperament totally reversed from just a few seconds before.

Gretchen's lips began to quiver and she started to sob.

"Oh my god!" Troy fumed. "I can't believe this!"

Gretchen covered her face with both hands and wept. "Please don't yell at me," she whimpered. "I hate it when you're mad at me."

"Well what do expect?" Troy replied, his tone just a touch lighter, but still not sympathetic to Gretchen's feelings. "It seems that every time we start getting close lately, you back off... You just said you still love me...Don't you?"

Troy stared straight ahead and pouted as Gretchen gazed out the passenger window. She didn't want to agitate Troy further, but her emotions for him were being twisted every which way. She couldn't answer him honestly at that point. She really didn't know anymore.

"Well?" he persisted. "Were you lying?"

Gretchen's cry turned into a bawl. She couldn't even look at him. She knew he had every right to question her love for him. By her actions, he could tell her heart was split. It was so obvious, and it really had been since the day he slapped her. Part of her still loved him, always would. But there was no denying that some of her also lived in fear of him since that afternoon. Their relationship would never be the same because of her fear.

"Well answer me. Were you lying?"

She didn't respond. She just kept on crying. It seemed to Troy her tears were answering his question. But deep in his own heart, he didn't really care if she loved him or not. He could live without her love, but he still needed her in his future plans. He tried to quell his anger. He wondered if now was even the time to drop a deceiving tear of his own. He gently touched her shoulder to calm her, but he immediately sensed her resistance to his touch.

"Gosh, do I bother you that much?" he said, before opening his car door and leaping out.

The slamming of the car door let Gretchen know she had hurt him. She got out of the car and walked around to him.

"I'm sorry," she cried. "I don't know what's wrong with me lately. I'm so confused."

Troy dropped his jaw and sighed. "Confused about what? I thought we had everything planned out. We were going to get married and live happily ever after." Troy sneered with sarcasm. "Now you don't even know whether you love me or not."

"I do love you!" Gretchen quickly replied.

"Well you have a funny way of showing it!" Troy snapped back.

Gretchen sniffled a few times before responding. "It's just that... well...I think differently about things now... Frankly Troy, you scare me."

"You didn't seem too scared a little while ago when we were making out. You seemed like you were enjoying yourself. Like we always used to do. Then all of a sudden you just...stop! I don't get it."

Troy began to pace in an effort to not blow up at her again. He was fighting his frustration valiantly. But it would be only a matter of time before his rage erupted once more. He rarely used to be like this, at least not much, until he began working at New Hope. He had not failed to see the correlation.

Franklin used to irritate him years back, whether it be on the racetrack or in the classroom. But Troy chalked up that anger as just a symptom of injured teenage pride. Gretchen had never fallen victim to his virulence then. She could always manage to tame his temper. Usually just a quick flash of her lovely smile was all it took to soothe his furious soul. But recently her calming influence lacked any lasting effect. A deep-seated culpability had crushed Troy's innocence in a way that no one close to him could ever have known. Only Cassie, it seemed, sensed the utter depth of the sin so submerged beneath Troy's outer facade. His fiancé's best friend was slowly chipping away at the cover he had so carefully crafted to hide his falling self-esteem. Gretchen now bore the brunt of Troy's misplaced hostility.

"I'm gonna tell you something Gretchen," Troy said, pointing defiantly. "That Cassie is ruining us."

"Cassie?" Gretchen replied with surprise. "What has Cassie done?"

"What has she done?" Troy retorted. "She's gotten too much into your head, that's what she's done. Since you've met her, you've changed completely!"

"No I haven't."

"Oh no! How come you used to always talk to me about anything, anything at all...You always trusted me to know what was good for us. Now if something's bothering you, you run to her. It's like I hardly even exist anymore."

Troy started to pace again as he gathered more verbal ammunition. Gretchen wanted to bolster her defenses as her heart sank further into dejection. She realized Troy was partially correct. She was a different person now, thanks in large part to Cassie's mentoring. But Troy had changed as well. He was no longer the dashing prince about whom she had always romanticized; the one who would sweep her away like a princess in waiting. His character had deteriorated so much since high school. Outwardly he appeared to be maturing, but his inner walk with the Lord had slowed to a crawl. That was the fundamental problem in their relationship. She knew she was growing in Christ, both in faith and obedience. He was stagnant, and she began to feel that fact most profoundly after they had become engaged. Still, she wanted to help him. Her heart stung for his.

"Troy honey, please don't blame..."

"Don't call me honey!" he shouted, a resentful scowl etched across his face.

Gretchen felt the bite of his resentment, but she pushed forward.

"What I'm trying to say is that all Cassie wants to do is love us like the Bible commands."

"What!" Troy interrupted. "Cassie doesn't love me. She hates me. I know it. Are you kidding me? Open your eyes why don't you?"

Gretchen never recalled Cassie saying a hateful word about Troy in her presence. She had warned her of his duplicity, but Cassie never uttered even a disparaging remark about her fiancé. Gretchen couldn't even imagine Cassie hating someone.

"Cassie does not hate you."

"Oh no. Well she acts like she does. Both her and Franklin."

"Come on, now you're just being paranoid."

Troy raised his hand in defiance. "I'm not going to argue with you over this. Either you're my girl or you're her girl."

Gretchen cast a bewildered look at Troy. "What's that supposed to mean?"

"I won't compete with her Gretchen."

"You're not."

"I feel like I am."

"How so?"

Troy bit his bottom lip and clenched his fist. If Cassie were there right then, he would have punched her. "For months now, every time I kiss you or hold you, I feel like at any moment she's going to rush in and pull you away from me. Like she can't stand to see us together. Like she wants you for herself."

"That's just crazy...Cassie is my dearest friend. She loves me and I love her. We're like..."

Troy pounded his fist on the hood of his car, startling Gretchen and leaving a small crack in the fiberglass. "Then why don't you make love to her! She's certainly preventing you from making love to me!"

Gretchen was aghast at Troy's comment. "Now you're just being disgusting!"

"Well you love her so much," Troy responded snidely. "Go on, love you're little sister."

Gretchen felt her body begin to tremble and the tears once again welling in her eyes. She couldn't fathom the bitterness in his remark. It was tainted with venom and intended to kill. She confirmed her deepest fears at that moment. Their relationship was dead. She pulled her mother's ring off her finger, grasped it in her palm and hurled it at Troy. It actually struck him in the center of his chest and bounced off inside the corvette, falling under the passenger's seat.

Gretchen burst into tears and turned and ran toward the building, not looking back until she reached the stairs. She turned around just in time to see Troy spin the tires on the Corvette and peel out onto the street.

As he sped down the boulevard, Troy felt indignation clutching the inner recesses of his gut. He reasoned his current circumstance couldn't be all his fault. The more he drove, the more the blame shifted. Those responsible would pay, he vowed. Cassie, Franklin, even his formerly beloved Gretchen, would face dire consequences if the plans for the future that he deemed rightfully his were thwarted.

But those problems were to be put aside for the time being. He needed something to calm his nerves. Troy whipped the Corvette into a convenience store and purchased a six pack of beer. He popped open a bottle, placed it between his legs and cruised down the boulevard looking for action. He found it waiting on a corner under a streetlight.

"Nice car," the young lady called out in a distinctly upper

Midwestern accent. She wore typical streetwalker attire, a form-fitting, full-body black leotard covered by a tan leopard-patterned mini skirt with accompanying black stockings and stiletto heels. Her glittery make up was caked on and her false lashes were so long they must have itched the upper parts of her deep-seated eye sockets. Troy snickered at the total cliché of her outfit. But he did find the bleached blond girl, who couldn't have been older than her late teens, kind of cute in a trashy sort of way.

Troy leaned over and pushed open the passenger side door. He figured she would serve his purposes for the night.

Chapter XIII

T he intolerable heartache could cease in a matter of minutes. The dark spirits haunting her mind at that moment told her as much. With two simple slices from the blade, her distraught existence would at least be made more bearable. That was the great deception Satan's minions whispered with taunting subtlety.

Do it, they urged. *God still loves you my dear. He always will. Hasn't he promised you as much? Go be with him. He's calling you home, isn't He?*

The tears rolling down Gretchen's face seemed to flow almost as rapidly as the water cascading over her listless, naked body. As she stood in the steaming shower with the razor knife clutched in her left hand, she gazed at the finger that used to play host to her mother's precious engagement ring. Where now was the tiny jewel that once so marked her place in this fading world?

She was, after all, to be the wife of princely Troy Battles, who soon would be king of an empire. For her whole life, at least as far back as she could remember, Gretchen Bjorn was adored like a princess in waiting. Her wedding was really to be a coronation of sorts, for both the Battles and the Bjorns had basically planned the affair since her birth. But now that day of regal dreams seemed as distant as the era of King Arthur's roundtable.

Her despair had been made even graver just minutes before, following the heartfelt phone conversation she'd had with Richard. The Battles family patriarch was none too pleased by Gretchen's forlorn disclosure. She spilled every lurid detail of the turmoil she'd endured over the past few months at the whim of his son. While sympathetic to the girl he loved like a daughter, Richard's apologies for Troy's behavior couldn't mask his displeasure with the break-up. When his tearful pleas that she reconsider her options were rebuffed, Richard displayed his disappointment in the same manner his son had done so many times before. She could now see where Troy's anger problems were manifest. Richard had never so much as spoke a cross word to her, but in his frustration his temperament brought her to despair.

Did any of her family love her anymore, Gretchen was left to wonder? She could understand her father's ambivalence to the situation. He'd never shown much of a backbone during times of confrontation. The soft-spoken Erik was the exact opposite of Richard, but the two personalities complemented each other well in business and each one knew how much he relied on the other's respective gifts. And they truly were brothers in Christ, if not in arms.

But Gretchen was feeling the love of neither at the moment. In fact, it felt as if her Heavenly Father had forsaken her as well. Her heart was so cold to the presence of the Lord. There was dread in her abandonment. Where were all who claimed to love her? Maybe God also had drawn away from her because of her fornication. The sense of her shame was deep. She didn't blame him. In fact, she didn't blame any of the men in her life from fleeing her. Gretchen reasoned a tramp would possess more virtue than she.

Do it, the demons uttered. *Maybe God is not with you anymore? Do you know? How could you? You haven't spoken to him, have you?*

Gretchen fell to her knees. "Stop!" she screamed. "Please stop!" She dropped the razor knife. It sliced her knee as it fell toward the drain, but she didn't feel a hint of pain. Her inner anguish had covered up any physical sensation. She rolled into a fetal position on the shower floor and wept in bitter sorrow as the steaming water pelted her back. Her wailing was uncontrollable.

Cassie suddenly burst through the bathroom door. Through the rolling mist now obscuring the room, she could barely make out the contour of Gretchen's body curled up on the shower floor. Cassie rushed over and pulled open the opaque glass shower doors. She saw a steady stream of blood slowly seeping down the drain. She gasped and stepped into the still-running shower. The water was nearly scalding.

"Oh my gosh, Gretchen!" panic-stricken Cassie screamed, pulling her friend out onto the tile floor. "What have you done?"

Gretchen was still sobbing profusely as Cassie inspected both her wrists. Strangely, there were no cuts on the either of them. By sheer reaction, she grabbed the back of the blond girl's steam-reddened neck and spun her head around. Her throat didn't have a mark on it.

"Oh honey, you're bleeding, where are you hurt?"

Again, Gretchen hadn't even felt the blade slice her skin when she dropped it. The evil voices urging her mind had so thoroughly entrapped her conscience that she responded submissively to their accusations. She lamented the proof of their guilt and her tears confirmed the verdict. Any punishment they cried for would be fitting. She had forsaken her will and was at the mercy of their judgment. She had never felt so low.

Cassie finally noticed the cut on Gretchen's knee when her friend buried her weeping face into Cassie's neck. Cassie pulled a clean white towel down from the rack above the toilet. The wound was not very deep, although it did bleed excessively. Cassie pressed down firmly on the gash to stop the bleeding as Gretchen continued to sob, still not speaking a word. Cassie held Gretchen tightly with her free arm and let the weeping girl release her grief.

After a few minutes, Gretchen began to ease out of her despondency. Cassie wrapped a bath towel around the naked girl and helped her into the bedroom they had been sharing for the past three weeks. The bleeding on Gretchen's knee had slowed greatly. Her tears had also run dry. The nearly-suicidal episode had passed.

Embarrassment soon began to set in. Gretchen adjusted the bath towel to better cover herself. She was thankful Cassie had come to her rescue, but disconcerted about the state in which she had been found. She didn't know how to explain herself.

"I'm so sorry," Gretchen said somberly, as if she were about to cry again.

Cassie, still soaking wet herself, quickly sat down next to Gretchen to calm her.

"Oh, hey, it will be alright," she said, hugging her friend closely. "We will figure this out together okay?"

Gretchen squeezed Cassie before pulling away and letting out a deep breath.

"I'm so blessed to have you. Cassie, I don't know what I'd do without you."

Cassie smiled lovingly at her friend and kissed her on the top of the head before walking over to her dresser to get a dry set of clothes for each of them. Although still quite worried, Cassie didn't press Gretchen for an explanation as they got dressed. She figured stricken girl would open up soon enough.

Cassie already knew about the broken engagement. She knew before Gretchen even told her and Franklin about it early New Year's morning. As they walked around the corner after their stroll on the beach, they had witnessed Troy speeding away from the church parking lot after his fight with Gretchen. Intuition told Cassie that something bad had happened. Cassie comforted Gretchen as best she could that morning, while Franklin unsuccessfully tried to call Troy's cell phone. Franklin left numerous messages, but Troy never called back. In fact, it was two days later, and Troy still had not been seen by anybody. Franklin believed Troy was avoiding further confrontation. He'd always known the Battles boy to flee when circumstances didn't go his way.

"I don't suppose Troy has tried to call here?" Gretchen asked.

"No, I haven't heard from him," Cassie replied, as she brushed her hair in front of the dresser mirror and spoke to her friend in the reflection. "But I don't think he would call me anyway."

"I still worry about him Cassie. I can't help it."

"I know you do honey. But really, you need to worry about yourself right now."

Gretchen nodded.

Cassie looked back into the mirror. "Do you feel like talking now about what happened? I was terribly scared Gretchen when I saw you bleeding on the floor in the shower. I thought you were dead."

Cassie looked down and swallowed hard so as not to choke up.

"I thought about it Cassie. I really did."

Cassie quickly got up and sat beside Gretchen at the foot of the bed. She was shocked at what she was hearing. Cassie knew Gretchen was upset by the breakup, but she didn't have any idea at all that her best friend might be contemplating suicide.

"Why honey?" Cassie asked, as she placed an arm around the somber girl. "You know so many people still love you so much. Me. Franklin. Papa. You're family. You have so much to live for."

Gretchen dropped her eyes downward. She couldn't bear to stare into Cassie's sympathetic gaze. She felt so foolish. She didn't know how to explain her actions. A truly wicked force had almost convinced her to toss away her life in an extreme effort to cast aside despair. Her sudden hopelessness had made suicide seem like a reasonable alternative to walking through a desperate maze of shattered dreams.

"Gretchen," Cassie said as she brushed the girl's long blond hair away from her face. "Why don't you continue to stay here for a while?"

"Oh Cassie, you don't trust me anymore do you?" Gretchen started to cry again.

"It's not that. Of course I trust you. I'm just worried." Cassie began to cry as well. "I'm scared...I love you."

The two you women hugged for a moment, each trying to convince the other that their worlds weren't really collapsing around them. God had really seemed to be blessing their lives up until a couple of months before. Cassie had even held out fantasies about a double wedding for the couples, although she hadn't mentioned the scenario to anybody. Troy's selfish actions had spoiled any chances for such an occasion.

"Cassie, I know you're mad at me, but..."

"I'm not mad at you. I'm just concerned."

"I know, but I think I'll be alright now. I think everything just hit me today and the devil took advantage of it."

Cassie didn't follow. "What do you mean?"

"I heard voices. I know it's crazy, but they told me to do it. I almost listened to them. I really did. But for some reason, I couldn't go through with it."

Cassie smiled at her friend. She realized fully what had taken place. Her concern about the state of Gretchen's psyche eased greatly.

"God stepped in," Cassie stated. "He always comes through for his children when they need him the most."

The two sisters clasped hands and went before their Heavenly Father in prayer. They thanked him for his tender mercy in a moment of sincere darkness. They would be forever grateful.

The trauma of the time continued as the trying week wore on.

Cassie ministered to Gretchen as best she could after the grief-stricken girl moved back into her dorm room on the UCLA campus. Cassie phoned her sister in Christ three or four times daily until classes resumed the following Monday. Gretchen didn't mind Cassie's concern for her well-being, she had given the pastor's daughter good reason to worry after all. Gretchen's heart still ached from missing Troy's presence in her life, but at least she no longer heard demonic voices prodding aberrant suicidal tendencies. God had indeed protected her soul and Gretchen knew it. And He was beginning to convince Cassie as well.

Still, it had been almost a week and no one had heard from Troy. The whole family was troubled by his absence, especially the young man's father. Richard had been trying to track down his son since receiving the unsettling phone call from Gretchen. He was about to fly out to Los Angeles to investigate the situation himself when Franklin phoned him.

"I really don't completely understand what happened Richard,"

Franklin said while talking on his cell phone in the New Hope Church office. "He hasn't come back here since that night.?

Richard nervously tapped his fingers on his desk in the penthouse suite of the high-rise office building he owned in downtown Fort Lauderdale. His mind flashed back to the beginning of the Holiday season. To Thanksgiving dinner, when his body did not seem stout enough to contain the pride bursting from within as Troy boldly bestowed Ingrid's ring upon Gretchen's delicate finger. It was quite possibly the most heartfelt moment he had ever witnessed in his life. His golden boy was betrothed to the precious little girl he had long wished his own. With the taking of the ring, Erik's daughter had finally enabled Richard to rekindle the flickering flame ever slipping away in the fading glimmer of ill-fated love. His glee flowed as freely as the expensive champagne pouring into the glasses held high in toast on that joyous evening of thankfulness.

But Troy somehow managed to shatter the grand illusion his father so coveted. Richard was beside himself over the trouncing of his dreams.

"I'm desperate to speak to him," Richard tearfully pleaded to Franklin.

"Oh I imagine you are brother. We all are very worried about Troy. We truly are. I know he must be hurting badly. We do want to help him. I've asked around, but no one has seen him. None of his buddies, the school, no one. I'm thinking about calling the police for help."

"Oh, don't do that yet," Richard quickly interjected, fearing Troy's disappearance might somehow become scandalous. "I'm sure he's physically okay. I called the bank and there has been some modest activity in his account."

"Yeah, but what if he was robbed or something?"

"Franklin, if he had been robbed, there would have been a lot more money taken out. The transactions were fairly normal. I ought to know, I have complete access to his account. No, I think he's just very angry and is avoiding us right now."

Franklin agreed, but wondered how much Gretchen had told Richard of Troy's actions toward her.

"I know Gretchen was very upset the night Troy took off," Franklin said, hoping Richard would let on what he knew about the couple's troubles. "She was heartbroken really. She said she spoke to you."

"Yes she did," Richard answered, his voice fading in remorse. "I'm afraid I wasn't very kind to her...I was so upset that they broke up that I kinda blamed her for it. I know it wasn't Gretchen's fault... My son can be such a louse sometimes."

Franklin heard the anger rising in Richard's voice.

"You know Franklin, I'd like to ring his neck. Gretchen loves him so much and he completely takes her for granted. When I finally get a hold of him, I'm gonna..."

"Richard," Franklin interrupted, "how much did Gretchen tell you?'"

Richard paused in an effort to regain his composure. "Everything. She told me everything."

Franklin took a deep breath and sighed. "Brother, I think Gretchen will eventually forgive Troy, but she just needs a little time. I know she loves him. We all do."

"I don't know what's wrong with him Franklin, he was doing so well," Richard's voice began to crack. "I know I haven't always been the greatest father in the world, but he's my only son and I've tried to love him so much. I've tried to love both of them so much."

Richard began to weep.

"And I know they both love you Richard. They're still just kids and they're gonna make mistakes."

"But how can I fix them?"

"You can't fix their mistakes. Only they can. We can help them, along with God's help. But sometimes they need to make their mistakes and learn from them. Our parents did the same for us. All we can do is love them and try to guide them in God's way."

"I know you're right. But it hurts to watch them go through it."

"I know. I know."

Franklin heard a click on his cell phone. "Is that mine or yours?"

"It's mine," Richard responded. "Oh, it's Troy! Hold on."

Franklin waited a few seconds as Richard answered the call.

"Franklin? Can I call you back?"

"Absolutely. Is everything alright? Is he okay?"

"Yeah, he says he is. He said he's been staying at a friend's house. Hey thank you for listening to me brother."

"No problem Richard. Anytime."

"I'll call you after I talk to Troy."

"Sounds good."

"Alright, bye."

Richard hung up and Franklin prayed that father would be gentle with his son. The boy definitely needed to be put in his place, but Franklin knew Richard could be brutal himself at times, like when Gretchen first informed him of the breakup. Franklin asked God to calm the hearts of both father and son. He was thankful that Troy was safe, if not sound. Franklin took comfort in God's unrestrained sovereignty in all situations in life. He had already observed such providence in his own walk.

He sought to keep his cool as he stared out toward the placid, blue ocean just blocks from the throne he had acquired through years of intense effort, but Richard could feel the heat building inside his usually-restrained temperament. Despite every fervent comment spewed forth by his wayward son, Richard fought to suppress the urge to blow his top. However, Troy was making the attempt seem extremely futile. The son's belligerent excuses laced with outright lies were forcing the father to lay down an ultimatum that would probably end with dire consequences.

To think only minutes earlier, Richard was so relieved to hear Troy's voice. More than a week of worry had been instantly calmed by just two words: "Hello father." Richard could immediately tell by Troy's tone, his boy appeared relatively unscathed by the tumultuous turn of events facing the family. But as their conversation further unfolded, Richard realized his son didn't grasp the seriousness of the charges before him.

"You just don't get it do you son?" Richard asked with a ruffled strain in his voice.

"What do you mean?" Troy retorted angrily.

"Some would call what you did to that lovely girl rape."

"Is that what she told you?"

"Not in so many words, but..."

"Gretchen wanted to father," Troy interrupted. "This was not the first time either."

"You mean you raped her other times too?"

"What are you talking about? I didn't rape her! She wanted it just as much as me. She always did."

"That's not what she said Troy. She said she told you to stop and you didn't. She said you coerced her into having sex. I talked to Franklin, he confirmed it."

"Franklin? What they hell does he have to do with it? Oh this is such bullsh..."

"Hey!" Richard screamed through the phone. "Watch you mouth! Remember who you're talking to!"

Troy was seething. He was so sick of trying to live up to his father's expectations. When was it going to stop? He had lived his whole life trying to win his father's praise. All he really longed for was Richard's love, but that was another merit not doled out frivolously in the Battles household. Unless, of course, your name was Gretchen Bjorn. Troy could not deny that as much as he loved Gretchen at one time, his father loved her more. The resentment that had built up over the years was staggering.

"You know, I give up," Troy roiled. "Believe whatever you want. I just don't care anymore."

"What kind of an attitude is that?"

"What do you care anyway? Gretchen is the one you love, not me. You always have father. You always will."

"I love both of you Troy. That's why this hurts me so much. I want you both to be happy."

"Well, we're not. We haven't been in a long time."

Richard was perplexed by that statement. "But you both seemed so happy at Thanksgiving. You seemed so in love when you proposed to her?"

"I did that for you father," Troy responded snidely. "Like everything else I've done in my life, I did that for your pleasure, not mine."

Richard was struck by the acrid honesty in Troy's venomous voice. His words pierced with an almost contemptuous sting. Their wound left Richard reeling, forcing a defensive posture.

"I'm sorry I've made your life so miserable," Richard lashed back. "I've only tried to love you the best I can. I've given you everything I could Troy. I don't know what else you want from me son."

"That's just it," Troy snapped. "Son. I only want to be your son!"

"You are my son. You're my only son. My heir if you want to be!"

"If I want to be?" Troy shouted. "I deserve to be! I've busted my ass trying to prove my worthiness to you! Trying to act like the great Richard Battles' son! It ain't easy father!"

"Nothing in life is son. Never has been. And it won't get easier either."

They both fell silent for a few seconds.

"You know Troy," Richard said in a more reserved tone. "It might be good for you to go it alone for a while. To see how the people who really struggle live."

"I have father. Why do you think I've been volunteering at New Hope Church?"

"You see, that's just it son. It's your attitude about life. Observing difficulty is a whole lot different than living it. I grew up dirt poor. I know what it's like to go hungry. To not know where your next meal is coming from. To have to work for everything you have. You have no idea."

Troy sighed. "That's not my fault. I can't help where I was born."

"No, but you can learn to appreciate what's been given to you little more. No, I take that back. A whole lot more."

"What do you want from me?"

Richard sighed. "What do I want? I want you to patch things up with Gretchen. I don't care what it takes. You make that girl happy. I want you to love her the way she deserves to be loved. Respect her like she deserves to be respected. Honor her the way she deserves to be honored. Just like the Bible says."

"What if she won't love me father?"

"Then earn her love!"

"Yeah, just like I have to earn yours!"

The sudden click told Richard the confrontation was over. He hoped he had made his point to Troy. A hit to the boy's wallet might accelerate the process of reconciliation. Richard's next action would help determine the result of his desired intention.

Richard immediately phoned Gretchen to apologize for his earlier frustration toward her. He was still unaware that she had briefly considered suicide. Gretchen didn't tell him either. She forgave Richard for his sternness during their last conversation. She was happy when he told her that Troy had called him. Richard noticed the lifting of her spirit upon hearing the news of Troy's well-being. She told Richard she missed both of them and prayed that they would all be close again one day.

It was the hopefulness in Gretchen's voice that Richard had so desperately needed to hear.

❧❖❧

The wine glass seemed to explode as it slammed against the plaster wall. Like tiny shards of crystal shrapnel, the pieces hurled their way throughout the small room Troy had reluctantly called home for the past two weeks. Some of the glass careened back onto Troy's drawn, sulking face. As he brushed aside the sharp fragments that stuck to his skin, each sliver took with it just a speck of blood.

The minute red splotches left behind displayed a fitting relevance to the crimson stain now creeping its way across the white wall. It had always been that way for as long as anyone could remember.

Even as a child, Troy's tantrums were noted to pain others more severely than he. A normally innocent scuffle for a wanted toy often left his playmates injured and crying for their parents. Growing up together, Gretchen bore the brunt of Troy's anger many times. On one occasion when they were youngsters, Gretchen was found bawling at the foot of the spiral staircase in the Battles mansion, her body scraped and bruised. Troy looked over the balcony with a sneer as his worried father comforted the seven-year-old girl.

Troy's violent disposition was treated pharmaceutically at the time when it was discovered he had pushed Gretchen down the stairs in a dispute over the way a game was to be played. Even at such a young age, Troy was ready to battle anyone if a challenge to his authority was presented. But neither his parents, nor any of the many doctors who treated him back then, could diagnose the deep-seated depravity that so controlled his unfortunate soul. The drugs calmed the boy for a while, but never fully cured him. So Richard continued to pray Troy's tumultuous spirit would be tamed before it someday proved fatal. He was presently unaware such disaster had already occurred.

Troy grabbed the keys to his corvette and left his friend's apartment where he had been a guest since a few days after his break-up with Gretchen. He was still stewing as he sped down the boulevard toward New Hope. He couldn't believe his father had followed through on the threat to disown him.

"Damn him," Troy muttered, as he peeled away from a traffic signal. "Damn all of them."

Troy vowed to regain everything he'd lost over the past month or there would be hell to pay. He promised himself as much. The only reason he wasn't completely broke at the moment was because his estranged mother had wired him some cash. He'd never had much use for his mom over the years, but she could prove helpful in times of trouble.

Heather Battles never really loved her son all that much either. But it was disdain for Troy's father that drove her every motivation. Their family saga was certainly unenviable at best.

Richard settled for the once-gorgeous gold digger on the rebound from abandoned love. Heather quickly discovered she never stood a chance at capturing Richard's wounded heart, but such was not her true desire anyway. She didn't really long for his love all that much, only his opulence. She secured her path to his affluence through cunning seduction. The way to his wealth was steered delicately through her bedroom. Inevitably, pregnancy became her passage to prominence. Heather knew Richard's faith, even as weak as it was during that fallen season, would not allow for abortion. He had no other choice but to marry the dubious vixen in order to save face. His reputation meant more to him than an inconvenient marriage that would eventually dissolve into mutual apathy.

Richard soon seized hold of the predicament and set a firm course for his unintended son's future. Meanwhile, unloved Heather would become a paramour to virtually every playboy on the peninsula. After one illicit affair struck too close to home, Heather was finally sent packing, albeit with a substantial severance that would ensure the most salacious details were kept out of the scandal sheets.

Heather's five-year hitch to Richard Battles had paid off handsomely. She invested well after the divorce and became extremely wealthy in her own right. She used every opportunity she could to try and show up her former husband, even if it meant propping up a son for whom she'd never harbored even the slightest maternal instinct. The iciness of the blood coursing through her veins had been copiously passed down to her offspring.

Troy planned to use his mother's resources to find his way back into his father's good graces.

He understood Gretchen was the key player in his grand scheme, but he knew he had a few other devices at his disposal. They were contained in the file under his bed at New Hope Church. What a fool he had been to rush off that New Year's night without grabbing the file. The papers inside contained incriminating evidence he could use to convince Gretchen to change her mind, either willingly or otherwise. Troy also knew the file held information that, if misunderstood, could ultimately prove detrimental to his own well-being. He shouldn't have been so careless with such vital material.

But he blamed his frenzy over the past two weeks on dejection over losing Gretchen. He was troubled by how much he missed her. Troy had to admit that deep inside, albeit very deep, he still sensed a certain fondness for her. It didn't matter whether those feelings were drawn from love or lust, most likely the latter he reasoned, but they were still there nonetheless. His derangement convinced him she belonged to him, regardless of either of their current emotions toward each other. He resolved himself to the fact that she would again be his or nobody's. And he told himself he didn't have a problem spilling blood if that was the course circumstances rendered.

Troy was pleased to find the parking lot nearly empty when he pulled his corvette alongside the church van. He didn't want to talk to anybody. He was just hoping to grab his file and get out of there quickly. He believed it was still under his bed in the spare room. He had hidden the file pretty well under a blanket and even if somebody had brought it somewhere for safekeeping, it was locked and only he had the key. He didn't figure Franklin or any of the others would have the audacity to break open the lock and peer into his personal papers. They claimed to be Christians after all, so Troy assumed they would mind their own business and leave his private belongings alone.

Unfortunately, when he opened the door to the room, his assumption proved to be incorrect.

⋘✦⋙

Cassie knew she was sinning, but the temptation was just too great to overcome. Besides, that occasion she wasn't just being a busybody, unable, or unwilling, to draw away from her magnetic curiosity. Lives might be at stake, maybe even her own she reasoned. What else could she do? She just had to sneak a quick peak. If she was careful, no one would know.

For some reason, unwitting courtesy perhaps, Cassie knocked before opening the door to the tiny bedroom. It had been weeks since anybody had stepped a foot inside. The bed was still neatly made. The top of the old wooden dresser was clear of any item, except for a small desk lamp. A few sets of shirts and slacks hung freely in the closet bolted on to the back wall. The night table held just an alarm clock and a few pieces of lint. For all his faults, Troy was definitely a tidy fellow, Cassie mused, the complete opposite of Franklin. And it was readily apparent Troy hadn't snuck back into his quarters since that fateful New Year's Eve nearly two weeks past.

Cassie knelt down beside the bed and looked underneath. She knew Troy kept the tan aluminum box under the bed. She had seen him put it back there while walking by his cracked-open door the day before he abruptly left the premises. She pulled back a green, woolen blanket from under the bed and found the standard file-sized box wrapped up in it. The box was locked.

"Darn!" Cassie fumed under her breath. She should have figured Troy would not have left his personal belongings alone with easy access. She wished she would have lifted the key from Troy's keychain when he'd left it there while delivering Christmas presents to needy children during New Hope's toy drive. How ironic, she thought, one of the most self-centered people she'd ever met helping to care for the poor during the holidays. Cassie realized they all had been fooled by Troy's deceiving motivation. She wondered what had been driving him all these months. Maybe the answer was to be found in the tin box. Somehow she had to get a look inside of it.

"You know, he hates me anyway," Cassie said to herself. She put the box on top of the bed and walked over to the maintenance closet down the hallway. A couple minutes later she returned with a small flathead screwdriver and a pair of tin snips. Cassie pried the screwdriver into a small gap in the lock and twisted it slowly. Surprisingly the lid popped right open. It also appeared the lock hadn't broken either.

"Well that was easy," Cassie said, not feeling even the slightest bit of remorse for breaking into Troy's privacy. She was so focused on the task at hand, that not the smallest concern about being caught entered her mind.

Cassie reached inside the box and pulled the contents out as a whole and placed them on the bed. As she began to set the box on the floor, she heard a rattle inside. It startled her when she looked inside the tin box and saw a small pistol. She carefully pulled out the revolver and looked it over. The gun frightened her so much that she gently placed it on the night table. She didn't know if it was loaded or not. Just touching the gun made her nervous. Cassie had no idea what kind of gun it was. She hated them, having seen such weapons used to snuff out so many young lives in their crime-ridden neighborhood. Maybe Troy kept it for protection, she thought. After all, the church was located in a dangerous part of the city. Her father would have a fit if he found out Troy had brought a gun into the building. Cassie figured that was just more ammunition she could use in building her case for Gretchen to permanently dismiss Troy from her life.

Oh how she wanted for Gretchen to find a beau who would love her the way she deserved to be loved. Cassie wished her best friend would find a mate like Franklin, a man who loved God with all his heart. He had proven that fact to Cassie time after time since the day they'd met. She loved him so much. She promised herself she would do anything to love and protect him for as long as they both shall live. Cassie longed for the day when she could respond to those vows for real.

Her mind continued to drift toward her wedding day, before she made herself set her sights back on the task at hand.

Cassie reached down and picked up the papers lying on the bed. She looked at each one before carefully placing them in order back on the bed. She wanted to try, if at all possible, to cover up her snooping. Among the papers was Troy's birth certificate, passport, banking information and some stock certificates for Battles Trading Corp. None of the information appeared useful to her, at least none of it seemed to harbor any deep, dark secrets. Cassie had gained no additional insight into the mind of the shrewd young rich boy. She only knew he was armed, and that could obviously still prove dangerous enough.

Frustrated, Cassie figured she better put the papers, and the

gun, back into the tin box. Maybe Troy wouldn't notice his belongings had been tampered with. She knew that if he did find out, he
would suspect her. But she also knew he couldn't prove that she
had looked through his things. Sure, there was still the matter of
the gun, but she would figure out a way to deal with that problem
later.

As Cassie was putting the papers back into the box, she noticed
a sealed manila envelope she had missed. Maybe this was the information she was looking for? With the edge of her fingernail, Cassie
tried to carefully slide open the envelope. But the paper ripped.
Oh well, Cassie figured, no need for care now. She pulled open the
envelope and took out the contents.

She found a fading newspaper article. The story was heartbreaking. It told of the tragic accident that claimed the lives of Franklin's
wife and little girls almost two years before. Cassie began to tear-up
as she read the article. It was rather mater-of-fact, like one would
expect to find in a newspaper story. Informative wording that lacked
any real emotion. Cassie knew better. She had seen firsthand in her
beloved fiancé how wrenching sudden death can be for those left
behind. But why did Troy save such an article, she asked herself? He
certainly didn't seem to care about other people's feelings. She had
witnessed that much on numerous occasions.

Cassie also noticed the ripped edges of a photograph inside
the envelope. She pulled it out and saw that it was a picture of
Franklin. The other half of the photo was still inside. Cassie felt
confused when she gazed at it. Smiling back at her was a beautiful
red-headed woman and two darling little pigtailed girls. Cassie
realized immediately they were Franklin's wife and kids. But she
was befuddled by the three red X's marked across their images.
What was that supposed to mean?

After studying the picture for a few moments, Cassie placed both parts of the photograph together. The fit formed a portrait of the ideal family, save for the X's defacing the departed members. Cassie shook her head in dismay. "He must really be a lunatic," she muttered to herself.

Suddenly, Cassie's world abruptly faded to black!

∽❖∼

Troy stood above the body, still clutching the gold-plated candelabra in his right hand. The rage that had erupted with fervor seared through his last rational nerve. With disgust, he hurled the candelabra at her head. It careened off the side of her face and landed next to her shoulder. Blood immediately began to flow steadily from her nose. Cassie never saw the vicious assault coming.

As she fell to the floor from the force of Troy's initial blow to the back of her head, the torn photograph dropped out of Cassie's hands and the pieces slid underneath the bed. Troy didn't notice where they had fallen. In fact, he didn't notice much of anything once he entered the room and found Cassie prying straight into his persona again.

Troy had felt the depths of her inquisition since that first night he and Gretchen knocked on Cassie's apartment door looking for work. He knew Cassie sensed his ulterior motives the minute she laid eyes on him. It wasn't long before her suspicion began to press on him like impending damnation. With each misgiving glance that cast judgment on his guilty soul, Troy's abhorrence for her thickened. He endured her circumspection for Gretchen's sake, but tolerance only provoked deeper hatred. It was because of Cassie, he had lost the love of his girl. But Troy deemed providence had allowed for vengeance. He was finished with Cassie's meddling once and for all.

He felt no remorse for striking her. He only felt relief.

For a couple of moments after the attack, time seemed to stand still for Troy. The voice who had taunted him for months came calling once more. He was well-pleased with Troy's actions.

Well done, my son. Well done.

Troy didn't move a muscle. He just looked down at Cassie's crumpled body. She seemed almost at peace in her current state. Maybe she's met her Lord by now, Troy thought. He realized he served a different master at that point. He reasoned he had probably always done so.

You've proven you are my seed.

Troy grinned and continued to stare at Cassie's body. He sensed a certain peace within himself as well. Confirming his destiny strangely seemed to offer comfort for his misguided soul. He was actually happy for the first time in many months.

My son, my son. Finish the deed my son'

Troy was confused. He didn't understand the request being made.

The girl is not dead. Finish the deed my son, my son, my son, my son...

The voice fled his conscience. Troy suddenly snapped back into the normal realm of reality. The place where circumstance meets consequence. Paranoia rapidly beset his mind!

Troy reached down and checked Cassie's pulse in her neck and both wrists. He felt no pulse anywhere. Maybe the voice had deceived him? She seemed dead. He rolled her onto her back. Her eyes were closed. He opened them with his fingers, but they closed again when he released. Troy placed his ear to her chest, but he couldn't hear a heartbeat through her bloodied white blouse. He quickly leaned his cheek against her face. He could feel a shallow breath seeping through her nostrils. Some of her blood stained his cheek. He didn't notice it.

The voice was correct. She was still alive.

"Great!" Troy muttered with disdain. "You can't even die properly you bitch!"

Troy kicked her in the ribs. She still didn't move. He sat down on the edge of the bed and stared at Cassie's wounded body, pondering his next move. He thought about leaving her there, figuring Ramon or Franklin would find her and think she had just fallen victim to a random attack. Maybe she would die before they found her? Maybe he should finish her off like the voice commanded him to do? He picked up the candelabra and thought about beating her brains out. It certainly would please him to do so.

As he gazed at her stricken body, Troy noticed the blood dripping from her nose and the back of her head had greatly stained the tan area rug next to the bed. He knew he was facing two choices: flee the premises quickly and hope that nobody had seen him enter the church; or kill Cassie somewhere else and dispose of the body.

Troy gathered up the papers and placed them back in the file. He quickly glanced at the contents, making doubly sure the stock certificates were there. He knew he would have use for them later no matter what decision he made about Cassie.

He then saw the pistol lying on the night table. He'd almost forgotten he had it. He picked up the gun and aimed it at Cassie's unconscious body lying face up on the floor. Troy smirked and pointed the gun at her head. His mind went blank as he squeezed the trigger. His deep loathing had managed to temporarily blot out his own consciousness. The revolver only clicked as it passed through each chamber. Troy had no knowledge whether or not the gun was loaded when he fired. His malice thoroughly coerced his every action. Cassie was spared only because the gun was empty. Troy remembered the bullets were in the glove compartment of the corvette. He would get them later.

Pulling the gun's trigger snapped Troy's rage. He slowly gathered his wits and realized the distress of the situation confronting him. A surge of panic began to bubble inside his belly. He had to rectify his problem quickly before someone returned to the church. He didn't know what information Cassie had discovered from looking through his file, but he wanted to make sure she never discussed its contents with anybody. He knew he needed to buy some time to sort out the situation. He reasoned leaving Cassie where she lay might eventually prove risky to his own health. She must be permanently silenced, but not there.

Troy ran out through the back door and surveyed the parking lot. It was still vacant except for his corvette and the church's old white work van. The van was totally enclosed except for the driver's side and passenger windows, neither of which rolled down properly, and the front windshield. Because he used the van to make food runs for the church, Troy still had the key on his keychain. He went outside and looked around again. It was a cool, quiet morning and none of the usual homeless folk seemed to be lurking about. Troy opened the back doors of the van and pushed aside enough of the tools and other junk to make a place to lay Cassie's body. He grabbed a roll of cotton twine and a roll of gray duct tape.

He went back into the church and knelt down beside Cassie. She was still unconscious, but the bleeding had stopped. Troy was so surprised she wasn't dead. His anger began to build again at just the sight of her.

"Calm down," he said to himself, squeezing both of his palms against his temples as if trying to physically subdue his inner frustration. "You can still work this out."

He placed his cheek against her nostrils once more just to confirm his diagnosis. The soft breath of air touching his cheek told him she was still alive, but severely injured. She might die soon enough, he hoped. Troy rolled Cassie flat on her back and folded her arms across her chest. He rolled off a few yards of the twine and wrapped it tightly around her wrists. The twine was thin, but proved very unbreakable when wrapped tautly several times. Troy did the same thing to Cassie's legs and ankles. Her tight blue jeans actually made the knots even more constricting. He duct taped her mouth closed, but kept her nose free to obtain air. He decided not to kill her until he could find a place to bury her body. Maybe the desert east of L.A. would be a good place, he thought.

Once he had Cassie bound so she could not escape, Troy pushed her to the edge of the five-by-eight rug. He rolled her up in it and wrapped the rug with twine at both ends and in to middle. Cassie was about five-and-a-half feet tall, so there was more than a foot of room at each end, enough space so that she wouldn't easily slide out.

He hoisted the rolled up rug and its damaged contents over his shoulder. The haul to the van would be heavy, but he knew he was strong enough to handle it. He was happy he had continued his stringent fitness routine since coming to college. He knew Gretchen had always admired the brawny cut of his physique, she had often told him so when they made love.

Troy thought of her as he carried his hated cargo to the van. He missed the intimacy he'd shared for so long with Gretchen. If only they had never come to New Hope Church that night six months ago. Gretchen would have never met Cassie and her prudish ways. The lovely blond girl would not have left his bed forever. He so much wanted to press his flesh to hers again. He desperately needed to. He absolutely must!

Once he slid the rug into the van, Troy locked the back doors. He went back into the church and grabbed the file and the rest of his cloths from the closet. He removed a pillow case from the bed and tossed his belongings into it. He returned to the van and started the engine. He began to pull out of the parking spot before noticing his corvette parked next to the passenger side. It dawned on him that if he wanted to make a cleaner break, he had to hide the car somewhere. He also knew someone could arrive back at the church at any moment and he'd be busted. He had to act fast.

When he got out of the van, Troy remembered the city parking garage located the next block over. That would be the perfect place to stash the corvette for a while. Even if it got towed away by the attendants after a few days, his beloved car would still be fairly safe in the impound lot and he could somehow figure a way to get it out later. Troy quickly drove over to the garage, parked the corvette, grabbed the bullets from the glove box and hustled back to New Hope. Thankfully, when he returned to the church about ten minutes later, neither Ramon, nor Franklin had arrived yet. He hopped into the van and drove off.

Troy still didn't know where he was headed as he cruised down the boulevard. He was confident Cassie wouldn't be able to cause him trouble in her current state. In fact, he almost felt giddy about his opportunity to pull out of his predicament. He still stubbornly believed he could work the dire circumstances to his advantage somehow.

As he passed a billboard touting the UCLA Bruins basketball team, Troy's mind immediately reverted back to Gretchen. He knew what he had to do. Somehow, someway, Gretchen must belong to him again. She was his woman and his alone. He would kill any man who ever touched her like he wanted to touch her again. Gretchen Bjorn would only know one lover in her life, Troy vowed. It was time to pay her a visit.

Chapter XIV

Shakespeare once called the prince of darkness a gentleman. So suave is his subversion that the discord left in his wake as he passes through the waters of an already-turbulent soul can appear placid, even docile, to those unwary. A deceptive manner is the inheritance bequeathed by the father of all lies to the diabolical seed of his loin. Troy Battles certainly reaped an abundant bounty from his infernal birthright. He had always been quite proficient with the talents generously bestowed by the gentleman from Hades. Troy hoped his fiendish charms would prevail one last time in order to secure the lifelong consort who could rectify his current misfortune.

❦

Gretchen was sitting on the front steps leading into the dormitory when Troy arrived in the van. She had no idea about the crippled cargo unmercifully stored inside. As long as Cassie remained unconscious, he still had the chance to permanently dispose of the nuisance who had so plagued his life for the last six months. Before pulling onto the campus, Troy checked his victim and made sure she was still incapacitated. He was pleased that Cassie seemed comatose and would not present a problem in the near future. He figured once he won back Gretchen, he could secretly finish off Cassie and bury her body in the desert on the way to Las Vegas. He swore to himself that Gretchen would be joining him for the journey, either willingly or otherwise.

Troy watched his childhood sweetheart closely as she got up and walked over to the van. How beautiful she looks, he thought, even dressed in a frumpy, old gray sweatshirt and a pair of faded blue jeans with a stylish hole in the knee. Her long blond hair wrapped tightly in a ponytail rushed forth memories of the sweet little girl he'd known his whole life. Sentiment tried its hardest to subdue him, but Troy valiantly fought back its consuming push.

A slight smile slowly slipped across Gretchen's genteel face when their eyes met for the first time in nearly three weeks. She usually beamed with delight when they came together, but so much had changed in the relationship in such a short span of time. She appeared reserved in her emotions as she walked up to the van to greet him. Troy knew then his task would be tougher than he'd previously thought. The instant spark of rekindled passion did not ignite like he had wished.

"Hi Troy," Gretchen said softly as he exited the van. "You look well."

"So do you my dear," Troy responded, taking her left hand and chivalrously kissing her ring finger. "Lovely as always."

She appreciated his manner. She'd observed his apparent gallantry many times before. "I was surprised when you called. Hey, where is the Corvette?"

"Uh, I had some errands to run so I borrowed the church van," he replied. "The vette is a little small sometimes."

Gretchen nodded in agreement. She assumed Troy had asked permission from either Franklin or Ramon. She hoped maybe he had cleared the air with them, and Cassie as well. She noticed a small smear of blood on his right cheek. As a subconscious reaction, she licked the end of her fingers and reached over and started to wipe it off.

"You have a little red spot on your face," she said as Troy brushed her hand aside.

"Oh, I probably just cut myself shaving," he responded, leaning down to look at his face in the van's side-view mirror, realizing right away the blood came from Cassie's wounds.

Gretchen smiled and rubbed his stubbled chin gently with the tips of her fingers. "You sure didn't do a very good job this morning"

"Uh...that was yesterday," he replied, aware that Gretchen knew his daily hygiene habits. Troy always took pride in looking his best when he would see her. He'd been slipping lately because she wasn't around. "I was kind of busy this morning. I probably just accidentally picked a scab or something."

Gretchen winced, but seemed satisfied with his explanation. "So what's up?"

"What do you mean?" he answered, rubbing his scruffy chin a couple of times.

"You called and said you had something urgent to speak to me about. Is everything alright?"

Troy looked down. It was the moment of truth. If he had still trusted God, he might have said a silent prayer, asking for help in convincing Gretchen to marry him. But Troy knew he was on his own at that point. He sensed no presence of the Spirit within him. He knew he really never had. He must rely on his own effort to fix the problems he himself had created.

"No," he sighed, looking straight into her stunning blue eyes while trying to conjure up a false tear in his own. "Everything is not alright."

"I know," she replied with a frown and somber tone in her voice. "I spoke to your father a few days ago. He told me what happened between you two."

"He would," Troy said, shaking his head in disgust.

Gretchen placed a hand on his shoulder. "He loves you Troy. We all do."

Troy covered his eyes with right hand and started to kneed his brow. He could feel the fury beginning to course through his veins once more. He had to subdue it quickly. "Well, you all have a funny way of showing it."

"We just want what's best for you Troy. We want..."

"What's best for me!" he retorted, his eyes flaring to reveal the state of his wounded pride. "What's best for me is for things to go back to the way they were before we moved here Gretchen! We should have gone to school in Florida and not Richard Battles' alma mater. It's like he's tried to plan our whole lives! I'm sick of it!"

"Are you sick of me too?" she asked, all too familiar with the battle raging inside him.

"No!" Troy pounded the side of the van with his fist. "I'm just sick of other people interfering with our plans. I wish they would just leave us alone!"

Gretchen just shook her head from side to side. She knew Troy had learned nothing during their time apart. If anything, she felt the distance between their hearts expanding ever more. It crushed her to understand they would never unite as one again.

"We can't go back Troy."

"Why not?"

"Because there is nothing to go back to." Gretchen covered her eyes and began to weep.

Normally, Troy would have placed his arm around her shoulders and pulled her head into his chest for comfort. But his heart had become strangely cold toward her feelings. Her tears used to immediately soften him. Yet now he hardly noticed them. In fact, her whimpering was starting to grate on him.

"I thought you loved me," he said.

"I do," she replied, tears streaming down her sullen face. "I always will."

"Then why can't we go back to the way we were? Tell me!"

"Because things are different now. I'm not the same person I used to be. And neither are you."

Troy knew she was right. He couldn't argue. He realized they were completely changed the minute they stepped foot into New Hope Church. It was just that Gretchen had changed for the better and he for the worse. Troy couldn't help but find the irony in that fact. That was supposed to be one of the vows to be recited at their wedding. But he knew she was better for losing him and he was worse for not having her. Any speck of goodness he may have previously possessed left with her when they broke up.

Still, Gretchen held a firm grip on any chances he might have to reconcile with his father, and of course, the family fortune. After all, that was the main reason he had driven to New Hope in the first place that day. Oh how he hated Cassie for screwing up his plans. He was elated she was probably lying near death in the back of the van not five feet away from them. She was the one who had placed second thoughts about him in Gretchen's head.

Damn her! he thought. *Damn her to hell!*

Gretchen was drying her eyes on her shirt sleeves when Troy managed to regain his focus. Regrettably, it was time to force her hand. He knew it shouldn't have had to be that way. He hoped he could convince her to think differently about him. Maybe undo some of the brainwashing he believed Cassie had administered. But at that point there was no chance for reason to prevail. Coercion had become the better option.

"I still want to marry you," Troy said.

Gretchen grinned and shook her head. "I'm sorry, but that's not going to happen."

He folded his arms across his chest and flashed a wry smirk toward his former beloved. "That's what you think."

Gretchen was taken aback by the bold statement. Her brow crinkled and her mouth pursed in anger. "You can't make me marry you Troy!" She turned in disgust and began to walk away. He grabbed her arm and pulled her back.

"Ow, you're hurting me," she cried, trying to struggle free.

Troy grabbed both of her slender arms by the biceps and jerked her face to face with him. He forcefully kissed her on the lips. She tried to pull away, but he was too strong.

"Let go of me or I'll scream! I swear I will!"

Troy shook her firmly. "You better not if you know what's good for you."

She stomped down on one of his feet causing him to release her. "You're not good for me!" she shouted vehemently and started to run off. "You never were! I can't believe I fell in love with you!"

Gretchen ran about halfway back toward the dorm building before Troy shouted to her. "If you love your father, you'd better get back here!"

The threat caused Gretchen to stop in her tracks. She looked back at Troy quizzically. He had an evil scowl strewn across his face that she'd never seen before, even at his lowest moments. It frightened her to the core of her being.

"That's right!" he exclaimed. "His well-being depends on you."

Gretchen had no idea about the significance of Troy's threat, but she walked toward him. He opened the passenger door of the van.

"Get in!" he stated.

Gretchen followed his demand. "What's going on?" she asked. "What's this about my father? Did you hurt him?"

Troy reached between the seats and lifted up the metal file. "He's fine...But he won't be if you don't do what I say."

"Troy! What are you talking about? You're scaring me!"

He reached into the file and pulled out the stock certificates. He handed them to her.

"What are these?" she asked nervously.

Troy snickered. "They're your father's reservations for prison."

Gretchen stared at the documents. She didn't have the slightest idea about their significance. She saw a bunch of legal writing along with Battle Trading Corp. and Erik Bjorn printed within the text. But she didn't know what to make of it.

"So what do these...stock certificates, mean to me? It looks like my father owns some stock in the company. So what? He works there."

A sinister laugh escaped from Troy's mouth. "He won't be working there, or anywhere else, for long."

Gretchen was getting frustrated with Troy's approach. "What do you mean? What did he do? Get to the point would you?"

The scowl returned to Troy's face. "They're forgeries. Your father doesn't really own a single share of stock in the company. Not one. I checked."

"Okay, so?" Gretchen held up her palms, still quite baffled.

"Forging stock certificates is a felony Gretchen. We're talking major prison time for your father."

She didn't say anything. She still wasn't grasping the full significance of the matter.

"That's right," Troy reiterated. "And when I showed them to him, he admitted they were his."

"Well how did you get a hold of them?" Gretchen shouted back.

"Don't worry about it. I have my sources."

"Does Richard know?"

"No. And my father doesn't have to know anything about it."

"What do you mean?"

Troy giggled snidely again.

"What? What do you want?"

A determined sneer gazed back at the confused girl. "I want you as my wife...And you will be or your beloved father will spend, oh I don't know, say the next twenty years in prison...I already researched the matter in case you were wondering."

She placed both hands over her face and burst into tears.

"It doesn't have to be so Gretchen. It's up to you."

"Why Troy? Why?" she continued to sob. "Why would you want to marry me when you know I'll never love you now they way you want me to?"

"Love!" Troy snapped. "Love! You think I want you for your love! I knew months ago I lost your love!"

"But...I thought you loved me. I thought that's what this was all about. Your proposal, our engagement...even our breakup. You seemed so sad when we broke up. I thought you were trying to get me to take you back...Why? Why are you doing this?"

Gretchen's sorrow had no effect on him. His heart was now hard as stone toward her.

"I want my inheritance back!" he exclaimed. "And you're going to help me get it."

Troy grabbed her arm sternly.

"My father said if we got back together, I would be welcomed home. You're gonna get me there Gretchen, my dear, or your precious father will also have a new home to call his own."

Troy stepped outside the van as she continued to weep. He wanted to give her a few moments to fully consider the consequences of her fateful decision. He lit up a cigarette to kill time. It was another harmful practice he'd secretly picked up over the last few weeks. He didn't know why he'd started to smoke. He'd always hated any form of tobacco product. But smoking seemed to have a calming effect on him for some reason. The health issues that follow such a terrible habit were certainly of no concern to him at that point. His financial affairs took precedence, thanks partly to the beautiful blond damsel now deeply distressed inside the van.

"If you'd only stuck to our plans," Troy muttered softly to himself as he watched at Gretchen sob into the palms of her hands. "Nobody would have to be hurt."

Troy shook his head in slight dismay as he took a drag off the cigarette. He looked at it burn slowly down, about halfway through. He gazed at the bright, fiery tip singe through the tobacco and paper. It burns so evenly and efficiently, he thought, like a miny, but intense conflagration with a staunch sense of purpose to its destructive force. It reminded Troy of his own life over the past couple of years. Yet he'd never imagined he would reach the point where his narcissistic actions would wreak such havoc on so many lives, especially those he thought he loved. But what was love anyway, he wondered? It was an emotion that had suddenly fled from his life, if he'd ever even truly possessed it in the first place. Love now signified failure to Troy Battles and the symbol of that failure was now crying her eyes out right in front of him. What a waste, he thought.

While Troy finished smoking his cigarette, Gretchen slowly began to regain her composure. She folded her hands together and bowed her head in prayer. She was desperate for the comfort of the Lord's Spirit and the guidance of His wise counsel. Her prayer life had deepened greatly since breaking up with Troy. She had sensed the presence of the Divine's affection during her despondency like never before. She again longed for that love in a most troubling time. Gretchen trusted God would direct her down the proper path. She was counting on it.

"Well, what have you decided?" Troy asked as he opened the driver's side door after stamping out his cigarette butt on the pavement. Gretchen was surprised when she looked up and saw him take the last puff before dropping the cigarette on the ground. She didn't say anything about his smoking. What would be the point after all? She dabbed her eyes with bottom front of her sweatshirt. Troy noticed her bare midriff as she pulled up her shirt. Her belly was still as taught as a high school cheerleader. Those were happy days he thought to himself. He wished they both could slip back to those years and start over. But he realized fate had cast a different lot for each of them. He vowed to make the best of his destiny.

Gretchen reasoned to follow God's will. Her conscience nudged her heart aside.

"I still can't marry you Troy," she replied. "I know now that the Lord doesn't want me to, no matter what."

"No matter what!" Troy shot back.

"Yes, no matter what," she answered softly.

"What about your dad? Don't you love him?"

"Of course I love him."

"He will go to prison, Gretchen, I promise you."

She looked downward. "I will ask him to confess what he did to the authorities. It is the only right thing to do. I know he will do what's right."

"You're unbelievable!" Troy said, shaking his head in dismay. "He didn't do the right thing before. What makes you think he'll do it now? He's in big trouble Gretchen. Big trouble!"

The passion behind his words stung her deeply. He seemed to take delight in her father's upcoming troubles. It was a stark contrast to how she'd always known Troy's feelings toward Erik. Her father had been like a favorite uncle to Troy since the children were toddlers. In fact, she often felt Troy was closer to Erik than he was to his own father. Richard Battles was always too busy to toss a ball around or go fishing with his son. Erik Bjorn made time for the eventual wayward boy and Troy acted like he loved him for his care. Gretchen couldn't fathom the reasoning behind Troy's sinister actions. She was still unaware of the depths of the depravity he was yet to display.

"What has come over you Troy?" she asked in angst. "All my father ever did for you was love you. You've taken his love, my love, all of our love, and turned it against us. Why Troy? Why?"

Gretchen began to cry again as she stared straight into Troy's sable, cogent eyes. The transparency of his soul appeared shallow. She could see only darkness. The light that used to radiate toward her from within the man she'd loved for so long was apparently absent. It was either buried too deep within his vengeance or had fled him completely, she couldn't tell. She felt helpless and he pounced on her vulnerability.

"I hate love!" he stated vehemently. "Don't you dare use that word around me anymore! If you or any of the family really loved me, loved me for who I am, all this wouldn't be happening now...I never loved any of you!...I hate you! I hate you!"

Troy slammed his fist on the hood of the van, but it was a relatively, slow morning around that part of the campus, so his anger drew no notice whatsoever.

"Stop!" Gretchen pleaded, covering her ears with both hands while tears streamed out of her eyes. "You don't mean that. You can't."

Troy jumped back into the van and grabbed both of her arms, turning her body toward his.

"You listen to me and you listen good!" he roared, clutching her wrists tightly. "You're going with me to Vegas right now and get married. Do you hear me woman?"

"I can't! I won't! You can't make me!"

Troy slapped her across the face. She tried to open the door and flee, but he pulled her back by her ponytail. She banged the back of her head on his shoulder. The blow made her dizzy. She didn't resist any further. His wrath frightened her too much.

"I will have what's mine, do you hear?" The shear terror reflecting back told him he was making his point. "I didn't tell you everything about your father Gretchen."

"What? What?" the panic-stricken girl cried.

Troy suddenly burst forth with an evil laugh. He delighted in making her squirm.

"Oh no! What's happened?" Gretchen began to sob uncontrollably.

"It's not what's happened," he replied, his laughter ceasing as abruptly as it had begun. "It's what could, or should I say, will happen, if you don't do as I tell you."

Gretchen continued to whimper as she stared intently at her ex-lover, hanging on every unmerciful word he uttered.

"You see," he calmly continued. "Your father told me the reason he forged those stock certificates was because he was desperate for money. I won't go into the details right now, but he used the certificates as collateral for a loan."

"A loan for what?" Gretchen interrupted. "We've always had money."

"Well, if you shut up and listen I'll tell you!" Troy angrily shot back.

Gretchen nodded her head and spoke no more.

"Anyway. It seems your father got involved in some kind of land-swapping scheme down in South America. The deal went sour and his investors wanted their money back. And they're not the kind of guys who take no for an answer. Your father knew what would happen to him if he couldn't hand over their money...Well, he didn't think it wise to get my father involved, so he went searching the banks for money. But they wanted some guarantee he could pay it back. It was like two million dollars. I guess that's when he conjured up the stock scam...Poor old Erik was a fool. I told him so."

Gretchen wiped her eyes again with the bottom of her already damp, gray sweatshirt. "But he paid those men their money right?"

"Oh sure he did. He knew better than to not pay them."

"So what's the problem then?"

Troy giggled snidely and stroked the back of Gretchen's head. "Oh you poor girl. So beautiful, but so dumb. Don't you see?"

Gretchen frowned and shook her head no.

"If I go to the authorities with these bogus certificates, Erik will not only go to jail. But there is a good chance, no a great chance, his South American buddies will be implicated when the whole story comes out. They won't like that much Gretchen, I promise you."

"What will they do?"

"Depends what your father tells the authorities. If those South Americans, Columbians I think, believe Erik made some kind of deal with the government, then they might kill him."

Gretchen fully understood the ploy Troy was implementing. She quickly knew the course her life would have to take to save her father.

"You know what you have to do now Gretchen, don't you?"

She dropped her head without even looking at him. He didn't need a response. He knew she only had one choice in the matter.

They had been traveling about an hour when they reached the western edge of the dessert. Not a word was spoken between the two of them since leaving the UCLA campus. Gretchen's silence was born of sheer terror. The evil young man driving the van bore no resemblance to the handsome guy she'd loved for so many years. Sure, his image was the same outwardly, but Gretchen had just witnessed firsthand the demon that had overtaken Troy Battles' inner being. The unadulterated iniquity which had beset her former lover left Gretchen speechless in a state of dread so dire it made her whole body quiver. Just the quickest of unintended glances when their eyes met caused her to tremble even more.

Her desperation was so deep. The only recourse Gretchen knew she had available was prayer. She closed her eyes and leaned her head against the passenger-side window, silently seeking the eternal counsel she understood would never fail her.

Troy looked over at Gretchen and believed she had fallen asleep. The quiet gave him a chance to get his own thoughts in order. He sought no heavenly being to call on for advice. The source of wisdom which drove him was summoned from an entirely different fountain of knowledge. That well of wickedness seemed bottomless and Troy easily tapped into the means of his current master.

He appeared to have frightened Gretchen into submission at last. Their marriage, although devious at best and now void of any kind of righteous love, could prove more than adequate to fulfill his needs. He felt her contempt for him, but such emotion would hold little consequence if covered sufficiently. He could force her if need be, not to love him, but convince others, most importantly Richard, that her affections were genuine. It would take some practice, but Gretchen could be made to do so. Troy believed his threats to that point, had already broken her will to resist further. He was confident he could conjure up more weaponry if she stepped out of line. His long-held plan for earthly glory, albeit ever tenuous, finally seemed attainable.

However, Cassie Ramirez suddenly disrupted his course of deception once again.

A couple of faint thuds sounded off from the rear of the van. Troy looked into the rearview mirror and noticed the rolled-up carpet twitch three times. He looked over at Gretchen, whose eyes were still closed. He then heard a couple of more banging sounds, a little bit louder that before. In the mirror, he could see one end of the carpet lifting up slowly.

"Great," he whispered to himself, knowing that Cassie appeared to be regaining consciousness. He had so hoped she would die on her own. She had been so quiet that he'd momentarily forgotten about her. Gretchen didn't even notice the roll of carpet lying on the floor of the old work van. One loud bang though, drew her attention to it.

"What's that?" Gretchen stated as the roll began to shake violently back and forth.

Troy quickly pulled the van over to the shoulder of the sparsely-driven road and slammed the vehicle into park.

"Hey what's going on here?" Gretchen shouted.

"Shut up!" Troy blasted back as he reached into the aluminum file box between the seats. He pulled out the revolver and pointed it at Gretchen. "Don't say a word! Just sit there and shut up!"

The terror returned to Gretchen's eyes. The peace she had been praying for passed abruptly. She did what she was told and watched Troy exit the van. He walked around to the rear door and slung it open. With the gun now tucked into the waist of his faded blue jeans, he slid off the twine that had been holding the rolled carpet together. When it unrolled, Cassie's battered body was exposed to Gretchen's startled eyes.

"I should have finished you off before!" Troy screamed at his still discombobulated victim.

"Oh my God!" Gretchen yelled. "What have you done?"

"Shut your mouth!" Troy shouted back as Cassie struggled to get free from the twine that was still binding her, though not as tightly as Troy had hoped. The duct tape over her mouth had also started to curl up on the sides. Cassie couldn't see Gretchen sitting in the front seat with both hands covering her own mouth in shock at the sight she was seeing. The pastor's daughter tried to focus her bewildered eyes on her assailant. Just as she was beginning to recognize him, Troy swung the butt of the pistol across her cheek, knocking her out once more.

Gretchen covered her eyes in horror and began to scream. Troy quickly turned over the gun and pointed it at her.

"Get back here!" he shouted. "Now! Hurry up!"

Sobbing intensely as she climbed over the seat, Gretchen made her way back to Cassie's limp body.

"You've killed her," she cried.

Troy reached down and touched Cassie's neck. He was able to feel a pulse.

"She's not dead, unfortunately," Troy huffed. "I just can't get a break."

Gretchen leaned over and gently swept the hair off Cassie's face. A couple of her tears dropped onto her friend's brow and rolled down the bridge of her still-bloodied nose.

"Oh you poor thing, what has he done to you?" Gretchen cried as she began to remove the tape from Cassie's mouth.

"Don't do that!" Troy barked before yanking Gretchen back toward him by her ponytail.

Gretchen screamed again as Troy pulled her out of the van and hurled her to the sand-covered asphalt shoulder. It was half-past eleven on the briskly cool desert morning and Troy could see a car coming toward them in the distance. He quickly hustled Gretchen and himself into the van and slammed the door closed before the oncoming car approached. Troy was thankful when the car sped by in the opposite direction without stopping. He really didn't want to have to pull his gun on an innocent bystander. He didn't need any more trouble at that point. He knew he already had more than enough to deal with at the time.

"Don't forget what I told you," Troy warned.

Gretchen uncharacteristically became combative. She held no concern for her own well-being as she began to pound on Troy's shoulder blades with her balled-up fists. "I hate you! I hate you! I hate you!" she wailed while continuing to strike at him. Infuriated, Troy forearmed her across the head, sending her flying into the back of the driver's seat. He then pointed the gun at Cassie's head.

"I'll shoot her right now! I swear I will!"

"No!" the dazed blond girl screamed. "No please don't! No, no, no..." Her voice faded as she pleaded through her unwarranted despair.

"Get over here," Troy commanded as he re-aimed the gun on Gretchen. "Do exactly as I say."

She slid over toward him. He tossed a roll of twine at her.

"Take this and tie it tightly around both of her wrists and ankles."

Gretchen wept profusely as she followed his command. It broke her heart to bind Cassie for him, but she knew she had to obey orders to save her friend's life.

Troy handed her the roll of gray duct tape. "Wrap this tightly over the other piece."

"But she might not be able to breath," Gretchen protested.

"She can breathe through her nose."

"It's all bloody."

"She did alright before. Just shut up and do what I say!"

Still crying, Gretchen ripped off a piece of tape, slightly larger that the one already covering Cassie's mouth. "I'm so sorry honey," she whispered as she placed the tape gently over the other one.

"Oh isn't that sweet," Troy sarcastically said, pushing Gretchen away from her fallen friend. "Now get over in the driver's seat. You're going to drive now."

Troy pointed the gun at his former beloved as he crawled to the passenger seat.

"Get going," he said.

"Where to?"

"Just shut your mouth and drive. I'll tell you where to go."

Gretchen sniffled a couple of times and started the van. "I don't even have my license with me."

It suddenly dawned on Troy he had made another critical mistake. By not allowing Gretchen to return to her dorm room for her purse, she wouldn't have any identification for the marriage license. They need ID to get married, even in Vegas. They certainly couldn't return to UCLA. It was one more costly blunder in his scheme. He became livid when he realized all was lost. The marriage would not take place and his inheritance was still out of reach.

"Damn!" he screamed at Gretchen. "You stupid bitch!"

Troy pounded on the dashboard. His action made Gretchen swerve off the road slightly. She was able to regain control of the van quickly though.

"You trying to get us all killed?" he shouted. "Watch where you're going!"

"Where are we going?" Gretchen asked, her eyes still clouded by streaming tears.

"Don't worry about it," Troy answered. "You have one more reason to do what I tell you lying in the back there, so you better just shut your mouth and do what I say."

Gretchen nodded her head and drove. She had no idea what would happen next. Her fate, as well as Cassie's, seemed to be bound to Troy's whim.

Where are you Lord? she cried silently. *Where are you?*

⁂

Troy's sanity had been teetering on the brink of rabid madness for weeks. The gods he had so willfully come to worship determined as much. Enticed by their lurid offerings of grandeur, Troy allowed his soul to succumb to mortal corruption. His psyche faithfully followed its dire course. There was no opportunity, nor desire, to turn back. He was no longer playing a sinister ploy for his future. His fight would now be for survival only, and he knew it.

Malevolence drove his rage toward the fierce pang of retribution. Those who had hurt him would make their amends in blood. How dare they scuttle his ship of dreams? He already had two of the culprits grasped firmly within his vengeful clutches. He determined in his ever-warping mind that they could still be used as bait to lure the primary contributor who caused his downfall.

Franklin Edwards always seemed to be linked in some way to Troy's misfortune. It was almost uncanny, Troy reasoned.

From the high school classroom, through their drag strip duels, to the recent months ministering at New Hope Church, Franklin had always managed to check Troy's ego. Because of his influence on Gretchen by way of Cassie, Franklin's meddling had again stifled Troy's will, at least from the perspective of the deranged man currently pointing a pistol at the former love of his previously fortunate life. Troy promised Franklin would finally suffer the ultimate penalty for the foul leading to his financial demise.

Thinking back to Franklin's woes immediately after the tragic deaths of Sara and the girls brought a pleasing grin to Troy's face. That he felt delight in Franklin's suffering didn't trouble Troy in the slightest. His sense of compassion had easily fled alongside his morality. Satan had sapped all sympathy, and pity was a virtue for the pious. Troy Battles desired to give neither. His vital principal now required only revenge. Once before Franklin had unfairly endured intolerable heartache brought on by mistaken intentions. This time Troy would be sure his old rival plainly knew the source of his suffering.

"Turn in there," Troy said to Gretchen, pointing to an abandoned silver mine about a half-mile down the highway.

"Why?" she asked, startled by his sudden demand after the two had not spoken to each other in more than an hour.

"Just shut up and do it!" he replied, aiming the gun at her.

"Hey okay!" she snapped back, "I'm only asking. Geez!"

"Well that's part of the problem. You ask too many questions lately... I make all the decisions now! You hear!"

Gretchen nodded, her eyes moistening once more. Consuming fear was beginning to tingle the last fragile edges of her nerves. She sensed the impending consequences of Troy's deepening degeneracy. She could see the diabolical rage searing within his piercing glare. She knew better than to not follow his command.

Turning left off the highway, Gretchen pulled onto a gravel road leading to the mine. She couldn't make out the name on the cracked wooden sign, most of the black lettering had faded or chipped away because of the intense desert sun. The mine obviously had not been worked for decades and Gretchen wondered why Troy would choose such a place to stop. She figured they were no more than an hour outside of Las Vegas by then. Her anxiety was becoming dreadful.

Gretchen stopped the church van just a few feet from a decrepit wood shack. Troy took the keys from the ignition and stepped outside the van.

"Don't try anything funny or I'll shoot the both of you right now," he told Gretchen through the open passenger-side door. "Just sit here until I come back, you hear?"

Gretchen nodded yes and began to whimper once again.

Troy shook his head in disgust and walked over to the wooden shack. When he pulled on the handle, the creaky door fell off its hinges and slammed to the ground at his feet.

"Well, I guess this won't do," he said, before turning and walking back toward the van. As he looked over to his left, he saw another small wooden door lying on the ground about twenty feet away. He walked over to the door and saw a rusty handle attached to it. When pulling up the handle, Troy discovered a hole about the size of a refrigerator. He couldn't see inside very well, as the sun was starting to set over the mountains to the west of the dessert. He did notice stairs leading down from the entrance to the hole. He had obviously found one of the old mine's emergency escape hatches.

He got an idea. "This place might serve a purpose after all," he mumbled to himself. He walked back to the van and opened the rear door. He saw that Cassie was still unconscious, but her state was okay for the time being. He would carry her if he had to.

"What's over there Troy?" Gretchen asked, still sitting in the driver's seat. Her nerves were about shot at that point. "What are you up to?"

Troy didn't answer her. He didn't even look at her. He just reached over Cassie's limp body and grabbed a large flashlight from one of the six shelves that lined the interior of the panel van. He switched it on and shined it on Cassie's bound body. It appeared the batteries were still quite strong. The light illuminated her injuries well. He slammed the door shut.

Gretchen was trembling as Troy walked around to her door. He yanked it open and grabbed her left shoulder, pulling her out the door. She stumbled to her knees on the sandy ground. Troy pulled her up.

"Ow!" she cried.

"Stop your bellyaching! You're coming with me."

"Where we going?"

"We're gonna check out this mine. Come on!"

"What for?" Gretchen asked as Troy hustled her over toward the shaft.

"Shut-up!" he said adamantly, forcing a deep sigh. "I'm not gonna hurt you. That is, if you just shut-up already!...God!"

Gretchen began to cry again. She couldn't believe how badly the man she used to love was treating both her and her best friend.

"Oh stop it!" he demanded. "Pull yourself together. Look at yourself. You're trembling...We are just going to do a little exploring."

Troy shined the flashlight down the mine shaft. It appeared the steps leading downward were clear of any debris, as far as he could see.

"Get down there!" he commanded.

Gretchen abruptly shot him a startled look. "I'm afraid Troy!" she pleaded. "You go first."

He shook his head. "Not a chance. I'm keeping my eyes on you."

"Where do you think I'm going to go? I'm stuck here! You have the keys! Oh please! I'm scared!"

Troy grabbed her by the arms and shook her, dropping the flashlight. "Look! Calm down! I'll be right behind you shining the flashlight over your shoulder. Now go!"

He pushed her down toward the opening. She fell, scrapping both of her knees on the wooden door. A splinter pierced her lower left thigh through her jeans. But the pain that it left behind had little of the sting in which her broken heart was feeling.

Troy picked up the light and shook it a couple of times. It seemed to still be functioning fine. He pointed the beam into the hole.

"Go ahead, get down there!" he commanded. Gretchen sniffled a couple of times and followed his orders.

The stairs dropped down only about fifteen feet before hitting bottom. They led into a chamber about the size of a small bedroom. Troy shined the light around the cold, stuffy, chamber, which was about eight feet high with a steel vent pipe leading up to the surface. He had noticed the pipe sticking out of the ground by the wooden door. This would make a nice tomb, Troy thought to himself, but that was a function for later. The chamber led into a descending corridor. The passageway was wide enough for two grown men to pass through walking side by side.

"Go that way," Troy told Gretchen, who coughed a couple of times. "I know you're not claustrophobic. We used to go exploring caves in Mexico together."

"But this one is more spooky!" she protested, remembering the happy times they spent with her father and Richard on vacation not so long before.

Troy had no sympathy for her anxiety. "Get going," he said, pushing her along.

They walked down the dark shaft probably about fifty feet before coming to a fork. The shaft on the right featured a set of what appeared to be two thin railroad tracks, previously used for carrying silver out from the depths of the mine. Figuring it would not be easy to walk between the tracks, and also not finding one of the carts used to carry the silver readily available, Troy decided to try the other shaft first.

The path was level and ran about twenty feet before opening into another small chamber. Troy shined the light into the area, which was about forty feet long and thirty feet wide. The top of the dark chamber was about fifteen feet high with another vent pipe leading above ground. The floor was rather damp from years of rain leaking through the vent. Troy figured the musty chamber probably served as some kind of storage area. He shined the flashlight along the walls and noticed a metallic cage formed into one corner. He and Gretchen walked over to the cage. It was made out of steel, firmly secured to the cave walls with large hex-shaped bolts drilled into the rock. There was also a steel door that opened into the cage. Troy found the key to the door tied to one of the steel bars with a piece of thin wire.

"This must be where they locked up the silver," Troy said aloud. "This is too perfect."

Gretchen started to shake again. She didn't like the tone of his comment. She wished she could flee, but she knew he would catch her quickly.

Troy jiggled the key and it easily fell away from the rusted wire holding it to the steel bar. He shut the door and heard it click. He placed the key inside the latch and the door unlocked right away. He swung open the creaky door once more.

"Get in!" he said to Gretchen.

"What?" the alarmed girl cried. "What are you doing?"

"Just get in!" Troy grabbed her arm and hurled her to the floor. He slammed the door shut, shaking it a couple of times to make sure it wouldn't open again. It didn't.

"Troy please! Troy!" Gretchen screamed. "Don't leave me here! Please!"

Her cries didn't faze him one bit. "Shut up!" he shouted.

"Where are you going? Don't leave me!"

Troy walked back over to the cage and slammed his fists on the door. "I'm coming back!" he shouted. "I'm not done with you yet! Not by a long shot!...I'm going to get Cassie!...This place ought to keep both you bitches for a while!'"

Gretchen sunk to her knees and wept as he left the chamber to fetch his other beleaguered victim. His ex-fiancé's sobs trailed him nearly all the way back to the entrance they had taken into the mine. He knew how much she hated the darkness; she had always been that way. Most children grow out of their fear of the dark, but Gretchen never did. To that day, she still kept a nightlight on while she slept. Even on the rare occasion when they were able to spend an entire amorous night together, she still insisted on a light to scare away her perceived night demons. Troy didn't mind though, as long as she fell asleep in the nude. Never a sound sleeper himself, he savored gazing at her lovely bare figure throughout the night. Gretchen's blooming, girlish curves could always stir the warmth his heart once held for her. It suddenly seemed strange that he now couldn't muster even the slightest passion, or much less compassion, for the delicate flower of his youth. Her cries of anguish just irritated him at this point. For a second, Troy thought about putting a bullet in her to cease the suffering, like one does for a wounded animal that has no hope of survival. But Gretchen had not yet outlived her usefulness to him. He still needed both her and Cassie in order to settle his score with Franklin. Troy knew it would be much more efficient to put all three of them out of his misery at the same time.

When Troy arrived back at the van, Cassie was still unconscious. He slapped her face a few times in an effort to revive her, but she refused to come to. He checked her pulse again to make sure she was still alive. He felt a throbbing in her neck and also noticed her chest rise when he leaned his ear next to her nose. She was still breathing, but would be of no assistance in helping him place her into the mine shaft.

He dragged her slumping body out of the van and hoisted her over his shoulders. Oddly, she seemed as heavy as when she was wrapped up in the carpet. Troy figured fatigue was beginning to sap his strength and it might be wise to hustle along his course of action.

He had to untie her in order to wrap her arms around his shoulders and chest as she rode piggyback down the mineshaft. He firmly held her right forearm to keep her body in place on his back as they descended the steps. He certainly hoped she didn't awaken at that point. Then Troy's foot slipped off one of the steps about two-thirds of the way down. They both crashed hard from the final five feet to the bottom of the shaft.

Troy landed sideways on Cassie's belly, breaking his fall. But the mishap caused her to groan in pain and slowly regain consciousness. The pain she felt was intense as she came to, though the full extent of her excruciation had only just begun. She immediately pulled the duct tape from across her mouth to breath better. The rush of cold air suddenly filling her lungs caused Cassie to begin to hyperventilate. She struggled desperately to steady her breathing pattern as her eyes vainly tried to search the darkness before her. She knew not the slightest inkling of the fate that had befallen her. The situation was precarious at best.

Meanwhile, Troy tried to shake the cobwebs from his own head. The fall left him dazed for a minute or so, but he regained his bearings quickly. He felt some blood on his left elbow and it hurt to bend the arm, but otherwise he was uninjured. He reached around the ground for the flashlight and found it a few seconds later. He switched the light on. Again the rugged flashlight had survived. The beam startled Cassie, whose panicked eyes also illuminated the misery besetting her beaten body. Her head was pounding and a sharp pain radiated from her lower left ankle up her entire leg. It took her a few seconds to recognize Troy. When she was finally able to fully focus on him, Cassie found herself staring down the barrel of a revolver.

"Troy!" she exclaimed, before leaning forward and wincing in agony.

Her desperate moans told him she wouldn't present much of a problem. Troy rose to his feet and moved toward Cassie. He pointed the gun at her throbbing head.

"Get up!" he commanded.

Suddenly, despite the tremendous pain still pummeling her broken body, she remembered all the reasons for her disdain of him. The memories came cascading back in torrents.

"I can't you fool, I think my ankle's broken!" she blurted out with disgust.

"I don't give a damn about your ankle, get your ass up!" he shot back, while pulling on her shoulder with his injured arm. He let go and shook off the pain.

Fright began to overcome Cassie and told her to follow his demands. "Help me, would you?" She reached up with her left arm. Troy reluctantly placed the gun in his waistband and pulled her to her feet.

"Ahh!" Cassie screamed in agony, the pain tearing through her ankle and head simultaneously.

Troy shined the light down the corridor to where Gretchen was locked up. "That way," he pointed, once again holding the gun. "Just feel your way along the walls as you go."

"Where are we?" Cassie asked, breathing heavily while fighting through the pain.

"Don't worry about it. Just shut your mouth and move."

She limped gingerly for a few steps before hearing cries coming from deep within the tunnel.

"Who's that?"

Troy smiled at her snidely. "You have a buddy of yours waiting for you."

Cassie now walked as fast as her struggling body would allow. When she got to the fork in the mine, she immediately recognized the cries she heard. "Gretchen? Is that you?" she yelled.

"Cassie!" Gretchen wailed. "Cassie! Help!"

Cassie amazingly found the strength to course the final twenty feet into the chamber. Troy was pleased at the increase in her pace. "See, you can move fast when you want to."

Cassie hurled a hateful look toward him and limped over to the steel cage. She reached out her hands and clutched Gretchen's through the bars.

"Oh Cassie," Gretchen cried. "I'm so happy you're okay."

"Honey, what did he do to you?"

Troy immediately pulled the back of Cassie's blouse, sending her tumbling to the floor. "You girls will have plenty of time to catch up with each other."

"You awful brute!" Gretchen screamed. "I hate you! I hate you!"

Troy whipped the gun around and fired a shot that whizzed by Gretchen's head. She dove back toward the rear of the eight-by-eight makeshift cell and covered her head.

"Gretchen!" Cassie screamed.

Troy spun and backhanded Cassie across the face, sending her sprawling onto her back. She hit her head and fell unconscious again. Troy took the key out of his pocket and unlocked the cell. Gretchen was too frightened to even move a muscle. Troy set the flashlight on the ground, facing the cell. He put the gun in his waist again and lifted up Cassie under her armpits. He dragged her into the cell and slammed the door shut.

Gretchen crawled over to her fallen friend and wept as she cradled her bruised head in her arms. She looked up at Troy with horror in her eyes.

"May God have mercy on your pitiful soul," she said to him, before looking back down at Cassie lying in her arms.

Troy blew Gretchen a kiss then turned and walked out of the chamber. He likened the mine to a way station along his predetermined path to the rancid bowels of hell. He knew his destiny was set.

Chapter XV

The commands of Christ are often disconcerting and formidable.

King Jesus decreed: "Love your enemies, do good to those who hate you, bless those who curse you, pray for those who mistreat you."

That his subjects are to bow humbly in obedience to such a divine ordinance is extraordinarily counterintuitive to the most conventional worldview.

Pray for your enemies whoever they may be? No matter how deep their sin? No matter how lost they are?

"Your Majesty, you can't be serious?" is the most probable of responses uttered by even the most loyal of the Lord's astonished servants.

Yet the Master's reply will always be trustworthy to those who are found to be his faithful slaves: "your reward will be great, and you will be sons of the Most High, because he his kind to the ungrateful and wicked. Be merciful, just as your Father is merciful."

❦

It was nearly dark when Franklin and Ramon drove into the

church parking lot in Cassie's small white sedan. Their day-long meeting with downtown civic leaders had gone quite well. New Hope Church had once again been blessed with an outpouring of donations from some of Los Angeles' finest citizens. The pastor and his protégé were pleased that influential businessmen had taken notice of New Hope's mission of mercy to the neighborhood's downtrodden. There was even talk of planting additional churches in some of the city's other blighted areas.

The brothers were praising God for his provision when Franklin noticed the back door of the church left wide open.

"Ramon look," Franklin said, pointing to the open door.

"That is quite odd," Ramon responded, a sudden sense of nervousness striking his gut. "I hope nobody broke in."

Franklin parked the car in front of the door and stepped out. "Better stay here and let me check it out first."

"Oh no, I will go in with you."

Franklin put his arm out and blocked Ramon. "It's okay man. One of us needs to be out here to call the cops if someone is inside. I'll holler for you if I need you."

Ramon reluctantly consented when he realized Franklin was correct in his thinking. The neighborhood could be very dangerous at times, even though most of the criminal minds tended to stay away from New Hope. However, the church had suffered a few minor break-ins over the years.

"Be careful," Ramon urged.

Franklin patted his brother on the shoulder a couple of times and went inside.

The place seemed to be fairly unruffled. The back door hadn't been broken open and nothing appeared to be missing at first glance. Franklin figured maybe Cassie had gone for a walk and just not latched the door properly. He dialed her cell phone number, but the call went directly to voice mail. Franklin left his fiancé a message to call him the first chance she could. He noticed the door to the room Troy slept in open slightly and went inside. He flipped on the light switch and immediately saw something was amiss.

The floor was bare and the closet was open. The clothes Troy had left behind when he'd scrambled from the premises on New Year's were also gone. Franklin could understand Troy sneaking back to retrieve his personal items, but why take the rug? Just then Ramon yelled down the hallway.

"Everything alright in there amigo?"

"Yeah," Franklin replied, leaning down to look under the bed. "There's no one here."

When he went to lay flat on the floor to get a closer look under the bed, Franklin noticed a reddish stain on the faded white tile. He touched it with his fingers and realized it was dried blood. A feeling of uneasiness came over him as Ramon entered the room.

"Something's wrong here," Franklin stated, gazing up at Ramon with a worried look on his face.

"What?" Ramon asked.

"There's blood on the floor here and the carpet is missing."

"Really?" Ramon responded quizzically.

"Yeah, and Troy's clothes are gone as well."

"I wonder if he was injured or something."

"I don't know. But it's strange that he would take the rug."

Ramon suddenly recalled not seeing the church van outside.

"Did you notice the van was gone?"

The two of them quickly rushed outside to look around the parking lot. They didn't see the van. They walked around to the front of the building and the van was not parked on the street either.

"He must have taken it," Franklin said, somewhat flustered.

"Yes, he had to have. I wonder what for?"

Franklin raised his palms upward and shook his head. "I don't know. Unless, Cassie has it."

Ramon shook his head no. "She could not have. I have her keys and only you and Troy have the other sets of keys for the van...No he probably has it."

"What for?"

"I do not know. Maybe his corvette broke down."

"Well he didn't ask to borrow it Ramon, did he?"

"No."

"Where I come from brother, taking things without asking first is stealing," Franklin said, his voice rising slightly in anger. "Maybe we should call the police."

Although he was also irritated with Troy, Ramon didn't want to jump to unproven conclusions. "Maybe we should try calling his cell phone?"

Franklin searched his phone for the number as they walked back into the church. Troy didn't answer, so Franklin left a message on the voice mail.

They returned to the bedroom and looked around again. Ramon then spotted some more blood dried into the dark brown comforter spread unevenly on the bed.

"Something happened here Franklin," Ramon said, pointing to the bloodstain. "I am getting worried."

"Maybe we better call the cops."

Ramon nodded yes and walked into the hallway to phone the police station. Franklin knelt down and looked under the bed once more. He saw a sheet of paper lying back against the wall. He slid the bed out a little and retrieved the paper. It was a torn photograph.

The image he saw sent a shiver slicing down his spine.

"Oh my God!" he exclaimed, staring at the photo of Sara, Brianna and Ashley with red X's drawn across their smiling faces. He immediately remembered where the picture had been taken. Sam Simmons snapped the shot more than two years before at Good Shepherd's church picnic. What a delightful time that had been, Franklin quickly recalled, nearly the entire afternoon flashing rapidly through his indelible mind. His absence from the photograph caused alarm. He should also be in the picture, but he could see where his image was torn out. Part of his right arm was still resting gently around his youngest daughter's shoulder. He looked under the bed again, but didn't see the other part of the photo. It had gotten stuck under one of the legs when Franklin moved the bed.

He sat on the bed and stared at the picture. His eyes began to well up. He felt a little guilty about not thinking of his lost family very often in recent days. So much had happened since they'd died. Franklin wasn't willingly trying to substitute his love for Sara and the girls with a growing devotion to Cassie, Ramon and the New Hope ministry, but essentially that's what had taken place. He knew there were days when he didn't once think of his departed loved ones. That only happened occasionally, but Franklin still felt he was slighting their memory sometimes. Just seeing the photograph brought the horror of their tragic demise racing back. He fully understood his weakness when recalling such awful events. He knew he had to shake off the recollections quickly if he were to deal with current circumstances.

"The police will be here shortly," Ramon told Franklin before walking over and sitting next to him on the bed. "What is that?"

Franklin handed him the torn photograph. "I found it under the bed."

Ramon was shocked by what he saw. "It is your wife and kids. Why is there an X across their faces?"

"That's what I'd like to ask Troy."

"Troy? What has he got to do with it?"

Franklin looked at his friend. Ramon could see the concern brewing in his misty eyes.

"Ramon, I've got a bad feeling about that Battles boy. Something happened here today."

The pastor nodded his shiny, balding head in agreement. "I know brother. I am worried. I tried calling Cassie, but I can not get in touch with her."

Franklin's heart sunk to the pit of his stomach. The photo of Sara and the kids had sidetracked his concern over Cassie. He was well aware of the disfavor she held of Troy and Gretchen's relationship. He also knew Troy didn't harbor much love for Cassie either.

"He's up to something Ramon, I just know it."

"Do you think he hurt her? Is this maybe her blood?" Ramon was beginning to get a little frantic.

"Hey, let's just try to remain calm and think rationally about this," Franklin said, patting his friend's knee a couple of times for reassurance.

Ramon hopped up and began to pace. "I tell you, if he hurt my daughter, God help him...It will take the Lord's own hand on me to stop me from killing him brother."

Franklin had never seen Ramon so agitated. He had often wanted to smack some sense into Troy himself, but others, including Ramon and Cassie, talked him out of it. Strikingly, it was his turn to do the same for Ramon. Franklin knew neither father nor fiancé would benefit by letting vengeance motivate their course of action. Too much appeared to be at stake to run off half-cocked.

"Ramon, we need to be smart about this. We don't even know yet if he has Cassie."

"He has her," Ramon replied with a deep scowl etched across his face.

"How do you know?"

"I just do. Call it father's intuition."

Franklin found it hard to argue that point, considering he was also fairly certain Troy was involved somehow. Just then, a squad car arrived.

"Look Ramon, let's be careful what we say to them until we get some more information about what happened here. I don't want to say anything that might jeopardize Cassie before we hear from Troy. We both know he's behind this somehow. Don't accuse him to the police just yet."

Ramon looked at Franklin rather startled. "Why not?"

"I don't know. I just have a gut feeling we better wait until we hear from him for Cassie's sake. Just trust me on this okay? I know Troy a whole lot better than you, believe me. We need to be cautious."

Ramon agreed. His instincts about Franklin had been proven correct ever since the first day they'd met well over a year ago. Besides, he believed God would send an angel to protect his daughter from ultimate harm. He had no choice but to trust his sovereign Lord.

The police took statements from Franklin and Ramon, as well as dusted for fingerprints and took samples of the blood stains for analysis. The two middle-aged officers agreed that some kind of an incident had occurred in the room, but since nothing was missing except for the clothes and the rug, it was difficult to determine whether a crime had happened or not. Troy might have just cut himself somehow while taking out the rug. And there was no real evidence Cassie had even been in the room at all. A few strands of medium-length black hair had been found on the bed, but since Cassie had recently had cut her hair short, the strand might have come from either her or the dark-haired Troy. The police advised Franklin and Ramon to wait twenty-four hours before filing a missing person's report on Cassie or Troy, as there might be a high-ly-reasonable explanation for their disappearance.

Ramon and Franklin kept their suspicions to themselves un-til the police drove away. They didn't let the officers see the torn photograph. They knew they probably should have, but figured waiting a day might bring more information. If Troy didn't call by then, they would give the police the picture. In the meantime, plac-ing a call to Gretchen might prove helpful.

⋘❖⋙

Like Cassie and Troy, Gretchen also failed to answer her cell phone. Becoming increasingly worried as they waited for any news about the girls' whereabouts, Ramon and Franklin decided it wise to pay a visit to the UCLA campus.

The security guard in the lobby of Gretchen's dormitory build-ing remembered seeing the young woman leaving in a white van earlier that day. However, the short, grandfatherly gentleman didn't recall noticing another woman accompanying her. He called up to Gretchen's room and one of her dorm mates answered the phone. She told the security guard she would be right down to speak with the pastor and his friend.

A few minutes later, a lanky, but stunning black girl exited the elevator and strode over toward the two men. There was a certain elegance to her walk, almost regal in a way, like a gorgeous empress from some exotic land. Her silky, scarlet dinner dress, adorned with a brilliant gold necklace, seemed out of place for a college dormitory. Franklin then remembered Gretchen speaking of the girl. She used to call the ebony beauty "The Queen of Sheba" because of the allure she cast upon wealthy men. Gretchen was amazed her roommate still took up residence in the dorm, but "The Queen" refused to be imprisoned as a kept woman in some hidden domicile paid for by any of her deliberate suitors. Gretchen had spent the past year and a half slowly sharing the gospel with the misdirected young lady, but her friend had not yet found the narrow path to the true King. Gretchen believed the girl had been making progress though.

"Hello, I am Mischa," she said in a rather deep voice for a woman, holding out her delicate hand to shake with both men. "How may I be of assistance to you gentlemen?"

"Greetings," Ramon replied in his usual polite tone. He was impressed by the girl's striking presence, despite his overwhelming worry over his daughter and Gretchen. "My name is Pastor Ramon Ramirez and this is my associate Franklin Edwards. We are with New Hope Church."

"Ah," Mischa interjected, "Gretchen has spoken very highly of you. It is a pleasure to meet you both. Will you sit down?"

The three of them sat facing each other around a small, glass, coffee table in the lobby.

"I hope we're not keeping you," Franklin said. "You look like you are ready to go out."

"I do have an engagement, but it is not extraordinarily pressing," the young lady answered demurely, as if trying to cover her discomfort in talking with a pair of holy men. She didn't know how many details of her aberrant lifestyle Gretchen had mentioned to them.

"We will get to the point of our visit," Ramon said, not knowing much of anything about Mischa. "We were wondering if you know where Gretchen is right now. We desperately need to speak with her."

Mischa appeared startled by the request. "I have not spoken to her since this morning. I hope everything is fine with her?"

"We don't know," Franklin said. "We've tried to call her cell phone, but there is no answer."

"Yes, I heard it ringing in her bedroom. I was going to answer it, but I did not feel it proper to do so. What is the matter? You look distressed."

"We are," Ramon said. "We think my daughter, and maybe even Gretchen, might be in some danger."

"Ramon!" Franklin said, surprised at his friend's bluntness. "We don't know that yet."

"I am sorry. I am afraid brother."

"I know. I know. Just try to relax."

Ramon looked away out the glass doors leading into the dormitory building. He began to shuffle his feet nervously. Mischa quickly took notice.

"What is happening?" she asked.

"That's what we are trying to find out," Franklin answered, noting the concern in the lovely girl's radiant hazel eyes. "You said you spoke to her this morning?"

"Yes, but she was on her way out the door. She went downstairs to speak with that dreadful boyfriend of hers."

"Troy?" Ramon asked, briskly returning to the conversation. "Troy was here?"

"Yes. Well he did not come inside. But I saw him through the window of our room upstairs."

"Was he driving a white van?" Franklin asked.

"Yes. Yes he was. Well, he was not driving the vehicle exactly. It was parked out front. He was standing next to it."

Franklin smiled at Ramon. They were both pleased to be getting some answers.

"Go on please," Franklin requested.

"Gretchen spoke to him for a few moments and then entered the vehicle, van you say?"

Ramon grinned, and nodded yes.

Mischa also smiled. She knew her English was still somewhat broken, despite spending nearly two years in the United States on a student visa from her native Somalia.

"The, van, remained still for a few moments longer, and then they went away. I have not seen her return since that time."

"Do you know where they were going?" Franklin asked.

"No I do not...But I thought it rather odd that Gretchen would leave without returning for her handbag. We women must have our cosmetics, you know."

Franklin laughed slightly. He enjoyed Mischa's foreign charm. He just wished they had met under less trying circumstances. He asked if she had seen Cassie.

"No. I did not see anyone else. Cassie? Is that your daughter sir?"

Ramon nodded yes. "We believe she may be with him."

"Gretchen spoke of her often," Mischa responded. "She said they were sisters."

"Sisters in faith, my dear," Ramon replied, his eyes beginning to mist. "Sisters in faith."

Just then, Franklin's cell phone rang. His eyes lit up in shock when he looked at the caller ID. It was Troy Battles calling at last.

"Hello," Franklin answered with Ramon looking at him intently.

"Edwards, is that you?" Troy barked.

"Yes Troy, it's me, where are you?" Franklin responded, looking sternly at Ramon.

"Never mind that!" Troy replied, his anger resounding loud enough to be heard by both Ramon and Mischa. "You better just listen carefully to what I have to say!"

"Okay, go on."

"I've taken Gretchen and Cassie."

"What do you mean you've taken them?" Franklin interrupted, his temper beginning to rise in reaction to Troy's commanding demeanor.

"Just shut up Edwards! You better just shut up right now!"

Franklin bit down on his bottom lip and balled up his fist. He would have punched Troy in the mouth if they were face to face. Instead, fearing for Cassie and Gretchen, Franklin just closed his eyes and listened to Troy's expletive-laden diatribe. He had never heard such foul vocabulary from Troy before.

"So do you understand Edwards? I'm not kidding! I'll kill those two bitches! I swear I will!"

Franklin took a deep breath before responding. He knew he'd better be careful with his words. Troy raved like a madman without yet giving any explicit instructions. His rants were demeaning and vile to both the girls and the men who feared for them.

"Okay Troy, calm down. Just tell me what you want me to do and I'll do it."

Like a man who had grown highly accustomed to wearing two faces to match each of his personalities, Troy suddenly switched over to his cool, but still blatantly evil side. Franklin quickly found either identity troublesome.

"This is what I will have you do," Troy said in a firm, steady tone. "Wait by the phone at the church. I will call you there on the church phone with further instructions. That way I will know where you are. Make sure Cassie's father stays with you. I will want to speak with him as well when I call. That's it for now. Any questions?"

"What about the girls?"

"They're alive. But if you want them to stay that way, you had better do everything I tell you."

"When will you call?"

"Later."

"Look Troy, we're not at the church right now. We will be back there in about a half-hour. Call me on my cell before then if you need to."

Franklin was beginning to become extremely nervous and tense, his voice exposed his uneasiness. Troy delighted in that fact. He knew Franklin would follow his instructions dutifully.

"I will call you after that. Just make sure you are there by then… Oh, and just a warning, don't even think about calling the police. If I so much as sense a cop, it will be deadly for your beloved. Chow."

With that Troy abruptly ended the hate-filled phone call.

Franklin just shook his head and kneaded his brow with his fingers. Ramon became anxious at his friend's reaction to the intense conversation.

"Franklin, are they alright? Are they alive?"

"Yeah, apparently they're alive," Franklin answered, glancing back and forth between Ramon and Mischa, whose eyes expressed a deep concern. "At least Troy says they are. He didn't go into any specifics. He just cussed me out really."

"Well, what are we to do? What did he say?"

"He told us to wait at the church for further instructions. He said he will call us there."

Ramon was frustrated. His anger burst forth into tears.

"Those poor girls," Ramon said, his face becoming redder with each falling teardrop. "Oh Lord protect them. That boy, he is crazy. He is crazy."

Mischa put her arm around Ramon to console him as he wept into his hands. "I knew that man was trouble. I told Gretchen so. But she loved him. Love can be so foolish sometimes."

Franklin offered a solemn smile to the black girl for her sympathy.

"What may I do for you?" she asked.

"You can pray for their safety," Franklin answered.

"I will try to do that," Mischa said, continuing to rub Ramon's shoulder. "I listened to Gretchen pray all the time. She is so in love with God. I learn from her."

"Thank you," Ramon whispered in between sniffles before grasping both of Mischa's soft hands.

Franklin realized they best get moving in case Troy phoned sooner than he said.

"Come on brother, we need go home," he said, patting Ramon on the shoulder. "Thank you for your help Mischa."

"Oh do please call me when you hear something." She reached into her tiny red, beaded purse and handed Franklin a business card.

"I will," Franklin responded. "Thanks again."

Mischa nodded and the men scurried out the door.

"Oh what a shame," she said as she watched them hustle to Cassie's car. "Oh what a dreadful shame."

Cassie's father and his would-be son-in-law waited up nearly all night, drinking coffee and praying in Ramon's office waiting for Troy to call with further instructions. He never did. Battles had planned on making their emotions squirm miserably.

While the girls languished in the dreary confines of the mine and the brothers endured the longest night of their lives, Troy Battles took pleasure in the seedy side of Vegas.

Around midnight, the slightly disheveled miscreant wandered into a rundown strip club just on the outskirts of town. The place was the kind of low-class establishment frequented by day laborers, who would rather feed their hard-earned wages into the garter belts of trashy pole princesses than the equally greedy one-armed bandits enticing fantasy at the casinos. Strippers were actually less expensive in the long run, and often rewarded a patron's investment with additional carnal dividends.

Troy had truly sunk to the very depths of his depravity. The onetime high society golden boy was now a meager bottom-feeder. Strangely, he felt fairly comfortable in his current lowly domain.

After ordering a beer, he took a seat at the foot of the small, round, wooded stage. Troy's interest was immediately drawn to the pretty, blond dancer performing just a few feet from him. His eyes met hers right away. The comely dancer's gaze was sad and lonely, like love had forsaken her long ago. The same sentiment departed from Troy the night Gretchen tossed Ingrid's ring back at him. It seemed disrepute had met its equal in one elicit glance. The dancer offered Troy a seductive sampling of her most intimate features. Her lewdness was matched only by her impudence. Troy appreciated her visual candor and tipped accordingly. He told himself he would have her that night.

When the last notes from the steamy ballad faded, the buxom blond found her way to Troy's seat. He signaled for the cocktail waitress to come over.

""Let me have another beer and whatever she wants," Troy said to the cute brunette before returning his attention to the dancer's ample chest.

"I'll have a glass of champagne please Dora," the blond girl ordered as she placed her hand coyly on Troy's knee. She could see that her routine had already aroused him.

Troy nodded approvingly. He was enjoying her boldness. "Good choice," he said. "I'm Troy. And who might you be my lovely?"

She appreciated the compliment and kissed his cheek. "They call me Davilla."

Troy giggled. "That's an interesting name."

Her smile broadened as she batted her glistening blue eyes. "I'm an interesting girl."

"I'll bet you are," he replied.

He placed his hand on top of hers as she glided it along his inner thigh while they both watched the next dancer, a sluttish red-head, perform her risqué act.

A great deal had changed in the life of Davilla D'Vine since the night she'd left Franklin Edwards destitute and practically hopeless. Her comeuppance for steering the pitiful downfall of one of God's own children was both swift and brutal. Franklin's financial demise also marked the decisive end to a successful run of trickery and deceit for lusty Davilla and her cagey boyfriend.

Just one month after bilking Franklin's bank account for all it was worth, Miss D'Vine's junkie lover was found facedown in a pool of his own blood behind a casino. Derek's murder remained unsolved, with police detectives still unable to identify the gun which unloaded the two bullets that had blasted the back of the hustler's skull. Davilla was still one of the primary suspects the cops deemed possessed motive for the crime, but as of yet they had been unsuccessful at sticking the rap on her. Derek's chicanery also left a slew of other dupes pining for revenge. But the drug addict was amazingly adept at his ruse and covered his tracks well. Identity theft can be extremely hard to trace if done correctly. Derek was a master at his trade, but a slave to his vices, of which Davilla was the most luscious.

She had catered to his every whim out of a delusive sense of devotion. He responded to her loving grace with demented obsession. It was inevitable their tempestuous union was bound for a bitter ending. Davilla was the only one left standing when their devious game ran its course. Her improper Midwestern upbringing left her ill-prepared to move along any noble path of distinction. She knew her fortune still lay only in her beauty, but the payoff was no longer as promising as it had once been. Dancing for dollars became a demoralizing means to an unfulfilling end. But Davilla was suited for the task at hand and she performed it well.

Troy Battles highly appreciated her erotic talents.

"I'm sure you hear this all the time," he said, his glassy, charcoal eyes again scanning her voluptuous figure, barely clad in a see-through white negligee, "but you are one of the most beautiful women I have ever had the pleasure to lay my eyes upon."

"And you've seen most all of me I believe," she cooed as she boldly ran her hand across the crotch of his trousers. Davilla still had no problem forcefully laying claim on a potentially lucrative strike. She had already noticed the abundant amount of cash Troy carried in his wallet when he'd tipped her dancing earlier. And the money wasn't only in single denominations either. "I'd be more than happy to give you a private showing in one of the backrooms if you'd like."

Troy hesitated for a few seconds. Davilla wondered if her advance had been too daring. She hoped not. She found him appealing, and not only from a financial point of view. Even scruffy and tainted from his bustling day, Troy still possessed untamed magnetism that women found difficult to resist. The lovely, blond stripper was no exception.

"It's not that I wouldn't like to know you more intimately," he finally replied. "I most certainly would. Just not here."

Davilla raised her perfectly-thinned eyebrows curiously. "What do you have in mind?"

Troy responded with a sly laugh. He knew he had become the one performing the tease. "Oh, I don't know. Why don't I order us up a few shots and we'll discuss our options. Are you still on the clock?"

"My hours are extremely flexible," she turned his face toward hers and kissed him lightly on the lips. "Any of us are allowed to skip our turn on stage if we want to. It just means more chances for the others to make money. That's what we're all here for."

Troy nodded. "That all?"

"Well maybe," Davilla giggled, rubbing the inside of his thigh again. "I can be persuaded to pursue other interests as well."

"Glad to hear that," Troy replied, then motioned to Dora once more and placed another drink order.

Four rounds of Tequila shots later, Troy and Davilla became fast friends. Watching the other girls strut on stage just made their lust for each other all the more intense. If they didn't find a place to satiate their carnal cravings quickly, one of the joint's back rooms might seem like a reasonable option. Troy was about ready to rip the negligee clean from Davilla's body. He knew she would hardly care if he did so.

"I saw a motel next door as I was pulling in here," Troy said, breaking a kiss with her, his hand still secretly slipped under her silky gown, cupping her breast. "We could go there."

Davilla shook her head positively. "It's a popular place. Open all night."

"Let's go." Troy got up and held his hand out for the dancer to take.

"Just let me go get my coat from my locker and I'll be ready."

"Don't be too long."

"I won't." She kissed him on the cheek and walked away.

Troy paid the bar tab while Davilla fetched her long, winter coat. Troy thought she looked elegant in the soft brown fur, which was one of the lone remaining luxuries she still possessed from her time of treachery with Derek. Those profitable days had long since passed. But she thought Troy might be good for a few quick bucks. He was extremely fine looking too, another bonus.

The stiff winter breeze struck them fiercely as they exited the club. The shot of cold air seemed to stimulate Troy's senses, reminding him of the dirty deed he still had to handle before turning his attention to Davilla. He decided to excuse himself for a moment and give Franklin a call.

"I need to phone someone real quick," he said.

Davilla became instantly suspicious. "Right now?"

Troy could immediately see her frustration. "Well, alright. Let's check into the motel first." He smiled and took her arm in his. They walked the hundred feet or so to the lobby of the sleazy motel.

The place was a total dive, but it would serve their purpose for the night. Troy opened his wallet and paid the short, boyish

Mexican night clerk in cash. Davilla subtly confirmed the wad try-ing to burst the wallet's seams. It was obvious to her that Troy held little regard for his money. Although she didn't know much about him, he had boasted that his wealthy mama supported his needs at his request. Davilla certainly had no idea that Troy's mom was just a refuge of last resort for the prodigal heir.

Troy fidgeted with the steel lock on the door of their room for a good minute before the key finally forced open the latch. He flipped on the switch and bore witness to the filthy dump they would call home for the night. It was after two in the morning. The dowdy room with drab greenish paint peeling off its plaster walls looked like it had not seen maid service for days. The dingy white bed sheets were ruffled, appearing as if they had been used for a recent romp. In fact, the whole room reeked with the pungent smell of promiscuity. Even the toilet in the pint-sized bathroom had been left unflushed, its caustic fumes permeating the tobacco-stenched air.

"Well isn't this delightful," Troy commented wryly, smirking at Davilla in feigned appreciation for ambiance of their rented quar-ters. "It's worth every bit of the twenty-five dollars they charge each night."

Davilla laughed and hugged her client. Although they hadn't specifically discussed compensation for the sexual favors she was about to dispense, she promised to reward him fully for every pen-ny he'd pay.

"I really do still need to make that phone call," he said, kissing her ruby lips with a mocking tenderness. "Do you mind my dear? It will take but a few moments."

Davilla offered a resigned smile. She knew he had his mind set. She returned his kiss along with a persuading caress on his rear end.

"Don't dally too long...I'll be warming up for you in the shower. Come and join me quickly."

She pulled away and dropped her coat on the floor. After pulling the negligee over her head to reveal her breathtaking bareness once more, she blew him another kiss and turned for the bathroom. Troy watched every step her stunning form took as it exited the tiny room. She winked at him as she closed the door. He promised her he wouldn't dawdle.

But once Troy reached the van, his mind quickly diverted to another matter. He pulled off the magnetic New Hope Church signs from the van's doors. He couldn't believe he had forgotten to take them off before going into the bar. Not that he was embarrassed for the church's sake; he couldn't care less about New Hope's image. But the fact that he had mistakenly left a clue for any possible pursuers rapidly drew his ire. He had so come to hate any symbol of the evangelistic mission that he blamed for thwarting his own self-centered calling.

He tossed the signs in the back and reached into the file between the seats. He made sure the gun was still there, fully loaded. It was. As he carefully placed the revolver into the back of the file, he decided to check the papers inside. The stock certificates were there, as well as the rest of his personal papers. As he closed the file, an alarming thought entered Troy's mind. He didn't recall seeing the photograph inside. He rapidly pulled out the entire contents of the tin box and scattered them all over the front seat. He searched and searched, but the photo was missing. A sudden shock struck his heart.

Cassie most likely was fully aware of his hidden crime and had the ability to implicate him. He had caught her red-handed looking through the contents of his personal file. She had to know his guilt.

The more he thought about the incident that morning, the more he convinced himself of that fact. Cassie Ramirez had comprehended his culpability in the deaths of Sara Edwards and the girls. She probably didn't understand the circumstances surrounding his sin, but Troy recognized Cassie would be trouble if she escaped his grasp. He determined then she had outlived her usefulness to him and the sooner she was disposed of the better. Troy realized he probably could no longer use the girls as a way of luring Franklin to his demise. His already tenuous plans would have to change once again.

He tried to call Franklin with his cell phone, but the batteries went dead. Frustrated, he slammed the phone to the ground. It splintered in half. Troy spotted a pay phone by the entrance to the strip bar. He grabbed the bag of spare change church employees used for freeway tolls from the van's glove box and walked over to the payphone. He dialed the church. Franklin picked up immediately after the first ring.

"Troy? Is that you Troy?" he asked, almost pleadingly.

Just the sound of Franklin Edwards' voice incensed Troy. His rage burst forth from the darkest corners of his wretched psyche. His loathing for Franklin, and all who had ever loved his unknowing rival, had finally reached its peak. Troy Battles' madness was nearly complete.

"They are as good as dead Edwards!" was all the raving man yelled before hanging up the phone and stomping into the bar. The phone rang back as the door slammed shut behind Troy, but he refused to hear it. He sat down at the bar and drank three more shots of Tequila. The place was nearly barren at that point, save for a few desperados foaming at the mouth over a couple of sleazy private dancers fondling one another in the far back corner. Their performance reminded Troy of Davilla waiting for him in the motel room.

As he stumbled out of the strip bar, the alcohol he'd consumed hammered its full effect into Troy's wavering head. He nearly fell as he opened the motel room door. Davilla was stretched out naked on the bed waiting for him.

"Where have you been?" she asked, quite perturbed at his nearly hour-long absence.

Troy waved his hand in front of his face and shook his head back and forth in a drunken stupor, not uttering a word in response to her demand. He collapsed face down on the bed next to her, covered his head and sunk into an intoxicated slumber.

Davilla sighed deeply and shook her head in disgust.

"That must have been some phone call," she said to the sleeping lush, as she removed his shoes and covered him with a blanket. She felt kind of sorry for the guy, but more so for herself. Sure he was really just another john, someone she was to have laid with for pay. But she was also attracted to him. She had sensed he would fulfill her animalistic sexual needs in a way rarely accomplished by her clients. Usually Davilla had to rely on her girlfriends from the bar or even her own measures of satisfaction to quench her thirst for sensual sin. But in Troy Battles, she had perceived a kindred spirit who could relate to her own devilish desire for lascivious ecstasy. Now he was useless to her. Just another loser in a seemingly eternal supply of forgetful players to grace her bed.

Davilla put on her fur and was about to leave the room when she remembered the cash Troy carried in his wallet. She quickly reasoned she should at least be paid for her effort. It wasn't her fault he had failed to live up to expectations. As Troy began to snore loudly despite lying on his stomach, Davilla snatched the wallet from his back pocket. She took out the cash and counted it.

"Wow, nearly a thousand dollars," she commented to herself.

She thought about taking the entire wad, which was her usual custom in such circumstances. But she sensed Troy might be the type to come after her for revenge if she cleaned him out. And he already knew where to find her. She couldn't flee into the darkness of the night, like she used to do when running scams for Derek. So she only clipped two hundred dollars from Troy and returned the wallet to his back pocket. He would probably figure he'd spent at least that much in the bar, she assumed.

Davilla D'Vine, after all, did possess a touch of mercy in her heart, contrary to the sleeping menace she was leaving behind to founder in his own regret.

Chapter XVI

The seed of the serpent and the seed of the woman have been known to co-mingle throughout this sinful age, their impiety birthing despair as certain as the dawn of death that must surely creep forward. Penitence for such a rebellious coupling always lacks any sufficient redemption. Atonement can only be met by either of two distinct submissions: forced humility at last buried deep in the potter's field; or by humble reverence bowing meekly at the foot of the cross. The contrast is as stark as it is eternal.

❦

Gretchen gently wiped away the dried blood she felt encrusted on Cassie's cheek, using only the wetness of her own tears as they fell down upon her fallen friend's face. She cradled the bruised head of the pastor's daughter in her arms as she wept in witness to Troy's brutality. The mineshaft felt nearly as dark and bitterly cold as her ex-lover's wicked heart. Gretchen's sorrow shifted easily between the battering of the innocent young woman lying unconscious in her lap and the tormented man who had apparently brought their lives to senseless ruin.

Did the Lord hear her cries? Was He present in her lament? Did

He even care at all, she wondered?

As she closed her eyes once more, pleading in prayer to a God who now seemed so distant, Gretchen heard a slight moan break through the stillness of their inevitable tomb. Cassie twitched a couple of times before moving her head slightly from side to side. Gretchen ceased her prayer and opened her eyes, not that she could see anything in the pitch blackness.

"Easy now Cassie," Gretchen whispered, slowly raising her friend's head. "Let me help you honey."

After a minute or so, Cassie managed to sit up. The calmness in Gretchen's voice told Cassie she was safe for the moment.

"Cassie, can you speak? How do you feel?"

Her throat was as parched as the desert surrounding the mine in which they were entrapped, but Cassie swallowed hard and eked out a few barely audible words. Gretchen leaned her head close to Cassie's mouth.

"Need water," she whispered, as Gretchen held her up.

"I know, I know. Troy left us in this cage with nothing. He wants us to die."

Gretchen sniffled a couple of times. Cassie laid her pounding head on her desperate friend's shoulder. Both girls had suffered so severely over the past eight hours, but each knew the other's only hope for survival rested on whatever individual resources they could still manage to muster from any God-given strength they had remaining. They knew they would only endure as a team.

Cassie circled her tongue around the inside of her mouth, trying to gather up enough saliva to wet her mouth and throat so she could speak more clearly. She coughed a couple of times and tasted the blood from her broken nose as it slid down her throat.

"Gretchen," she moaned.

"Yes honey."

"Why Gretchen? Why?"

Gretchen leaned her head against Cassie's, and then interlocked right hands with her sister for comfort.

"I've been trying to figure that out Cassie. He's not the same person I grew up with. I don't even know him anymore."

Cassie squeezed Gretchen's hand tightly as she winced in pain and tried to adjust her body into a less agonizing position. She laid her head back down on Gretchen's lap. Her skull throbbed less that way.

"Try to rest honey," Gretchen said as she gently stroked Cassie's matted hair. "I know God will get us through this. I know He will."

"Just keep talking to me Gretchen...If I pass out again..." Cassie took a couple of deep breaths. "I may die."

"You're not gonna die!" Gretchen mournfully exclaimed as her eyes began to well once more. "I won't let you...Save you strength honey. Don't talk anymore. Just rest now."

Gretchen prayed to the Lord for the willpower for Cassie to survive. She begged for her friend's life. Cassie found instant resurgence through Gretchen's prayer.

"Where are we Gretchen?"

Cassie sat up again.

"Easy honey, easy," Gretchen warned, placing her arm around Cassie to steady her.

"I'm okay...Thank you for your sweet prayer."

Cassie wheezed a few times before catching her breath. While her condition was tenuous at best, she did feel a bit more comfortable. Although still scratchy, her mouth and throat were now less dry than when she first regained consciousness.

"How long has he been gone?" Cassie asked, beginning to re-member the circumstances that had led to their dire situation.

"Troy probably left us here two or three hours ago."

"What is this place?"

"It's some kind of an old mine near Las Vegas."

"Las Vegas? I don't understand."

"Troy kidnapped us Cassie. I don't fully know why. He was trying to force me to marry him, but I wouldn't...I'm sorry Cassie. Just so sorry."

Gretchen began to cry. Cassie leaned against her friend's shoul-der. It hurt too much to raise her arms.

"It can't be your fault. Don't cry...How could it be your fault?"

"Oh Cassie," she continued to sob. "If I would have just done what he said, we would both be better off...He has always con-trolled me...Now he's hurt you..."

Cassie patted Gretchen's knee a few times. "We'll be alright. God is with us. I promise."

Gretchen regained her composure after a few more sorrowful moments. Her mind began to wander back to her childhood for some reason. To a time when she and Troy were like brother and sister. She had loved him so much. She knew her deep love for him even as a youngster.

"We used to be so close Cassie, me and Troy," Gretchen stated, as Cassie lay back down on her lap again. "I often thought we were of the same blood. For a while, others thought so as well."

"What do you mean?"

"It's a long, troubling story."

"Tell me," Cassie said. "We have time."

Gretchen lightly stroked Cassie temples. The motion was soothing.

"Well," Gretchen sighed. "I've told you our families are close."

"You have."

"Well, they're closer than most. Sinfully close in fact."

Cassie wheezed and coughed.

"Go on, I'm still listening."

Gretchen hesitated before continuing. "It's kind of embarrassing Cassie."

"You can tell me anything, you know that."

Gretchen took a deep breath. It hurt her to unsettle old family dirt, but she felt doing so might help Cassie understand their current circumstances.

"You see...back in the eighties before either I or Troy was born, my mother and Troy's father had an affair. Although they were each married at the time, Richard and my mother were in love, so it wasn't as trashy as it sounds. But she became pregnant."

"With you?" Cassie asked.

"That's what they thought at first."

"What about your father? Did he find out?"

"Yes they confessed everything to my father. Their affair. Her pregnancy. Everything."

Cassie again sat up, still trying to find a way to decrease the pain from her injuries. "Go on please."

"Well, my mother naturally wanted to keep the baby. She didn't believe in abortion...And since Richard and my father were best friends, as well as business partners, they tried to cover up all the sorted details."

"You mean your father forgave Richard and Ingrid?"

"He did."

"Wow! That showed a lot of grace."

"It was not as graceful as it seems Cassie. My father has always been weak, most often to a fault. He knew he needed Richard's money, and my mother's strength and guidance. He really had no choice in the matter. He's always done what he's been told to do."

"Didn't your father love your mother?"

"Everybody loved my mother. She was one of the most wonderful people the world has ever known. But you have to understand something Cassie about the world from which I come."

"What?"

"Things are arranged in high society, especially in the old country. You see, the marriage between my mother and father was set when they were children in Sweden. Their families arranged the whole thing. My mother and father were forced to get married. He loved her, but she didn't feel the same for him. She liked my father, but she didn't love him."

"So that's why she went looking for love elsewhere."

"Yes, I know it's difficult to understand, but yes."

But Cassie still didn't comprehend the entire story. "So what about you? Richard is not really your father is he?"

"No he's not. But they didn't know that until after I was born. The blood types didn't match. Richard was heartbroken."

"So what about you mother?" Cassie asked, the story diverting her mind from her pain temporarily. "She remained with your father, no?"

"Yes, until her death when I was nine. She was the dutiful wife to my father always, obviously even during her affair with Richard. That's the way she was raised in the old country. You know, for better or for worse, until death do us part."

Cassie still wondered how Troy, and his sinister ways, fit into the whole mess. The evil had to be born from somewhere.

"But how does all that explain Troy's actions now Gretchen?"

Cassie asked, lying down on Gretchen again, her head beginning to pound once more.

"He's not like his father at all," Gretchen replied, coughing twice as her throat was beginning to dry up from telling the story. "I love Richard, like my own father. And he loves me like his own daughter, probably because he never stopped loving my mother. He probably sees her in me. That's why he was so set on Troy and me getting married some day. Just like in the old country, it was to be arranged. And I imagined I would be Mrs. Troy Battles some day. That's really all I ever wanted, until now."

Gretchen began to choke up. Cassie could feel her sister's sorrow at the course fate had already set unchangeably in place. Gretchen's childhood fantasy had been forever shattered. Cassie forced herself to sit up and hug the fallen princess tightly.

"What happened to Troy honey?" Cassie asked. "Where did his wickedness come from?"

"It comes from his mother!" Gretchen quickly replied. "I love Richard, but his ex wife is truly hateful. I've never met a more wicked woman...Heather passed on that gene to Troy. It's not his fault, really...I feel so sorry for him."

Gretchen started to weep again. Despite Troy's miserable behavior of late, she longed to forgive him. But they were past that point. She could no longer offer forgiveness to someone who wanted no part of grace. Her charity would never cover the multitude of his sins. Only God himself could grant such a pardon for Troy's callous deeds, no matter the source from which they came.

Cassie's suffering confirmed that rueful fact.

❧❖❧

Franklin Edwards had literally been down this road before in more ways than one. His travel early that morning touched a place in his worried heart not felt in nearly two years. The sense of impending doom surely eating away at the resoluteness he had so steadily built up since his previous journey by bus on the highway between L.A. and Vegas was beginning to consume his trust in God's promises of restoration. The only well of relief for his bitter torment was prayerfully sitting next to him en route to a destination quite possibly filled with disaster. Ramon's steadfast faith was all that kept Franklin's hope for perseverance alive.

"I just couldn't bear to lose Cassie like I lost Sara," Franklin said, choking back the tears he knew would cloud not only his vision of the highway ahead of him, but also his mind's ability to react with sound judgment to the intolerable task Troy Battles had so miserably set before him.

"Brother, sometimes it may be that only God knows the forces at work in the plan of Satan," Ramon responded, patting Franklin on the thigh a few times to try and calm him. "I am worried also about my daughter and her friend, but God is not absent now. He is with them, and us as well. I am certain He will protect them. Remember, Satan can only travel as far as God's leash allows."

"But you don't think God would allow them to die do you? They are so young. So loving, so precious, so..."

Franklin slammed his palm in anger against the steering wheel of Cassie's little white car as it briskly scurried along the sparsely-traveled desert road. The car swerved slightly in response to Franklin's act of frustration, which had been slowly ramping up since Troy's sobering call three hours earlier.

"Please son," Ramon calmly replied, "we must keep our composure. We have to for the sake of the girls. I believe God will provide an opportunity for their rescue. Troy is not in his right mind, he will surely make another mistake. He has already made one."

Ramon's wink and slight smile offered fresh hope to Franklin. He knew his future father in-law was correct in his assertion. Troy had indeed already committed a critical blunder in his drunken rage by using a pay phone to call Franklin. From the caller ID, Franklin recognized that Troy was not calling him from his cell phone. The number that showed up on the phone's call log was easily traceable. With one courteous call to the phone company, Franklin was able to find out the address to the pay phone Troy had used to make his threat to kill Cassie and Gretchen. Franklin plugged the address into his computer at New Hope and out popped directions and a map to the location of the pay phone. Franklin was confused that Battles was calling from a motel near Las Vegas, but that was the only lead he and Ramon had to go on, so they followed it promptly. Franklin tried to call Troy's cell again, but the line was apparently out of service, with the call not even going to voicemail.

Ramon drove the first half of the apprehensive trip to Vegas. Franklin loathed the fact he was heading back to a city that had caused him so much trouble. He had vowed never to return there, but he knew he had no choice in the matter. He was glad Ramon would be with him this time.

On their way out of L.A., Franklin decided to phone his old friend Sam Simmons in an effort to get any additional information that might prove helpful in his quest to seek out Troy. Sam was quite valuable, telling Franklin that Troy and Richard had a major falling out over some sort of family scandal. Although Sam didn't ascertain the full details of the scandal, Franklin was fairly certain it had something to do with Troy's behavior toward Gretchen. Sam told Franklin that Troy had been cut off from the Battles' fortune, but according to Sam's wife Sandy, Heather had been wiring her son money. Sam didn't say how Sandy knew such a personal detail, but the gossip lines flow freely among the society women in Franklin's old hometown.

The background Sam gave Franklin was insightful, but still didn't explain why Troy had kidnapped Gretchen and Cassie. And the information gave neither Franklin nor Ramon any reason behind the disturbing torn photograph found under Troy's bed at New Hope.

"You know Ramon, something else has really been bothering me," Franklin stated, his composure seemingly stable once more.

"What is that?" Ramon replied, watching the sun boldly make its assent through the crisp, blue, dessert sky.

"The picture I found in Troy's room. I don't get it. Why would he have such a picture?"

Ramon frowned and shook his head, bewildered. "I do not know. Another mystery from a very strange boy."

"But why the X's?"

Ramon again shook his head. He noticed the still-stinging lament reflected in Franklin's weary brown eyes. Ramon knew how cruel it was for Franklin to be reminded of his family's tragic demise while dealing with the fierce mental anguish of their current dilemma concerning Cassie and her best friend.

"It's almost like Troy was happy they were gone," Franklin commented. "Like the photo was a memento or something."

"A memento of what?" Ramon asked.

"I don't know. There were times when I was teaching class and I knew Troy didn't like me very much, but he was usually pretty respectful toward me. Even when we were racing and I beat him... I don't know Ramon, it was almost like he wanted me to find that photo."

"Why?"

Franklin shook his head quizzically. "The way it was torn. The way my picture was torn out of it...Sort of like, oh I don't know, like they were gone and I was next."

Ramon was shaken by what he was hearing. ""Franklin, you do not think he had anything to do with their deaths do you?"

That thought really hadn't crossed Franklin's mind at all. He didn't know how to consider Ramon's suggestion.

"I don't see how," Franklin said with doubt in his voice. "The police report seemed pretty straight forward. Sara overcompensated on a wet road and flipped the car. She made a mistake." Franklin swallowed hard. "She really wasn't a very good driver Ramon. I was always on her about not paying attention to what she was doing... No, I think Troy kept that photo for other reasons."

"Like what?"

Franklin sighed deeply. "Maybe to use against me somehow. To hurt me in some way in the future. To hold over my head like I was at fault somehow for their deaths...I did blame myself for the longest time, you know."

Ramon quickly leaned over and put his hand on Franklin's shoulder. "Look, brother, you know there is no way it is your fault they died. We know everything is the Lord's will. His perfect will. He took them home because He wanted them home."

"Oh I know you're right," Franklin interrupted. "I know God is in control of everything...I'm just saying maybe Troy was going to give it to me some day to get back at me for something. Maybe he hates me for something, I don't know."

"That is diabolical if that is what he was going to do," Ramon responded in disgust. "Pure evil, I tell you. Horrible, just horrible!"

Franklin saw the anger brewing in his friend. He didn't want to make Ramon more anxious about their circumstances than he already was.

"I guess I shouldn't make accusations when I don't know. The photo could mean anything I suppose."

"It means something alright," Ramon replied. "We just do not know what it is...He took those girls for some reason. He said he was going to kill them if we did not do what he said...He is very wicked Franklin, very, very wicked."

Franklin hadn't told Ramon that Troy had already said Cassie and Gretchen were as good as dead. He didn't feel his fiancé's father needed any further hardship striking his wounded heart until absolutely necessary. There would be time enough for that if Troy followed through on his threat. Ramon still harbored hope for now, more hope than he held for sure. Franklin knew time may not be on their side for much longer.

"I guess we will find out when we catch up to Troy," Franklin said. "Just keep praying brother. Pray that God allows us to find them soon."

Ramon didn't need to be asked twice. He bowed his head and went before the Lord of all life. Only God knew the answers to the many troubling questions circling feverishly through both men's minds. Their hope lay in their faith, and in their faith alone.

❧❦❧

Troy's mood when he awoke was as sour as the pungent breath bouncing back from his saliva-drenched pillow. All the tequila he had downed the night before was demanding payment for the shameful services it had dutifully rendered. Yet as much as his body felt the self-inflicted punishment he so deserved for his overindulgence, Troy's conscience remained relatively unscathed.

The absolute consequences for his depraved conduct no longer piqued his mind toward any significant form of repentance. His soul was fully prepared for the impending doom it was bound to encounter. Troy Battles sensed his ultimate fate would be sealed shortly. He didn't care.

After sprucing up for appearances sake, he left the seedy motel and drove the van toward Vegas to pick up a few supplies. He still planned to murder Cassie and Gretchen, but not quite yet. In the deep recesses of his twisted mind, Troy was still enjoying the cruel dominion in which he governed the fate of the two beleaguered girls. He wanted to hold on to that misguided command a while longer. He found the power over life and death thoroughly exhilarating, godlike in a way. They would surely die when he was ready, but Troy knew the girls required food and water until then.

Just before hitting the main drag in Vegas, he pulled into a convenience store in a small strip mall. He purchased some bottled water, a few prepackaged sandwiches, cigarettes, another flashlight and some batteries. When he opened his wallet to pay for the goods, he noticed some of his money was missing. It only took a minute to figure out where the cash had gone. He promised he would take the missing funds from Davilla D'Vine's hide later that evening.

As he was getting back into the van, Troy saw an erotic boutique at the far end of the mall. A slew of dastardly ideas cluttered his head. He went inside and looked around. The small shop was actually quite crowded for a weekday morning. Troy gazed at all the lingerie hanging throughout the place, but knew there was no need for such romantic attire now. At one time, he would have loved to see comely Gretchen donning such sexy clothing, but his attraction for her had waned substantially in the last twenty-four hours. Davilla was more his type now. But he wasn't looking to make a purchase for her either. His needs were found in the fetish section. He quickly collected the items he required: two pairs of handcuffs, a choker collar and a cattail whip.

"Planning a little party tonight?" the tall, freaky-looking redhead at the checkout counter asked, the multiple piercings sprouting up from her face perfectly complementing the silver grill accenting what looked to be an ordinarily well-kept smile.

"Something like that," Troy answered, his devilish grin somewhat detailing the true intentions of his purchase. His mind told him the clerk would most likely find satisfaction herself with the sadistic items.

She rang up the transaction and placed the purchase in a discreet plastic bag.

"Well, enjoy yourself," she said with a playful smirk, handing Troy the bag.

"Oh, I will," he responded. "A lot more than some I know."

Troy was feeling much better as he drove back toward the mine. His hangover had subsided greatly since eating one of the sandwiches and rehydrating himself with water. He felt totally prepared to inflict more punishment on the women who had sidetracked his life. He considered it a bonus to have a little fun before disposing of them. A time of pernicious pleasure to be savored, he mused.

On his way out of Vegas, Troy stopped at a post office to mail Eric Bjorn's bogus stock certificates to the federal authorities, who would undoubtedly bring dishonor to Gretchen's fraudulent father long after his daughter's piteous demise. Troy wanted to ensure all who had pained him would not soon dismiss their contributions to his unforgettable infamy.

The girls were huddled closely as Troy shined the flashlight into the steel cell holding his victims.

"Aw, isn't that sweet," he said mockingly to the duo clinging tightly to each other, trembling at the mere sight of the ruthless perpetrator.

"It's freezing in here!" Gretchen screamed at Troy, who unlocked the cell and stepped inside.

"Quit your bitching!" he yelled back. "Or I'll give you something you can really complain about."

Cassie grabbed Gretchen's arm as she started to stand up and confront Troy. The pastor's daughter knew they needed to bide their time against the armed madman. Any hope for survival would depend on reacting rationally to Troy's violent temper.

"Besides, I come bearing gifts." Troy opened up one of the three plastic bags he was carrying. He tossed each one of them a sandwich and a bottle of water. "Don't say anything else, either of you. Just sit there quietly and eat...Oh, in case you've forgotten." He pulled out the gun from his waist and pointed it menacingly at each of them. "We're all gonna have some fun when you're done."

With a snide laugh, Troy walked out of the cell and locked the door behind him. He left the flashlight shining on the girls inside the cell so he could watch them as they ate while he smoked a cigarette.

Gretchen was famished as she unwrapped her soggy, processed ham and cheese sandwich from its plastic container. As she scarfed down what she thought might be her last meal, she wondered what Troy meant by "fun." He had made the statement with dreadful anticipation. She soon became too frightened to ponder the meaning further.

Cassie could manage just a few nibbles of her sandwich because of her injuries. Chewing brought wretched pain to her broken nose and swollen jaw. Troy's battering had also loosened a few back teeth. But the cool water sliding down her throat proved mercifully soothing. She thought Troy would most likely have taken it away if he knew how much relief it was giving her. His loathsome stare always reminded her most assuredly how much he despised her. His gaze was eerily penetrating, as if she could herself almost feel the demon piercing the soul from within him. It would be only a matter of moments before she would once again meet that demon face to face.

Troy stamped out his cigarette as the girls finished eating. He unlocked the cell and walked back inside, carrying the other two plastic bags with him. His peccant smirk told both girls trouble was looming.

"Gretchen, get over here!" he commanded, pointing the gun at her.

She began to cry as she stood up and approached him.

"Oh stop that!" he screamed, "I'm not gonna shoot you. Like I said, we're just gonna have a little fun, that's all."

"What? What do you mean?" she whimpered. Cassie thought about trying to rush Troy, but she knew her legs were too weak to even stand, much less charge the deranged man pointing a gun at her best friend.

Troy reached down into one of the plastic bags by his feet and pulled out the stainless steel choke collar, like one used to discipline an unruly puppy. He handed it to Gretchen.

"Put this around your neck."

"What?" she screamed, startled by his demand.

"Do it!" he shouted, holding the gun to her forehead.

With tears streaming down her once-delicate face, Gretchen did as she was told. Troy yanked the chain with his left hand, the force of his tug driving the girl to her knees. Cassie grimaced as Gretchen yelped, gasping for breath. Troy pulled her back up to her feet with the leash and shoved the gun in her back. The force of his weapon in her rib cage quickly straightened her posture, but at least she could breathe again.

Troy pushed her over to Cassie and shoved her down to the ground. He took out a pair of the hand cuffs and threw them into Gretchen's lap.

"Put your hands behind your back Cassie," he demanded

"Oh Troy, leave her alone," Gretchen pleaded, "can't you see how hurt she is?"

"Shut up!" he yelled, yanking on the choke collar again to silence his charge.

Cassie followed his order. She feared for Gretchen's health more than her own at that point.

"Put these handcuffs on her," Troy stated to Gretchen. "Now!"

Gretchen hesitated. Troy yanked on the collar once again.

"Do as he says honey," Cassie said somberly. "I'll be alright."

Troy flashed another evil grin as Gretchen followed through on his command. The control he was exerting made his loins tingle. The power was intoxicating. He desired it in abundance. He became more depraved with each passing second.

Once Cassie was secure, with the bottom of his foot, Troy pushed Gretchen away. She fell back and hit her head against the rock wall. She was dizzied, but remained conscious. Troy reached down and grasped the front collar of Cassie's thin white blouse. He yanked it hard, causing the buttons to fly off and the sheer material to easily rip open. The force popped the front of Cassie's bra, exposing her bare chest to the brisk mine air. She immediately began to shiver, equally as much from her embarrassment as from the cold. She began to weep in her shame. Troy fed on her suffering. Retribution leaves such a sweet taste, he thought to himself.

"Gretchen!" Troy barked, "your girlfriend is cold. Warm her up."

He pulled his former fiancé up by the choker and dragged her over to Cassie. She fell on top of the handcuffed girl, knocking her backward. Gretchen quickly sat up.

"Go on, kiss her," Troy shouted. "You love her so much. Kiss her breasts!"

Gretchen started to cry also. Troy pulled on the chain once more.

"What's the matter dear? I thought you loved her. You always said you loved her so much. Go on make love to her. Go on!"

"Troy stop!" Gretchen wailed miserably. "Please stop! I beg you!"

Troy began to laugh out boisterously. "I guess you really don't love her so much do you? You used to love me too, remember?" His howl became decidedly wicked. "Maybe I should put a bullet in her right now? Huh? What do you think? Huh?" Troy yanked on the choker once more with his left hand and placed the gun to Cassie's head. The pastor's daughter defiantly didn't flinch. She would have been ready to pass on at that point, if not for the concern over her friend's well-being.

"No! No!" Gretchen screamed. "No don't. I'll do anything you want. I promise. Anything. Don't kill her please. Please. Please..." Gretchen's fading shrill echoed throughout the mine.

Troy pulled her up by the leash again to cease her cries.

"You'll do anything huh?" Troy exclaimed.

"Yes, yes, just leave her alone."

Brutally tugging the choker, Troy forced Gretchen to her knees in front of him. The tears were rolling in torrents down her cheeks as he released his grip on the chain. He began to unbuckle his belt with his free hand while firmly clutching the gun in his right. He felt his domination was limitless. Gretchen understood the thoughtless task she was resolved to perform. Something they had never done together as a couple, although Troy had often hinted at the deed.

Cassie wasn't about to let Gretchen demean herself at any cost.

"Gretchen stop!" she shouted. "He's not worth it!"

The statement immediately rankled Troy to the core of his deluded mind. His reaction was swift and furious. He pushed Gretchen away from him and ran over to Cassie. He backhanded her across the face, sending her reeling to the ground.

"I'll shut that mouth of yours if it's the last thing I do!" He yanked Cassie up by the back of her hair. Blood began to slowly trickle out of her mouth. "Gretchen grab those two bags and get over here!"

Gretchen followed orders quickly. She feared to say anything.

"Take off her shoes and socks!"

Gretchen did as he commanded. Troy balled up one of Cassie's socks and stuffed it in her mouth.

"Oh Troy!" Gretchen yelled.

"Shut your mouth or I'll do the same to you!"

Troy let go of Cassie, whose face was now stricken with fear.

"Get that duct tape and wrap it around her mouth and hair until I tell you to stop!" Troy pressed the gun against Cassie exposed chest. "Do it now!"

Gretchen did as she was ordered, wrapping the tape tightly around Cassie's mouth and hair three times until Troy told her to stop. She wept profusely as she bound and silenced her best friend ever. Cassie's teary eyes told Gretchen to claim no blame for her actions.

Troy pulled Gretchen to her feet and took out the other pair of handcuffs. She didn't protest at all when he forced her arms behind her back and snapped the cuffs shut. He duct-taped Gretchen's mouth shut like Cassie's, but left out the filthy sock. Instead, he propped Gretchen against the wall opposite where Cassie was sitting. The two girls faced each other as Troy finished off the roll of tape by wrapping it tightly around Gretchen's pants, binding her legs together.

He took out the whip from the plastic bag and ran his fingers along its leather straps. With a wicked smile, he cracked it a couple of times. Both girls' eyes lit up in horror. Troy tossed the whip down between the two of them.

"That's what you bitches will receive when I come back," he sneered. "I think it's better if I give you some time to think about what's coming."

Troy giggled a few times, locked the cell door and walked back up the mineshaft.

They saw that he had mistakenly forgotten the flashlight; its illumination easily displayed the savage abuse both girls had endured. Cassie was shivering greatly as Gretchen looked over. It took about fifteen minutes, but she managed to slowly wiggle her way the ten-foot distance to Cassie. She pressed her back up against her friend's bare chest for warmth. Cassie's shiver stopped within a couple of minutes.

Neither could speak to the other to offer words of comfort. They could only rely on their prayers. The two young women's savage trauma had ceased for the time being. They prayed the respite would last a while before the beast returned as promised.

⋟⋄⋞

Franklin's lament had abated for the most part as he and Ramon drove into the Sandy Motel parking lot. Both men convinced themselves that they should just keep pushing forward in their desperate search. They knew God had already determined the outcome of the girls' plight. The men believed they must remain faithful in the Lord's governance over all circumstances. They understood they really had no choice but to do so.

"Are you sure this is the place?" Ramon asked as Franklin turned off the ignition to Cassie's car.

Franklin looked up at the faded wood sign above the entrance to the run-down motel and confirmed the name on his computer printout. Sure enough, the Sandy Motel was definitely the listing of the payphone Troy Battles had called from the night before. The place reminded him of the decrepit haunts he had seen in many of the old film noir movies from the 1940's and 50's. The type of establishment where a weary traveler would unwittingly stop for a good night's rest and end up resting permanently. It was tough for him to imagine preppy Troy would resort to calling such dreadful digs even temporary quarters. But Franklin reasoned Troy might be running low on cash since he had been separated from the Battles fortune.

"Should be it," Franklin replied. "That's probably the phone he called from over there next to that other building. Let's check it out."

They walked over to the payphone. It was still early afternoon on that cool January day. Except for the rugged, dry surroundings, the crisp temperatures hardly made it seem like the men were conducting their search in the midst of a desert. It was almost cold enough to snow, save for the complete lack of precipitation. Franklin picked up the pay phone and checked the number under the receiver. It matched the one he had written down off the church's called ID.

"This is it Ramon. This is where he called from."

Ramon quickly glanced around the gravel parking lot. There were a few cars and a couple of old beat-up trucks parked in front of the motel and the other worn-out wooden building, which Ramon surmised was some kind of drinking establishment from the beer signs flashing above the two porthole-sized windows next to the front door.

""I do not see the corvette or the church van brother," Ramon said with a slight frown on his pudgy round face. "Maybe he left already."

Franklin put the phone receiver back on the hook with frustrating force. He had hoped Troy could be found there. He knew of no place else to look.

"Come on," Ramon replied to his friend's anger, rubbing his shoulder in a calming manner. "We will go inside and ask someone. Do not give up."

"I'm not," Franklin sighed deeply. "I just want to get to the bottom of this mess."

"I know, we both do."

The two men walked inside the motel office. The same Mexican clerk who had checked in Troy the night before was again on duty. Although Franklin and Ramon shared most of the details they could about their dilemma, the clerk didn't seem to care a whole lot and didn't forward much information. Ramon placed a couple of twenty-dollar bills in the young man's slimy hands and his memory clicked in a lot more favorably.

"I can't let you see the register," the clerk said, licking his greasy fingers in between bites of his fried chicken lunch, "but there was a man who looked like you said. He stayed here last night."

Franklin's eyes lit up. "Really? Is he still here?"

The clerk rudely cleared his nostrils with the tip of his pinky. "Naw man. He checked out this morning before I came on."

"Damn!" Franklin exclaimed. "That's just great!"

Ramon patted his frustrated buddy on the shoulder. "It will be okay." Ramon turned to the chubby clerk, who was now devouring a drumstick like he'd not eaten in weeks. "Was there anybody with him? Like a couple of young women?"

The clerk finished off the drumstick and wiped his mouth on the sleeve of his green flannel shirt. "He did have a lady friend with him."

"What did she look like?" Franklin interrupted excitedly. "A pretty blond or a black-haired Mexican girl?"

"She was a blond, very pretty."

Franklin and Ramon looked at each other, hoping it was Gretchen.

"Was she about five-foot-six, kind of slender?" Franklin asked.

"Naw, she was very, oh how you say?" the clerk cupped to hands in front of his chest, "booxum...You know, big-chested."

They acted surprised by the clerk's description.

"Yes. I have seen her before," he continued. "Very beautiful. She works next door."

"Next door?" Ramon asked.

"Yes. The nudie bar next door. Many of the girls bring men over here. We ask no questions. Not our business what they do. As long as they pay, no?"

Franklin shook his head in dismay, but he was grateful to at least know that Troy had been there.

"Why do we not go and ask around the bar Franklin? Maybe we can find the girl and ask her where Troy went...Thank you for your help senior'."

The Mexican grinned and winked. "Enjoy yourself over there. I wish you find what you looking for."

Ramon nodded and he and Franklin began to walk to the bar. They saw the bar's owner, a short, stocky, man with slick-backed dark hair, brooding eyes and a pencil-thin mustache, leaving his shiny black Cadillac. Tony was a middle-aged fellow of Italian decent, who seemed like his already-sour mood could suddenly change for the worse with just the slightest twinge of irritation. Neither Franklin nor Ramon wanted to test the temperament of the foul-mouthed man, whose favorite adjective began with the letter F.

Like the motel clerk, Tony didn't immediately forward much assistance. He bluntly suggested the men patronize his club and ask his girls to help out. Just as Franklin and Ramon were about to decline the offer, a taxi dropped off one of the girls for work. Franklin immediately recognized the stunning blond woman who exited the cab.

"Hello Davilla," Franklin said, briskly striding over toward the cab.

The girl's heart sunk when she saw who was speaking to her. She also remembered him instantly, even his name, Franklin Edwards. Davilla had never forgotten what she and Derek had done to him. Of all their many marks over the years, Franklin was the one she regretted duping the most. Since the night she left him reeling, Davilla sensed her deeds had finally crossed some dubious line that would ultimately result in divine retribution. He was a stain on her conscience she couldn't wipe off. He even seemed to haunt her dreams occasionally, yet in a pleasant sort of way. Never ranting at her, as would seem appropriate because of her cruel transgression, but instead softly whispering kind words of forgiveness. Through the mist of her mind, his gentle smile affirmed his pardon of her miserable iniquity. Davilla wondered if the man she was now facing in the flesh would be as merciful.

"Do I know you?" she asked, hoping her feigned surprise might somehow confuse his apparent certainty of her own recognition of him. The attempt was futile.

"You know me very well, intimately in fact," he replied, his wide smile forceful, yet still calming.

Davilla couldn't help but immediately drop her guard. She wanted to in fact. There was no use trying to explain herself and what she had done to him. She sensed he already knew the reasons behind her actions, even if not any of the pertinent details. Such facts were irrelevant at that point anyway.

"What do you want?" she asked, her heavily-shadowed blue eyes beginning to mist and her pouty red lips quivering ever so slightly in confirmation of her guilt.

"Don't be frightened," Franklin answered, his placid smile signaling little desire for combat. "We just want to ask you a few questions."

"Who's he Franklin?" she asked, pointing at Ramon, who was standing a few feet behind Franklin.

"Oh, I'm sorry," Franklin quickly replied, "this is my friend, the Reverend Ramon Ramirez. Ramon, this is Davilla...Uh, we go back a ways, you might say."

Davilla uneasily held out her hand to shake Ramon's, not knowing how much Franklin had shared about their previous acquaintance. "Nice to meet you."

"Likewise," Ramon responded with a firm handshake, covering his confusion well.

So far, so good, Davilla thought. Both men seemed nonconfrontational for the moment at least. "You said you wanted to ask me some questions?"

"Yes, we are looking for two young women," Ramon blurted out suddenly.

Davilla's eyes nearly popped out of their sockets at Ramon's statement. She was surprised that such a comment would come from a man of the cloth. Franklin choked back a cough and giggled at his friend's mistaken remark, especially its utterance in front of a strip bar. Ironically, it was the first time he'd managed to laugh in two days.

"What my friend means," Franklin said, looking at Ramon and rolling his eyes, "is that we are trying to locate his daughter and a friend of hers. They've been missing for two days now and we're very worried."

Ramon rubbed his eyes in embarrassment. Davilla grinned at Franklin. Ramon's faux pas seemed to lighten the mood unexpectedly.

"Do you think they're working here?" she asked. "Because I know all the girls and they have been here for a while now."

"Oh no," Ramon interjected. "We believe they have been kidnapped. By a boy named Troy Battles. Have you seen him?"

Franklin turned quickly to Ramon and placed his hand on the overly-excited man's shoulder. "Ramon, easy. Relax."

Davilla obviously didn't fully understand the situation the men were inquiring about. But she was glad neither of them was after her. She felt obliged to share her knowledge with them.

"I met a man named Troy last night," she confessed, her shameful eyes revealing to Franklin that not much had changed in the stripper's life since he'd last seen her.

"Were you the one who stayed with him at the motel?" Franklin inquired with a careful tone, trying not to seem judgmental. "The clerk said he checked into a room with a blond dancer."

"That was me...But we didn't spend much time together. He left right after we checked in..."

"Did he say where he was going?" Ramon interrupted.

Franklin raised his hand and smiled at the pastor. "Let her finish Ramon."

"Oh, I am sorry," Ramon said to Davilla, placing two fingers over his mouth.

Davilla smiled at him. "That's okay...As I was saying, he left right after we checked in to make a phone call. He said it was important. Then he didn't come back for an hour. When he did, he was totally plastered and passed out on the bed. I left him there shortly after that and went home."

Franklin frowned and looked downward. Ramon sighed loudly.

"I'm sorry," Davilla said. "There wasn't much use for me to stick around."

Franklin realized his reaction was inappropriate, even toward a wanton woman. "Oh dear, no," he responded apologetically, grasping her hand in regret for his unwitting expression. "I'm glad you didn't. Troy is dangerous."

"He did seem kind of brash, and he was mad about something after he came back to the room."

Ramon looked at Franklin with distress. "I bet that is when he threatened you."

Franklin nodded in agreement. "Probably right."

Davilla suddenly became concerned. "He threatened you? About what?"

Franklin gazed into her disconcerted eyes. "That's why we need to find him, and fast. He didn't really threaten me." Franklin began to choke up. "He threatened to kill the girls...He said they were as good as dead and hung up."

Ramon quickly put his arm around Franklin, who was failing in his effort to hold back tears. Davilla swallowed hard, trying to gulp down the lump that had developed in her throat.

"My daughter is also his fiancée" Ramon told Davilla as he hugged Franklin. "The other girl is her best friend."

Davilla suddenly wanted to help the two men in any way she could. She felt the urge to make amends to Franklin for her past indiscretion. To pay a penance in some way, if that was possible.

"He may come back to see me," she said. "I know I gave him reason to. If he does, I will call you right away, I promise."

"Like I said," Franklin quickly replied, "he's very dangerous. I couldn't ask you to risk harm to yourself."

"I want to!" she exclaimed with a quiver in her voice. "I need to! Please! Please let me help you!"

Ramon looked at Franklin with resignation. Both men knew the lovely dancer might be their only hope at safely bringing home the two women.

"Franklin, we could check into the motel and see if Troy comes back."

Franklin wiped his eyes and rubbed his chin. He agreed with Ramon and Davilla. Staying at the motel was their best shot at catching Troy.

"Why don't we do that Ramon? Would you mind checking us in? I need to talk to Davilla about something else."

She felt a staunch blow to her insides. She knew she had it coming and deserved it. She only hoped Franklin would find some way to show mercy in the requital he had a right to inflict upon her. She was ready to accept it fully.

"No problem brother," Ramon answered with a smile. "Take your time. I will find you when I am settled."

Franklin nodded and held out his arm for Davilla to take hold of. She smiled nervously and interlocked her arm in his, saying nothing while they walked inside the bar. She was at his disposal for the time being. She knew she owed him more than she could ever repay, but she was willing to try somehow.

They sat down together at a small booth tucked discreetly in the far end of the nearly-empty club. It was normally used for lap dances, but the booth would serve a more genteel purpose this time. Davilla was still wary, but Franklin's smile calmed her.

"Can I get us something to drink?" she asked.

"You know, I am thirsty," he replied with a relaxed sigh. "A cold beer might taste real good about now."

"I'll be right back," she said, then walked behind the bar and drew two beers from the tap herself.

While Davilla was away, another dancer slithered her way over to Franklin's booth. Before he had the chance to tell the young lady that he was already being tended to, she began her sales pitch. She was a frail, freckled, redhead with drawn hazel eyes that seemed ready to burst from their sockets. Her slight chest was barely hidden by the sheer white nightie covering her torso. The black g-string blasting through the skimpy material made her slim attire quite unattractive, Franklin thought. She leaned down and put her arm around Franklin, causing him to feel highly uncomfortable.

"Hi handsome," she squealed in a tone like a teenager, but her rather unkempt appearance had already revealed that those years passed by long ago. "May I dance for you?"

Franklin smiled courteously at her before politely declining the invitation. Davilla strode back to the table and set down the two beers.

"Beat it Patsy," she said, her scowl warning the hopeful floozy not to test the waters any longer.

The girl frowned and started to walk away. "I swear Leah," the redhead shot back, "why do you always have to take the cute ones for yourself?"

"Because I can!" she retorted.

Patsy huffed and scooted over to the bar to search out different prey.

"I didn't mean to cause any trouble," Franklin commented.

Davilla offered up the sly grin that had led Franklin to surrender his virtue the last time they'd met.

"You didn't." She slid Franklin's beer mug over to him and lifted up her glass. "Cheers."

They tapped glasses together.

"I wish these were more cheerful times," Franklin said, a worried expression once again casting an ashen pall across his face.

They each guzzled down half of their beer. Davilla wished she had ordered a shot of whisky for each of them as well. She knew she could have used one at that moment. Her nerves were already frazzled, fearing Franklin was about ready to lay down the hammer because of her sorted past.

"Oh, why did she call you Leah?" he asked, forgetting that she had already let the name slip out the first time they saw each other at The Wild Side in Vegas.

"That's my real name," she replied, casting her eyes shamefully downward for a second. "Leah. Leah Jacobs. Nobody uses their real name in my business that's for sure."

She was well aware using a false moniker was the least of the lies she'd told over the years.

"So how is business?" Franklin smiled and coughed slightly, realizing the question hadn't come out quite the way he intended. "I mean, why are you working here?"

"You mean in a dive like this?"

"Well, yeah. You're a very beautiful woman. You could do so much..."

Davilla's eyes began to well up. She suddenly couldn't look him in the face. Her shame became deeper than it ever had been in her entire life. She covered her face and wept into her left hand.

"Hey, hey." Franklin reached over and gently grasped her other hand on the table. "I didn't mean to upset you. I'm sorry."

She sniffled a couple of times and looked at him again, tears of remorse rolling down her flushed cheeks. "I'm so sorry Franklin. I'm so sorry for what I did to you." The dam of emotions that had been building for years suddenly burst. She could not hold back the torrent of her guilt any longer. Franklin got up and sat down next to her. He put his arm around her shoulders.

"It will be fine my dear, everything will be fine now. I've forgiven you."

Davilla was stunned by his words. Was he kidding? She had ruined him. How could he forgive her? She must have misunderstood?

"Really?" She tried to wipe her eyes with her fingers. Franklin handed her a napkin from under his beer mug. It was still dry enough in parts to sop up some of her tears.

"Of course," he said. "I forgave you a long time ago."

The gleam immediately began to return to her sullen eyes. She knew he meant what he'd told her. He couldn't hide the truth that his gentle eyes clearly spelled out for her. She had never known before what it felt like to be forgiven.

"Davilla, I mean Leah." He smiled tenderly. "In my life now I try not to dwell on the past too much. I live for the future, for eternity. That's what counts for me. That's what God wants me to do. He wants me to forgive those who need forgiveness; just like He has forgiven me...Oh don't you see dear? It's never too late to forgive someone, or accept forgiveness."

Franklin softly kissed the top of her head, not in a romantic way, but more like a brother would when providing comfort to a wounded sister. Her heart melted at the virtuous gesture. No man had ever displayed such pure affection toward her. She had previously sensed his kindness that amorous night they'd shared before. She wished he would whisk her away toward a new life they could explore together. But she knew his heart had already been touched by another. She was happy for him, though still envious.

"Your fiancée is a lucky girl," she commented, dabbing her still-teary eyes. "You have to be the sweetest man I've ever met. I hope she treasures what she has in you."

Franklin now began to get teary himself.

"I treasure her as well. That's why I have got to find her. I just have to."

He shoulders slumped and he rubbed his weary eyes. He hadn't slept in nearly two days. Davilla put her arm around him for comfort.

"I promise you I will do everything I can to help you find her. I swear it."

Franklin looked up and smiled. "That's sweet, but I don't want you to get hurt. Troy is a dangerous man. There's no telling what he might do to you."

"I can handle myself," she quickly replied. "Don't you worry about me. I've dealt with rougher guys than him before, believe me."

Franklin became concerned she was trying to cover her past sins.

"You don't owe me Leah."

She didn't understand, but liked hearing her real name spoken by his lips. "What do you mean?"

He shook his head. "There's no need to pay me back for the past. God will help me find Cassie if it is His will."

"That's her name, Cassie?"

"Yes. The other girl is Gretchen, Troy's ex girlfriend. They were going to be married as well. Then something happened."

"But what can I do for you Franklin?" she asked, her eyes almost pleading. "There must be something I can do."

Franklin hated to think she was going to dance at the bar that night, but he didn't have time to convince her otherwise. "Are you working tonight?"

"Yes," she replied, "but I'm not dancing. I'm going to be bartending. That's why I'm here so early. Why?"

Franklin was thankful for that. "Well if you see Troy come in here for some reason, would you call me right away on my cell phone?"

He opened up his wallet and handed her a business card.

"Absolutely, I will."

"Great, but don't confront him. Just call me okay?"

She nodded.

"I'm going to catch up with Ramon. Will you be alright?"

"Yes, I'll be fine," she answered as he stood up and began to leave. He turned back around and kissed her on the cheek once more before returning to the motel.

She watched him leave, wishing their paths would have crossed under different circumstances the first time they'd met. She knew her life would have been so much different somehow.

Chapter XVII

T roy couldn't fool himself for long. He knew his cruelty toward Cassie and Gretchen was really just a cover-up. His malevolence was baffling, especially to the true patriarch of his soul -- the Father of all Lies. The incarnation of Evil understood the genuine nature of the heart ruling his charge, but Troy was failing to live accordingly. The young prince needed a not-so subtle reminder to stay on task. The evil one who always lurked in the bleak regresses of Troy's conscience was eager to provide the necessary prompting.

My son, my son. Have you forgotten your vow my son?

The voice had not spoken to him since the day before. As he drove the church van back toward Vegas, Troy realized he couldn't hide from the echo reverberating through his mind. It demanded an answer.

You said you would kill them my son.

Troy's shoulders slumped as he loosely gripped the steering wheel. He couldn't shake the fact that his resolve was waning. The girls should have been slain already. He had convinced himself that torturing them was too enjoyable to stop too soon, but he was really trying to deceive his own mind. The voice was calling him out on that fact.

Have you lost your nerve my son?

"No father!" Troy screamed back, his eyes beginning to mist like a young child who knows his culpability has been exposed.

Have no fear for I am with you.

The tone was soothing, immediately bringing calm to Troy's wavering confidence. The voice only requested submission, all that it had ever asked of him. He had always found peace in its pleasing manner. That occasion would be no different, he errantly surmised.

"What should I do?" Troy asked, hoping to draw upon the well of dark grace which had abundantly supplied his needs in the ignoble journey for reprisal. "Don't fail me now. We're too close."

The voice was well pleased with Troy's subjection to eternal bondage. Assistance could be offered much more easily.

Think of your courage last night my son.

Troy quickly remembered the anger he harbored the night before toward those he hated. How just the sound of Franklin's voice brought forth such fervent disdain that murder was an act that could be committed as easily as crushing an annoying insect with the palm of his hand. The crime would be so easy to commit within the proper frame of mind. Troy knew he had to recapture that state once more. He reasoned whiskey would provide the confidence he was lacking to carry out his dreadful duty.

Before reaching the city, Troy stopped at a liquor store on the main highway. He hustled inside and grabbed a bottle of tequila, which had done the trick the night before. But once he reached into his back pocket as he approached the checkout counter, Troy realized his wallet was missing. He felt around the outside of his trousers, but with no luck.

"Damn!" he exclaimed, placing the bottle down hard on the

counter, startling the elderly clerk, who peered at Troy cautiously through bottle-thick eyeglasses. "Just leave this here. I forgot my wallet. I'll be back shortly."

The slight old man appeared frightened by Troy's frustrated manner and didn't say a word. He just nodded his head in agreement and placed the bottle off to the side. Troy hopped into the van, squealed the tires and sped off toward the mine. He figured he had left his wallet there somewhere, remembering he last felt it in his back pocket as he sat down smoking a cigarette while the girls were eating. The only place he'd been since then was in the van. He pulled off the road and searched around the driver's seat and on the floorboard, but the wallet was nowhere to be found.

About a quarter of the way through his ten-mile trek back to the mine, Troy came upon the old motel and strip bar. Davilla's thievery dawned on him. He didn't know if she was working that night, but he certainly wanted to find out.

Davilla noticed Troy the minute he stepped into the bar. He quickly scanned a couple of the sleazy dancers performing for the still-sparse, late-afternoon crowd before spotting Davilla working behind the bar. He briskly walked over to her. She saw the scowl strewn across his reddening face.

"I need to talk to you now!" he demanded.

She became immediately defensive, reaching under the counter to tap the button that buzzed Tony's office in the back room. The silent alarm had been installed a few months before after one of the dancers had been accosted by an unruly patron after the joint had closed. Tony would be out shortly, a weapon concealed on his person just in case.

"How can I help you Troy?" Davilla replied, a feigned smile opposing her cautious blue eyes.

"You know," he replied, firmly grabbing her wrist over the bar.

"Hey," she protested, pulling her arm away. "You better watch yourself buddy!"

Tony opened his office door and saw the confrontation developing. He rushed over to the bar and yanked the back of Troy's collar, pulling him to the ground.

"What seems to be the problem here pal?" Tony asked forcefully in his heavy Bronx accent, pointing his right index finger at Troy, who was still sitting on the floor.

"This little tramp here owes me some money," Troy responded, quickly glancing between Davilla and Tony with simmering anger beginning to flare up from his charcoal eyes. "And she's gonna pay up."

Troy rose to his feet and balled his fists, trying to ready for any assault Davilla's boss might hurl his way. He'd wished he hadn't left his revolver in the van.

"Ya lookin' for a fight pal?" Tony said, pressing his finger into Troy's chest, "cause if ya are, I can give ya one."

Davilla reached over the bar and placed her hand on Tony's shoulder. "It's alright Tony. This is between me and him. I can handle it, okay?"

Tony looked back at Davilla, whose stern grin told him that she hit the buzzer only to place him on standby in case circumstances got out of hand. He knew Davilla was quite capable of putting rude patrons in their places, having seen her martial arts training put into practice on more than a few occasions. He had experienced her skills firsthand a couple of months back. She flipped him on his keister after he got too fresh with his roving hands while closing up the bar one night.

Although he wanted to smack the defiant smirk off

Troy's face himself, Tony reluctantly agreed to Davilla's wishes, muttering a few choice expletives under his breath as he walked over to the far end of the bar and began to clean some glasses.

"Now Troy, do you want to talk peacefully?" she asked, knowing he had no alternative in the matter and remembering Franklin's need to find the kidnapper.

He rolled his eyes and nodded yes.

"Good, pull up a seat," she said.

Troy sat down at the bar.

"Can I get you something to drink?"

"I'd like one, but I don't have any money," he said snidely.

Davilla reached under the bar and picked up a bottle of tequila. She poured some into a shot glass and slid it over to him. He stared her down as he slugged the shot and then placed the glass firmly on the bar. She poured him another.

"Look," she said with a resigned expression, "I know I owe you, but I didn't clean you out last night. What happened to the rest of it?"

Troy downed the second shot with the same brooding stare. "I still have it," he said. "I just left my wallet somewhere."

"Well then, I guess that's your problem, isn't it?"

"Oh, I know where the wallet is," he sneered. "It's just a couple hundred bucks light."

Davilla glared back at him, hate for the smug young man began to brew in her heart. But since talking to Franklin earlier, she did feel guilty about stealing the cash from Troy. Franklin had touched a remote place in her conscience and she was beginning to see the error of her ways. She wanted to return the money to Troy right then and there, but she didn't have it on her. She had deposited the cash in her bank account that morning and she normally never carried more than cab fare with her to work. Then she realized that she might be able to use the situation to her advantage. Davilla wanted Troy to stay put until she phoned Franklin.

"Look, I don't have the cash on me, but let me make a phone call real quick," she said, pouring Troy another shot. "Why don't you wait here and have another drink on the house?"

Troy glared at her beautiful eyes which baited him to accept her request. "Fine," he sighed with a suspicious grin. "Don't dawdle now."

Davilla winked at him coyly and then asked Tony if she could use the phone in his office. Troy scanned her body with his lecherous eyes as she left the room. Even in blue jeans and a red tank top, she was a stunning sight at which to gaze. He told himself he would rather let her keep the money and have her pay him back with the erotic talents she had boasted about the previous night. He was becoming more visibly excited at the thought of collecting his due. But suddenly, his mind abruptly refocused on the murderous duty for which he knew he'd been so luridly called. He was aware that Davilla D'Vine was a pleasure who would have to wait until his dirty business was finished.

Troy polished off the drink and left the bar.

A few minutes later, Davilla returned from Tony's office.

"Where did he go?!" she exclaimed, panic-stricken because Franklin had told her to try and stall Troy while he and Ramon traveled back from a small grocery store just down the highway.

"I saw him leave about five minutes ago," Tony answered.

"Oh no!" she cried. "Why didn't you stop him?"

"What the hell for?" Tony replied, somewhat perturbed at Davilla's tone. "I'm glad he's outta here. What are ya doin' with scum like that anyway, huh?"

Davilla began to rub her eyebrows. She didn't want to fail Franklin. It would crush her if he was hurt again because she had let Troy slip away. She knew she had to act fast.

"Tony, I need to borrow your car."

The manager finished dumping a bucket of ice into one of the bins behind the bar and tossed a confused look at the desperate blond.

"Hey what are ya up to huh?" he said, holding his palms upward and shaking his balding head from side to side.

"Please Tony!" she pleaded, "I don't have time to explain now, but a friend of mine may be in deep trouble!"

"Ya don't even have a driver's license!"

"Come on! I know how to drive! You've seen me! We're wasting time!"

Tony sighed and reached into his pocket. He pulled off the car keys from the rest of the keys on his long chain and handed them to Davilla.

"Ya be very careful," he warned, handing the keys to flustered girl. "I hope ya know what ya doin'. I don't trust that guy. If he hurts my favorite girl, why I'll..."

Tony balled up his fist and gritted his teeth. Davilla grinned and took the keys from him. She had learned to appreciate the way he trusted her loyalty to him over the past months, both on the dance floor and behind the bar. Davilla found the brash Italian's sweet spot for her most charming. She kissed her boss on the cheek and thanked him before dashing from the club.

As she was running to Tony's car, Davilla saw Patsy standing next to the pay phone smoking a cigarette.

"Hey, did you see a guy leave here in a white van?" she called out while unlocking the door to Tony's nearly new, jet black Cadillac Seville.

"Tony lending you his ride?"

"Never mind that, did you see him?"

"Yeah, I saw him. What's it to you?"

Patsy and Davilla had been rivals for Tony's generosity since both came seeking employment on the same day. Their ill will toward one another was enhanced once Davilla brushed off the scrawny girl's sexual advances toward her after they'd danced together on stage during their first week at the club. Davilla's attraction for girls had subsided greatly since Derek's untimely death. She had always enjoyed her female lovers very much, but a sadistic incident between one of her girlfriends and her former brutal beau helped drive his demise. Davilla had severe difficulty loving anyone since his death. Franklin was the only man who had stirred any emotion in her frigid heart in a very long time. She longed desperately to help him.

"Come on Patsy, which way did he go?"

The skinny stripper stamped her smoke out on the ground and pointed west.

"He went that way, toward the hills."

"Thank you!" Davilla exclaimed, hurling a curt smile and a sneer at the girl, who shot back a middle-fingered salute.

Davilla shook her head in disgust and jumped into Tony's car. She squealed the tires as she sped off onto the highway, hoping to gain ground quickly on Troy. She loved the feel of Tony's well-kept vehicle. It handled brilliantly on the wide open highway, which was good because Davilla was speeding ahead at close to ninety miles per hour. Traffic was extremely light as she motored along toward the hills, which were fast awaiting the approaching sunset. She knew there were only a few stop-offs along the way in the wide-open desert terrain, so she figured to catch up to Troy's white van quickly.

About fifteen miles down the road, Davilla approached the dirt road leading into the old silver mine. She figured it wouldn't hurt to check it out. As she turned onto the narrow road, she noticed some fresh tire tracks. She cautiously drove toward the mine, fearing Troy might see her as she approached the entrance to the facility. It had been a few years since she been there, a place where her and Derek would go to practice shooting off pistols. They both had developed a love for guns during their scheming together. Both knew that passion would produce tragic consequences one day.

Davilla pulled the car behind the abandoned security shack at the front of the main entrance, about a hundred yards from the mine. She parked the car at an angle behind the shack and a crumbling wood fence, where it could only be seen by someone entering the area, not leaving. She certainly didn't want Troy to catch her if he was inside.

It wasn't long after Davilla left the car and walked around the sharp curve in the dirt road when she spotted the white van about fifty yards away. She quickly hid behind a large cactus cluster and observed the scene before her. She noticed Troy walk around the van and head toward the mine. He knelt down beside a hole in the ground and picked something up. He looked over the object and slapped it on his palm. Davilla could tell from the smile on Troy's face that he was pleased to find the object, which she still couldn't make out. He jumped back into the van and began to drive off. Davilla crouched as low as she could get behind the cactus, hoping he wouldn't see her. She was relieved when he raced past her and headed back out toward the highway.

She suddenly remembered she had not spoken to Franklin since leaving the bar in Tony's car. She figured he and Ramon had to be there by then. She knew she had to warn them in case Troy might be heading back their way. She ran back to the car and phoned Franklin's cell.

"Hello, it's me," she said when he answered the phone.

"Leah?" Franklin asked. "Where are you? Are you alright?"

A smile immediately covered her flushed face. She loved the fact he called her by her real name. Just hearing it spoken in his caring manner made her feel like she was special to him. Like he respected her enough to speak to her properly, even after the way she had treated him in the past. She thought it may have been the first time in her life that she had felt truly forgiven by someone. Her long-troubled heart was beginning to feel renewed, quickened suddenly by just hearing the tender call of her name by someone who cared enough about her well-being to address her with concern.

"I'm fine Franklin. I've found Troy. He was at the old mine outside of town. He came looking for something and seemed to find it." Davilla spoke so fast Franklin was having trouble getting a word in. "I bet it was the wallet he said he lost..."

"Leah, Leah, calm down honey," Franklin interrupted. "Is he still there? He doesn't know you've followed him does he?"

"No. He left. I think he might be heading back toward the bar. Where are you Franklin?"

"Ramon and I just got back to the motel. Listen, did you see anybody with him?"

"You mean your girlfriend?" she asked, forgetting Franklin was engaged.

"Yes, and another girl," he replied.

"No. He appeared to be alone...But maybe..." she paused, pondering the possibility the girls maybe hidden somewhere on the premises.

"What?" Franklin asked. "What are you thinking?"

"This would be a good place to stash somebody Franklin. Oh I'm sorry, I didn't mean to put it that way."

Franklin realized she might be right. His thoughts quickly changed from tracking down Troy to finding the girls, dead or alive.

"Leah, don't do anything. Tell me how to get to you."

She figured Franklin might have a hard time finding her on his own, so she told him to meet her by the highway.

"Do you know where the big "Welcome to Las Vegas' sign is west of town?"

"Yes, I saw it driving here with Ramon."

"Meet me there. I'm driving Tony's black Cadillac. It should take you about ten minutes to get here from there."

"Okay, I'm on my way right now," he replied. "Watch carefully in case Troy comes back before I get there. I don't want you to get hurt. He's very dangerous Leah."

"I know. I'll be careful. I promise."

Franklin hung up the phone and filled in the details for Ramon, who was anxiously standing next to him. Franklin told Ramon to wait for his call at the motel in case Troy returned there and the mine turned out to be a dead end in their search for the girls. Ramon reluctantly agreed after recognizing Franklin's plan made sense. They had to cover all the bases they could. Such prudence really might mean the difference between life and death for those they both loved.

⋰⋯⋱

While Franklin headed out to meet Davilla, Troy made his way back to the liquor store. He knew he still needed the boost of liquid courage a bottle of whiskey would provide for his looming task.

But it was fortunate that Troy's struggling nerve provided Franklin the time he needed to explore the first real hope he'd had in days.

The knots began to form in Franklin's stomach as he made the ten-minute jaunt to Davilla's location. What if Cassie was there at the mine? And Gretchen too? What if they were both dead? Franklin knew he had to quickly usher such dreadful thoughts from his mind and trust in God's mercy toward the girls. He remembered Ramon's truth earlier in the day, that God would only allow Satan and his followers just so much leeway during their terrible deeds. It saddened Franklin that he now had to consider Troy Battles one of the many disciples of darkness. But Troy's dastardly actions only served to prove where his loyalty lay. Yet even Franklin couldn't have known how far his former student had so pitifully tumbled into the unredeemed depths of depravity.

Davilla waved feverishly at Franklin as he pulled off the highway. He drove around the small hill that lofted the weathered billboard, which had easily summoned many foolish travelers toward their revelry in false hope. Just a couple of years back, Franklin recalled how he too had been lured into despair by a similar sign on the opposite side of town. He thought it ironic that the pretty lady who had so devastated his trust in women back then was the same one who was trying to help him find the woman who had so beautifully restored his faith in true love. Franklin vowed he would be forever grateful to the troubled stripper if his beloved Cassie could be found alive and well. He begged God such would be the case.

"I was just getting ready to call you again," Davilla said, breathing heavily with excitement. "I was hoping you'd get here quickly. I'm afraid he might come back."

Franklin softly rubbed her bare shoulder to settle her down. She loved his warming touch, especially since in her haste to follow

Troy, she had forgotten to grab her coat from the bar. It was becoming bitterly cold as the sun began to fade behind the western hills.

"You must be freezing out here," he said, removing his brown flannel hunting jacket and wrapping it around her shoulders. The maroon USC sweatshirt Cassie had given him for his last birthday would have to suffice for the moment.

"I am," Davilla said, her teeth chattering. "I was in such a hurry to catch up to Troy that I left my coat behind. I wasn't about to go back and get it."

Franklin smiled at her, appreciating her zeal in the pursuit of Troy Battles. "How long has he been gone?"

"Probably about twenty minutes or so I guess...He sped out of here pretty quickly once he found what he was looking for."

The mine wasn't visible from where they were standing so they walked up the short hill that hosted the sign.

"You see that building over there?" Davilla said, pointing about a quarter-mile toward the northwest.

"Uh huh," he answered, scanning his eyes around the dilapidated complex.

"Well, a few yards to the left of that is a hole that leads down into the mine. I've only been down there once. It's pretty creepy... Anyway, I didn't see Troy go inside the hole. He just picked up something off the ground. He told me earlier at the bar that he'd lost his wallet, so maybe that's what it was. He seemed pleased to find it..."

"He didn't go into the hole, you say?" Franklin interrupted, scratching the two-day-old whiskers irritating his dried out skin.

"I didn't see him go in, but he was already here when I got here."

"Hmm, I wonder," he said, looking over at Davilla inquisitively.

"I was thinking the same thing. It would be the perfect place to hide someone. Oh Franklin, do you think they're in there?"

"I'm gonna find out," he replied. "Is that the road leading into the mine?"

Franklin pointed to the entrance off the highway, just west of where they were standing.

"Yes," she answered, before starting to walk to Tony's car. "I'll drive you over there."

Franklin grabbed her arm. "No Leah. I need you to wait here and keep an eye out for Troy, in case he comes back."

She sighed with reluctance, but she knew he was correct in his thinking.

"I'm afraid Franklin. Why don't you call the police?"

He smiled and hugged her. "I can't. Don't have anything to tell them yet...I'll be careful...If you see him, call me and then call the cops."

She reached up and kissed him on the forehead. "For good luck."

He kissed her cheek and jumped in Cassie's car and drove off.

From the hill, Davilla watched Franklin drive into the mine complex as dusk was fast approaching. He hid the car as best he could behind the rundown building next to the mineshaft. But Davilla saw that the vehicle could still be noticed from the dirt road if Troy were to look close enough. She got more worried by the moment. Franklin found the hole and lifted the cover. Before entering the hole, he looked up toward the hill and waved to Davilla. She waved back, and then blew him a kiss she knew he couldn't see.

As the daylight grew dimmer, she hoped it wasn't the last time they would ever see one another.

With flashlight in hand, Franklin called out both Cassie and Gretchen's names through the cold, grim tunnel. His anger and worry both grew evenly as he pondered his surroundings. If it was where Troy was hiding the two women, the place was despicable and he would see to it that Battles paid dearly for his crime. But Franklin's concern for the girls became even tenser the further into the mine he traveled. He continued to cry out their names. "Cassie, Gretchen," he repeatedly called in desperation, hoping for a reply. But unknown to Franklin, the girls could not respond.

Franklin approached the fork in the mineshaft. He suddenly heard a soft tapping coming from the corridor to his left. He shined the flashlight into the mineshaft. The tapping abruptly changed from a soft tap to a loud metallic clang.

The girls had heard his calling. Though their mouths were still muffled from being taped shut, they had seen the glow from Franklin's flashlight and knew he was close by. They were determined to summon him by rapidly banging the metal handcuffs against the cell bars. They each pounded the steel so hard that blood began to drip from the back of their hands where the cuffs firmly clasped their wrists.

Franklin ran so fast down the tunnel that he slipped and fell on the slick rock floor, bruising his right knee. Yet he felt no pain as he limped into the chamber holding Troy's prisoners. Just seeing them alive brought joyful relief to his worried heart.

"Oh, thank God!" he exclaimed, rejoicing tears starting to fill his eyes.

Then, he saw the awful condition in which they had been left to suffer. The evidence of Troy's abuse brought repugnance to Franklin's normally placid demeanor. Battles would most certainly pay for his cruelty, Franklin vowed.

Gretchen saw Franklin first and immediately began to roll her way over to him. The duct tape still binding her legs had loosened a great deal, but it was still preventing her from standing up and walking. The rocky ground scraped her skin greatly as she rolled the ten feet to the door of the cell, but she endured the pain. Cassie was unable to move because of her injuries, but just seeing Franklin had already softened her suffering. She knew her ordeal would be over shortly. His loving smile told her so.

Once Gretchen reached Franklin, he placed his hands through the bars and pulled up a corner of the tape across her mouth.

"I'm sorry, but this will hurt," he said with sympathy in his eyes.

Gretchen nodded her head and braced for the pain. Franklin quickly yanked the tape from across the blond girl's mouth. She winced and took a couple of quick breaths. Franklin began to pull the rest of the tape down off her hair.

"Just leave it!" Gretchen cried, her eyes bugging out from the pain.

Franklin stopped pulling. "I'm sorry," he said.

"That's okay, at least I can breath better, thank you."

"Gretchen, are you injured? What's wrong with Cassie? Oh you poor girls," Franklin was nearly frantic as he lightly rubbed Gretchen's cheek, his tears reflecting the conflicting emotions of elation and turmoil at the sight of the beleaguered women. "What has he done to you?"

"Oh Franklin, we will both be okay now that you're here," Gretchen responded, sobbing with relief herself. "Cassie's pretty hurt. She has a head injury and a broken ankle I think. She can't move."

Franklin shined the flashlight on his beaten fiancé. He wished he could rush over to her and hold her. Cassie's normally bold onyx eyes were glassy and a miserable pained glare shot across the frigid cell, but he could tell she was content at that point with just having been found. She knew God had brought Franklin to her rescue and medical care would soon be forthcoming.

Franklin saw Cassie begin to shiver as the chilly air again pierced her exposed chest. He removed his sweatshirt.

"See if you can cover her with this, she's freezing," he told Gretchen. "Here let me pull that tape off your legs."

Franklin reached into his pants and took out the pocket knife he always carried with him. He cut off the tape from Gretchen's blue jeans.

"Ah, that's a relief," she sighed. "It feels good to stretch my legs again."

She backed against the bars and took the sweatshirt from Franklin with her cuffed hands. Gretchen walked over to Cassie and tried to slip the garment over her shoulders, but it fell off. After two more futile backwards attempts, Gretchen turned and fronted the now blue-faced girl.

"Try slipping the neckline over her head and then pulling it down," Franklin suggested.

"Good idea," Gretchen answered, stretching the neck open as wide as she could with cuffed hands. "Cassie honey, lean your head forward and try slipping into the hole."

Cassie managed to do as Gretchen asked, despite trembling from the hypothermia now penetrating her entire body. Gretchen backed up against Cassie and pulled the sweatshirt down enough to cover her friend's bareness. The sigh emanating from Cassie's bloodied nose told Gretchen she was already beginning to warm up.

"We need to get this tape off her mouth Franklin, let me use your knife."

Franklin had been using the screwdriver on the pocketknife to try and tinker with the door's lock. But it wasn't working. "Here," he said, handing the open blade to Gretchen. "Be careful now, you'll be doing it backward."

"I know. I will. She'll be just so much better off if she can breathe through her mouth."

Gretchen knew the easiest way would be to cut the tape through Cassie's hair.

"Lean your head to one side now honey," Gretchen asked, dropping the knife temporarily on the ground between them and feeling for a weak area between Cassie's hair and the tape. After a couple seconds, she found the spot just behind Cassie's left ear. Gretchen delicately slipped the blade in place and slowly sliced through the hair and tape. Franklin's knife was sharp and cut through easily, but nicked Cassie's ear on the last slice. Gretchen dropped the knife again.

"Oh I'm very sorry honey," she said, looking back and seeing blood dripping from Cassie's earlobe.

"Did you cut her?" Franklin asked.

"Not too badly I think."

"Okay, do you think you can pull the tape off now?"

"Yes, it's really loose now."

Gretchen held the broken end of the tape while standing with her back in front of Cassie's head.

"This is probably really gonna hurt honey but you'll feel much better when I'm done."

Gretchen didn't give Cassie the opportunity to tense up and quickly ripped the tape away from the stricken girl's mouth. Franklin winced as Cassie let out a muffled yelp. The filthy sock was still stuffed in her mouth. Gretchen reached back and pulled the sock from Cassie's mouth with her cuffed hands.

Cassie began to breathe heavily, but more fully as the cold air rushed into her lungs. Her jaws were sore from being held open for so long with the sock.

"Oh gosh that's so much better," Cassie said in labored relief, still trying to get her bearings straight from the painful ordeal.

Gretchen knelt down in front of Cassie and wept onto her neck and shoulders.

"I wish I didn't have to hurt you so bad," she cried. "I didn't mean to."

Cassie leaned her head against Gretchen, wishing she could hug the girl in comfort, but unable to because of her own cuffed hands. "I know, I know you didn't," she whispered, barely able to talk because of her parched throat. She looked over at Franklin and saw the tears streaming down his face. She winked and blew a kiss at him to show she was going to be alright. He blew a kiss back.

"I've got to get you girls out of here," he said, rattling the cell door back and forth.

Gretchen stood up and dried her eyes. "How Franklin? Troy has the only key."

Franklin's eyes suddenly lit up. "That's right, Troy!" In the excitement of finding the girls, Franklin had almost forgotten that the madman could return any moment. He took out his cell phone and flipped it open. He quickly saw that he had no service so deep underground. "Gretchen, Cassie, I need to call for help outside. The phone won't work in here. I'll be right back. Hang in there."

Cassie smiled and nodded, still not able to speak audibly.

Gretchen walked over to pick up one of the water bottles Troy had left them earlier. "Please hurry Franklin." She went to Cassie and carefully held the water bottle behind her back for Franklin's woman to drink from.

Franklin wiped a couple of tears from his eyes. He hated to see either girl in such a frightful state. "I will, I promise." He turned and started to walk away before stopping. "I love you both so much," he said, before turning and heading back out the tunnel.

"We know Franklin," Gretchen replied. "We know you do."

⚶⟡⟞

From the top of the hill by the Vegas sign, Davilla saw Franklin exit the mine and make a call on his phone. But her cell phone didn't ring right away. She saw Franklin open the trunk of his car and pull out a crow bar while he was talking. Still no call to her though.

After about five minutes, he waved to Davilla and her phone finally rang.

"Franklin, what's going on? Did you find them?"

"Yes I did," he answered, quite hurriedly.

"Are they, well, alive?"

"Yeah, they're alive, but they are locked up inside the mine... Look Leah, I need you to something for me, okay?"

She sensed the nearly frantic urgency in Franklin's voice. "What Franklin? Anything, you know that."

"I've already called Ramon and the police. They're sending an ambulance. They should be here in a little while. I told Ramon how to get here and he is going to take a taxi, but it might take some time before he gets here."

"Why you have the crow bar?" she asked, figuring he might use it for protection.

"Wow, you see very well from up there. I'm going to try and use it to free the girls...Anyway, listen, I gave Ramon your cell number and told him where you were. He is going to meet you there. Keep an eye out for him, alright…Listen, I have to get moving. Thanks for your help."

"But Franklin, I want to…"

She saw him hang up and rush back down into the mine. She found herself getting a little perturbed at his suddenness. An almost selfish jealousy began to creep into her repentive attitude, like a disappointed sweetheart who had been passed over for a more desirable preference. Davilla caught herself and quickly squelched such childishness. Franklin needed her, and she loved helping him in any way she could.

About five minutes later, Davilla glimpsed a sight that made her shudder. It was a vehicle turning into the mine. Troy Battles was returning in the white church van. Her heart dropped in anguish.

She hurriedly tried to call Franklin on his cell phone to warn him, but he couldn't pick up inside the mine. Troy stopped for a moment near the security shack where Davilla had hidden Tony's car earlier. He got out of the van and walked around the back of the shack. She noticed him drink from what appeared to be a whiskey bottle. After a couple of slugs, he got into the van and drove inside the compound.

Davilla freaked out! She tried calling Ramon's cell, but the batteries on her own phone were nearly dead and she could no longer dial out. She reached into Tony's glove box, hoping he might have a car charger that would fit her phone. Naturally, he did not. But she did find another item that could prove helpful to the dire cause.

※❖※

"Help will be here shortly," Franklin said to the girls as he tried to pry open the cell door with the crow bar. "Try to stay calm okay."

Cassie laid her wobbling head on Gretchen's shoulder while they both watched him struggle to free them from captivity. The old steel catch on the door was proving difficult to budge, but Franklin kept working the crow bar into it, hoping to somehow pop it open.

"We've been praying together since you went outside Franklin," Gretchen remarked. "Thanking God for allowing you to find us."

"Keep on doing that, please," he responded, forcing the crow bar forward with all his might. "Pray that He will give me the strength to get you out of here before Troy gets back."

Suddenly, Franklin heard the cock of a gun and found a bright light shining into his eyes.

"Too late Edwards!" Troy snarled, coolly pointing the revolver at Franklin's head.

Gretchen screamed as Franklin stepped back from the cell door and dropped the crow bar on the ground. Troy swung the gun around toward the girls.

"Shut your damn mouth Gretchen!" he screamed, "or I'll shoot you both right now! I swear to hell I will!"

Franklin quickly tried to intervene and calm the rapidly intensifying rage engulfing his former student. He was shocked by Troy's wrath. He had never before witnessed firsthand the sheer madness the girls had endured for the past two days.

"Troy, just calm down man," he said, holding his palms out in a defensive posture.

Troy swung the gun back around and aimed it at Franklin's head again.

"Don't tell me what to do!" he shouted. "I'll do the talking now!"

"Alright, alright, whatever you say," Franklin replied, quickly glancing over at the girls who were whimpering in fear.

"Sit down and shut up!" Troy commanded, the hand holding the gun beginning to shake ever so slightly.

Troy walked over to the cage and shook the door to make sure it was still locked. It was. He reached into his pocket with his free hand and pulled out a cigarette. He placed the smoke in his mouth and lit it, never taking his eyes off Franklin. He signed out a couple of puffs.

"Now Edwards, I don't know how you found us, but we're all very glad you could make it to our little party." Troy giggled snidely a few times before taking another drag off his cigarette.

While Franklin sat there dumbfounded by the pure wickedness that had overcome the apparently drunken young man, Cassie suddenly found an unexpected dose of courage and the voice to expel it.

"He killed your wife Franklin!" she screamed.

Troy wheeled around and fired off a shot toward the girls. A bullet ripped through the left side of Cassie's abdomen, sending her slumping on to Gretchen.

"Cassie!" Franklin screamed, diving toward the cell door.

"Get back!" Troy yelled, as he fired a second shot, that one whizzing by Franklin's head.

Franklin jumped back, clutching his head with both hands and looking mournfully at Gretchen, who was holding his fallen love.

"She's still alive Franklin," Gretchen cried, placing her bare hand against Cassie's wound to try and stop the bleeding. "Oh stay with me Cassie. I have you honey. I'm here baby. Stay calm. Stay calm."

Franklin looked up at Troy, shaking his head as he stared at the relatively composed gunman. Troy felt nothing after firing the gun. No remorse. No regret. Certainly no shame. Nothing, absolutely nothing. He reached into his pocket and calmly took out another cigarette. He lit it as Franklin watched him, saying not a word because of the shock that had beset him following Troy's actions.

Smoking the cigarette seemed to break Troy out of his eerie mental silence. He was surprised Cassie had figured out he was responsible for the deaths of Sara and the girls, although Troy knew there was no way Franklin's doomed fiancée could have comprehended all the pertinent details of the tragedy.

"She should have just minded her own business Edwards," Troy said, shaking his head in mock regret. "All of us would have been better off."

Franklin boldly picked up his flashlight and shined it on Troy.

"What do you think you're doing?" he demanded, cocking the trigger once more.

"If you're going to shoot me, then I want to look you straight in your cold-blooded eyes," Franklin answered defiantly. "But before you do, let me ask you a question."

"What?" Troy said curtly.

Franklin took a deep breath and sighed out loud. "Why? Simply why? My family never did anything to you."

"How do you know I did it?" Troy answered. "Maybe your girlfriend's lying."

"She isn't. I saw the photos Troy. I don't know what happened, but I bet you do, don't you?"

Troy began to laugh maniacally. "Oh Edwards, you think you're so smart don't you?" He continued laughing. Gretchen looked over at Troy, tears streaming down her face. She didn't recognize at all the man she had once loved so deeply.

"Oh Franklin, be careful. He's crazy."

Troy turned and fired another shot, which sailed past Gretchen's head. She covered up quickly.

"Shut up!" he screamed. "Damn you! Shut the hell up."

Troy whipped the gun back around at Franklin.

"You want to know why Edwards?" he shouted. "Do you!?"

Franklin pursed his lips in defiance and nodded his head yes.

Troy took another long drag from his cigarette before responding.

"I wasn't trying to kill anybody," he said, with finally a slightly regretful grin seeping across his face. Franklin continued to shine the light on Troy, who for some reason, didn't seem to mind. "I was just hoping to make you wreck your precious race car. You were never going to use that car to embarrass me again Edwards. Do you hear!?"

An insane scowl erupted from Troy's face, like he was reliving the last race between him and Franklin in his mind all over again.

"But Troy, it was only a race."

"Shut up! Shut up!" The rage began to inflame the disturbed young man. "I never lose at anything! Do you hear!?"

Franklin didn't respond. He was shocked by Troy's lunacy.

After spitting out the cigarette dangling from his lips, Troy reached down and picked up the tequila bottle he had brought with him. He slugged a few shots worth of liquor and flung the bottle against the tunnel wall. The shattering of the glass seemed to shake Troy mentally back into the present.

"You see Edwards, their deaths are really kind of your fault," he snickered deviously. "I fixed those brakes so that the fluid would leak out slowly. It should have lasted until the next weekend when we raced...I didn't know you would let your wife drive your race car. What were you thinking man?"

Franklin saw that Troy had obviously deflected responsibility for the deadly wreck from his twisted mind. But he also saw an opening to try and talk some sense into the deluded man.

"So it was just an accident Troy," Franklin claimed with a forgiving smile on his face, as if trying to convince Battles that the current situation could be rectified. "Why make matters worse?"

"Because there ain't no other way!" Troy retorted.

"Sure there is," Franklin pleaded. "Cut you losses now. Repent. Turn yourself in. Ask for God's forgiveness. If you confess what happened, God will forgive you. He always will Troy."

Battles started to howl with laughter. "You just don't get it Edwards do you?"

"What Troy? What don't I get?"

He continued to laugh like a lunatic hearing a joke only he could understand. Troy then abruptly stopped laughing.

"I hate you!" he exclaimed, aiming the gun at Franklin's head again. "I hate all of you. My father, my mother, everybody!...You talk to me about God." Troy spit on the ground with disdain. "Talk about repentance. Repentance is for Christians Edwards. You know that. I'm no Christian. I never have been."

Troy walked over to where Franklin was sitting and placed the gun to his forehead.

"I know now that my real father is Satan. That's right Edwards. Satan!"

Troy pressed the gun further into Franklin's forehead, almost like he was trying to crush the front of his former teacher's skull with the tip of the barrel.

"Get ready to kiss your father Edwards."

Franklin closed his eyes. He knew this was the end. In a split second, he would meet God face to face. He was ready. There was nothing he could do. Troy Battles held his fate for the moment.

A shot rang out!

But Franklin felt no pain. He didn't know death could be so painless. He heard the girls screaming. He opened his eyes and looked at them. He didn't think one could still see the world after he had passed. He glanced back at his killer. But Troy wasn't in front of him any longer.

Franklin looked down and saw Troy lying on his stomach. Blood was gushing from the back of the boy's head. Franklin touched the wound and felt a gaping hole in Troy's skull.

He looked over at the girls, who also had puzzled expressions on their faces.

"Franklin, look out!" Gretchen screamed.

When he looked toward the entrance of the mine chamber, Franklin saw Davilla step out from the shadows. She smiled fondly at him and then dropped Tony's gun on the ground by her feet.

Chapter XVIII

S cripture is assuredly clear on the most precious of promises: God's plan of salvation will not be thwarted. He will certainly use any means He sovereignly chooses to gather his elect. These are the children the Father has loved with grace and mercy since before time itself was created by the command of his holy voice. Children, whose destinies were set in motion by his eternal hand long before their entrance into this fallen world. Through the shed blood of the Son and the quickening power of the Spirit, they have been redeemed, and adopted forever into a family secured by the precious love of the Divine.

Although the darkness hates the light, the future of God's chosen children will always shine bright. As Saint Paul so inspirationally wrote to his Roman brothers and sisters, "I am convinced that neither death nor life, neither angels nor demons, neither the present nor the future, neither height nor depth, nor anything else in all creation, will be able to separate us from the love of God that is in Christ Jesus our Lord."

❧❖❧

Franklin kissed Cassie tenderly on the cheek before the

paramedics gently rolled her battered body on board the ambulance. Cassie reached up and lightly caressed Franklin's scruffy chin one time. That motion took all the strength she could muster. But the warming smile on her bruised face matched the hopeful gleam in her blackened eyes, telling her beloved that from then on all would be well with them. He was just relieved she was going to pull through her horrible ordeal.

Gretchen, although still in shock over Troy's final comeuppance, was physically in much better shape than her sister in the faith. But the tears flowing freely from the blond girl's eyes as Ramon held her hand on the stretcher, told the story of the inner grief that easily surpassed her bodily pain. The anguish over watching love perish would sap her vitality for a long time to come.

After the ambulances carrying each wounded girl sped away toward Las Vegas, Franklin walked over to where the police were questioning Davilla. A heavy-set officer placed her in handcuffs and began to read the pretty dancer her rights.

"Miss Jacobs," the cop calmly stated, "you are under arrest for the murder of…"

"Whoa, wait a minute!" Franklin boldly interrupted, looking surprised by the proceedings. "She saved my life. He was going to kill me…"

"Sir please," the cop responded.

"But officer, you don't understand. She didn't…"

Davilla smiled at Franklin with resignation, knowing full well the reasons behind the circumstances unfolding in front of them.

"Mr. Edwards, calm down, please." The cop's agitation increased.

Franklin shook his head, confusion marking his face.

"Miss Jacobs, you are under arrest for the murder of Derek

Mulholland. You have the right to remain silent. You have the right to have an attorney present while being questioned. You have the right..."

Davilla dropped her eyes toward the ground as the officer continued. She didn't want to look at Franklin. She didn't want him to witness the guilt her eyes could no longer conceal. He would then be able to gaze into her soul and see the real depths of her despair. For the first time since Derek's killing, a consuming sense of shame had overcome her. Davilla could feel Franklin's sympathetic eyes upon her as the cops placed her in the squad car. She made sure not to look back at the only man she'd ever known whose compassion was true. She loved him for that.

But Davilla always knew the day would come when the authorities would piece together enough evidence to pin Derek's murder on her. For more than a year, she had managed to shrewdly throw investigators off track with evasive answers to their interrogation. They knew she had motive for killing her devious cohort, but could not produce a murder weapon or enough incriminating facts to charge the stripper with the crime. Apparently they finally had secured sufficient evidence.

Franklin asked the officers where they were taking the troubled girl whom God had used to save his life and the lives of those he loved. The arresting officer gave him a card with information about the jail where Davilla would be held. Franklin asked the cop to tell the girl he would contact her later. Franklin felt the need to help her any way he could. His gratitude to her would be endless.

Just before the police car drove her away, their eyes met for the last time. Davilla mouthed "I love you" to Franklin. He returned a pleasing smile and noticed a single tear gently roll down the woman's remorseful face. Both sensed the deepness of the moment.

Paths had crossed for an eternal purpose, of which only God could fully comprehend.

⚜

The next two weeks proved understandably eventful.

Gretchen healed first and headed back to South Florida to help Richard Battles take care of Troy's funeral arrangements. Richard blamed himself for never completely comprehending his only son's derangement. Troy's rancid behavior toward Gretchen devastated his father more that anything else. Richard deeply mourned the loss of his son, but lamented Gretchen's heartache even more. The wealthy entrepreneur knew there wasn't any amount of money that could make amends for his son's actions toward the young woman he thought of as his own daughter. Riches would secure no comfort in the debacle. Only God's grace could provide the solace required to move forward. Richard and Gretchen were forced to lean on each other's faith to get through the first few weeks of the tragedy. Eric Bjorn could only stand by and offer minimal support to his daughter and best friend. Troy had been correct in his assessment of Erik's terminal weakness. It was a personality fault Gretchen's real father could never overcome and would shortly prove terribly detrimental.

Cassie was held in a Las Vegas hospital for twelve days before Ramon and Franklin were able to take her home to convalesce. Her injuries had been severe, but not life-threatening. A small skull fracture, a broken ankle and a gunshot wound which called for the removal of a shell fragment that nicked her bowel before lodging in her ribcage, provided ample evidence of Troy Battles' ruthlessness. But Cassie's spirit never waned during her hospital stay. She drew strength from her renewed faith in God's providence and Franklin's heroic devotion to their love. During her violent upheaval in Troy's brutal clutches, Cassie sensed her man would somehow come to her rescue. She knew God wouldn't let Franklin fail to save her even when Troy had the gun pressed to her fiancé's forehead.

Franklin also explained to his betrothed Davilla's role in the girls' rescue. Cassie remembered seeing the blond woman wearing Franklin's flannel jacket after dropping the gun in the mine. Franklin kidded his fiancé that only a woman would notice such a detail in the middle of chaos. After being released from the hospital, Cassie wanted to thank the beautiful dancer in person for her courageous act, but Davilla refused to see them at the jail. She gave Franklin no reason for her refusal.

The six-hour drive back to Los Angeles allowed Franklin, Cassie and Ramon time to reflect on the unsettling events of the past few months, as well as lay plans for their future.

"You know," Franklin said as he drove Cassie's car down the highway home, "it's truly amazing how the desert can look so desolate, and yet so beautiful at the same time."

"Life is much the same my son," Ramon remarked from the back seat. "Every hour God gives us on earth is precious and not to be wasted."

Franklin glanced over at Cassie and smiled fondly. She looked extremely radiant that cool February morning. It was Valentines Day and she wore an appropriate bright red turtleneck sweater with a gold heart-shaped pendant pinned just below the collar. The sweater was offset by white slacks that hung loosely to allow her abdominal staples room to breath. But it was the Mexican girl's glistening coal-colored eyes which especially drew Franklin's notice that day, just as they had the first time he saw them more than a year before. The bruises on her delicate face were almost fully healed, makeup covering nicely any remaining discolor. Franklin swallowed hard and choked back a few joyous tears that were beginning to swell. Cassie noticed as he quickly refocused his eyes on the highway ahead.

"What's on you mind sweetheart?" she asked, lightly rubbing her hand on his shoulder.

Franklin leaned his head against her hand. She glided her fingers along his clean-shaven face.

"Oh, I'm just taking in what your father said." Cassie kissed Franklin's cheek. "Ramon, you're right. There is no time to waste. I think the last few weeks proved that."

"They most certainly did son," Ramon replied, before gazing out the window at the large, lonely cactus which seemed to sprout up randomly across the vast sandy terrain.

Franklin grinned at Cassie. "I love it when your father calls me son...and when you call me sweetheart." She slid over toward him as far as her bucket seat would allow and then leaned her head against his shoulder. He put his arm around her. "I am so happy we are all together again."

"And we always will be," she whispered aloud.

"That's what I was thinking about honey. I want to start our new life together as soon as possible. I almost lost you." Franklin sniffled, causing Cassie to sit up straight. "Honey, I don't mean to rush you. I know you have been through a lot. You still need time to heal, but..." Franklin began to cry.

"Oh baby, what? Don't cry. I'm here now and I'm going nowhere else." Cassie smiled sweetly and rubbed his back. Franklin had been solid as a rock since finding the girls in the mine, but the trauma of the past two weeks had finally caught up to him.

"Do you want me to drive son?" Ramon asked, leaning forward

and touching Franklin's shoulder.

"No, I'm fine, really," he replied, placing his right hand on Cassie's thigh and steering with his left. She leaned her head back on his shoulder. "Honey, let's get married soon. I mean as soon as you're well enough to. I love you so much. I just...I just have to know that you're my wife. I just have to."

"Oh Franklin, I will be. I will be your wife whenever you want me to. Today, tomorrow, whenever." She kissed his neck and then his cheek once more. "I adore you. I can't wait to be Mrs. Franklin Edwards. The sooner the better." She kissed his neck and cheek again, and then playfully nuzzled his ear with her teeth.

Ramon cleared his throat loudly.

"Oh papa, I'm sorry," Cassie placed her hand over her mouth and giggled. "I almost forgot you were back there."

Franklin noticed his future father-in-law's broad grin in the rearview mirror as Cassie sat up ladylike in her seat.

"Maybe we should not have left Las Vegas so soon, no?" Ramon suggested.

Franklin let out a boisterous laugh. "Yeah, we could have gotten married real quick there, I guess. Maybe even a drive-through ceremony."

Cassie slapped Franklin on the thigh and hurled a fake pout toward her fiancé.

"Yes, and a drive-through honeymoon too," Ramon giggled as he reached over and tickled his daughter behind her ear like he used to do when she was a little girl.

"Papa!" she protested, as she brushed away his hand with her cheek.

Ramon patted her gently on the head and sat back in his seat chuckling. Franklin delighted in the playfulness. It was the first time in weeks they'd been able to laugh together like that.

"Seriously though," Franklin said, glancing quickly into the mirror at Ramon and then over at Cassie. "I think we should be wed soon."

"I totally agree sweetheart. I don't need a big wedding. Just friends and family would be fine. I just want to be your wife. That is most important, no?"

"Yes it is," her father responded from the back seat. "But I would like it to be as nice as possible. You are my only daughter you know."

Cassie turned and smiled lovingly at her father. "I know papa. It will be nice. But it doesn't have to be extravagant. Maybe just a small ceremony at the church and a small reception in the banquet room."

Both Ramon and Franklin shook their heads in agreement.

"But when should we do it?" Franklin asked, reaching over and softly placing his hand on Cassie's thigh. She winked coyly, understanding the hidden meaning in his question.

"Well, you will probably need at least two months," Ramon answered.

Cassie opened her purse and flipped to the calendar in her checkbook. A week before while Cassie was still recovering, Franklin and Ramon had driven the van and car back to New Hope and gathered a few of Cassie's personal items for her return trip home. She was glad to have a few of her belongings with her since Troy snatched her with only the clothes on her back.

"Well, two months from now would be right around Easter," she said. "We will have to wait until after that...How about the first weekend in May. Oh that's such a lovely time of year."

"Sounds good to me," Ramon replied. "What about you my son?"

Franklin thought about it and then nodded his head without saying a word. Cassie saw that something about the date had struck a nerve in her fiancé.

"Is that alright sweetheart?" she asked. "Is that not soon enough? Or too soon, maybe?"

Franklin smiled at her. "No that day would be fine."

"Then what sweetheart?" she asked. "I can see you're thinking about something."

Ramon looked on curiously, not following whether there was a problem.

"Oh no," Franklin answered. "My mind just wanders sometimes." He rubbed her thigh.

Cassie smiled demurely at him. A few seconds later, a startled expression raced across her face.

"Oh my God, I'm so sorry."

"What?" Franklin asked.

"Oh sweetheart, how thoughtless of me. That's too close to Sara's passing isn't it? I'm so sorry."

Cassie covered her mouth and looked away.

"Hey, hey, that's okay," Franklin responded, touching her cheek lightly with the back of his hand. "I think that would be a wonderful time for us to get married."

"Really?" Cassie's eyes began to mist.

"Sure it would...Look, ever since Sara and the girls died, I've been trying to get my life in order. I've had my ups and downs, we all have. But I know God has walked alongside me the whole way. He will continue to be with me...I think this is the next step in my journey. Our journey honey."

Franklin squeezed her thigh. Cassie reflected a comforting smile, her teary eyes acknowledging her sympathy to the love of her young life. Ramon kept silent, absorbing the heartfelt moment he was proud to witness.

"Sara's journey is complete," Franklin continued. "She is with the Lord now. We all will be there someday as well...I want to complete my journey with you, honey. I know God wants me to. I think He's proven that by saving both our lives in that mine. I think it's his will."

Cassie sniffled a couple of times. "I think it is his will too Franklin. But we can pick another time to get married. I really don't mind. I want to do whatever makes you happy. I love you so much."

A few sniffles echoed from the back seat. Franklin smiled at Ramon through the rearview mirror.

"Honey, I think May would be a perfect time to begin the rest of my life with you...Besides, I think your father probably believes its time for you to make an honest man out of me."

Franklin winked at Ramon and then reached over and pulled Cassie to him. They touched their lips together quickly and drove toward their future together.

❧❖❧

The touch of envy Gretchen felt was only natural as she helped Cassie wiggle into her wedding dress. The silken white gown that fit perfectly over her best friend reminded Troy Battles' former beloved of just how far out of sync her life had become during the past two years.

Gretchen could easily picture herself in the wedding dress so beautifully adorning Cassie's still-virginal figure. The fine lace gently caressing her olive-toned shoulders drifted daintily down to her bosom, the V-shaped cut allowing Cassie to offer her betrothed an alluring, yet proper taste of the delicacy he had for so long waited to enjoy. The snowy silk snuggly girdled itself around the bride's girlish waist before flowing freely over a hidden hoop drawn to a laced hem that barely touched the floor. Gretchen noted that the way Cassie wore the gown would have brought beaming pride to even the most striking of southern belles. A ribboned bow accented Cassie's shinning raven hair.

"You look absolutely dazzling honey," Gretchen commented, gently brushing back a wisp of curly hair that had fallen across the bride's face. "Wait until Franklin gets a look at you...He'll be out of control girl."

Cassie blushed slightly and then quickly scanned the dress in the full-length mirror on her closet door. She had to agree with Gretchen's assessment.

"This is the most beautiful dress I've ever worn," she said. "I used to dream about wearing it when I was a little girl. Oh, when I looked at my mother's wedding pictures I would fantasize how I would look in it...I wish she could be here Gretchen."

Cassie sniffled a few times and began to weep slightly. Gretchen placed a hand on her friend's shoulder and hugged her. "I know you do. But you're mama's here in spirit. She would be so proud of you honey."

"I know she is. It's just that sometimes I miss her so much."

Gretchen kissed Cassie on the cheek and reached down and grabbed a couple of tissues off the dresser. "Here, here, now," she said, gently tapping under Cassie's eyes with the tissue. "You're gonna mess up your makeup honey. Don't cry no more, okay?"

Cassie sniffled twice and nodded her head. Gretchen gave her the tissues.

"I'm so happy you're here with me today," Cassie said, hugging her sister in the faith tightly. "You're my best friend in the whole world. I'm so glad God brought you into my life."

It was Gretchen, who then began to cry.

"Maybe you wouldn't have had so much trouble if He hadn't?"

Cassie turned quickly around and pointed her finger at Gretchen.

"Now, don't do that," she lightly, but firmly scolded. "We both know what happened to me, and you, is not your fault. It was in God's plan. You know that."

Gretchen took a couple of tissues for herself. "I know, I know."

Cassie smiled and hugged Gretchen.

"Now, no more of that okay?"

"Okay."

"You promise?"

"I do."

Cassie kissed her friend's forehead. "Good. Now let me pray for us okay?"

Gretchen nodded yes and smiled with resignation. She knew Cassie was right. Troy's actions were all of his own doing and yet somehow still part of God's eternal plan for their lives. She was elated Cassie was marrying the man of her dreams. But Gretchen still felt sorrow in her own heart for the crushing loss she had suffered. Sure, she ended up hating Troy, but yet she still found her mind wandering back to the joyful times they had shared together. She felt Troy at least loved her at some point during their closest years. But those wayward memories were destined for a tomb that would eventually be sealed shut until the Day of Judgment. Such a fate was only a matter of time itself.

Cassie held Gretchen's hands as they sat down together at the foot of the bed.

"Most gracious Father in heaven," Cassie prayed. "Thank you

first and foremost for the love you have given us, most preciously through the sacrifice of your Son, our Lord and Savior, Jesus Christ. May we always be grateful for that love...Father, I pray for my sister. I pray for her comfort during this time of recovery. I know it has only been two months, but while her body has healed Father, Gretchen's heart is still hurting. Please heal her heart as well Father. I love her so much, but not nearly as much as I know you do. Let her feel your love for her Father. Please calm her heart and let her know how close you really are to her...Please do the same for all of us Father. Me, Franklin, papa, all of us Father. We need you so much as we all begin new lives together. We can journey nowhere safely without your Spirit. Help us to always follow you in faith. I ask this for today and forever. In the loving name of Jesus, I pray. Amen."

As Cassie began to get up, Gretchen clutched her hands and pulled her back.

"Let me pray for you now honey," she stated, her eyes welling.

Cassie smiled and closed her eyes again.

Gretchen sighed deeply before beginning.

"Dear Lord, I am so sorry for not crying out to you more. I am in pain still, but I know you feel it as well. Please strengthen me so that I can be more loving to all my family, both here and back home. We all need you so much God." Gretchen sniffled and whimpered a few times. Cassie clutched her friend's hands tightly. "Lord, I do pray for my sister and her new husband. I pray for your blessing on their wedding today and their marriage always. I pray that their life together will be blessed by constantly knowing your presence. Surround them with your love Jesus. Oh God, I love them so much. Help me to always be there for them. Cassie, Franklin, and Ramon too Lord, I feel like they are the only family I have left now.

Help me to show them how much I cherish them. Please. I ask this with love, in your name Jesus. Amen."

The women hugged for a moment before Gretchen caught a glimpse of Cassie's alarm clock.

"Oh my gosh, we better get a move on!" Gretchen exclaimed. "You don't want to be late for your own wedding now do you?"

"Ooh, it is getting close, isn't it?"

"Yeah, I better get dressed."

Gretchen, still wearing just her bathrobe, hustled over to the closet door and removed her light blue silk dress from the hanger. She slipped it on quickly as Cassie put the finishing touches on her makeup. Gretchen would be the only bridesmaid at the intimate ceremony of family and friends. Always frugal, Cassie wanted to keep the wedding party small to save on expenses. Besides, she knew Gretchen was her only truly close Christian girlfriend. She wanted her dearest friend to have a special place in one of the most glorious days of her young life. Gretchen cherished the honor.

⚜

One by one the guests congratulated the blessed couple. Ramon's still-teary eyes gazed fondly at the precious daughter he had just given away to his best friend. Cassie made for a stunning bride, he thought, just as beautiful as her mother was on her own wedding day more than a quarter-century before. The moment was still bittersweet, however, for the middle-aged pastor. During the years since Ilianna's passing, he had been both father and mother to their only child. The reality that his baby would now be cared for by another suddenly swept over him like a rushing river. The droplets slowly sliding down his round cheeks easily displayed the conflicting emotions he felt inside. Resounding joy mixed with just a touch of pensiveness. Cassie, the little girl who had always been the focus of his spirit, was now a proud young woman who had captured the heart of a man who loved her equally as well. Ramon began to smile broadly as the splendid couple made their rounds through modest reception hall at New Hope Church.

"Penny for your thoughts?" Gracie asked, as she sat down next to Cassie's father at the family table. She sensed he was struggling with issues of his only child's inevitable departure from the nest. She had felt the same way after Franklin and Sara's wedding.

Gracie's question broke Ramon from his train of thought.

"Oh, hello Mrs. Edwards," he replied, nodding respectfully to Franklin's mother. "Just a lovely ceremony, no?"

"Quite lovely," she answered, her always-disarming smile tearing down the awkwardness of the moment. "Please, call me Gracie."

"Why certainly...Gracie."

She chuckled to herself. Ramon looked at her quizzically.

"You know Ramon, it just occurred to me that there are two Mrs. Edwards again...And I couldn't be more delighted."

Ramon nodded twice. "This is true. This is true...I am very happy that my daughter and your son found each other." He choked up for a second. "I have grown to love Franklin very much. He is a wonderful man for my Cassie...May God bless them both."

"He most certainly will Ramon. I know He will, especially after what they've been through."

The pop music the DJ had been playing slowed to an elegant waltz. A few of the older couples in the crowd of about fifty, made their way to the dance floor.

"May I have this dance Gracie?" Ramon asked, holding out his hand.

Franklin's mother smiled demurely and placed her glass of wine on the table. Ramon helped her to her feet and they joined the others. Cassie quickly noticed her father and new mother-in-law dancing, and whispered something into Franklin's ear. They both giggled and stared at their parents. Ramon and Gracie didn't look back.

The song lasted about five minutes, plenty long enough for all the generations in the hall. Gracie thanked Ramon and walked over to where her son was standing, talking to Sam Simmons, who stood up as Franklin's best man that day. Cassie, Gretchen and a bunch of the younger women were kicking up the dance floor to the rapid beat of a disco tune.

"You looked great out there Gracie," Sam commented. "I remember when Sandy and I would dance all night long. Those were the days."

"You should have danced with her Sam," Gracie replied. "It was a lot of fun. Ramon is a very fine dancer...You and Sandy used to be great dancers."

"That was a long time ago Gracie." Sam shook his head in mock disgust at himself. "Before busted hips and brittle bones. We'd probably hurt ourselves now."

Gracie laughed. "Oh Sam, I'm older than both of you."

"Yeah, but Gracie, you're still very spry. Have been ever since I've known ya."

Franklin's mother hugged her dear old friend. "You ain't too old for me to squeeze you though."

Gracie released her embrace and looked at her son. "Franklin can I speak to you for a moment please? I've got something I've been meaning to give you."

Franklin's eyes lit up. "Ooh, a present mommy?" He rubbed his hands together in mock anticipation. Sam excused himself with a nod and a roll of the eyes.

"Come on son," Gracie said, leading Franklin into the hallway and then to Ramon's office.

They sat down on the old, black leather couch.

"What's up mama?" Franklin asked with a smile.

Gracie reached over and took hold of her son's right hand. "I've been meaning to give you something since I got here, but I haven't had the chance."

"Yeah, I know mama," Franklin responded apologetically. "I haven't had the chance to spend as much time with you as I would have liked the past two days. I'm sorry."

"Oh that's alright dear. There's a lot to do before a wedding. God knows. It's a busy time."

Franklin leaned over and kissed his mother on the cheek.

"Close your eyes and hold out you hand," she said.

He did as she asked. Gracie placed an object into her son's palm and rolled up his hand. She held it shut for a moment.

"Okay, now you can open your eyes," she said as she released his hand.

Franklin opened his eyes and hand simultaneously. He was shocked when he gazed at the item lying in his palm.

"It's daddy's watch!" Franklin exclaimed in amazement. "How did you get it back?"

Gracie coughed lightly a couple of times to clear her throat. The dancing had left her rather thirsty. "It was actually pretty easy, really."

"But when did you go to Las Vegas?"

"I didn't."

"But how? What?" Franklin stammered, still stunned to once again be holding Jordan's prized gold watch. "I thought it was lost forever when I pawned it."

Gracie stuck out her chin proudly. "Well, your mother has become quite savvy on the computer. When you finally called me after you arrived in L.A. and told me what happened, I went on line and got a list of all the pawn shops in Las Vegas. And I want to tell you, there are a whole lot of them."

Franklin looked somewhat somberly at the floor. "Oh, I know. I remember."

"Oh dear, I'm not trying to make you feel bad," she reached over and tenderly rubbed her son's shoulder. "It was a very bad time for you. You did what you had to do. I didn't blame you."

"I know mama." Franklin looked up with misting eyes at his sympathetic mom. "I'm just happy you were able to get it back. Daddy loved this watch."

"And I know you do too."

Franklin stared glumly at the watch and opened it up and looked at his mother's tiny photo inside. "Yeah, but I don't deserve to have it.? He snapped the locket shut and handed it back to his mother.

"Oh no. I got it back for you. I want you to have it. I insist." She placed the watch firmly back in her son's hand.

Franklin began to cry. He leaned over and wept on his mother's shoulder. He remembered the comfort that he had always found there, ever since the days of his childhood. Mother's shoulder would always be waiting for him, whether the actions that drew him to it were of his own fault or not.

"Honey, I didn't mean to make you cry on your wedding day." She rubbed his back. "I'm sorry. I wanted to give you the watch as a wedding present from your father and me."

Franklin sat back and sniffled a few times. "I know mama. I'm not really crying about the watch."

"Then what baby?" she asked, her eyes welling with tears.

Franklin smiled. "Holding daddy's watch again makes me feel like I truly have another chance to start over again...I don't know. It's like God has given me back the watch as some sort of symbol of his grace. His forgiveness. At least, I finally feel forgiven."

Franklin laid his head back onto his mother's shoulder. The two of them just sat there in silence for a few minutes, treasuring the glory of the blessed day.

"Anybody seen my husband?" Cassie called to the church volunteers cleaning up in the kitchen the next room over.

Gracie kissed her son on the cheek. "Your wife's calling for you."

Franklin nodded in delight. "Now that's something I think I can get used to again mama. A wife calling for me."

Mother and son got up and left the room with their arms around each other's waists. Franklin gazed adoringly at his father's gold watch. He did think of it as a symbol of God's grace, just like the woman calling for him in the hallway. He knew he had been blessed tremendously.

"Here I am honey," he cried out to Cassie.

❧✦❧

Gretchen hugged her forever sister tightly, thinking all the while how strange God's ways can be. She knew she would see Cassie again in the future, but had no idea when that time would come. Though thousands of miles would separate the best friends, both understood the trauma their hearts had endured together would always unite them in spirit. Gretchen figured she probably would be the one eventually moving back to South Florida, but God had once again made other plans for her life. He had instead called

Cassie to the east coast, as an integral part of Franklin's spiritual homecoming.

Nevertheless, Gretchen had been obliged to return home over the summer for one more extremely trying ordeal, the incarceration of both her father and Richard. She was forced to witness one last coup de grace by demonic Troy Battles, this one from beyond the grave. The evidence of Eric Bjorn's crimes had indeed found its way to the appropriate government authorities, courtesy of Troy. One of the demented man's last desperate acts did prove successful in staggering the Battles empire. Gretchen's dad's embezzlement and stock fraud unwittingly also brought down Troy's own father. Richard Battles' culpability in shady business practices, which had long been under government scrutiny, especially since many were tied to the local political elite, finally became exposed to the light. To his credit, however, Richard quickly came clean and took the punishment he had coming. Both he and Eric pleaded guilty to federal corruption charges and traded in their designer suits for prison blues, the only attire they would need for the better part of the next decade.

Gretchen was devastated by their sentences, but pleased with their remorse and repentance. Virtues she had never witnessed in Richard Battles' hell-bound son.

"I'm going to miss you so much," Cassie tearfully said as she broke her embrace with Gretchen. "But I am so happy you are going to work with papa."

Gretchen wiped her eyes and then picked up one of Cassie's suitcases off the bedroom floor. She remembered how just the night before Ramon had spoken about emptiness that would linger in the old apartment once his daughter embarked on the next phase of her Christian walk. Under that roof, he had seen Cassie mature from a frightened little pre-teen who had just lost her beloved mother into a boldly faithful young woman on fire in her love for Christ, and her mercifully restored husband. Over dinner the previous evening, the newlyweds, the pastor and Gretchen ironed out the final transition details in the mission church's life. New Hope's vision of caring for the needy while spreading the eternal security of the gospel would still remain in devoted hands.

"I guess God has given all of us new jobs now," Gretchen remarked, as she held open the bedroom door for Cassie, who carried a suitcase in each hand. "It seems like Franklin is very happy to begin teaching again."

"Oh yes, he's elated," Cassie answered, her own beaming smile reflecting the joy she knew her husband felt in his heart the very moment Herman Steponophlitz informed him that Good Shepherd Christian School had never satisfactorily filled his old position.

"Franklin was great teacher there," Gretchen stated. "We all loved him...well, most of us anyhow." She quickly pulled her eyes from Cassie and stared somberly at the floor, realizing Troy had usually been in opposition to Franklin's views on just about everything taught in the classroom. She certainly understood the reasons behind Troy's antagonism. She had felt the defiant punch of his enmity firsthand.

"Oh honey, try to focus on the future," Cassie pleaded.

"It's going to be so hard," Gretchen replied, putting the suitcase she was carrying on the floor before covering her eyes and weeping into her hands. "Especially without you around."

Cassie immediately dropped the suitcases and again put her arms around her friend.

"Gretchen, Gretchen," she said, gently rubbing the blond girl's back as they hugged, "what am I going to do with you?"

Gretchen continued to release her tears. She was frightened of the future. She had lost so much. Her dearest friend would be all the way on the other side of the country.

"I'll always be just a phone call away," Cassie said. "You know that. You can call me any time you want, day or night. You know I will pray for you every day, right?"

Gretchen smiled and nodded her head. She was slightly embarrassed by her sudden emotional outburst. She hoped it was a final release, brought about by Cassie's impending departure, although deep down she knew there would probably be many more teary times as the months marched on toward full recovery. Gretchen realized by ministering to the neighborhood needy, God would heal her own soul as well.

"I will covet your prayers Cassie. I truly will."

Cassie smiled reassuringly and kissed her friend's forehead. "Good. You will have them."

Gretchen wiped her eyes with the sleeve of her bright orange New Hope tee shirt. Cassie reached into her purse and handed her a tissue instead. "Thank you...Cassie?"

"Yes honey."

"You trust me right?"

"Of course I do," Cassie answered with a quizzical look. "What do you mean?"

"Well," Gretchen rubbed her finger across her lips, glancing up at the ceiling, as if asking for guidance from the heavenly source. "You always did so much around here. I know your father depended on you a lot. I just hope I don't mess things up too bad."

"You'll do great! I know you will...Besides, papa wouldn't have hired you if he didn't think you could do the job...He trusts you and so do I."

"I know, it's just like I told you guys last night. With my switching majors, I feel like I'm starting my education all over again. I hope I can do it."

"You can Gretchen, I know you can...Just keep asking the Lord for help. Remember, without his guidance, you can do nothing on your own."

Gretchen shook her head in affirmation to Cassie's statement. She knew following her best friend's career choice in social work would require God's assistance. He had placed the desire to help society's downtrodden on her heart and He would give her the resources to follow through if she remained faithful to his will. Gretchen resolved to do so.

"I will make you proud of me Cassie. I promise I will."

Cassie hugged her again. "You already have honey."

The girls grabbed the suitcases and headed downstairs. Franklin already had the U-Haul loaded up and hitched to Cassie's car. Everything was in place for the long journey to South Florida. As the four of them said their final tearful goodbyes, they all sensed God's providence in the rearranging of their lives. He had carried them through their respective destinies thus far. They trusted that He would guide them through the rest of life's adventure as well.

Cassie was beaming as she exited the bathroom of the rented Fort Lauderdale apartment. She quickly rushed over to the bed, where Franklin was just waking up. He was still yawning and clearing the slumber from his eyes when he noticed the towel slip off his wife's freshly-showered body. The sight was still pleasing, even in the dim, early-morning light.

"Kiss me here," Cassie said, pointing her index finger just below her bare belly button.

Franklin grinned mischievously. "I would love to honey, but I probably shouldn't start something I don't really have time to finish. Don't want to be late for work my first day on the job, you know."

Cassie giggled and leaned down and kissed his lips.

"No silly, I wasn't talking about making love to me," she said, blushing slightly. "Just kiss my belly, okay?"

Franklin obeyed and planted a firm smooch on her soft, tight abdomen. He laid his head back down on the pillow. Cassie sat down next to him and caressed his whiskered face. An almost sheepish grin crept from her lips, as if she was too timid to reveal what was on her mind.

"What?" Franklin queried, looking confused by her actions.

Cassie bit down lightly on her bottom lip.

"I have a surprise for you."

Franklin laughed deviously, wondering what his wife was up to.

"Okay, tell me. I love surprises, well sometimes."

Cassie started to giggle again. "You're gonna love this one, I promise."

Franklin was getting anxious. "Alright, alright. Tell me would you. I'm dying to know. What?"

Cassie took a deep breath and sighed before responding. "That kiss on my tummy was an introduction of sorts."

Franklin tilted his head in wonder. "I don't get it. Introduction?"

Cassie rolled her eyes and looked up. She then began to giggle again.

"What honey?" Franklin smiled in confusion. "I just kissed your belly." The significance of the kiss then suddenly dawned on him. "No! Really?" His brown eyes lit up brightly as he rose from the bed.

Cassie nodded her head. "We're going to have a baby!" she screamed and hugged her husband.

Franklin kissed her on the lips. "Are you sure?" he asked.

"Of course, I'm sure," she replied.

"Well, how do you know? I mean..."

Cassie rolled her eyes again. "Well, I'm over two weeks late and this was the third different test to come up positive, so yeah honey, I'm pretty sure I'm pregnant."

Franklin embraced her again. Tears of joy began to flow from his eyes. "Oh honey, I love you so much. I can't believe I'm gonna have another child."

He kissed her passionately, almost as if he was rewarding her for the blessing God had so graciously bestowed. After a few moments, they broke their embrace and readied for the day ahead. Both knew it was the first of many days of praise and thanksgiving.

As Franklin and Cassie talked over breakfast on that eventful morning, their discussion reflected the growing grace they knew they had received.

"You know honey," Franklin said. "I feel like God has totally restored me now into his good graces."

"What do you mean?" Cassie asked as she nibbled a bite off her bagel at the kitchen table.

"Well, I have a beautiful, new wife."

Cassie smiled and blushed slightly.

"We're going to have a baby," he continued. "And today I return to my job at a place I've always loved to work. I don't think I could feel more blessed at this moment."

Cassie reached her hand across the table and clasped Franklin's hand. He blew her a kiss.

"You know Cass, I remember teaching my students about the tulip the last time I was here."

Cassie looked at him with slight confusion.

"You know, the acrostic for reformed theology."

She realized the gist of his discussion and nodded her head while she chewed on her bagel.

"The P was always my favorite letter in the acrostic," he said while spreading a dollop of cream cheese on his own bagel.

"Why's that sweetheart?" she mumbled between chews.

"Because it stands for perseverance," he explained. "Honey, I think the point of this whole long season for me is to realize God's presence in every aspect of my life. I mean, I know now that God is always in the lives of his children. He guaranteed his love for them with Christ's death on the cross and his resurrection...We will persevere in hard times, whether self-inflicted or not, because he preserves us. I know that's what He did for me."

Cassie smiled proudly at her husband. "Sounds like a good lesson to me. I've always known you were specially touched by God. I knew it the first time I saw you. Your life will be a good lesson for the kids you teach, including ours honey."

She got up and cleared their plates from the table. Cassie kissed Franklin and let him finish getting ready for the first day of the new school year.

On the drive to Good Shepherd, Franklin assessed his life at that point. He knew with Cassie by his side, it would be much easier to deal with the memories of Sara and the girls. God had given a helper who would lovingly walk with him through the challenges presented in his restored life. God had not forgotten him during the season of tragedy he had endured. Franklin realized he loved God even more because of the turbulent times.

In fact, as Franklin looked over the twenty fresh faces in his classroom that first day of school, he pondered to himself if there was a Troy or Gretchen among the group. There were so many different types of high-schoolers staring back at him. He didn't recognize any of them, which was surprising, considering he figured at least some of them had to have attended the school when he taught there two years before. Where were they in their walks with Christ? he wondered. Did some of them not even know Jesus as their personal Lord and Savior? Could he do anything do help those who may wander from the Light to find their way again?

Franklin then remembered that only God himself knows for certain the destiny of any of those created in his image. It is God alone who determines a person's fate. He said so in his Holy Word. And that truth has remained in place for thousands of years and would exist for all eternity.

After greeting his new students and asking each of them to give a short statement about themselves, Franklin slowly scanned his eyes around the room, smiled coyly and then posed a question to his class: "What is your favorite flower?"